A Dirty Death

REBECCA TOPE

Allison & Busby Limited
11 Wardour Mews
London W1F 8AN
allisonandbusby.com

First published in Great Britain in 1999.
First published in paperback by Allison & Busby in 2012.
This paperback edition published by Allison & Busby in 2019.

A CIP catalogue record for this book is available from
the British Library.

10 9 8 7 6 5 4 3 2 1

ISBN 978-0-7490-2556-4

Typeset in 10.5/15.5 pt Sabon LT Pro by
Allison & Busby Ltd.

The paper used for this Allison & Busby publication
has been produced from trees that have been legally sourced
from well-managed and credibly certified forests.

Printed and bound by
CPI Group (UK) Ltd, Croydon, CR0 4YY

Dedicated to Liz, as promised
all those years ago

Chapter One

It had already been a spring laden with mortality. News reports were full of mutating killer viruses, terrorist bombings, earthquakes and floods. Both God and man, in equal measure, seemed intent on eradicating the human race. There had, too, been smaller tragedies at home: the family dog had died only a few weeks before, and a whole herd of prime beef animals had been wasted on the altar of BSE-phobia, despite the farmer's confidence in his organic status.

So it was with a strange momentary lack of surprise that Lilah found her father, early that morning, half-submerged face-down in the slurry pit. She looked at his back, at the familiar mustard-coloured milking coat which had in any case always been stained with splashes of cow muck, slowly sinking into the stuff. All around him the crust was broken, stirred up by what she supposed had been his frantic thrashings, his struggle to live. Fresh streaks of muck spattered the sides of the pit and dotted the concrete which led to the edge. In those first few clear seconds, she supposed he must have somehow skidded over the brink, on the side which had no protective fence – and landed with a great splash.

Against her will, she visualised what must have come next. Everyone knew how treacherous slurry could be, with its sucking quicksand effect, and almost no hope of gaining a foothold. Full from a winter of mucking-out, and no chance yet to get out in the fields with the spreader, the pit was perhaps four and a half feet deep. A man on his knees could not have kept his head above the surface.

An unbearable conflict gripped her. She should get him out – of course she should. But then she might drown in it too. The pit had always been so strictly forbidden, and Guy was so very obviously beyond all help, that she spent two or three long minutes simply hovering, helpless.

At last she called Sam, her voice unnaturally shrill. She knew that, as always at this time, he would be across the yard in the outside lavatory, performing his essential morning defecation. But he was at her side in seconds, struggling with the orange bale string which held up his moleskins, his cheeks flushed with effort and embarrassment. Now that Lilah was twenty and no longer his little helper, he knew she was too old for such casual intimacies.

'Oh,' he said, and made as if to jump into the pit immediately. Then he stopped himself. 'He'll be dead, by the look of it.' Lilah noticed how wrong it felt for Sam to be using ordinary English words to describe something so entirely cataclysmic. There ought to be a special language reserved for moments like this.

'We'll have to get him out of there,' Sam added, swallowing something nasty in his throat, twisting his face in disgust. At the sudden vivid picture of what the farmer would look like when turned over, slurry in his mouth and nose, down inside his clothes, Lilah was abruptly sick, her morning cereal and toast slithering over the sloping edge of the pit to join her father.

'Go and get your brother. And your Mum—' he heaved a brief sigh of anguish before continuing '—and then phone 999.'

By this time, they were both shaking with the shock; severe, uncontrollable shivering, as if they were out in a blizzard with no coats on. Lilah looked down at her own hands, dancing and jittering of their own accord, and clenched her fists hard. Jerkily, she turned and tried to run back to the house. It was like running in a dream.

Dad was dead. Drowned in slurry – wet, brown, stinking, lethal slurry. How often had his children been warned of its dangers, *told* and *told* to keep away from the pit? How often had they joked about what an awful way it would be to die? *Dad was dead.* Like a cloud of attacking bees, the implications of this began to descend upon her. Tears ran down her face, fogging her vision when she tried to telephone.

'Emergency. Which service do you require?' said a ludicrously calm voice.

'Police. Ambulance. My dad – he fell in the slurry – he's dead.' Her voice came in breathless gasps; she couldn't believe she was saying the words. She wondered if she had said them correctly, or had she just gibbered? The woman asked for her address and phone number, and then requested a precise spelling of the farm's name, twice. '*Redstone*, for God's sake,' screamed Lilah. 'How many ways can you spell that?'

'Please try to keep calm, madam,' said the woman, and Lilah hated her with horrifying ferocity, as she was promised immediate co-operation. There were no policemen or ambulances nearer than ten miles. There would inevitably be a wait.

She went up to Roddy's room then, knowing she should hurry, but reluctant to involve him, to have to bring him such distress and deal with his shock.

Roddy slept like an Egyptian mummy, wound tightly in his sheet. It had been a warm night, making the duvet superfluous. Lilah paused a moment, then laid a hand on his thick black hair, and he came instantly awake.

'Something's happened,' she whispered. It wrung her with a bitter pain, having to force him outside to witness the horror, but if she didn't do it, Sam would, and Sam was not always gentle with Roddy. 'You've got to come and help Sam. I warn you, you'll probably be sick. I was.'

'*Sick?*' He looked alarmed. 'What on earth are you talking about?'

'It's Dad. He's in the slurry. You'll have to help fish him out.' Roddy swallowed a small giggle, looking hopefully at his sister, wanting to be told she was playing some horrible joke on him. But her face convinced him otherwise. 'You're crying,' he said, in real shock.

She put a hand to her face, surprised. 'He's dead, you see,' she explained. 'Drowned in slurry.' The last word broke up on the loud sob she could not prevent. 'It's awful, Rod. Terrible. Now get dressed. Wear something old. I'll have to tell Mum.'

Miranda Beardon was lying cosily in the big double bed, stretched diagonally across it, occupying all available space. A small transistor radio, tuned to the local station, whispered in her ear. She looked up at her daughter, displaying some

10

resentment at the disturbance. Lilah expected that a mere glance at her would be enough to denote tragedy, but her mother just sighed.

'What's happened now? I could hear there was some kind of goings-on out there. Noisy lot. I suppose the cows are in the road again?'

'No—' *The cows! They'd be waiting to be milked. The tanker would come at ten, and there'd be nothing ready. Dad'd be livid . . . Oh, God!*

'No, Mum. It's much worse than that. Dad's—' She couldn't say it. A great black cloth wrapped itself around her tongue, and she couldn't say the word. More tears fell, and her mother finally grasped that this was much bigger trouble than she had bargained for. She sat up in the bed, naked, urgency suddenly gripping her.

'What? Lilah, tell me. What's happened?'

'Dad's drowned. In the slurry pit. Sam and Roddy are getting him out. The police will be here soon. And an ambulance, I suppose.'

'No! He wouldn't fall in the slurry. He wouldn't be such a fool. Are you sure it's him?'

Lilah nodded, then turned to leave the room. Her mother's nakedness offended her. This was no way to receive the news that you'd been widowed.

'Lilah? What am I going to do?'

'Put some clothes on, and come down. I'm going back to help Sam.'

The policeman, when he arrived, was familiar to Lilah. His long smooth cheeks and sand-coloured hair hadn't changed in seven years. She had last known him as Bus Prefect on the daily trip to and from school. He had been in the first-year sixth when she started at the comprehensive, and for two years they had wordlessly shared transport for over an hour each day.

He knew exactly who she was, of course: the Beardons had farmed Redstone for the past fourteen years. Nevertheless, he had to do things properly.

'Miss Beardon?' he enquired, as she walked up to his car in the yard. She nodded, confused as to how to address him. The 'Miss' seemed strange, coming from him. It made her feel she was no longer herself.

But then, she *was* no longer herself, of course. She was fatherless now. A half-orphan. It made sense that this status should acquire a new unfriendly title.

Denholm Cooper, the policeman was called. Den, for short. She had always identified with him in having to explain his name. People thought Den was for Dennis just as they assumed Lilah was really *De*lilah, and she had felt a bond with him accordingly – enough of a bond, at twelve years old, for a brief but profound schoolgirl crush to blossom. Looking at him now, she remembered it all, and blushed.

Human beings adjusted very rapidly to calamity, it seemed. Lilah had already assumed that she would have to make special efforts to put people at their ease, so that they wouldn't shy away from her – tainted as she now was by the death of a loved one. She must not cry or vomit in front of anyone. She must act naturally, observe the normal rules of social intercourse. Den, however, already seemed unperturbed by what had happened. She had taken a step to one side, to allow him to leap eagerly from his car and run with urgency to the scene of the tragedy. Instead, he remained sitting where he was for a full minute, which hinted to Lilah of arrogance. What if Dad hadn't quite drowned, but needed instant resuscitation? How strange that the woman on the telephone hadn't questioned her more closely when she had said her father was dead.

'Your Mum at home, is she?' asked Den, calmly.

Lilah waved towards the house. Then she looked across the yard to where Sam was clumping towards them. Slurry had splashed him extensively, and he held his hands out stiffly from his sides, as if unable to abide himself. Suddenly decisive, the policeman unfolded his legs from the car, standing over them, taller than anyone Lilah had ever before stood close to. Perhaps that was why he stayed so long in the vehicle, she thought; his height intimidates people. An hysterical urge to say 'Goodness, you've grown,' seized her, but she fought it down.

'Got him out, did you?' said Den. 'I'd better come and have a look, then.' They walked the thirty yards to the pit and stood motionless for a moment. 'You shouldn't really have done that.'

Sam looked mutinous. 'Couldn't leave him in there,' he stated flatly. 'How would you like it?'

The farmer was covered with a sheet of black plastic, lying near the spot where Lilah assumed he had first slipped. The splashes of muck were no longer visible, and she gave them no further thought. 'I washed him off a bit,' said Sam, as he pulled the sheet back. No one tried to keep Lilah away. She stared down at the face, splotched in nostrils and eye sockets with the khaki-coloured manure. The mouth, too, was open and muck had got into it. That was the worst. She had been kissed by that mouth, every night and every morning of her life.

Then Roddy and her mother were standing beside her. Mum gave a strangled cry, but no words came from her. *This is the language of catastrophe*, Lilah thought. *This is how we ought to be communicating – in sobs and groans and muffled shrieks.* Roddy's face was bilious, his lips drawn back in a terrible grimace. Den nodded to Sam in a silent instruction to re-cover the body. His own face was a poor colour, and he put a hand to his mouth.

'Right,' he said, very quietly. 'Right. Well . . .' Like a man looking for escape, he strode back to his car and reached in for the phone. They heard him, across the silent yard, saying, 'Send the duty doctor out, will you? ASAP. Then ask the undertaker's men to fetch him. No need for an ambulance. Yes, a p.m., definitely. It's not nice, Jim. Not nice at all.'

Time passed in a whole new way. Another two policemen arrived, and with Den they fastened white tape around two sides of the pit, looking helplessly at each other when the roll ran out. 'Nobody is to come past this point,' they ordered the huddled family.

A middle-aged doctor with a loud voice turned up and made a mysterious sequence of examinations, glancing disapprovingly at Lilah and Miranda, clearly wishing someone would remove them. Not long afterwards, two black-coated men arrived in a big estate car and took the body away, making surreptitious and somehow comical attempts to avoid touching any of the muck. Lilah noticed a large moist dollop fall onto one man's shoe; he kicked his foot frantically, trying to get it off.

Den explained about the coroner and the delay in getting a death certificate. He produced a notepad and asked who had found the body, what time, how long since anyone last saw him alive, whether there had been any odd circumstances. Lilah tried to tell him the whole story; how she'd searched for him, wondering why he wasn't in the milking parlour; how she had eventually gone to the slurry pit and glanced in, never for a second expecting to find what she did. Den wrote carefully on his pad, repeating details in unfeeling interruptions of her tale.

When he had finished, he cast an eye around the yard. 'Must have been an accident,' he said. 'Don't you think?'

She couldn't answer. Following his glance, she scanned the unfenced edge of the pit as if searching for an action replay of what had happened to her father. There was an uncoiled hosepipe lying close by, which Sam had used to clean away some of the muck, and a stack of rotting timber which had once been a derelict shed, recently demolished. The concrete close to the pit was slippery and sloped downwards.

'He could have skidded on a wet patch,' continued Den. 'Or is there a dog, perhaps, that might have accidentally pushed him in?'

'The dog's dead,' said Roddy, harshly.

Den didn't react. He told them there would be a further police visit, questions, more formalities. Then he drove away.

Lilah looked after him, wondering at the vivid memories he had aroused in her. It seemed almost shameful that she could think about a childish passion at a time like this. His face stayed in her mind – she had known those flat stretches from his cheekbone to his jaw in intimate detail after so many journeys spent watching him in the bus driver's mirror. His seat had been at the back, of course, and she was down near the front. The random coincidence of images in the mirror had seemed to her to prove that Fate had intended them for each other. But, when he left school, she had forgotten all about him.

Sam attended to the cows, with distracted help from Lilah and Roddy. The widow, Miranda Beardon, forty-five and now the head of the house, telephoned her mother, and wept down the line for a long time. Two policemen came back, with a long tape measure and a camera, but their examinations were brief. Lilah heard one say 'Weird way to top yourself,' and for the first time the possibility of suicide hit her, only to be brushed impatiently away again. No one who had known her dad could imagine such a thing.

Through the rest of that day Lilah struggled to make sense of what had happened. *Dad has drowned in the slurry. He's dead. He fell into the pit.* And finally, as if it had been waiting quietly to pounce, came the most obvious question: *How?* How in the world had a fit man, not yet sixty, in the bright summer morning light, managed to succumb to such a stupid accident? She tried to imagine how it would be to fall in. The stuff was slippery, of course, and it might prove difficult to get any sort of purchase. But surely, a person could lift his face out, enough to avoid drowning? The pit was deep – the whole winter's worth of muck, waiting to be spread on the fields this very week. Too deep to be able to get up on hands and knees and hold your face clear. You'd have to stand up, and that may well be impossible. It was even conceivable that the sheer horror and panic of being in such a thoroughly grim situation would kill you before you actually drowned.

Very deliberately, Lilah forced herself to think it all through. If she didn't do it now, while already immersed unavoidably in the facts of the situation, she doubted if she could ever persuade herself to come back to it again.

There was some small nub of self-satisfaction in the process, too. *See*, she told herself, *how much tougher and braver you are than your mother! All she can do is cry and moan. She never was any good in a crisis. You, however, have risen to the occasion splendidly. After this, life is going to be pretty smooth sailing. Nothing as bad as this can ever befall you again.*

But she cried bitterly into her pillow that night. After supper she'd gone for a short walk with Roddy, needing to talk to him, and to find out how he was enduring. At sixteen, her brother was a handsome adolescent, his dark skin free of blemish, his preoccupations transparently wholesome. Lilah had always liked him and admired his straightforward nature. From toddlerhood, they had both been closely involved in the farmwork, and took turns in less demanding aspects of the work.

They walked up the slope behind the farm buildings, where the fields rapidly became steep and less fertile. The hill rose to thick woodland, belonging to the neighbouring farm – a large estate owned by Jonathan Mabberley. Though only a mile from the centre of the village, Redstone felt isolated in its folds of hills crossed by crooked narrow lanes. Farmhouses seemed to rise at random from the ground, some on hillsides, some hidden deep in natural hollows. Redstone was one of the latter, its buildings and yard fitted snugly into the bottom of a shallow bowl, with all the land around it sloping uphill. It was an ancient land, barely scratched by humankind: the nearest major road was six miles away, and the sound of traffic was no more that an occasional swoosh as a single vehicle used one of the lanes. Lilah had not yet even tried to escape from this rural life into a faster, more exciting, more urban setting. One day, she told herself, she might give it a try. But the necessary courage was a long time coming.

As he strode unseeingly in a straight line up the hillside, Roddy fought his tears, choosing rage over grief. He smacked one fist into his palm, over and over, emitting tight phrases of fury. 'It's *stupid*, Lilah. A stupid way to die. Why wasn't he more careful? What are we supposed to do now? Everything's ruined. What a mess. Oh sod it. Fucking sod the stupid fool.' A few hot tears shook themselves free, but he viciously swept them away without acknowledgement. He hardly seemed the same boy who had slept so safely in the embrace of his sheet that morning.

Lilah was shocked by his anger. Somehow, it seemed almost wicked, and entirely inappropriate. Then she remembered Tamsin, the half-breed collie they'd had when she was younger. She had been prone to chasing cars, and finally one had come too close and run over her leg. Lilah had witnessed the whole incident. As the tyre had cracked Tamsin's bone, the dog had bitten and snarled furiously at it, fighting the enemy that was hurting her. Bravely she had tried to take on the thing that was so much bigger and stronger than herself. Roddy seemed to Lilah like Tamsin, now – snarling at Death, shaking his fist defiantly at the most powerful adversary of them all.

Chapter Two

Father Edmund Larkin was hot in his black clothes. He hated summer funerals for making him stand out in the sun with too much on. He hated this funeral more than most.

'In sure and certain hope of the Resurrection to come' were hollow words when spoken on behalf of a man like Guy Beardon. If anyone deserved to lie rotting and forgotten forever, it was him. The vicar had disliked Guy almost from their very first meeting, six years earlier. Burying a person you disliked might naturally be expected to bring a small twinge of satisfaction – but when you were God's spokesman and a minister of the Church you were forbidden such pleasures. Common human antipathies were out of order: you were supposed to pray for their extermination from your sinful breast.

The vicar knew with near certainty that Guy was damned – if such old-fashioned notions could still apply. Selfish, rude and domineering were the words he mentally used about him, when preparing his oration for the funeral. Intolerant, secretive and hypocritical also came to mind.

Something of an amateur psychologist, Father Edmund believed that Guy had a lot to hide. He had seen it in the farmer's shadowed eyes.

He had a host of excellent reasons for his intense dislike of the man. The open personal slights which Guy had directed at him had been infuriating; the contempt for the particular brand of Anglicanism Father Edmund practised had been uncomfortable; moreover the admiration Guy attracted from the majority of the villagers had incensed the vicar, who was only too well aware of his own fading popularity. And there were other reasons; reasons he didn't even want to acknowledge.

Guy's end had, of course, rocked the village. Not since near-blind Joe Thrussle had fallen head-first into his butterwell, long before Father Edmund had come here, had there been such drama. Speculation ran rife. Had Guy been drinking? Did a cow or dog nudge him in? Some even sniggeringly suggested that ol' Sam might have done it, to get himself a bit of peace. Everyone had heard the way Guy had mocked Sam, day in and day out for decades now. Everyone had also heard – though none could say where – that Sam had many an illicit encounter with Miranda, while Guy was safely ploughing the farthest fields, or spending a day at Newton Abbot races. The rumours seemed self-generated; no one had any concrete evidence for them. Perhaps, thought Father Edmund sourly, it just stood to reason that any man and woman in a house together would make the most natural use of the opportunity.

The vicar himself tried subtly to propound the theory that Guy's death was suicide. He had his own good reasons for this, though even without them, his innate sense of mischief might have led him to the same course. Suicide was a subject Father Edmund knew a good deal about. Hadn't he once found himself poised on the edge of just such a slurry pit, looking down at the deep dark stuff, thinking blackly of immersing himself in it? A devilish kind of baptism that would be, he'd said to himself. And much of the devil's best work had an insidious appeal for this particular man of the church. In the quietest stretches of the night, when the owl or the fox in his garden woke him with their predatory howls, he could not prevent his thoughts from turning to practices that were agreed by any community to be beyond the pale. Practices which were forever barred to him. Dirty practices, which would horrify any decent-minded person. Activities which he knew would bring the most intense of pleasures and the deepest of shame.

Perhaps, he surmised, Guy had been free in his indulgences. Living on a farm, he had opportunities in abundance for many of the shocking imaginings of that lonely vicarage bedroom. Father Edmund had slowly convinced himself that Guy Beardon lived a life of debauchery, for which he ought to be severely punished. Wasn't it obvious from his uncouth language? Wouldn't any amateur psychologist come to the same conclusion? A man whose expletives were all 'shit' and 'bugger' and 'sod' had to have a tendency in a certain familiar and forbidden direction.

And now the man was dead. The vicar had had considerable difficulty in constructing his funeral peroration without explicitly mentioning how he had died. His main motive was to avoid, if possible, inducing tears in the women of the family.

Crying women were yet another repellant aspect of his work. More than once, when a weeping parishioner had come to pour out her troubles, he had needed to fix his hands rigidly around the seat of his chair in order to prevent himself from rushing from the room. He had learnt, from long experience, that there were certain phrases at a funeral which could almost guarantee that the waterworks would start. 'Sadly missed' was one. Almost anything nice about the dead person's character was taboo, too. The trick was to be very subtly annoying; to get small details wrong, to hint that this person may be better off dead, and best of all, to try and work in some just-perceptible element of farce. His favourite was to get the coffin positioned too close to the lectern, so that he had to squeeze his generous girth painfully between the two, before he could say his piece. This almost always set any young mourners giggling, which forced the adults to shush them, and thus took their minds off their grief for a blessed minute or two.

But this funeral did not readily lend itself to any of these gambits. He scanned the full pews in the small church, noting with some irritation that people who had openly loathed the man had nonetheless shown up for his funeral. There were his neighbours – the Mabberleys and the Grimsdales – with whom Guy had scarcely exchanged a civil word; and there were Tim and Sarah Rickworth, the affluent young incomers, who could surely have little reason to regret Guy's passing. Father Edmund presumed that they thought it was village etiquette to come to all the funerals held at the church. Not that there were many – this was only the second one since Christmas.

Carefully, the vicar launched into his well-prepared address. 'We are here today to perform a melancholy necessity. Farmer

Guy Beardon has been taken from us by the most tragic accident. The whole community has been deeply shocked by the sudden and unkind way in which he lost his life, and our profound sympathies go out to his family. Guy was a well-known figure in the village, having farmed here for sixteen years . . .' (The one deliberate error he permitted himself. He noted with satisfaction that Miranda and Lilah simultaneously looked up with a new attention.) 'He took an active part in all our local proceedings. An involved member of the Parish Council and other organisations, there will be many areas where his shoes will be hard to fill . . .' (*Why can't he just say, 'He'll be sadly missed'?* wondered Lilah). 'Very often the quality of a life will compensate for an untimely end, and this may be some small consolation. Guy Beardon had a loving family around him, he made a success of Redstone Farm – some say against serious odds; he led a healthy outdoor life. His devotion to the ideal of organic farming was beyond doubt, and forced him to be outspoken on the subject on many occasions. There are those who might envy him, despite his shocking end. Now, let us sing the hymn chosen by his family, "Abide With Me".'

The deep soulful eyes of the lovely Lilah had been fixed intently on him since the mistake about the time they'd been at the farm. He had acted up accordingly, giving the best performance he could manage. Like a Madonna, the girl was, Father Edmund thought sadly. An intelligent modern Madonna, remote and serene. A woman to dream about, if you were the type to dream about women. No need to worry about *her* breaking down. It was the widow, Miranda, who bothered Father Edmund more. Throughout the service, the woman had kept up a constant irritating sniff, dabbing endlessly at her nose with a man's large white hanky. She held onto her daughter's arm like a drowning person, virtually ignoring the wretched young Roddy on her other side.

Father Edmund could identify only too well with Roddy. Grimly, the boy had set his jaw against any unseemly weaknesses. He sat as if alone in the world, suffering in that hidden, brave British way which makes some unworthy souls yearn to keep jabbing until the pain became apparent.

Finally they got to the graveside. The late May sun blazed down, the air was filled with smells of newly cut grass, honeysuckle, privet flowers. Not so much as a hint of the malodorous slurry which still filled everyone's mental nostrils, and remained clinging to the walls of Guy Beardon's bronchial passages. The four black-suited bearers – one of them, Lilah noted, the very man whose shoe had been splashed with slurry when Guy was taken away – sweated masochistically, preparing to lower the stout coffin deep into the ground. Nobody bothered to scatter soil or flowers on the lid, as Father Edmund intoned the final words. Miranda had never been to a funeral before, and presumably knew nothing of the procedure. With a small shrug, the vicar let it go. What did it signify anyway?

Lilah couldn't watch at the last moment, when the coffin was lowered ceremoniously into the hole lined with violently coloured artificial grass. She turned her head away and was immediately distracted by the sight of a young woman watching from beyond the hedge bordering the churchyard. The woman was standing completely still, her gaze fixed intently on the proceedings. Almost everyone who had been in the church was now hovering awkwardly between the church door and the lychgate, but this observer was not just another villager, come to join the party. This was Elvira, who lived in the old stone cottage opposite the churchyard with Phoebe, her mother. Elvira had been born damaged in some way, so that she stared at everything with the same unrelenting hunger. Her stare was legendary; few could meet her gaze for long. She must have seen funerals before, living as she did so close to the church; Lilah could imagine that they made a welcome diversion for her, as would the weddings and the carol services. All the same, it was unsettling to see her there, and Lilah turned her attention quickly back to the coffin, out of sight now unless you leant over the edge, and this was something she had no desire to do.

The Beardons were forced to run the gauntlet as they walked away from the grave, passing a line of villagers, each keen to convey condolences and make their presence felt. It was, after all, something of an effort to attend a funeral and they did not intend that their generous gesture should go unmarked. One by one, people took Miranda by the hand. Mrs Axford from the shop; the gentlemanly and forbearing Wing Commander Stradling; Martha Cattermole – 'Oh, I didn't see you in the church,' said Lilah in surprise. 'How nice of you to come.'

Martha was another familiar face from school, but unlike Den Cooper, she had been on the staff and Lilah a favourite pupil of hers. They had kept in touch after Lilah left. Martha and her sisters were so well born that they almost qualified as aristocracy; they lived in a huge and beautiful house outside a larger village, four or five miles away. Today Martha wore a long cotton skirt and an embroidered waistcoat, her frizzy hair – the colour of apricots in the bright sunshine – tied back, showing the sharp definition of her jaw. She stood out in the line of so-called mourners like a Siamese cat in a row of tabbies.

'I was so sorry when I heard,' she said. 'It must have been such a shock. And I liked your father. He was an original.'

Lilah couldn't reply. This was the first time anybody had paid tribute to Guy as if they really meant it. It highlighted the deficiency of regret amongst Guy's acquaintances and Lilah had to blink hard for a moment. 'Yes,' she said.

She and Martha had talked before about the similarities between their families. Although from different social classes, they were both misfits in the rooted community. The Cattermoles were bohemian, with exotic, well-connected friends. Martha had adopted teaching as a profession out of a passionate sense of commitment. 'And the money comes in useful,' she said, more than once. 'We're nothing like as rich as we look.' She was in her mid-thirties and her friendship with Lilah was yet another topic for local gossip.

The line continued. Miss Trott and Miss Singleton, who lived in adjacent cottages in the main street and felt they somehow represented the village as a whole by virtue of the geography of their homes: they shook hands with all three Beardons, and nodded solemnly in acknowledgement of Miranda's mumbled thanks. Next came Mr Spencer, the family's solicitor. He bent forward and murmured to Miranda, 'If I might make an appointment to see you within the next few days?'

She widened her eyes. 'You'd better phone me,' she said. 'I can't think about it now.' Next came Amos and Isaac Grimsdale, brothers and close neighbours to the Beardons. 'You must come back to the house with us,' said Miranda.

'You've known us such a long time, you're almost family.' Lilah gasped inwardly at the gross exaggeration. But it was beginning to look as if the funeral gathering would be uncomfortably sparse if some reinforcements weren't found, and the Grimsdales did have some claim to be included.

Finally there was Den Cooper. Lilah had seen him as she followed the coffin out of the church, and had hoped he would wait long enough for her to speak to him. But now she had the chance, she couldn't think what to say.

'I hope you didn't mind me coming?' he said to Miranda, who had automatically shaken his hand. She looked at him in some confusion; he was not in uniform.

'It's Den, Mum. The policeman who came—'

'I know who he is,' lied Miranda. 'I just wondered why—'

'Mum!' Lilah felt a clenching embarrassment. Would her mother never learn to guard her tongue – or would she herself never learn to mind what was said? She turned to Den. 'It was very kind of you to come,' she said firmly.

Den cleared his throat. 'Well, it's not so much *kind*,' he demurred.

'You mean it's all part of the job?' Miranda asked. 'I wouldn't have thought it necessary for you to turn up at the funeral of every accidental death you come across.'

'Well—' He looked to Lilah for rescue.

'Mum, you're being very rude. Go and talk to the vicar.' She looked into Den's eyes, remembered again, with a rush of vivid images, how friendly they had always seemed when she'd met his reflection in that bus mirror.

'It wasn't just duty,' he started to explain. 'I felt – well, *connected*. Having been there so soon after it happened.'

'It doesn't matter why you're here. It's just nice to see you,' she said. 'It's interesting, who's here and who's not. Mum's best friend is away on holiday. Both lots of neighbours showed up . . .' She indicated Amos and Isaac with a little tilt of her head. '. . . but the Mabberleys seem to have rushed off already.'

'Interesting,' he agreed blandly. 'Now you should go. I'll be seeing you.'

Now for Father Edmund. As they straggled back to the cars waiting outside the church gate, Lilah laid a hand on his arm. 'Thank you, Mr Larkin,' she said. 'You did it very nicely.'

Two emotions fought within the vicar. Gratitude that she had acknowledged him wrestled with annoyance at the 'Mr Larkin'. Nobody *ever* called him that. The influence of the heathenish Guy was at work here, he realised. The man had been obsessed with removing people's formal titles, like some crackpot Quaker, and 'Mr' was as far as he would ever go. The chief victim in the village had been Wing Commander Stradling. Guy made an elaborate ritual of always addressing him as 'Mr Stradling'. He would call to him in a loud voice across the hall at the Parish Council meetings, or refer to him in ringing tones within the man's hearing. The fact that Father Edmund himself had some sympathy with the principle only made it more maddening. He knew he would never have had Guy's courage when face-to-face with the long-retired airman.

He smiled thinly at Lilah, automatically switching into his occupational demeanour. He bowed his head slightly, and patted her upper arm with a limp hand. 'I'm glad to be of service to you at such a difficult time,' he whispered. 'Look after your poor mother, won't you. Come and see

28

me, if there's anything at all I can do.' The words flowed spontaneously, without conscious thought. Once in a while, he almost caught himself adopting an Irish inflection. True priestliness was somehow done best by the Irish, he believed. It was perhaps bad luck that he'd been so firmly entrenched in Anglicanism from his earliest days. Much of the passion and the acceptance, the hypocrisy and the good cheer of the Romans appealed to him in his more whimsical moments.

Beyond the church gates, villagers were gathered in knots. This was in effect the last real chance to have a serious gossip about the event; now that Guy was buried, ten days after his death, the thing was over and there'd be little more to be said. An inquest had been opened and adjourned to some future date, but the Beardons had already been told by a laconic man who announced himself as the Coroner's Officer that it would probably be brief and undramatic. He mentioned that there was always an excess of formality in the case of an accident with no witnesses, but since the post-mortem examination had found sufficient matter in the lungs to drown Mr Beardon, it would take very little to convince the Coroner that the circumstances were unsuspicious. Nobody would be churlish enough to take matters any further than 'death by misadventure'. Nobody was unduly keen to dwell on the details of what happens when slurry enters the lungs, either. It was already virtually a foregone conclusion as to what the final verdict would be.

Guy had died by accident, the official judgement would ordain. He had slipped on the edge of the pit, and fallen in, possibly knocking his head in the process, and blacking out. The stuff in his mouth and throat was more than enough to suffocate him. Gruesome, by general consent, and reason enough to give rise to a knee-jerk demand for special security measures for such pits.

With the verdict already taken for granted, the villagers felt justified, however, in extensive idle speculations. A stranger passing through might have observed a series of pantomimes, as people enacted their own pet theory of how Guy might have met his death. Lengths of hose lay about the yard – he could have caught his foot. There had been light rain during the night – perhaps enough to make the ground unusually slippery for rubber boots. Or he might have been muzzy with sleep, and just stepped off the edge thinking he was somewhere else.

The slurry pit was fairly new to Redstone, and Guy had typically not bothered to apply for permission from the Council to build it. Pleased with his own cleverness, he had positioned it at the foot of a natural slope, thirty yards from the big back door of the shippon. At the same time he had reconstructed the floor of the cowshed and the yard outside with channels for the muck, so that it could be sluiced out and straight down into the pit. Strong fencing protected it on three sides, but the fourth was open. In Guy's usual fashion, safety had been assured by a total ban on any of his family going within six feet of the edge on that side. Everyone obeyed Guy's edicts, including this one. So compliant was Lilah that she had felt distinctly disobedient when she finally went to the edge of the pit in her search for Guy that dreadful morning.

Father Edmund watched his parishioners with some cynicism. It seemed that few of his quiet hints as to the probability of suicide had taken root. This was a shame, but at the same time, almost nobody seemed to have seriously considered foul play. How foolish, how naive of them, thought the minister. Did they think such wickedness impossible in their peaceful, forgotten little corner of the world?

With his customary fixed smile, Father Edmund scanned their faces. Sam Carter, the Beardons' worker, was driving the family home. Stiff in his dark suit, the man seemed pathetic. His brief exposure to public attention had clearly been uncomfortable to him. Sam had intrigued the vicar for a long time, yet they'd rarely exchanged more than a morning nod in six years. Sam was said to be a professed atheist – the very fact that he had once expressed such a definite position on the matter made him interesting. *One day*, thought Father Edmund, *one day, I shall really get to know that man.*

The group of Beardon family mourners and close friends climbed into an assortment of cars and drove away. Guy's two brothers and Miranda's parents swelled the numbers. Father Edmund went back to the vicarage, having politely declined Miranda's murmured invitation to accompany the family to the farmhouse for some sandwiches. Guy Beardon was really dead, then, he repeated to himself. Who in this small community could ever have guessed it would come to this? No one else, he believed, knew what he knew about the dead farmer. And, knowing what he did, he was entitled to a small complacent smirk when the villagers spoke of accidents.

Chapter Three

The funeral wake was typically noisy. Martin, Guy's elder brother, was a large oafish man in his sixties, who hadn't been near Redstone for five years or more. He seemed to have taken it upon himself to lift Miranda's spirits, and he hung around her, a lumpen hand on her arm, telling stories of Guy as a child, always getting into trouble. 'Stubborn wasn't the word,' he chuckled. 'That boy – sometimes we thought he must be a gypsy child, swapped for our real brother in the pram. Always into something, breaking the rules, getting himself hurt. He's probably told you about most of it himself.'

Miranda had to bring herself back from the hazy unreality in which she had spent the days since Guy's death. She looked up at the strange man who had attached himself to her. What had he asked her? Something about Guy as a little boy . . . 'He said his father was always chasing after him with a stick. It sounded a violent sort of upbringing. He never raised a hand to Roddy, to my knowledge.'

'Aye, Dad didn't stand any nonsense. Never did much good in Guy's case, though. He always skipped out of range. He must have mellowed in his ways if he's never thrashed your Roddy. He was still pretty wild in his twenties – and later. I can remember, oh, must have been thirty years ago now—'

'Mum,' Lilah interrupted without apology, 'Grampa says he's got to go in a minute. Something about missing the traffic.'

Miranda cast a vague look around the crowded living room, hoping to find her friend Sylvia. People stood about with cups of tea and plates full of the food which had been prepared by women of the village. Most of them were dressed in black or dark blue, but with smiles on their faces. Roland, Guy's other brother, was sitting in an armchair, his thighs spread wide and his shoulders pressed well back, as if the chair was too small for him and he was trying to stretch it. Roddy stood beside him, looking down resentfully at the unfamiliar uncle and proffering a plate of small cakes as Roland chatted volubly to Sam, who perched uneasily on the edge of the sofa close by.

Miranda's father, a small, elderly man in an expensive dark suit with worry writ large across his features, stood by the door, obviously hoping for a rapid escape. Hetty Taplow from the village skittered back and forth with trays, acting the part of maid with enthusiasm. She had arrived unasked, as she did at most funerals, knowing she would not be rejected, and knowing too that the stories gleaned would keep her in friendship for months to come. Everyone, including Hetty, considered the Beardons to be remote, almost mysterious, with the mismatched parents and self-sufficient children. Hetty cleaned three mornings a week for the Cattermoles in the big Georgian house in a nearby village, as well as serving behind the bar at the pub on Saturdays. There was very little local gossip that passed her by.

'Where's Sylvia?' Miranda asked her daughter. 'How am I supposed to manage all this without Sylvia? And will you look at the Grimms. What are they doing here?'

Lilah followed her gaze. Standing together, in crumpled grey suits dating back no less than thirty years, were the Grimsdale brothers, Isaac and Amos – close neighbours in rural terms, their house a little over a quarter of a mile away, on a facing hillside. Miranda had given them their nickname in an attempt to convince Lilah and Roddy that they were nothing to be frightened of. 'Like the Brothers Grimm,' she'd explained. 'I shouldn't be surprised if these two write the odd fairy story, as well.' But when Lilah told Guy this suggestion, he laughed dismissively.

'Neither one of them can write at all,' he'd said. 'Signing their names is just about the best they can manage.'

Guy had bought the Grimsdale farm, piecemeal, over the years, leaving the brothers in an island of weedy meadow, their stone house slowly disintegrating about their ears. For Roddy and Lilah they had been bogeymen, crazily irascible, always on the edge of their awareness, only two fields away from their own house. But now Lilah would not be distracted.

'You invited them yourself,' she sighed. 'And Sylvia's away. You know she is. You were supposed to be feeding her animals – remember?'

'Oh, God! They'll have starved by now!'

'No they won't. It's all taken care of. Pull yourself together. Say something to Grampa.'

34

But it was Miranda's mother who next grabbed the widow's attention. She wore a good dark suit to match her husband's, and now stared disapprovingly at Lilah's short skirt and cotton top. 'Hasn't she got a proper suit?'

'Of course she hasn't,' snapped Miranda. 'What would a girl like her want with a suit?'

'You must let Grampa buy her one, dear. It's an awful embarrassment to be caught at a time like this with nothing suitable to wear.'

'Really, Mum, I don't think people bother about clothes so much these days. It would be a wicked waste of money.'

Her mother sighed. 'This is all so terrible, I don't think it's sunk in properly yet. I mean, *Guy*. He was always so full of life. *Too* full of life, some might say.'

Miranda just nodded. Her mother was of no help to her; her father was even worse – dithering, talking nonsense a lot of the time. Lilah had been saying for months that she thought he was developing Alzheimer's, and Miranda could see this afternoon that it might be true. He hadn't once mentioned Guy, but talked earnestly about the forty-mile drive they'd endured to get here and how he didn't know how he'd ever get them home again, with so many holiday-makers on the roads, and the car making a very odd knocking sound. Mother didn't drive, but sat stoically beside him, offering navigational help and soothing reassurance.

'I've a good mind to ask Grampa to stay and help with the milking,' said Lilah, crossly.

'Well don't,' said Miranda, with a small giggle. 'He'd only spoil that suit. Why don't you ask the Grimms instead?' Her giggle took on an hysterical note.

'You'll have to come and see Granny and Grampa off,' Lilah insisted, firmly. Miranda turned belatedly back to Martin, still with his mouth open, poised to continue his interrupted story. With a little shrug and a smile, she left him, letting Lilah take her place.

'I was just telling your mother about Guy, when he was a youngster,' Martin began again.

'How much older were you?' she asked, to be polite.

'I was eight when he was born, and Roland was six. Quite threw us sideways it did, for a bit. Ma was ill having him, which meant half the work didn't get done, and he yowled all the time. We hated that baby, but he never seemed to mind. Once he could walk and get about outside, he was always as happy as a cricket.'

Lilah tried to see the images as her uncle was seeing them. The isolated family, on a farm deep in the Devonshire countryside, the little latecomer, upsetting the harmony, going his own wilful way despite all reproaches. She felt a pang of affection for the difficult child her father had been. Martin went on, 'Left home when he was sixteen, you know. Didn't see him for years after that. We thought he'd gone into the army, lying about his age, but Roland always said he'd never do that. Too much of a rebel for that. Prison was more like it, he said. Lucky for Guy that National Service finished just as he reached eighteen. We just sort of forgot about him after a while. Ma never got over it, though. He came back two days before she died, as if he'd known. Weird business.'

Martin shook his head wonderingly, helpless in the face of telepathic magic. Lilah felt a tension between wanting to hear more and knowing it wasn't the right moment. 'Uncle

Martin,' she said, 'I wish you came to see us more often. We should talk. Dad never told us anything about his early life.'

'Well, that doesn't surprise me,' said her uncle. 'There'd be quite a bit he'd rather keep quiet about. But it's been good to see you again, though it's a sad occasion. Makes you think, this kind of thing. Makes you see things different. I never thought our Guy would pitch himself into the slurry. What a way to go!' He pulled the same disgusted face that Lilah had been seeing on practically everyone since the fateful morning.

'I'll have to go and circulate,' she excused herself. 'It was good of you to come.'

'It was worth it to see you so grown up,' he responded gallantly. 'Quite a change from the last time.'

She smiled and turned to go. She wanted to find Roddy, check that he was all right – he must be feeling lonely amongst all these adults. Apart from her, there was nobody else under thirty. She found him in the kitchen, helping Hetty. Her musical Devon voice flowed constantly. 'Y'ere, my lover, do you take the plates through,' she ordered him, giving him two big plates of sandwiches to carry. Lilah waited for him, and took one of the plates.

'How're you doing?' she asked.

''Tis fair mazed I be,' he quipped. Conversing in pseudo-Devon dialect was a game they had always played. Neither of them could manage the real thing; Guy had worked hard to eradicate it from his own voice and had successfully prevented his children from adopting it. Or so he had believed. The fact that their mother had grown up in a middle-class family in Surrey was overlooked as a formative factor.

'Pity Jonathan isn't here,' Lilah said.

'You're joking. He wouldn't dare. Dad loathed him.'

'Lots of people didn't bother coming, when you think about it. Tim and Sarah, the Cattermoles, half the Parish Council—'

'They didn't *like* him, Li. They're just being honest. You have to admire them for not being hypocrites. Most of the people here only came because of Mum. Like the Grimms.'

'She misses Sylvia. You'd think a person's best friend would cut short a holiday for something like this.'

'Does she know about it?'

'Good question. Maybe she doesn't. She went off the morning we found Dad. She was probably at the airport before the news got out.'

'Sandwich?' Roddy proffered his plate to Sam, who had drifted aimlessly into the kitchen, instinctively seeking the two people he knew best. He put up a resistant hand and shook his head. He pulled a pained expression at the youngsters, indicating both discomfort and sorrow.

'Don't worry, they'll soon go,' Lilah assured him. 'Then we can get back to work.'

The sandwiches proved unwanted by almost everybody when Roddy did a dutiful circuit of the living room, so he took them back to the kitchen virtually untouched.

'Silly sods,' said Hetty. 'Food for free, this be.' Alongside her role as information exchange between a small network of villages, Hetty also acted as the focal point for a complex bartering system, so that nothing was ever wasted. Outgrown clothes, surplus plants or animals, second-hand tools and equipment – Hetty always knew someone who was looking for the very thing. She eyed the plates as if trying to remember just who had asked her to watch out for the cheese and tomato in granary, or ham and cucumber without crusts.

'Phoebe!' she said suddenly. 'Her's been poorly and missed work for nearly a month.' She looked hard at Lilah, and then back at the sandwiches.

'Oh yes, take them,' said the girl. 'I didn't know Phoebe wasn't well. I haven't seen her for ages.'

Back in the living room, Lilah realised that more people were on the verge of leaving. Once the momentum got going there was a barely dignified scramble for the door and within minutes, there were just Sam, Roddy, Miranda and Hetty left.

'Mum, I told Hetty she could take some leftovers for Phoebe Winnicombe. She's poorly, apparently, and if she doesn't work she doesn't get any money. That's all right, isn't it?'

'Fine,' said Miranda vaguely. Lilah wasn't even sure she'd registered who she was talking about. She smiled at Hetty and was rewarded by seeing her tip almost every morsel of uneaten food on to a tray, to be covered in cling film. *Lucky Phoebe*, she thought grimly.

'Uncle Martin's nice,' she commented later, to her mother and brother. 'Did you know that Dad left home at sixteen, and didn't go back for years and years?'

'That was a long time ago. He was thirty-six when I met him. It was ancient history by then.'

'Funny how you never think much about people's pasts when they're alive, and then as soon as they die, you wish you'd known all sorts of things about them.'

'It makes sense, if you think about it,' said Miranda. 'It's easier to hold onto the memory of them if you know as much as you can. It makes them more real.' Lilah was impressed, but she tried not to show it.

'Well I'm off to help Sam and Roddy. See you later.'

Miranda sighed. 'Busy, busy,' she commented. 'I can't wait until we sell this bloody place.'

Lilah stood rigid, turned to stone by her mother's words. 'What?' she whispered. 'What did you say?'

'Well, we can't keep it up without Guy, can we? Surely you realise that. It was almost the first thing I thought, when you told me he was dead. Now I can get away from this wretched shitty hole, and live somewhere civilised. I'm sorry if you don't like it, but it happens to be true.'

Lilah realised her mother had been drinking, but that wasn't enough to negate her words. Possessed with rage, she could hardly speak.

'We are never *never* going to sell the farm,' she shouted. 'It's my inheritance, and Roddy's. It's our *home*.' Without waiting for a reply, she swung out of the door and crossed the yard erratically, shaking almost as much as on the morning that Guy died. She knew she was on the verge of war with her mother, and was determined to battle to keep Redstone going, whatever might happen.

Nothing more was said on the subject that day. They all went to bed very early, drained by the emotion of the day and knowing the business of the farm had to be tackled first thing next morning, and every morning while they remained at Redstone. Lilah thought of the naughty little boy she'd been told

about and wondered bleakly for a moment about the passage
of time and death and whether any of it meant anything.

They woke next morning to a steady drizzle, which cast a
sullen gloom over everything from the first moment they
opened their eyes. Sam, in his self-contained room which
opened directly onto the yard, struggled with his clothes
in the semi-darkness, forcing his thoughts away from the
terrible morning, only a week and a half ago, when Lilah
had shouted for him. The ghastly business of retrieving Guy
from the slurry haunted his dreams, and he feared it would
do so for the rest of his life.

As he went out into the yard, a sack held over his head
and shoulders against the rain, he cast his eyes up the rising
slope to where the roof of the Grimsdales' house could
be seen. It was something he did every morning, without
knowing why. The sun rose over that roof; perhaps that was
it. In winter months, the first pale suggestion of dawn came
to that stretch of sky first. There was also the telltale plume
of smoke, rising from the chimney, indicating the wind
direction. However early Sam and Guy might have risen for
the morning milking, Amos and Isaac were always earlier.
Once or twice Guy had joked that he thought they must be
vampires or zombies, living a nocturnal existence. Sam had
disapproved of such remarks – weren't the youngsters scared
enough of the brothers already?

The fact that there was no smoke on this particular
morning did not strike Sam as odd; the drizzle would have
obscured it anyway. He could barely even see the house.
Glumly, he trudged to the field gate, halfway down the

lane, and called the usual 'Ho! Ho!' at the cows, to bring them trooping submissively into the milking yard. He had convinced Lilah and Roddy that he could manage on his own. The cows behaved much better for him than they ever had for Guy, and if they pushed into the stalls in the wrong sequence, what did it matter? They all got dealt with, one way or another, and the milk yield was just as good as it had ever been.

Lilah's alarm clock was set to coincide with the final minutes of the milking, so that she could play a part in returning the cows to their field, while Sam sluiced down the equipment and tidied up. As she emerged into the persistent rain, she too glanced up towards the Grimms' house. What she saw did not give her any indication of the day's weather. Running clumsily, a hand held to the side of his head, which was splashed grotesquely with deep red, was Amos Grimsdale. As he came closer, she could see how sunken his eyes were, his mouth a dark circle of suffering and horror. He was trying to speak.

Hesitantly, she moved towards him, remembering all the times she had run away and hidden from him, creating a bogeyman with which to frighten herself. Now, she had no choice but to behave responsibly. A few moments later she could hear his words: 'Isaac! Help me! Isaac – he's dead.'

Chapter Four

Sam and Lilah both followed Amos back to his house, trying to soothe his babbling, numbly prepared for whatever horror they might encounter. Lilah had run back to her own house first, yelling at Miranda to wake up, phone the police, send them to the Grimms' house. She wasn't sure that anything would be done as she'd ordered.

'He won't really be dead,' said Sam, repeating it like a mantra, trying to convince Amos or perhaps himself. But when Lilah looked at the vicious lesion on the side of the old man's head, she was not reassured. When they found Isaac, lying in his jumbled bed, not bleeding, but staring with sightless eyes at the ceiling, they had to agree with Amos. A ghastly cavity beside Isaac's right eye showed where a savage blow had been struck, forceful enough to kill him. The clear assumption was that the same attempt had been made on Amos, but with less skill or effectiveness. Together they turned to him.

'Who was it?' asked Sam. 'What bloody bugger did this, eh?'

Amos sat down heavily in a chair beside the bedroom door, ignoring the pile of clothes draped over the seat and back. He looked dazed, vacant. At first Lilah thought he was groping for a description of the murderer, remembering the face and trying to put a name to it. But then he began to slide sideways, like a badly propped-up doll, and she realised they were not going to get any answers from him.

'Sam!' she cried. 'Catch him!' Carefully they laid him on the floor, and then scrambled around and over each other, putting a pillow under his head, covering him with a grimy blanket.

'He's still breathing,' Lilah whispered, after a few moments. 'What about his pulse?'

Sam shrugged. 'No good at first aid. Never mind all that, so long as he's breathing. Let's just hope your Mum makes that phone call.'

'Poor old chap. Doesn't he look pathetic.' She stared curiously at the man she'd been afraid of for years. A ragged beard covered his lower face; his hair, which had been brushed for the funeral, was reverting to its normal scarecrow style. His skin was like the bark of a tree, so weathered and ravaged and unwashed was it. At least his wound seemed to have stopped bleeding. 'Just a poor old man, who's minded his own business all his life.'

'Not sure about that,' grunted Sam. 'Blessed tinkers, these Grimms are. Not so old, either. What a way to live. Look at it!' He glanced around the room, one of two bedrooms; at the filthy window, the unsavoury pile of old clothes in one corner, the heavily cobwebbed ceiling.

Lilah looked, and couldn't restrain a little laugh. 'Makes Redstone look like Buckingham Palace,' she commented.

'Funny – I've never been in here before, and I've lived next door for most of my life.'

Sam grunted again, and turned to look at the inert Isaac. 'Two dead bodies in two weeks is going it a bit,' he muttered. 'Don't like to think what the police'll say.'

Lilah's mind slowly absorbed what Sam had said. She stared at him. 'But this is nothing to do with Daddy,' she told him, earnestly. 'How could it be? Daddy fell in the slurry.'

Sam nodded at her. 'He did, lovey. He did indeed.' And then came the slamming of a car door and the familiar tones of the young policeman. Despite the awfulness of the situation, Lilah felt a stab of pleasure as she recognised the voice. Meeting Den again so soon was at least a crumb of consolation.

A moment later, an ambulance siren was audible, and all was bustle amidst uniformed men and gentle questions. Amos was rushed away in the ambulance, which did little to reduce the sense of a very crowded little farmhouse. Sam and Lilah were banished from the bedroom while Isaac was examined in the greatest detail, as well as photographed. Then another carload of police arrived. All was suddenly serious. Den took Sam and Lilah out into the yard, and they explained what had happened.

'Two sudden deaths, only ten days apart,' Den said to himself. 'That's likely to change our view about how Mr Beardon died.'

'Told you it would,' said Sam to Lilah. 'No such thing as coincidence – I've always said that.'

'Don't be stupid,' she snapped back at him. '*Of course* there's such a thing. It makes no sense at all to try to connect the Grimms with Daddy.'

Sam raised his eyebrows and clamped his lips together, a picture of stubborn patience. But then his eyes narrowed and he decided to speak. 'It's time you woke up to a few things about your precious father,' he said. 'You're old enough now to give up some of your rosy ideas about him.'

'What do you mean?' She tried to keep the little-girl vulnerability out of her voice, knowing she often exploited her position when with Sam, just as she had with her father. Adopting adult behaviour when acting as a very junior farmhand had been impossible, and there had been a collective game – almost a conspiracy – to prevent her from growing up. To have Sam tell her now to act her age was an unkind shock, particularly in the present circumstances.

Den picked up Sam's remark in a different way. 'Are you saying there are things about Mr Beardon that the police should know?' he enquired. 'Things you haven't told us?'

Sam rubbed one boot against a cobble set into the yard. 'Bound to be,' he mumbled. 'You never asked me about him, did you? Him as a person. Just about finding him in the muck.'

Den drew a sharp breath and glanced at the group of police officers emerging from the house. Lilah was immediately aware of how different things were this time. This was a crime, deliberately violent. Nothing could be touched, not even the body, until a full examination of the scene had been made. It was horrible – and oddly exciting, she realised with a twinge of shame.

'Perhaps you two could come with us,' an older man said to Lilah and Sam, with a nod at Den. 'Thanks, Cooper. We'll go through your findings when we've finished here.' Lilah cast a desperate glance at Den, seeking explanations, reassurance. But although he met her eyes, he gave nothing away.

In an untidy procession, half the party left the house and crammed into one of the police cars. As they drove cautiously down the rutted, twisting lane, they met the undertaker's men, in the same Renault Espace which had collected Guy's body. Lilah felt a lurch of agony as she recognised it. The two vehicles could not pass in the narrow lane, and hesitated, nose to nose, before the Espace began to reverse. When they finally came alongside, the two drivers wound down their windows to speak.

'Take him straight to Pathology, will you?' said the policeman.

'Right you are,' agreed the undertaker's man, neutrally.

'Can we go round to Redstone and tell my mother what's happening, please?' Lilah asked, in a flat tone. 'We're not in any great hurry, are we?'

The man driving the car glanced at the policewoman next to him. She gave no perceptible response, but he seemed satisfied.

'That'll be all right,' he said. 'If you're quick.'

They were eventually taken to a police station ten miles away and questioned separately. It took a long time for Lilah to explain about the Grimms, and how they were virtual strangers to her, despite their close proximity. She knew nothing about any relatives they might have. No, she had no idea who might want to kill them. Her father had said they were tinkers, gypsies, but only as an expression of scorn – they weren't really. She thought they'd been born in that house. Perhaps they had shady acquaintances. They were poachers, probably. She threw out random suggestions, hoping to strike the right answer, as much for her own sake as for the requirements of the law.

'Am I right in thinking they've been your close neighbours for – what? Fourteen years, did you say?'

Lilah nodded.

'And you don't know anything more than you've told me about them?'

'No. Sam might, or Mum. But I really know nothing about them. They live on the money Dad gave them for the sale of their fields, I think. I have absolutely no idea who might want to kill them.'

At last, the interview ended, and they gave her a cup of tepid coffee. The atmosphere relaxed, and Den Cooper came into the room, clearly sent to look after her.

'Oh, God,' she sighed. 'I think I must be in a nightmare. This is all so weird. Is there any news about Amos?'

'They think he'll live. He came round for a minute, apparently, but he's badly shaken up.'

'Aren't we all,' said Lilah grimly. 'Why on earth did this have to happen, just when we were trying to get back to normal?'

'You poor thing,' he sympathised. 'It must have been like a rerun of last time.'

She thought about it, staring up at the small window, and the tree pressing close against it outside. 'No,' she said. 'It isn't anything like last time.'

'Well, we think it is.' He fell silent, and started to fiddle self-consciously with the notepad still lying on the table. 'We think we should probably have opened a murder inquiry on Guy Beardon, from the start.'

Lilah was dumb at first. Then: 'But *why?* It doesn't make sense. You haven't got any reason to think that. There's no evidence—'

'That's a problem, yes. There might have been some, but your Sam washed it all away. Not his fault. But we can't just let it go. Not now. There'll be a file opened and more interviews. They'll probably let me do some of it.'

'So we've got to live like that, have we? As an open file which could at any moment turn into a prosecution for murder?'

'Until there's evidence one way or the other, yes. But for now it's Isaac's killer we'll be concentrating on. Poor old chap. What a way to go.'

They took her and Sam home again. The rain had stopped, and they could see Roddy in the barn, cutting a sack of calf nuts open with a penknife. Sam made a click of annoyance, and Lilah knew without his saying anything that Roddy should have opened it by pulling the string at the top. She remembered her father ripping ferociously at the obstructive fastening, which would only ever yield to a gentle touch. The harder a person pulled, the more impossible it became to unravel the string. 'Lateral thinking,' she said. 'Roddy's a lateral thinker. And he likes to use that knife whenever he can.'

The four of them gathered in the kitchen, which still had the remnants of the funeral foods – the scraps that Hetty had left behind – scattered on the worktops. Lilah spoke explosively, feeling the words echo inside her head, after she'd uttered them. 'They think Daddy was murdered. They think the same person killed Isaac and possibly Amos as well, if he doesn't get better. They'll be coming to empty the slurry pit as soon as they can, to look for anything suspicious.'

Miranda's face was white. 'What exactly are they going to do?'

'They're sending round a forensics team, later on this morning. If they can't find anything, they'll have to let it go, I suppose. Have the inquest, and accept whatever the verdict says.'

'It's just a horrible coincidence,' said Roddy, on the verge of tears. 'It must be. Or if there has to be a connection, it could just be that somebody's read about Dad in the papers and came snooping round, and—' he tailed off.

'And decided to try and murder two old men. Why would they do that, Rod? I can only think of one reason – to shut them up, because they'd seen or heard something about what happened to Daddy. And Sam says there's no such thing as coincidence – don't you, Sam?'

'That's what I think,' Sam confirmed quietly. 'And I told the police as much. The Grimms aren't just two innocent old men. They've had their share of trouble. I told the police – ask around the village. Ask Hetty Taplow, for one. It was she that told me, years ago now.'

'Told you what?' Lilah and Miranda asked together.

'I'd best not say.' He ducked his head, defiant. 'If Amos gets better, he can tell them himself. Anyway there's work to be done. If those forensics chaps are coming, we'd best be ready for them.' He clumped out into the yard, glancing automatically up the hill to the Grimms' roof, and then he turned away with a grimace. Roddy followed him.

'Somebody better start thinking about what'll happen when

I have to go back to school and take my exams,' he grumbled, as he went. 'I'm only on study leave, in case you've forgotten.'

That day seemed like a whole week of turmoil and confusion. Lilah took the forensics people all around the slurry pit, trying to describe how she'd found Guy, what exactly she and Sam had done, what she had heard and seen. Then they questioned Sam, Roddy and Miranda, in turn. It was obvious that nothing any of them said suggested a deliberate killing. Then the police widened their examinations by going into the milking parlour, Guy's office, and finally the house.

'I've read about this sort of thing,' Roddy murmured to his sister, as the men went meticulously through the drawers of Guy's office desk, picking up letters and bank statements and putting them carefully into plastic bags. 'Though I thought they'd be much rougher than this.'

'It's not a drugs raid,' she replied indignantly. 'They've no reason to suspect us of anything.'

The police instructed Sam to empty the pit as quickly as he could, listening with some impatience to his explanations of the procedure and how long it would take. They would have to hire in a tanker, not having one of their own, and the muck would have to be spread on the fields.

'Now, hang on a minute,' said a senior policeman. 'We can't wait while you do all that.'

'So where should we put it?' demanded Lilah. 'It's a health hazard if we just let it run across the yard and it might get into the stream if we're not careful.'

The men looked around the yard, exchanged glances, and

finally nodded reluctant agreement. 'Take it onto the fields, then,' they said.

A wide-diameter flexible hosepipe was lowered into the pit, and the tanker's pump set going. Gradually, with a prodigious stirring-up of the slurry smell, the level fell. Soon the tanker was full and Sam drove off to a designated field to spread the muck. The job would take all day, at least, and Lilah's help was only sporadically required. Aimlessly, she drifted away, unsure of what needed her attentions most. Roddy, true to form, had vanished to his room to revise for his GCSEs. Miranda was chopping brambles away from the garden gate. Lilah watched her for a moment.

'Pity to cut them now,' she called. 'We'd have got some good blackberries from them later on.'

'Not these bits,' Miranda corrected. 'They're new growth. I swear they make a good three inches' progress a day at this time of year. Another week and they'd be right across the gate. We couldn't get in or out without being scratched.'

'Mmmm,' murmured Lilah, losing interest. An uncharacteristic apathy had gripped her, and she remained unmoving in the yard, with a few hens scratching close by and a large airliner rumbling overhead. The bustle of the forensics people had abated; most of them had already departed with mysterious plastic bags containing tiny scraps of who knew what.

Sam's return with the noisy tractor and malodorous tanker came as quite a relief. It would take a dozen or more fill-ups to empty the pit, and then the distasteful job would be over until the coming winter. *By then, we probably won't be here anyway*, thought Lilah, with a sharp sense of grief.

The bottom of the pit was not smooth and obvious, as the bottom of a swimming pool might have been. The straw content of the slurry sank to the bottom, creating hillocks and valleys; a miniature landscape. Once all the semi-liquid matter was gone, there was still a lot of work shovelling the dense slabs of residue into a pile in one corner, and then left to dry out further, for use on the garden. Various objects then came to light.

The three attending policemen lined up with Lilah and Roddy, watching Sam fish the objects out. A brick; a horrible shapeless lump which turned out to be a dead hen on closer examination; several chunks of wood, apparently fallen from a dying oak tree growing above one end of the pit; and a shoe.

The last created real excitement as Sam presented it on the end of his shovel, and Roddy fetched a bucket of water to wash it in. He and Lilah stood back and let the officials get their hands dirty. Before long they held it up. A training shoe, complete with laces, its original colour blue or grey.

'I'd say a size six, or thereabouts,' said one of the men.

Lilah wished passionately that she could say it was hers, lost months ago after some silly game with Roddy. Or that it was from an old pair, no longer used, and given to the puppy to play with. There was a boxful of outgrown footwear in the house, she told the policemen. They were welcome to sift through and see whether this shoe's partner was in there. Even if it wasn't it might still be possible that someone – Miranda was the most likely – had impulsively removed their shoe to throw at an errant cow or cat, and it had landed in the slurry. Nobody was going to bother to get it out again, if that happened. Easier to go into town and get another pair from the stall in the weekly market.

They all looked at each other and again at the shoe. 'It's quite a new one, I'd say,' said the man holding it. They carefully sifted through the shoebox in the house, without finding what they sought.

'Seems as if this trainer belongs to someone from off the farm,' concluded the man, and bagged it up with impressive ceremony. The police left then, wrinkling their noses at the stench of slurry.

Restless and suspicious, Lilah began to walk down the lane to bring the cows in for milking. The lack of a dog still felt strange at moments like this; normally Lydwina would have come wagging up to her, knowing it was time for her to assist, running around the stragglers and chivvying them gently along. Guy had never permitted more than one dog on the farm at a time, but had insisted on that one receiving all the attention and affection it needed. He had taken dogs more seriously than other animals, training each one in turn to respond to words and whistles which made it more useful than any human assistant could have been. *If Lydwina hadn't died, nobody could have got away with murdering Daddy*, Lilah thought. The dog's untimely death made her feel that the hand of fate was over them, victimising them however much they tried to resist.

The image of Guy face down in the slurry remained with her, more vivid than it had been at the time. Although today she had been scrupulous in calmly describing what she had seen, she knew her answers conveyed only part of the whole event. There were facets which evaded description. Guy's character; the normal reliable routine; something intangible in the air when she finally found him – she had mentioned none of these things, but as the men drove away Lilah was slowly beginning to entertain the idea that her father had been murdered, however much she tried to cling to her insistence that it was an accident. She desperately wanted it to have been accidental. If it was murder, then he had been killed by somebody who hated him with a profound passion. The sheer cruelty of the act was almost beyond imagining.

But even Lilah, devoted daughter, with nothing to reproach him for in his role as her father, knew that quite a substantial number of people had hated Guy Beardon.

The afternoon had turned dry and warm, and that evening, after milking, Sam sent Lilah to the bottom field to have a look at the grass. 'See if it's ready to turn the cows back in there tomorrow,' he said. 'It's had over a week now – should be enough.'

She hadn't known how much she would welcome the chance of a spell alone until she was clear of the farm buildings and into the soothing rhythm of a brisk walk. And inevitably she thought about her father, remembering him as he had been with her, trying to blot out the manner of his dying. All her life she would carry memories of their relationship. Her mind swarmed with them: the summer evening when she was seven and had just been given her first pet rabbit. Dad had walked her around the orchard, and the many weedy paths between the outbuildings, showing her which plants the animal could safely eat. Plantains, dandelions, chickweed, dock (in small quantities), groundsel as well as clover and plain grass. 'But never give them buttercups, pet. Buttercups are poisonous to rabbits. If they do get poorly, or off their food, parsley is the best medicine.' Lilah had remembered every word with crystal clarity. Even now, when the rabbits had all gone, she couldn't pass a lush patch of plantains or clovers without itching to gather them.

Dad had been patient in that way. Patient and kind and magically understanding. He seemed to know what she was thinking and feeling. He knew, for instance, she was really, genuinely, frightened of spiders, and so he would deftly remove them from her room, or the bath or wherever one threatened her. Mum, in contrast, mocked the fear as nonsense, accusing her of hysteria and attention-seeking.

When she had been poorly, it was always Dad who nursed her. He took her temperature twice a day, sponged her hot head with a cold flannel, cut wafer-thin slices of white bread and spread softened butter on them. And he listened gravely and knowingly when she described the terrible feverish nightmares she suffered. When she babbled about ladies who got fat and then thin again, he seemed to know what she meant, whereas Mum simply backed away, almost as frightened as Lilah had been. Both the children had learnt very early that when someone reliable was required, it was Dad, not Mum, they must call on. Endless small proofs of the wonderful success Guy had made of fatherhood filled Lilah's memory.

But had he been a wonderful *man*? She had been aware that most of the villagers did not like him. Over the years she had overheard too many references to his bad temper, his arrogance, his disregard for the usual rules of behaviour, to be able to convince herself that he had been popular. She had noticed only too acutely all the things the vicar had not said about him at the funeral. Successful, high-profile in the village, yes – but not a word about his character. Had he been good or charitable or courageous? An effective farmer – but what about his showing as a husband, a friend? What was it he had done to justify being killed, as she now felt certain he had been? And who was it who had been so afraid of capture that he had murdered poor old Isaac for good measure?

Chapter Five

Two more days passed and Lilah took over many of her father's routine tasks on the farm. She checked all the cows' feeding programs on the computer, and adjusted the charts in the milking parlour accordingly. She dealt with the endless sheaves of papers from the Ministry, claiming compensation for the young beef animals which had been incinerated because of the hysterical public response to the so-called BSE crisis. 'It'll all be forgotten in two years' time,' Guy had raged, almost in tears at his helplessness in the face of implacable officialdom. Lilah had shared his feelings, and waded through the paperwork now, grinding her teeth at the stupidity of it, the waste of money, the waste of those innocent bovine lives. They should have gone to feed people, not to be dyed purple and rendered down to nothing. Guy's rage had been all the more bitter for knowing that through a single act of carelessness, he had neglected to complete all the Soil Association paperwork the previous year, and was therefore unable to save his beef animals from the exemption they were perfectly qualified for.

At moments like this, Lilah could convince herself that in a sense she *was* her father, that he had somehow taken over a share of her body in a benign sort of possession. Restless with the need to explore her feelings, she roamed the places that Guy had spent most time in. His big old chair in the living room became a favourite spot, as did the barn outside. If it had been winter, she would have spent long sessions leaning against the chrome bar of the Rayburn, as Dad had always done. As it was, she wore one of his lighter jumpers, hugging it to her, savouring the smell of him.

But none of this was enough to help her make sense of her fears and suspicions as to what had befallen her father. More than anything, she needed some support from her mother. Surely Miranda must be the person who knew Guy best? She must hold the answers to at least some of the nagging questions. Lilah rehearsed how she might ask them, how she might slip them into casual conversation – 'Tell me, Mum, what was he *really* like?' It sounded so stupid, when she already knew the answer: he was big and kind and sweaty and angry and funny and . . . the list went on and on. But Lilah knew this was all much too subjective. This was stuff that any daughter might say about her Daddy. Lilah wanted much more than that. She wanted nothing less than to know why he had lived, and – supremely – why he had died.

But her mother was no help at all. For the first week of her widowhood, Miranda Bearden had retreated to her bedroom for the best part of each day. It was a large, light room at the front of the house, cluttered to bursting point with the kind of massive furniture that tended to find its way into farmhouses. Much of it had been bought by Guy at giveaway prices in local auctions, when they first came to Redstone with their two little children. Every surface was crammed with a miscellany of dusty objects, many of them untouched for the past ten or twelve years, and almost all of them generated by Miranda rather than her husband.

Miranda collected small useless knick-knacks because they struck a chord with her. She liked wood and stone and clay. She liked corn dollies and rush baskets and raffia mats. She very much liked the idea of herself as a real countrywoman, living on the land and surrounding herself with the products of country crafts. In practical terms, she was shockingly incompetent; entirely ineffectual in persuading a cow or pig to turn a certain way, limp and slow in the fieldwork, ineluctably ignorant about matters which were part of her husband and children's blood. One cause of her near-prostration now was a helpless despair at the prospect of making decisions regarding the future of the farm.

Guy's impact on the bedroom had always been minimal. His clothes were confined to one side of the great yellow wardrobe with art deco designs stencilled onto it, and a single drawer of the tallboy. His daily working things were permanently kept on an old chair near his side of the bed. On the wall, some years ago, he had tacked up a large poster of a blue whale that Roddy had given him. It now had cobwebs holding it to the wall as well as some fossilised BluTack. A cupboard, once used for the chamberpot, stood beside the bed on his side. Inside it were three old copies of *Farmers Weekly*, a large white dusty hanky scrunched into a hard ball, (evidence of a cold which had swept the family two years earlier – Guy had crossly put his hanky in there, saying it was the only way he could be sure of retaining at least one for himself), a defunct biro, and a thermometer in a metal case.

On top of the cupboard there was a bedside lamp, a torch, his watch and a pottery pig which Lilah had made for him at school. Guy was not a man to read himself to sleep at night. His evening routine had been unwavering. Promptly at ten, he would round up and eject the four cats from their places in the Rayburn fender or on the kitchen table to do their duties out in the barn; and (until it died) he would take his dog a dish of the complete dry food it lived on, pausing to stand listening a moment in the yard; switch off any lights; and plod heavily upstairs to bed. Washing and teeth-cleaning took only moments, before he climbed beneath the heavy old blankets, sighed once and fell into the sort of sleep which only a man who spends his day in physical labour knows.

Now Miranda lay full-length on the bed for hours at a stretch. Sometimes she glanced through a magazine, almost experimentally, as if testing to see whether she could still make sense of the words. Sometimes she made odd little lists – 'pension, insurance, bank loan, phone school, relief milker??', jotting down thoughts as they occurred, one concern after another. Sam must be given his days off, despite his insistence that she could leave all the farm business to him. Were Lilah and Roddy capable of doing the milking on their own? Who was going to make the decisions now? Guy had been like the great central pole of a tent; without him there, they all flapped and fussed and fought their way through the confusion he'd left by his going.

And yet – despite all the worry, the blank inability to foresee any viable future – Miranda's prime emotion following

61

the funeral was relief. It was relief, more than panic, which had stranded her helplessly on the bed. The abrupt cessation of the tension she had lived with for over half her lifetime was like having her spinal column removed. With every new day that came, she reminded herself that there was nobody watching her any more, nobody despising her feebleness, or keeping her on tenterhooks with his volatile changes of mood. No more casually cruel jokes at her expense, no more hysteria if a meal was ten minutes late, or she was out five minutes longer than she'd said she would be. The repressive habits of the past twenty-two years could be abandoned now. She was free, and the heady intoxication of it paralysed her more effectively than any alcohol or drugs might have done.

Relief was sometimes mixed with darker feelings. Two decades of bottled-up resentment came surging to the surface, and although it was physically exhausting, she let it take its course, until it left her weeping and cursing into her pillow two days after the funeral.

A faint 'Coo-ee' at the back door saved her. She sat up, wiping roughly at her face.

'Hello!' she responded, as she rolled herself off the bed. 'Is that you?'

The visitor was already in the kitchen when Miranda got downstairs. Eagerly, they embraced, holding tight. Then the newcomer rested her cheek lovingly against Miranda's head, leaving it there for a moment. Sylvia was a good four inches taller than her friend and proportionately wider. Miranda freed one hand, then slid it with absent-minded affection up and down the other woman's bare arm.

'It's lovely to see you,' she said. 'Do you want some coffee?'

'Not really, thanks. Tell me how you are.'

Miranda blew out her cheeks, and rolled her eyes. 'We-e-ell, let's see. Li's cross with me, because I said we'd have to sell up and live like normal people. I'm cross with Sam, because he's behaving as if I'm some kind of time bomb. Roddy's cross with everyone. The police think Guy was murdered, because of what happened to the Grimms. Did you hear about that?' Sylvia nodded. 'Yes, well, it was horrible, but honestly, it can't have had anything to do with Guy. The vicar seems to think he committed suicide, which is even more idiotic. They're all working their backsides off out there and resenting me for sitting in here like Lady Muck.'

Sylvia gurgled in an attempt to stifle the laugh that erupted. Miranda only slowly understood why.

'Oh, yes, *muck*'s a taboo word now, I suppose. Do you think I'll have to spend the whole of the rest of my life avoiding it?'

'Either that, or you'll have to say it twenty times a day to everyone you meet, to assure them that it's all right.'

'Oh, God. Who'd be a widow!'

'Me, for a start. However much you miss the bugger, there are any number of compensations. Especially if you have a clear conscience, like me.'

'Hey! Who says I haven't?'

'Several people, I imagine. I blame Hetty Taplow, though I've got no proof. Don't forget that I hear all the gossip where I am. Not only about you.' She began to digress. 'This business with Guy has got everyone crawling out of the woodwork and swapping stories. All kinds of stuff's getting passed around – nothing to do with you and Redstone, half of it.'

'For example?'

'Well, Phoebe's got her knickers in a twist about Elvira, apparently. They've been screaming at each other, and Elvira's taken to storming off and refusing to go to her day centre.'

'That doesn't sound very earth-shattering. Go back to Hetty Taplow. Feeling unwanted as usual, is she?'

'Not noticeably. But you're not her greatest friend, I must admit. Some would say she has good reason.'

'Oh, don't start that again. It's all in your imagination – you know it is.'

'It isn't, Em. I know for certain that she's fancied Sam since she was about eighteen. She won't look at anyone else. And she blames you for coming between them. Ever since that time—'

'Shhh. Li might come in and hear you.' Miranda glanced nervously out at the yard. 'It's all nonsense, anyway. I'd have been delighted for Sam to marry Hetty. It would have been very convenient for everyone. If anyone got in the way, it was Guy, not me.'

'Oh, well, it doesn't matter now, I suppose. Though, come to think of it, maybe it will come right for Hetty yet. Unless you've already moved Sam in here?'

'Far from it. He hasn't been anywhere near me, since . . . He has a very perverted set of values, that man. It was fine when Guy was alive, but now he's dead, it's all very different.'

'Well, I guess I can see his point,' sighed Sylvia, suddenly looking sad. 'I have to admit I'm a bit surprised that you don't feel the same. It's called having respect for the dead.'

'Oh!' Miranda shouted, suddenly angry. 'Why is everyone always so *superior*? How is it that I can never be mature or sensible, compared to all of you? Even my own daughter makes me feel like a foolish child.'

'Come on, Em. That's just you – the way you are. We all love you for it. We're not superior – just dull and boring and hidebound. Even Li. But we admire you – and envy you, too. I mean, who else would dare name a child Lilah, for a start? I probably already told you that when I heard that was your daughter's name I was determined to be your friend. It said it all.'

'Except it was Guy's idea, not mine. He was always one for fancy names. Even the dogs had to be Chloe and Tamsin and *Lydwina* rather than Lassie or Blossom. Some of the cows' names are completely over the top.'

'It doesn't matter.' Sylvia firmly shook her head. 'Only one wife in a million would have *agreed* to it.'

'Well, I'm not going to argue. I'm just happy you're here. Without Guy I'm all at sea.'

'I can imagine.' Sylvia paused, according Guy his moment of silence. 'But he was a bit of a despot, too, in some ways.'

'Oh, Syl, I do love you. I've been needing to talk to someone sane for ages. I don't know how you could have stayed away so long.'

'Neither do I, now I'm here. Look, haven't you got some wine or something? I've got all afternoon, and you don't seem to be going anywhere. Time we caught up with it all.'

They talked for three hours. They remembered Guy, and their own past history, and glanced at the future, and debated money and widowhood and Lilah and Roddy, and went back again to remembering Guy. For Miranda it was like plunging into a hot scented bubble bath after not washing for a month. She revelled and basked in it, and was almost glad that Sylvia had stayed away so long, such was the delight and relief she now felt.

Action followed her restored good humour. Firstly, she tackled Guy's side of the bedroom. Pulling open the wardrobe and the tallboy, she took out all his clothes and piled them onto the bed. There was no sense in keeping the suits or shoes for Roddy – she knew he'd never wear them – so she bundled them up to go to the charity shop in town. Casting her eye around the room, she began to imagine how she might rearrange it. The bedside cupboard on Guy's side could go, and instead she could have a bookcase there, containing her favourites which were currently down in the sitting room. She might get rid of the wardrobe and buy a smaller modern one for her own use. She could even throw out the bed and replace it with something less monumental, something more her size.

Miranda had known at the time that she was taking a calculated risk in marrying Guy. He had been thirty-five to her twenty-three. He had a world-weariness about him which she took for real maturity. Sexually, he had astonished and annihilated her. There had been a time, almost forgotten now, when you could almost see the electricity passing between their bodies, whenever they were within twenty feet of each other. He had been noisy, hairy, wicked and wholly irresistible. Those had been her best years and Miranda felt her gamble had been justified on that basis alone. Whatever Guy had turned into later, however contemptuous he became of her once she was floundering in maternity and he was pushing himself to the limits to pay for the farm – she had accepted it for the sake of those early times.

She had been thankful, too, that he had never once made comparisons between her and Barbara, his first wife. Barbara and her two sons had been completely expunged from the Beardon consciousness; Lilah and Roddy only knew that there had been an earlier family, which had no bearing on their existence. Neither had ever shown any interest or curiosity concerning their half-brothers.

That first marriage had not ended with any great crisis; it had just withered away. Guy had been teaching, after putting himself through years of self-motivated study, unhappy and angry at the daily grind and repetitive timetables – feeling like an exile from his native land. He supposed, he told Miranda, that he'd been a dull husband. Privately, she thought he'd probably been unbearably sorry for himself, even occasionally violent. Whatever Barbara might have felt, it was certain that Guy would neither have known nor cared. He had been a young man heading haphazardly up a blind alley.

He had told her the story, flatly, before he'd asked her to marry him. Quitting his teaching career had been part of quitting his marriage. At thirty-two, he had turned back to farming in his native Devonshire and sought a new wife. The quest had taken three years, during which Guy had taken on one of his former pupils – Sam – and set himself up on a small rented farm, intent on rediscovering the agricultural skills learnt as a boy. With the birth of Roddy, and the onset of his forty-fifth birthday, he had set about finding and buying a bigger farm. Two years later they had moved to Redstone.

Chapter Six

Den Cooper's notebook was almost full. He had spent a whole day in the village interviewing as many of the inhabitants as he could find, starting with those who had been at Guy's funeral. After all, they had been amongst the last to see Isaac Grimsdale alive.

His opening remarks were always the same: 'Good morning/ afternoon Sir/Madam. I expect you've heard about the violent death of Mr Isaac Grimsdale yesterday? I'd be grateful if you'd answer a few questions. I'm afraid it's a murder investigation, which means we do require the full co-operation of everyone we approach.' From there he worked down a list of endless repetitive questions. One of the more interesting was: 'Have you any reason to think that Mr Grimsdale's death might be connected in any way with that of Mr Guy Beardon?' One of the more difficult was: 'Can you please account for your own whereabouts between five and seven o'clock yesterday morning?' Nobody liked to be asked to provide an alibi.

After nine of these interviews, Den's head was spinning. Before reporting back to the Chief Inspector he sat in his car for twenty minutes, trying to make sense of everything he'd been told.

He had started with Wing Commander Stradling, who lived in an impossibly neat bungalow with his disabled wife Doreen. The old man had taken Den outside and given him a chair on the patio, so as not to disturb Mrs Stradling. His responses to most of the questions had been brief to the point of gruffness. He had lived in the village for eight years. He and his wife had had the bungalow built to their own design, as she needed special facilities. They had purchased the land twelve years ago when the village school and its playing field were sold off. Yes, he was acquainted with both the dead men, though much more so with Beardon than Grimsdale. No, he hadn't the slightest reason to think the deaths might be linked. Hadn't Beardon simply tripped and fallen into his unguarded pit? Short of entering into ludicrous flights of fancy – which he was sure the constable would prefer him not to do – he could not provide the slightest connection. He had been asleep in bed until six-thirty the previous morning, and had been seen by the postman at seven-fifteen, when he had been sitting with his morning tea on this very patio. A slim alibi, admittedly, but perhaps better than nothing. Doreen would confirm it, for what that was worth.

Lastly Den had put the question which Chief Inspector Smith had so often insisted was the most revealing: 'Did you like the two men?'

The Wing Commander's face had filled with a colour close to that of port wine. He drew in a long breath. 'Grimsdale was innocuous, as far as I know. Beardon was a crass, insensitive pig. He went out of his way to offend people –

69

me in particular. He made fun of people to their faces. No, constable, I cannot pretend to have *liked* him.'

Den made an appropriate note and closed his book. 'Thank you, sir, you've been most helpful.'

Next stop was Father Edmund Larkin. Den quailed slightly at the prospect of questioning the vicar; they had come into contact before in their respective dealings with calamity and crisis, but Den doubted whether Father Edmund would remember him. He did not seem like a man who took much notice of people. Scrupulously he went through his questions. The Reverend Larkin answered ramblingly, giving minute detail where none had been invited. He had been in the incumbency for nine years, serving this parish and two others, covering a wide geographical area, which kept him fully occupied. The vicarage was old and too big for one person, but the PCC had yet to find him something more suitable. It was very close to the church, however, and adjacent to the village street, so parishioners dropped in frequently, and he felt he was *au fait* with most of what went on, at least in the centre of the village. He had not known the Grimsdales or the Beardons very well. Neither household came to church, and as they were both positioned in a somewhat isolated corner of the parish, he seldom encountered them. They had experienced no deaths, weddings or christenings in his time here until now, and had therefore never availed themselves of his services. He had been in bed until seven-thirty the previous day, although there was no way at all that he could prove it except to assume that someone would probably have noticed him if he had made his way to the Grimsdale place and killed Isaac. People in this area rose early, after all.

The last question gave him pause; like the Wing Commander before him, his colour heightened, the sallow cheeks turning a pinkish brown. 'I had no particular feelings towards Isaac Grimsdale. I can't say I found any reason to be fond of Guy Beardon, but, as I say, I hardly knew the man. My eulogy at the funeral summed up virtually everything I did know about him. He seems to have been successful according to his own lights. His family seemed to hold him in some esteem.' Den's brow wrinkled at that: what an odd phrase to use about a husband and father! He jotted it down verbatim.

Behind the vicarage was a smallholding of three or four acres, run by a Mrs Sylvia Westerby. This was Miranda Beardon's best friend, only just returned from a fortnight in Corfu. Her name had already been mentioned more than once and he was curious to meet her. After a long delay she opened the front door of her oddly misshapen little house and to Den's surprise he found he had to lower his glance only slightly to meet her eye. She must have been close to six feet tall. At eleven in the morning she was wearing a flowery blouse and bright red shorts, which struck him as an outfit unsuitable for farmwork. She had wide bony shoulders and slim hips, giving her the silhouette of a young man. She held a cigarette between her fingers and a towel was wrapped round her head.

'Sorry. I was washing my hair,' she said. 'Come in.'

She took him into a living room that looked as if it had just been ransacked by a very determined burglar. 'Sorry about the mess,' she said carelessly, obviously not sorry at all. They sat together on a sofa, forcing Den to twist at an awkward angl in order to watch her face as she answered his questions. She answered readily in a husky voice. She had lived in this house for twenty-five years. She and her husband had moved here from Bristol and produced three children, the youngest of whom had died in an accident when she was five. The husband had left her not long after and then died of cancer. ('Served him right!' she laughed.) The surviving children were now in their twenties and living in Wales and Spain respectively. Sylvia herself made a precarious living by breeding Angora goats – which were a real pain, breaking out all the time and never doing what you wanted them to – as well as keeping fifty free-range hens of various kinds, and teaching a few hours a week in the evenings. When asked for more detail, she explained that she currently ran classes in rug-making, plant propagation and recovering from divorce. 'Funny mixture, I know – but I reckon to turn my hand to almost anything. Most people are more ignorant than me,' she said, 'though I say so myself.' She had got back from Corfu the evening before last, landing at Gatwick and driving herself home. 'Bloody airport car park – cost nearly as much as the flight,' she grumbled. She had been fast asleep, dead to the world, until at least ten the previous morning, and no, she couldn't prove it. No, there couldn't possibly be any connection between the two deaths. She was still getting over the news about Guy – it had been a complete shock when Miranda phoned her yesterday. She had liked the Grimsdales very much. She always stopped for a chat on the rare occasions they came into the village. 'Isaac was two sandwiches short of a picnic,' she said, 'if you know what I mean.' Asked for elaboration, she explained that the younger brother had been very dependent on Amos, although perfectly able to do outside work and drive a tractor. 'It's lucky it wasn't the other way around,' she said. 'He'd never have coped on his own.' As for Guy, well, she'd liked him. Under his bad-tempered and bullying veneer he had been an intelligent and trustworthy man. It was true that he'd been awful to Sam, and sometimes much too sharp with young Roddy, but she'd met worse. Miranda seemed to cope with him, which was the main thing.

She visited Redstone all the time. She and Miranda were best friends. They had coffee together at least once a week, and had minded each other's children and animals over the years – Miranda's children and Sylvia's animals. They had met the first week the Beardons had arrived at Redstone, in the shop. They'd just clicked instantly. They made each other laugh.

'Oh, one thing,' she said as he was leaving, 'see if you can catch Phoebe Winnicombe. She'll tell you plenty about the Grimsdales.'

But Phoebe and her daughter Elvira had not been there when he knocked on the door of the stone cottage overlooking the churchyard, so instead he had made his way to the Rickworths', an expensive, modern house on a slope, with a small paved garden. He was expecting to be similarly disappointed on a weekday morning, but surprisingly both Tim and Sarah had been at home. Tim, not much older than Den, opened the door and smilingly invited him into the main room, where Sarah sat in front of a computer with headphones over her ears and a microphone attached. She was clearly interrupted by Den's intrusion: when she saw his uniform, she removed the headphones and sighed audibly.

Once again the questions were put, the replies noted. The couple repeatedly hesitated, each waiting for the other to answer – not from politeness so much as caution, it seemed to Den. When an answer did eventually come, the other partner would often disagree, especially over matters of fact. Tim said they had lived in the village for four years; Sarah said five. Tim said he worked as a consultant to a software firm; she said he was a self-employed computer games salesman. They did agree that she worked as a hardware designer specialising in sound reproduction. They barely knew the Grimsdales or the Beardons, but were good friends of the Mabberleys, on the next farm along from Redstone. They could think of no earthly connection between the two deaths, and they had no feelings about Guy or Isaac, except that they knew Guy had made himself unpopular with the likes of the Wing Commander. This caused another disagreement: Tim found it rather amusing, while Sarah thought it was unkind to tease the poor old chap. They'd both been in bed until about seven-thirty the previous morning, and could only provide each other as alibi. The atmosphere in the house was brittle and Den was relieved to conclude his interview.

By this time he was hungry, and he called at the Ring o' Bells pub for some lunch. Maggie Dansett, the landlady, made a big production of cutting a round of ham sandwiches. She leant over the bar towards him as he ate, more than ready for a gossip. 'That Guy Beardon, he were a proper tartar to they chillun of his'n,' she confided. 'And worse to poor old Sam. You'll have heard, I reckon, what a tongue 'e had on'n? Sharp as fish hooks and festered near as bad, too, I'd say. Now poor old Isaac, who never hurt so much as a fly. What a thing! You police people trawling all over the village, 'tis a bad business and no mistake. Folks is axing, who'll be the third? There's always a third, everyone knows that. Sooner you catch the bugger as did for poor Isaac, the sooner us'll sleep at night.'

Den smiled deprecatingly and finished his sandwich. He hadn't intended to interview Mrs Dansett and her stream of consciousness was disconcerting. As far as he could tell she hadn't said anything worth writing down, except for the reference to Guy's ill-treatment of Sam. It went without saying that Sam had to be everybody's first choice when it came to wondering who – if anybody – had pushed Guy into the slurry.

Scanning the list he'd made first thing that morning, he realised he had seen all the main players; all those whom he considered most likely to be of assistance, having observed them closely at Guy's funeral. Hetty Taplow came next, and her house was a mile away, in a row of workers' cottages set close to the road, and comprising a tiny settlement all of its own. It was in the opposite direction to Redstone and the Mabberleys', and he hesitated as to which course to take first. The decision came readily: Hetty was another Mrs Dansett – a gossip who knew everything and nothing. No hard facts, little but second-hand tales and wild suppositions, spiced with tight-lipped judgements. Hetty could wait.

He turned right out of the pub's small car park and followed the winding lane past Redstone's roadside entrance. Half a mile further on he turned left into another farm driveway.

The approach was lined with stately horse chestnut trees, heavy with their white flowers. To his left, towards Redstone, lay a dense wood of oak and beech and ash: Jonathan Mabberley's greatest asset. There had been talk, a year or two back, of the National Trust taking it over as a safeguard against the magnificent trees ever being destroyed. But Jonathan had resisted, giving every assurance that there was no threat to the trees from him.

The house was of an old colonial style, improved and extended until it straggled over a considerable area. It stood sideways onto the drive, with a broad verandah at the front and a terrace leading down to another paved area at the back. Wisteria smothered many of the walls and a walkway linked the house to an old stone barn. It was immaculate; there were neither the sounds nor the smells of a farmyard.

Den parked in a wide gravelled semicircle beyond the house and crunched his way to the front door. A red Irish setter stood wagging its plumy tail fatuously at him, as if he were an old acquaintance. The door stood open, but there was no sign of any occupants. He bit his lip, wondering what the dog would do if he tried to go inside.

'Can I help you?' came a well-modulated voice from behind him. Spinning round, Den came face to face with the owner of the house. It seemed impossible that Jonathan Mabberley could have reached his side without making any sound on the gravel, and Den's mouth dropped open stupidly. As the farmer stood there, waiting, Den struggled to repeat his little speech. 'Um – you'll have heard about Mr Isaac Grimsdale's death—' he began.

Jonathan nodded gravely, but said nothing. 'Well, I'm here to ask if you'd help our investigations by answering a few questions,' Den plunged on, feeling more in control as the words began to run smoothly, automatically, once again.

'Of course,' replied the charming voice. 'I'll just call my wife. I'm sure you'd like to speak to her as well?'

'Thank you,' Den mumbled.

'Cappy! Cappy?' the man called, turning his head towards a large, well-made shed close to where Den had parked his car. 'Just a moment – I'll fetch her.' And he set off, moving as gracefully as a dancer – or as his own lovely dog, which followed him.

A small dark woman emerged from the shed, brushing her hands down her white cotton trousers. Den had wondered at the funeral just where she had originated from; her skin was too dark to be European, her features impossible to place. Her accent, when she spoke, was American.

The Mabberleys offered him a seat on the verandah and the red dog laid its long muzzle on his leg and watched him with liquid eyes throughout the conversation. He found this unnerving. Especially when he became uncomfortably aware of a patch of doggy drool seeping through his trousers.

He ploughed through his list of questions, feeling increasingly that he was being humoured, even toyed with, by this uncannily relaxed couple. Jonathan had lived all his life in this house; Cappy had joined him when they had married five years ago. They knew the Beardons quite well, and as for the Grimsdales – well, they were part of the local furniture, so to speak. They'd been born in that cottage. Jonathan had sometimes gone with his mother to visit them, as a youngster, but had to admit he'd not had much to do with them since then. There wasn't much by way of a link between Guy and the Grimsdales, except of course that Guy had bought up almost all of their land. Jonathan had wondered whether that was entirely sporting, but Amos and Isaac hadn't seemed to mind. It didn't seem very likely to the Mabberleys that Guy's death had any connection with the murder of Isaac. At least, neither of them could think of anything that might suggest such a connection. They had been in bed till nearly eight the previous morning – since giving up the milking cows there hadn't been any need to rise at dawn like the olden days. Now they kept beef cattle, God help them, which could wait until a more civilised hour before needing any attention.

Asked how they had felt about Guy Beardon, they looked at each other, part amused, part doubtful. 'What can we say to that?' Jonathan asked his wife in an ironic tone.

'Well,' she drawled, 'all we can *truthfully* say is that he was a very exasperating man. Unreasonable. Volatile. Not an easy neighbour.'

'He was bloody rude,' added her husband. 'Especially to you, my sweet.'

'But he did care about his animals and his family. He doted on Lilah – nobody could argue with that. Treated her like a little princess, even when she'd left school and ought to be growing up a bit. A good farmer, a good father, but . . . a difficult man,' she summarised.

Driving away again, Den thought grimly that everyone he'd questioned seemed to have prepared their answers in advance. They had at least provided a consistent picture: a community prepared to tolerate an irascible neighbour with general good humour. Not one person had a respectable alibi for the murder of Isaac; but nobody seemed worried by the lack of one.

It was four o'clock when he reached Hetty Taplow's cottage. Contrary to his expectations, she was by far the least forthcoming of all his interviewees. She seemed frightened of him, impatient for him to be gone. Her round cheeks, normally rosy with good cheer, were pale and creased, making her look older than her thirty-five years. Her brother, who lived with her, arrived home from work while Den was there and glared at him suspiciously. No, Hetty insisted, she had no idea why anyone should kill poor old Isaac. It was a shame and a sin to do such a thing. And Amos not much better, lying there in hospital – he'd hate that, away from all his things. Scarcely been outside the village in their lives and now look what'd happened. 'You go and talk to that Phoebe Winnicombe,' she said as a parting shot. 'Her's the one you need to ax all these questions of.'

But Den was too tired to try Phoebe's cottage again. That would have to wait for another day. It was time to return his overflowing but repetitive notebook to the Incident Room and let old man Smith make what he could of it.

Chapter Seven

As the days passed, letters of condolence continued to arrive, along with cards etched in silver, some featuring religious themes, proffering hope of a life beyond this one. 'This is all very strange,' said Miranda. 'Like a morbid sort of Christmas. When are they going to stop?' It seemed that the news was rippling outwards very slowly, as if passed by osmosis. People who had known Guy and Miranda in South Devon on their first rented farm; people who had sold them cattle feed or grass seed; parents of Roddy's schoolfriends; all wrote, sending futile words of sympathy and encouragement. Other letters came, too, addressed to Guy himself. Bills, mostly, but also a long-awaited diploma for Agatha, his prize cow. For six consecutive years, Agatha had produced prodigious quantities of top-quality, super-creamy milk; her butterfat content was phenomenal. Now she was rewarded by a fancy piece of paper, which would have made Guy glow with pride. A highly competitive character, he was justly boastful of the way he had built up his milking herd from nothing, his pretty, little, fawn-coloured Jerseys, fed organically and treated as individuals, a deliberate deviation from the endless repetition of black-and-white Friesans with numbers stencilled on their backsides. His small beef herd, now victim to the BSE regulations, comprised mostly crossbreeds.

Miranda didn't know what to do with Agatha's prize. Helplessly she showed it to Lilah, tears in her eyes. It was the small things that jumped out and snagged your emotions, she was discovering. The girl was equally ensnared. 'Oh, no,' she choked. 'And he isn't here to see it. Oh, Mum, it's so sad. After waiting for it so long. It doesn't mean anything now.'

'It'll make Agatha more valuable,' said Miranda, before she could stop herself. She didn't mean to be callous, she inwardly defended. It was just her way, to try and see the bright side.

But Lilah was offended. 'We're not selling Agatha,' she shouted, through tears that made her seem terribly young. 'We're not selling *any* of the cows. We're not selling anything. This is my farm, now. I'm going to see that we keep it going just as it was.'

'It's not your farm, Li. Don't be silly. Whatever makes you think that? If we have to sell, then it'll be my decision, and Sam's, whatever you might think about it.'

She hadn't meant to sound so harsh, but Lilah had been provocative. Without another word, the girl turned and ran outside, slamming the door behind her.

Miranda knew what Lilah had meant, of course. She was aware of a higher moral law which decreed that the farm certainly ought to be her daughter's. Guy had always assumed that Lilah would take over as he got older, and had begun to train her years ago. Roddy had never shown the same interest; his academic courses at school would over-qualify

81

him for a life of mud and EC regulations. Guy had never tried to hide his pride in his clever son, talking about Oxford and the satisfactions of an indoor life with complete sincerity. Miranda understood that he was claiming both children as his own, doubly possessive now because of the two abandoned and neglected sons from his past. Roddy was reliving Guy's early professional dreams, and making them come true this time; Lilah was to continue the work he'd done at Redstone, and build on the milk herd until it was the best in the country. Always a man to have his cake and eat it too, she remarked to Sylvia, more than once.

Now Miranda wandered through the house, the certificate in her hand, trying to think where to put it. Everything to do with the cows was in the office outside, where Guy had an old filing cabinet and a second-hand computer. She put the certificate down on top of a dusty pile of magazines beside Guy's armchair and forgot about it. The farm office was foreign territory to her; it didn't occur to her to enter it now. If anyone were to inherit mastery of the office, it was Sam, not her.

Sam's mood was one of conflict and confusion. His grief for Guy was muted by self-pity. His workload was doubled, and nobody remembered to thank him properly or to reassure him that this situation wouldn't last forever. Counterbalancing this was the strong sense of obligation that he carried towards Miranda and the children. They were the only family he had, and it satisfied him to know they were dependent on him now. As he fell exhausted into bed each night, in the little annexe to the main farmhouse which was his home, having ensured that the cows were all as they should be, and the equipment clean and ready for the morning, his customary last thoughts were grimly contented. Once the family settled down a bit, they'd be grateful, all right; until then he just had to make sure he carried out his duties as Guy would have wished and expected.

Lilah was his chief helpmate; he was pleased by the effective team they made. Both were in agreement that morning milking would always be the worst part of the day. The ghost of Guy hovered in the yard at any time of day, but those moments after breakfast, when Sam and Lilah met to begin their day, were hard to bear. They exchanged looks of pain and understanding; they avoided glancing towards the now empty slurry pit. 'Will they send an official to make us fill it in, do you think? said Lilah.

Sam shrugged. Who knew? Officialdom had never much disturbed him – other people had always handled that side of things on his behalf. How he would manage now, without Guy's individual mix of scorn and kindness, was something he still couldn't think about. *Wouldn't* think about. That way lay grief and fear.

Lilah got up early the day after the attack on the Grimms, and went to help Sam in the final stages of the milking. Not having a dog to help bring the cows in was a nuisance. Lydwina, the most beautiful, intelligent collie they'd ever owned, had died, tragically, on Easter Monday, carelessly kicked in the head by a frisky young heifer let out into a field for the first time. The family's grief had been intense; Guy had threatened to shoot the offending heifer in the first hysterical moments of the disaster. They'd had the dog only a year, a special acquisition beloved by everyone. Roddy, however, had taken her to his heart the most, and many of her skills were learnt at his instruction. When she died, Roddy had gone numb and cold with disbelief. *Perhaps*, thought Lilah, *that has something to do with the way he is now.*

She talked a lot that morning: a stream of words coming from her, about the cows and the weather and the clock – would they finish in time for the tanker? Would Cornelia finish her heat before the AI man arrived? Would the hay be spoilt if they didn't get it cut by the end of the month? Would the heifers escape if they didn't patch that gap in the hedge today? Much of what she said was lost beneath the steady throbbing of the milking machine. Sam understood that she was talking more to herself than to him, that she required only the occasional nod and smile in reply. Perhaps he realised also that unleashing so many anxieties was cathartic, a welcome release. Sam was surprised at how much the girl knew about the farm; he had previously seen her only as a useful second assistant to Guy, given peripheral tasks. Now he understood that she knew and understood the daily routine very nearly as well as he did. But then it was only what you'd expect, he thought with some sourness; her father had always given her his undivided attention. A girl her age should have been off working at a proper job, a career, not hanging about at home with her father, merely enrolling for occasional short courses at the local college as the whim took her. Still, if she hadn't stayed under Guy's wing for so long, Redstone would have been finished now.

Roddy, by contrast, was almost useless. He came out to the parlour or the barn, looking helpless and lost, and stood waiting for orders he clearly wasn't keen to fulfil.

'That mouldy hay's got to be shifted,' Sam had said hopefully, a few mornings ago, cocking his head at the grey musty bales.

'Shifted where to?' Roddy vaguely asked, hands still in his pockets.

Sam had shrugged. Mouldy hay was just . . . *shifted*. It came in useful as bedding for calves, or mulch for the vegetable patch, or . . . It ought to be obvious. But he couldn't show his irritation with the boy. Sam could see how tightly the jaw was clenched, how desperately Roddy wanted to be somewhere else. Partly he sympathised. He knew Guy had been as unpleasant with his lad at times as he had been to Sam himself. If either of them made a mistake, the vitriolic tongue would reduce them both to ashes, effectively killing any tendency to show initiative. Without him, they were headless. Lilah, by contrast, had been encouraged and praised by her father much more than she'd been criticised, and thus sustained a self-confidence that the others lacked. Sam knew that Guy had always wanted a daughter just like her; pride and pleasure had shone from him whenever he was with her.

The police displayed an odd mixture of suspicion and neglect. Two men came back, that morning, and asked Miranda to explain the precise connection between the two properties – Redstone and the Grimsdales' smallholding. In some detail, she recounted the process whereby Guy had bought the eighty acres which had once belonged to the brothers. The first purchase had been ten years ago, three large fields amounting to nearly forty acres, triangular in shape, running alongside the road. She found a map and showed them. Five years later, a similar transaction had been conducted, this time involving a patch of woodland on the other side of the road, which Guy had used for keeping free-range pigs. 'It

85

was nice, having those pigs,' she added wistfully. 'I like pigs.'

'That's all right, madam,' said one of the men heavily. 'We don't need to know what he used it for.'

'Sorry,' shrugged Miranda. 'I have no way of knowing what you think is relevant.'

'No pigs now?' queried the other, younger, officer, more polite and less cynical.

'No. They kept getting out into the road, and they'd served the purpose of clearing the land. Guy took all the trees out, only last year.'

'Bet that made him popular,' commented the second man.

Miranda pulled a face. 'You can say that again,' she agreed. 'Woodlands are emotive things around here. Fortunately, the Mabberleys do the right thing in that respect, maintaining their ancestral acres.'

'These land purchases,' pursued the first man. 'Were they all done amicably? I mean, the Grimsdales were happy to sell to your husband, were they?'

Miranda's brows rose. 'Oh, yes. They got a fair price. They bought a new tractor, and a car. Even had the roof fixed, after the first lot. They needed the cash, you see. They had no idea how to farm effectively. Couldn't keep up with the times.'

'Sad,' said the nicer man. 'Seems a shame.'

'Oh, I think they accepted it. And the tractor was their pride and joy. You must have heard about the way Isaac used to drive it up and down the main road every summer. Caused traffic jams for miles, on a Saturday, holding up all the summer visitors. Even Guy thought that was funny.' She laughed at the memory. 'We all enjoy teasing the grockles, don't we.'

The men pursed their lips and said nothing. Clearly Miranda had said the wrong thing. The older policeman summarised: 'Can we ask you one more time, Mrs Beardon – have you any idea at all who could have attacked the Grimsdale brothers?'

'My answer is still the same. I have no idea at all. Just guesses, which are all the obvious ones. A passing tramp. A burglar who went too far. Someone who'd committed a crime further up country, and thought the Grimsdales had somehow found out about it . . .' She tailed off. 'Anyway, I expect you'll be able to ask Amos any day now. Then everything will be explained, won't it.' She settled back in her chair. 'And then let's hope we can all get on with our lives in peace.'

'You seem remarkably unafraid,' commented the unsmiling policeman. 'Two deaths and a serious assault happening on your doorstep, and you talk about getting back to normal. Most ladies in your position would be seriously frightened.'

'We lock the doors at night,' she said crisply. 'And keep ourselves busy. I must say I really can't see any reason to fear. Perhaps I lack imagination?'

She could almost hear him thinking, *Or perhaps you have reason to know there's nothing to fear* . . . Forcing herself to say nothing more, but to show them out calmly, she only realised how tensely she'd been holding herself in when they'd gone. Expelling a great breath, and letting her shoulders slump, she threw herself into her chair by the Rayburn. 'Oh, God,' she murmured aloud. 'Let this whole mess be over with, before it drives me completely mad.'

* * *

Lilah had been too busy to think much about Constable Den, but her heart did a decidedly interested double-flip when he turned up the following day. He met her in the yard, having parked beyond the gate and walked in. She wondered whether he'd been exploring the sheds which stood close to where he'd left his car.

'Could you show me your father's office, please?' he said. 'Forensics have suggested we go through the computer files.'

'Really?' was all she could say. 'You'll be very disappointed. Dad never really got to grips with the computer, apart from keeping track of the milk yield, and the prices he paid for feed. You can see it's a very outdated system.'

'Let's have a look then.' He switched the machine on, and scanned the screen. 'Hmmm, I see what you mean. This is a 286 – a real dinosaur.'

'He was talking about getting a new one, only a few weeks ago. He wanted to keep up with all the latest technology. He never wanted to stop learning.' Her voice sounded hollow, in her own ears. Words with the emotion shut away, reciting facts which threatened to trigger tears and misery if they weren't kept carefully neutral.

'He'd been a teacher, I understand.'

Lilah stared at him. 'Who on earth told you that?'

He spread his hands, a caricature of innocence. 'It's in the files somewhere. Perhaps he got a pension? That's probably it.'

'Well, it was a million years ago. When he was in his twenties. I wasn't born until he was nearly forty. Do you always go back into a person's past history like this?'

Den's face was carefully inexpressive. 'This is a murder inquiry. We go into everything.'

'So the file on my father's death is still open, is it?' She stared hard at him.

'It certainly is,' he said primly. 'Nothing concrete yet, but . . .' He scratched his head gently with the tip of one long finger. 'It's all rather complicated. My Chief Inspector's been looking through all the interview notes and he's got a hunch.'

'That's supposed to mean something, is it?'

'It means we'll all be out for ten hours a day asking a lot of questions. I've got to speak to your mother. Is she in?'

'Oh yes.' Lilah flipped a hand towards the house. 'She's always in these days, playing the tragedy queen act to the hilt. And never lifting a finger to help us out here.'

Den ran a tongue over the front of his teeth, too professional to make any response to Lilah's bitterness. He raised his gaze to the sky, giving her time to change the subject. Watching him, she could read his thoughts as if they were written in highlighter on his brow.

'You can't blame me for being cross,' she complained. 'We're expected to just get on with our lives, not knowing anything, whether there's some crazy killer loose out there – or whether you're going to turn up at five o'clock some morning and drag one of us away under arrest. It's not a good way to live, believe me.'

He put out a hand, and rested it on her shoulder. The effect was extraordinarily soothing. She took a small step towards him, yearning to rest her head against his chest, against the smooth-knit, navy-blue jumper. But she couldn't do that. If she gave in now, letting weakness flow through her, she might never again find the strength to keep going.

'Let me ask you straight,' he said, letting the hand fall.

'Do you believe your father was killed deliberately?'

She looked up at him, running the picture past her inner eye, yet again. Guy in the slurry, on a clear May morning that was just like any other day. Guy didn't have accidents. Guy would never even allow the thought of suicide into his mind.

'I don't know,' she dithered wretchedly. 'Every time I think about it I end up believing he must have been – but I can't bear to imagine who might have done it.'

'There were certainly plenty of people who disliked him,' Den said with a little frown. 'Except maybe your mum's friend, Mrs Westerby. She doesn't seem to have made much effort to win friends.'

'He was impatient with people,' she agreed. 'But that was just because he had strong opinions. He was brave enough to be honest. He was really . . .' Her tense voice broke, and she felt her face crumple. 'He was a great father to me. I can't bear to think of never seeing him again.'

With a great effort she swallowed the tears and tilted up her chin. Den rested his hand once again on her shoulder, saying nothing, watching her swing from acting like a lost little girl to accepting heavy responsibilities, taking control of herself. His respect for her grew considerably as he observed the transformation.

'Go and talk to Mum,' she dismissed him. 'I've got too much to do.'

Obediently, he walked towards the house.

Chapter Eight

Amos had never been in hospital before, not even when he got his hand caught in the turnip-chopper and lost the tops of two fingers. Isaac had bound it up with dock leaves and then salved it with his own glycerine-based ointment, and it had healed up perfectly. The other time, when he trod on a four-inch nail, hadn't been so easy, but it had never occurred to them to consult a doctor.

Now, here he was with young girls fussing over him, bringing him plates of inedible, unfamiliar food, sticking glass tubes under his tongue, forcing pills into him three times a day. It was, at least in the first few days, worse than any nightmare. The bed was stiff and hard, the sheets so white they made his head ache, and no blankets to speak of. Of course, it was smotheringly hot in the ward, and blankets would have made it worse, but it felt all wrong to be lying in a bed with no proper weight to it. And he badly missed having the cats for company.

He and Isaac had got themselves a television six or seven years ago, and he was quite familiar with the world of a hospital through programmes like *Casualty*. He knew many of the technical terms, and how the doctors were always tired and the nurses always fresh and kind. But he had discovered that the reality was utterly different. He hadn't known that they would bring him a funny-shaped bottle to piss into. He hadn't known about the long, empty hours in the afternoon when you couldn't sleep, and nothing happened, and all you could do was lie there and think. On the telly, everything was constant rush and bustle and panic bells ringing. Here, everyone was old and confused and endlessly complaining.

One night he had been woken by something grabbing his wrist. Terrified, he tried to see what it was, but there was apparently nothing there. Only when the grip tightened did he look down on the floor to find an old lady sitting there, her nightie obscenely rucked up around her waist, tugging mindlessly at him. When their eyes met, she croaked, 'Take me home, Daddy. Please take me home.' Horror gripped him, and he cried out, a long peal of anguish and despair, which brought two night nurses rushing to the bedside to bundle the poor old creature away.

The police came to speak with him, nearly every day. They asked him if he remembered what had happened in the house that morning. He knew they were being careful about Isaac, not sure whether Amos knew his brother was dead. He did know, of *course* he did, but it was too difficult to speak of it. He mumbled at his questioners, disconnected words, which didn't make any sense even to him. It was much easier not to talk. When the nurse asked him if he'd prefer chicken or pork for his dinner, he made no response. What did it matter? When the food came, it was impossible to determine which it was, anyway.

He lay there, on those long afternoons, with his head throbbing and the brightness of everything too much to bear, and let his thoughts drift where they would. And they almost always drifted to Miranda Beardon. He remembered, as clear and vivid as a memory can be, the day the family first came to Redstone. The lithe young woman, with brown arms and a lovely head of hair, had come running up the field to introduce herself to him and Isaac. Her two little children followed her, laughing and rolling in the long grass, like some advertisement for butter or toilet tissue. Isaac, the younger brother, had been red-faced and shy with her, but Amos had seen a vision, and was not going to spoil it with oafish behaviour. He had drawn himself up, squared his shoulders, and asked her in. The house hadn't been such a mess then, with Mother not long dead and money coming in from contracting work.

She had spoken quickly, breathlessly, about having no idea how to be a farmer's wife, but facing the challenge eagerly. The cows were to be Jerseys, which had such sweet faces, and seemed small and docile enough, from what she'd seen. Which wasn't much. She had chattered on for fifteen minutes, not letting him get many words of his own in. Then she'd gone back down to the big farmhouse and the older husband – older than Isaac, but not quite so old as Amos, by the looks of him. The husband who moved like a bull, always sure of himself, always quick to anger, shouting at that wretched Sam and, as the years went by, his own boy child, too.

Amos could watch a good deal of what happened at

Redstone, either from his bedroom window or from the corner of his sole remaining field. It was not so far distant, and his eyesight was good. As Guy purchased their land, each time with absolute politeness and prompt payment, the brothers felt diminished. They put the money in the bank, and bought a few things – the television, a better car, and a new tractor – but the money never seemed to go down. 'Why are we doing it?' Isaac demanded, the last time. 'We've got enough money already.'

Amos had shrugged. ''Tain't easy to gainsay that Beardon. And he'll make a better job of it than us'll do. Money'll be there for us, when it's needed.' The truth was, he'd lost the will to keep on farming, trying to grapple with the constant stream of documents and regulations that came in the post. Applications for this and that; returns to tell them what animals you had, and how old they were; people trying to sell you things. It was all rubbish, but rubbish you daren't throw away. The brothers would struggle to read it all, then shake their heads and carefully stack the papers up on their mother's old bureau, until the pile was halfway to the ceiling.

Amos's adoration of Miranda had taken deep root, and over the years it blossomed prodigiously. The sight of her would lighten his day and colour his dreams at night. If it hadn't been for her husband, he'd have found ways of speaking to her, wooing her with gifts, offering her anything at all. He knew how delightful a woman's body could be, had more experience in that department than most people suspected. He was haunted constantly by imaginings of himself and Miranda in lustful embrace, but he never even came close to doing anything about it. Even when he saw that Sam slipping into the house when the husband was away, and Miranda there all alone, and coming out half an hour later, hitching at himself in that obvious way, Amos knew he could never aspire to a similar privilege. It gave him cause to detest Sam, but it only enhanced Miranda in his opinion. A goddess such as she was clearly needed homage of that sort. More fool Guy, for leaving her unguarded.

If she'd been his, he'd have built a ten-foot fence around her, and fed her on cream and peaches. He'd have wound wild flowers into her hair and knelt nightly at her feet. Amos dreamt, quite contentedly, of his alternative existence as a sultan with a single concubine.

Before the Beardons arrived, the Grimsdales had been much the same as other farming families round about. The brothers scarcely ever talked of those times, now. They made little effort to pinpoint where it all began to go wrong, where they'd fallen off the bus that had taken everyone else headlong into prosperity. Once in a while, Amos would blame Isaac for their plight. He would grumble, in a long monotonous tirade, 'I don't see how I'm meant to do anything, with you a drag on me, the way you are. Never wanting to do anything, scared of your own shadow. Look at you. Can't even give the place a good clean, or wash your sheets. And that cat – it's expecting again, when I told you to keep it in. We're overrun with the bloody things as it is.' And on he would go, obsessively listing every grievance, pausing only to draw breath and fix Isaac with a resentful stare, knowing there would be no response.

Isaac would grin crookedly, and cock his head almost to his shoulder, in the way he had of taking criticism. Almost always there'd be a cat on his lap, or squirming round his legs. The cats loved Isaac, and he loved them, and for all anyone could tell, that was enough for him. That and his potions, mixed from flowers and leaves; docks and buttercups, comfrey and feverfew all gleaned from Mother, who'd known everything about plants that there was to know.

'Time for tea, Mr Grimsdale,' came a chirpy voice, followed by a crashing clatter of metal and china, heralding the tea trolley. Having roused him, the woman went away, and there was a long, frustrating interval while cups were slowly handed round to all the other beds but his, or so it seemed. When the drink finally arrived, it was weak and tepid, and tasted like nothing he had ever called tea.

Sometimes, after tea, the patients would be ousted from their beds and sent to the day room to watch television for an hour. Amos had been excused from this so far, after a glance at his chart hanging at the end of the bed. At first, when he moved, his head had throbbed and seemed to swell, and he would moan and lie back with closed eyes. This seemed to make the nurses nervous, which was a convenient discovery. Now, when his head was feeling a lot better, he sustained the moaning act, as a way of gaining some peace.

He had noticed how carefully he was treated, by comparing himself with the other patients. Little groups of nurses talked about him, at their 'station' as they called it, shooting glances at him and widening their eyes. The police would come at odd times when there were no other visitors, and sit beside him, hot and intimidating in their dark uniforms. Amos gave them no help for a week, but then he grew tired of the whole business and began, all of a sudden, to speak lucidly.

'Young thug,' he spat, working his mouth with rage, 'came in the night, in the dark.' The policeman almost fell off his chair with excitement, and fished in his pocket for a pencil.

'Did you see him? Can you give us a description?'

Amos let his head sink into the pillow, experimenting with his stiff face, wondering whether he'd ever be able to frown effectively again. 'I saw 'un,' he said. 'Dark eyes, he had. Thin.'

'And he was young, you say? How young?'

'I'd say around thirty, or less. Course, I couldn't see his face.'

The policeman lowered his pencil and stared bleakly at Amos. 'Pardon?' he said.

'No, he had one of those woolly things over his head. Just a gap for his eyes. 'Cept he'd pushed it back, like it was too hot. Sweating, he was. Hair stuck to his head.'

'What colour hair was it?'

'Dark, I said. Like his eyes. Savage look he had.'

The policeman scribbled. 'Can you tell me what happened?'

'I was asleep, and something waked me. Some noise. I put my lamp on, by the bed, and called out to Isaac. He has nightmares once in a while. I thought maybe . . .' The breath suddenly caught in his throat, as he remembered that Isaac would have no more nightmares. Grief collected somewhere behind his nose, stinging and cruel. He struggled to sit up, and the policeman tried feebly to assist him.

'Then he came into my room holding the crowbar high. I knew he was going to hit me. He came right at me, mad-looking. His shadow was big behind him, on the wall.' Amos shuddered. He would dream of that shadow, he knew. 'I rolled off the bed, but he came after me, swinging the bar at me. It got me, and knocked me out. When I woke up, he'd gone and it was light outside. I went to find Isaac—'

'Yes, we know the rest. Had you ever seen this man before? I mean, despite the mask, did you recognise him?'

Amos shook his head, wincing slightly. 'Looked like a gypsy. Rough clothes.'

'Did you notice his hands?'

Amos considered for a long time. 'No,' he said. 'Can't say I did.'

'Would you know him again?'

'I might, sir. My light was right on his eyes. You don't forget the look of a man who's wanting to kill you for no reason. We had nothing to steal. And Isaac – poor harmless old chap like him. Where's the sense?'

The policeman had no answers. 'Thank you very much indeed, Mr Grimsdale. Now that you're able to remember, we're in a much better position to proceed. This description, as far as it goes, will be circulated, to begin with. Now you just rest, and leave it to us.'

Amos lay back and watched the man walk away. He felt a faint regret at having broken his silence. It made the whole business seem trivial, ordinary. A masked madman had come into the house, swinging his crowbar, and casually murdered poor Isaac, who'd never done anyone the slightest harm. Nobody but Amos would care. Where was Isaac now, he wondered for the first time. Had they gone ahead and buried him, with a handful of villagers as witnesses? Or was he in some cold metal drawer somewhere, waiting until Amos was well enough to be there, and pay for it? And what about the cats? Was anybody feeding them?

Questions flew around his head, like the troubles from Pandora's box, biting at him and making him feel sick. He held a hand to his damaged head, the flesh pulpy beneath his fingers, scabs coming loose on his cheek. He knew he couldn't stay in hospital any longer. The time had come to confront what had happened, and go home to find a way of resuming his life. And to pursue the evil swine whose murderous eyes bored into his mind every moment of the day.

Chapter Nine

Den drove away, taking two floppy disks with him, containing copies of Guy's few computer files, and a few more pages of notes, mostly relating to his interview with Miranda. Lilah hung about in the office, savouring the sense of Guy in the one room where his orderly streak had manifested itself. Shelves of farm requisites lined the walls, dusty but methodical. If an animal got into trouble, or a machine broke down, it was essential to be able to find the right medication or spark plug quickly. Guy had not been a man to waste time or endure frustration.

Before she could decide whether the room might hold any important revelations as yet overlooked by the police, she glanced through the window. She must have subconsciously seen movement from the corner of her eye, because a man was walking down the drive to the gate. A man with a spring in his step, and a graceful Irish setter running ahead of him. Only Jonathan Mabberley would have such a dog. A dog only marginally susceptible to discipline, unable to resist running after sheep until they dropped, and utterly useless for any of the normal work a farm dog might be expected to undertake. But she was gorgeous; she adored the entire human race and would never dream of inflicting deliberate hurt on anything.

With a sense of something close to relief, Lilah went out to meet him. Roxanne, the setter, flung herself at the girl, her front paws hooking expertly onto Lilah's forearms, her smiling jaws drooling against her human friend's chest. The paws were muddy, the jaws a little disconcerting, but Lilah wasn't worried. 'Hello, you beauty,' she crooned. 'You bad, beautiful dog. Hello, Jonathan.'

'How are you?' he asked, and it was clear he really wanted to know. 'Get down, Roxy. Behave yourself.' The dog took no notice.

'Not so bad,' Lilah smiled, feeling the crookedness of her mouth. How quickly a person could forget how to smile. 'About what you'd expect, I suppose.'

'I meant to come before this. We never got a chance to talk to you at the funeral, and . . . well, there's not really any excuse. Time just goes by—'

'I know. Don't worry, Jonathan. There wasn't anything you could have done, anyway.'

'I wondered if you wanted some help. I could manage the odd afternoon, if you need me.'

'That's a nice offer. We're coping, I think. Mum seems to have come through the worst, and she's talking about getting down to some work. We're trying not to think about the hay, though. How are you at grass-cutting?'

'Middling, I think would be the word. Slightly better than nothing.'

Lilah laughed. Smiling, laughing, two minutes into Jonathan's visit: the man was a tonic. And yet Guy had loathed him so passionately, it felt disloyal even to be speaking to him, here in broad daylight out in the yard. Lilah still half expected her father to emerge from one of the buildings and start some raging argument with the man.

She herself had always found Jonathan Mabberley intriguing. Although officially he was 'the enemy' – the neighbour Guy fought with constantly on every minor issue, despised for his sloppy farming practices and carefree demeanour – his charm was unavoidable. Wickedly, he would visit Redstone when he knew Guy was away, and flirt disgracefully with both Miranda and her daughter. In his late thirties, well-spoken and relaxed, he had treated Guy as a mildly amusing neurotic, to be humoured but not taken seriously. The sheer blasphemy of this approach had been enough to seduce the Beardon women.

Jonathan had a lot to forgive Farmer Beardon for. Guy spared nothing in his raging tirades against the man when one of his beef bulls got in with the Jersey heifers, on the day that three of them were in heat; or when the Mabberley bullocks found their way through the threadbare hedges into clover which was being conserved for a later time. The names Guy called him, the aspersions on his background and value systems, the threats and aggression, all rolled off his neighbour's back. 'Jonathan is the most Christian man I ever met,' Miranda said, more than once, when Guy wasn't listening.

Only Roddy seemed unimpressed by Jonathan. 'It was terrible what his bull did,' he pointed out, coolly. The heifers had been given abortifacients, and their planned calving dates thereby significantly delayed. Roddy's orderly mind was outraged by that.

'Am I interrupting you?' Jonathan asked now. 'What were you doing?'

'It's silly, I suppose, but I was having a look in Dad's office. The police seem interested in it, and I wondered whether there might be some sort of . . . well, *clue*. Sounds daft, doesn't it.'

'Clue? It really is a murder inquiry then?'

She hesitated. There was something indefinably dangerous about Jonathan. He gave off an aura of a kind of intimacy that was exciting, but nonetheless disturbing. He spoke to everyone in the same way, she knew that, and yet he made her feel that she was one of the most special people in his life. He invited confidences which he hadn't truly earned. And Dad had hated him. Now, more than ever, that had to count for something.

But it was very tempting to talk to someone about her certainty that Guy had been murdered. Someone from outside; someone neutral. Miranda was too distracted to be rational, and Roddy sheered off if he came within spitting distance of anything serious. But perhaps Jonathan wasn't the person: he must be rather pleased, she supposed, that Guy Beardon was out of his hair, and that had to put him on a list of people to be wary of.

'They seemed sure it was an accident at first. But when Isaac was killed, that changed their minds. Apparently it's impossible, in the official mind, for two deaths to happen in the same area, within two weeks of each other, by coincidence.'

'Well, you can see their point,' he nodded. 'And I dare say they're always on the lookout for a nice juicy serial killer. They can do wonders for a copper's career.'

She grimaced, half amused, half offended. 'Nobody's said anything about a serial killer. That's going a bit far, don't you think?'

'Sorry,' he flipped a careless hand. 'Trust me to say the wrong thing. Maybe I should take my dog and go.'

Roxanne was sniffing idly around the big barn, across the yard from where they stood. Her feathering rippled as she moved, light glinting on her glossy coat. Jonathan had made a great thing of it when his dog's uncle had won Best in Show at Crufts that year and Guy had ratcheted up his mockery accordingly. 'It'll still be just as dead when it gets shot for chasing sheep,' he'd glowered. 'Then he can have a champion pedigree hearthrug made out of it.'

'Don't go,' Lilah pleaded. 'Come and say hello to Mum. She'll be glad to see you.'

'It's a kind thought, but I won't stay now. I just came by to see how you were. It must be a strain, keeping things going on the farm, and coming to terms with your Dad dying, all at once.'

She shrugged. 'It helps, really, having to keep on top of the work. And Sam's a marvel.'

'Of course. Actually I thought I saw him just now, in my woods.'

'*Sam*? No, you couldn't have done. He's doing some fencing in Top Linhey. Right the other side from your woods.'

'Oh, I know. I realised it wasn't him after a minute or two. It was a younger chap, and he had a girl with him. I was going to shout at them, until I saw the girl was Elvira Winnicombe. Not much point in shouting at her.'

'I thought she was going to that day centre in town. She's meant to go every morning. Last I heard, she was doing very well, making rugs and stuff.'

'Poor lass. Maybe she's having a holiday.'

'I'm surprised her mother lets her go out with a boy – she never lets her out unsupervised. Although I think Phoebe's poorly. Hetty said something at the funeral. Maybe she's losing her grip over Elvira. It must be quite a responsibility.'

He grinned. 'Well, to be honest, I deliberately looked the other way, pretended I hadn't seen them. She deserves a bit of fun, if you ask me.'

Lilah felt a surge of exasperation. Jonathan's irresponsibility seemed to know no bounds. Elvira, though twenty-three years old, had the capabilities of a child of eight or nine. The precise nature of her handicap was not fully understood. Some maintained that living with Phoebe Winnicombe would send anyone off their rocker; others that it was an age-old fact that children of sin would always turn out badly. But on the whole the mother and daughter were treated with the typical mix of affection and impatience that country people show the disadvantaged in their midst. Some years ago there had been talk by the health visitor and local doctor of having Elvira sterilised, which had given rise to a wholesale outraged defence of the girl's rights. Nobody in the village or neighbouring area would force themselves on her, and if she met a boy she could love and live with, then where was the harm in that? But as she became older and more voluptuous, the community became more uneasy, and Phoebe openly and loudly worried about what could happen. By mutual consent, the people of the village took it upon themselves to supervise Elvira and keep her safe.

All except Jonathan, it would seem. 'Honestly,' Lilah said. 'Anything might happen if you let her wander off with a boy. You should have taken her home.'

'I don't think it was a *boy*. He looked well into his twenties. And she was quite happy, laughing and chatting. I'm sure there's nothing to worry about. It looked like some sort of nature ramble. Probably it's some carer chap from her day centre, giving her some fresh air. There might even have been others with them, who I didn't see. If you like, I'll go back that way, and make sure nothing untoward is happening.'

'That would be a good idea. Now, I'd better get on. It's nearly lunchtime already, and I've hardly done anything yet.'

'By the way, Cappy's doing one of her barbecues on Saturday, about six. Will you come? Bring your Mum and brother, too. Just turn up – there's always more than enough.'

'Who's going to be there?'

'Oh, the Rickworths, the vicar, various odd bods.'

'Okay, then. It sounds fun. Thanks. I'll try and come, though I might be late. I can't vouch for the others.'

'Whatever.' He shrugged easily, whistled to his dog, and swung along the path that ran past the slurry pit, alongside a hedge and through a gateway onto the small lane leading to his farm. Lilah watched him go, wondering whether he'd remember to check that Elvira was all right. She wished she hadn't told her about seeing the vulnerable girl. She had too much to worry about as it was, without that nagging at her. Most of all, she wanted to think about Den, and that moment when she could have used him as a comforter and friend, and perhaps even more than that. In a desert of fear and sadness and bewilderment, Den shone like a beacon of hope. Despite – or perhaps because of – his role as junior detective in the investigation into Guy's death, he seemed to her someone she could trust.

'We've got two more weeks until the recorder comes,' noted Lilah, when she and Sam were finishing up that evening's milking. 'I wonder if she's heard about Dad? I wonder if we can keep the yield up. So far, we're doing really well.'

The recorder was a brisk woman, youngish, with a friendly manner, who visited every dairy farm on a strict monthly routine. The days when she came were memorable because the milking took longer, and she often brought gossip from neighbouring farms. Guy was always charming in her presence, and did all he could to impress her. The yard was invariably brushed before her visits . . .

'Sam!'

He was clattering some of the equipment and didn't hear her. Then the new heifer, last to be milked, kicked her unit off and all was consternation for a few minutes. They both remembered how Guy would beat the novice milkers if they did that, training them into docility from the outset.

'Sam?' she tried again, when things had calmed down. He turned, questioning. 'If we cleaned the yard last time Maggie came, how come it was so filthy again only a few days later?'

He looked blank.

'You said you hosed it all down because it was mucky everywhere – you know, that morning. Especially beside the slurry pit. It's not usually bad there, anyway, not when the cows are lying out. So why was it like that?'

He turned his attention back to the last minutes of the milking, and then seemed not to want to answer her questions. 'Wait a minute – you can switch the motor off now.' He went on dismantling the units and pipes while she went through to the little room containing the motor and flicked the switch up. The sudden silence, as always, came as a profound relief. Silence, and stillness; the throbbing was a physical sensation, which left a calm pool of relaxation behind it when it stopped. She almost forgot what she had been saying.

Almost, but not quite. 'Sam, you heard me. Why should it have been so mucky?'

He still seemed not to understand her. 'You were there,' he growled, abruptly angry with her. 'You know as well as I do how it was.'

She paused, trying to think back. She had been on the house side of the pit when she first saw Guy. Sam had fished him out on the opposite side. A picture slowly developed in her mind. Before Sam had come out of the privy, before anybody had done anything, she remembered that there had been a great splurge of slurry up that side and over the lip to the yard beyond. Perhaps she had assumed it was made by Guy struggling to get out again. But of course it couldn't have been. Because the marks were of someone who *had* got out . . .

She gave a small gasp as the implications hit her. 'Jesus, Sam. Sam!' But she said no more. *Trust nobody* came a warning from somewhere, ringing in her ears.

Sam looked impatient. 'What? What's the matter with you?' Another of her father's phrases: it cast a chill over her.

'I'm sorry. It just came over me again, that's all. I'm all jangled this morning. I think I had a bad dream and it's making me jittery. Take no notice.' She held out a hand in front of her and was alarmed by how much it was shaking. Sam seemed to soften.

'Bound to be like that sometimes,' he sympathised. 'Best thing is to concentrate on the work. That's what I try to do.'

Finished at last, they closed the doors and went in for their second breakfast.

For once, they found Miranda dressed and downstairs. She was wiping down the worktops with a pungent cloth, tackling the build-up of splashes and stains that no one seemed to have noticed.

'Morning,' said Sam, cheerily. 'Going to be a nice one. Thought we might get started on clearing out the big barn today, but the weather's more suited to an outdoor job.'

'I could help you,' Miranda offered. 'It's time I pulled my weight. We can't go on as we have been, can we?'

Lilah looked at her, considering. 'I'm not sure what you could do,' she said. 'I mean, it'd take so long to explain things to you—'

Miranda hovered between offence and amusement. Finally she chose the latter.

'I know,' she laughed. 'I never was any use as a farmhand. But there isn't much to do around the house, so could you give me a try?'

'S'pose so,' Lilah conceded. 'You'd be better off asking Sam than me.'

109

Sam looked cornered, but gave a brief nod. 'There's sure to be something needing doing,' he agreed. 'Come out and find me when you're ready.'

Miranda left it for half an hour, and then went to look for Sam. She had woken that morning with an urgent need to speak to him. The offer of help was as much a ploy to gain an opportunity to be with him as a genuine urge to do her bit. It seemed to her that there was a great deal to be said between them.

She found him in the milking parlour, where he was still finishing off the essential end-of-milking procedures. His back was to her as he sluiced all the disassembled units in the sterilising tank. In Guy's coat; she felt, as Lilah had done, that he had taken on something of her husband's personality along with the garment. His movements seemed more deft than usual, his shoulders less bowed. He even seemed to her an inch or two taller than before. She watched the back of his head, the springy hair longer than he normally kept it, and felt a surging pulse between her legs. She moved forward to touch him.

He turned to meet her; he'd known she was there. 'There you are,' he said, not meeting her eyes.

'I wanted to talk to you.' But this was such a reversal of their usual encounters, where he would hurry into the house to see her, snatching opportunities as they occurred, that she didn't know what to say.

'You talk to me every day, at mealtimes,' he said, deliberately obtuse.

'Not alone. What's the matter? You seem to have lost interest.'

'The man's *dead*, for God's sake,' he blurted, harshly. 'Do you think I could . . .' He went back to his work, shaking his head, closing the matter. Miranda was stunned. The pulse became more urgent, mixed with panic.

'That's *stupid*,' she hissed. 'Damn it, you can't be saying you'll never do it again.'

'That's how I feel now. As if all this is *because* of what I did.'

She was beyond words. She had encountered the over-developed morality of men before and always found it misplaced and inconvenient. Now she felt insulted as well. For an androgynous moment, she could feel the kind of fury that she presumed led a man to rape. If she had been equipped for it, she would have thrown Sam onto the wet concrete floor there and then and plunged into him, in a rage of frustration. The more hurt and humiliation she could have inflicted in her revenge, the better she'd have liked it.

As it was, she took up a large metal bucket standing near the doorway, and dashed it against the wall, wanting simply to cause noise and confusion. The rolling clatter it made was disappointing, but enough to cover her departure and convey to Sam precisely how she felt.

Chapter Ten

Lilah hadn't been into town since her father's death. Each morning, she had made the farm her main priority, and found the day disappearing in an endless, insistent stream of tasks. Guy had very often given himself a long break in the afternoons, but Lilah hadn't dared do the same. Even when Miranda started to take over some yard-based work, there suddenly seemed to be new things to do in the further fields.

But on that Friday, she finally decided she could manage a brief shopping trip. The prospect of meeting some different people, perhaps bumping into a friend, rediscovering something like normality, was very attractive. Her two best friends had moved away, and had not been available during the crisis days, but she had lived here almost for ever, and knew virtually everyone who would be assembled at the stalls of the Friday street market. If there was time, she might even go into the big comprehensive school during the lunch break and look for Martha Cattermole.

Feeling shy and very exposed, she took the smaller of their two cars and drove herself the eleven miles into town. Passing through the village on the way, she noticed Father Edmund coming out of the Post Office. He spotted her instantly, and gave her such a piercing stare that she almost stopped, thinking he wanted to speak to her. When he made no move, she pushed harder on the accelerator again, wondering at the sudden tightness in her chest. There had been something very disturbing in the look he'd given her.

It was a bright day; the hedgerows and fields seemed to shimmer with life and weeds grew almost as you watched them. The narrow lanes sported pink campion and cow parsley and the occasional excessive hogweed, towering high and arrogant above everything else. Guy had called them Triffids, and took delight in felling them with a well-judged chop from his bill-hook.

As she drove, Lilah became aware of a sense of escape. Forgetting the weird vicar and all the events of the past weeks, she began to hum brokenly 'Oh my darling Clementine', which had always been the song she and Guy sang together in the car, from the time she'd been a tiny infant. The memories were still there, intact, she found, and was cheered. She only had to sing 'Thou art lost and gone for ever, dreadful sorry, Clementine', to feel her father with her, laughing and intimate and warm. The obvious meaning of the words themselves was irrelevant. Sentimentality would have been a betrayal. For the moment, feelings about Guy had been put on hold, waiting for the inquest into his death – due the following week – to be over.

As she drove into town, she had to stop at a T-junction. The traffic was heavy – tourists mostly, she noted – and she had to wait some time. Then a police car turned from the

113

main road into the one where she waited, and she recognised Den. Without thinking, she waved hard at him, anxious to catch his eye. At the very last moment, he saw her, and she could see every step in the process by which he remembered their last encounter. Then he braked, a few yards back from where she was, and leant out of his open window.

'Can I talk to you?' he called. 'Pull in for a minute, will you? I'll just turn round.' He indicated a farm entrance a little way ahead as his intended turning place.

Easier said than done, she thought. Several cars were behind her, all wanting to get out into the main road. What was she supposed to do? As a gap appeared in the traffic, she pulled out, turning left, and drew in at the roadside, fifty yards beyond the junction. Someone hooted at her, and she almost drove off again. Everything seemed difficult, confused. Cars whizzed past her, and she felt frightened and breathless.

Then he was at the passenger door, leaning down from his immoderate height, smiling through the glass at her. He was in uniform, his smartness making him seem important and reliable. 'I can't leave it here,' she said helplessly. 'What do you want me to do?'

He opened the door. 'Sorry. I didn't mean to flummox you. But I wanted to see you and it seemed too good a chance to miss. Are you in a rush to get somewhere?'

'Not really. Sort of. It's not important.' His long face was the epitome of patience. He gentled her, sensing the tension.

'Drive round to the car park, then. I'll meet you there. Is that okay?'

'I'll never get out into this traffic again. Look at it!'

'Allow me.' He stood up straight, and went round behind

114

her car. In a state approaching disbelief, she watched while he stepped into the road, and held up one hand. The closest car ignored him, but the next one hurriedly drew to a halt. Fumblingly, she started off, jerking the clutch and steering an amateurish arc as she got under way.

He took her to a small backstreet café for coffee, and gracefully folded himself into the cramped seat. He asked her how she was feeling and whether things on the farm were still under control. She watched him, knowing he had something more to say. The sun had caught his cheeks, roughening the skin. Again she remembered how she had admired him as a schoolgirl.

He began talking as soon as they had their coffee in front of them. 'Amos is doing well,' he said. 'They think he'll make a good recovery.'

'Thank goodness for that. Though it'll never be the same for him, without Isaac. I don't suppose he'll want to stay in the house, by himself. Poor old chap. He looked so awful, staggering down the field to get help, covered in blood.'

She was prattling, much as she'd done that morning with Sam. Talking helped, she'd discovered. Just stringing words together, letting them pour out to anyone who would listen, was comforting in a strange way.

Den nodded briskly, and stirred his coffee, even though he hadn't put any sugar in it. 'Don't you want to know what he's been saying?'

'What? Has Amos been telling you about the attack? Gosh, that's progress, isn't it. Was it somebody he knew?'

'Well, he's talking properly at last. And he's given a bit of a description of the attacker. But it isn't a lot of help, really.'

She frowned at him. 'Is this some kind of test? You want to see if I'm nervous of what Amos might tell you? Surely you wouldn't be that devious?'

He laughed, showing no sign of embarrassment. 'No, I didn't mean it to sound like that. I just thought you'd be keen to know, for your own purposes. I mean, aren't you scared that there's some maniac loose in the neighbourhood, hiding out somewhere, ready to kill again?'

She smiled. 'You've been reading too many tabloid headlines,' she said, feeling older and wiser than him. 'My Dad would call this typical police scaremongering. You know – every time there's a child killed or woman raped, some police person comes on the telly and says every woman and child should stay indoors, and behave with great caution. Making it our problem.'

He shook his head. 'I don't get it. Whose problem should it be, then?'

'I don't mean *problem*, exactly. Almost our *fault*. Blaming the victim. You'd have to hear Dad on the subject to follow the argument. He was brilliant at putting the other point of view. And he brought us up to be sensible. It's no good – you're not going to make me believe in some monster hiding in the bushes.'

'Then who killed Isaac?' He leant forward, staring her in the face. 'And who killed your father?'

'I don't know,' she replied carefully. 'But I think it must have been someone who hated him, or who would benefit from his death.'

'And yet when it happened we all thought it was an

accident. There are quite a few red faces over that, I can tell you. And I haven't come out of it smelling of roses, by a long way.'

'Why, what should you have done?'

'Well, we didn't look very thoroughly for marks where he might have skidded. We didn't ask ourselves why he was so far from the edge – I mean, why did he go so far in? Lots of little things. The slurry wasn't all that deep, really. He could have stood up in it. I've had a right telling-off, to be honest. Letting Sam move things about and clean up, not examining it right at the start. We just filled in the G5 and more or less left it at that. The post-mortem just confirmed what we assumed.'

'We all felt sure it was an accident, then,' she said. 'It never occurred to anybody that it might have been anything else. It must happen all the time – I mean, murder isn't the first thing that comes to mind when a person dies, is it? If the Grimms hadn't been attacked, we'd probably still be talking about an accident. Although—'

'What?'

'I don't think I could ever really believe that. Dad wasn't the type to have accidents. I keep saying that, don't I? He just *wasn't*, though. He always had everything under control. And he didn't have a heart attack or a stroke or anything, according to that Coroner's man. Somebody *must* have pushed him in, and then I suppose held him down.' She shuddered. 'What a terrible thing to do.'

'And the inquest is next week.' He spoke as if this was the real point that he had to discuss. Lilah waited for what might come next.

'It's sure to be embarrassing,' he explained. 'Foul play now looks much more likely than it did to start with, but there's scarcely any evidence available to indicate what happened. Coroners don't like that kind of set-up. It's messy. "Unlawful killing by person or persons unknown" is what he'll probably say. And nobody likes that. It puts a lot of pressure on the police, and makes the whole thing very public.'

'There'll be an inquest for Isaac as well, I suppose?'

Den nodded. 'That's much more straightforward. And everyone's hope now is that we'll find this gypsy—'

'What? Who said anything about a gypsy? What are you talking about?'

'Oh, Amos's description. Sounded like some vagrant. Rather what we'd been thinking. Given that there's nobody in the world could possibly have a proper motive for smashing that poor fool's head in.'

'Wait, wait. This isn't making sense. You think this tramp or whatever went from Redstone to the Grimms', randomly killing Daddy and Isaac, for no good reason, and now that Amos has told you what he looks like, you'll just stumble across him one day and arrest him for a double murder.' She raised her eyebrows at him, feeling again the sensation of her father somehow inside her, projecting his own clear-sighted cynicism onto the matter.

Den grinned uneasily. 'Well, not quite like that. But you must admit it fits the facts.'

'It doesn't fit the *people*. It doesn't fit with real life and what makes people do things. Surely you can see that?'

'Okay, Miss Freud. Tell me where we're going wrong.'

'I already have. I don't believe in psychopaths lurking

in the bushes, killing for the sake of it. It's fairytale stuff. I know it would be highly convenient for all of us if it was true, but it's too bloody easy. Something's going on, right here amongst people we know, and you're supposed to be figuring it out. You haven't been asking the right questions. Oh – this is so *frustrating*.'

She wriggled on the plastic seat, gripping her hands together in a double fist. 'This is unreal,' she blurted. 'You and me – we were at school together, for heaven's sake.'

He laughed, and leant back, stretching out the long legs that had been folded up uncomfortably to fit beneath the meagre formica table. 'What's that got to do with it?' he said.

She grinned back at him. 'Nothing, really. It's just – here we are, trying to make sense of two horrible deaths and you're just Den Cooper, who used to be on the school bus. It doesn't match up.'

He looked hard at her, his gaze flickering slightly, as he focused alternately on her two eyes. It made her feel very thoroughly inspected. She could see him thinking again.

'I'd forgotten that feeling,' he said slowly. 'The job does that to you. You see crime and death and awful misery, even in this little place, and you forget what ordinary life is like. To me, *everything* is ordinary now. They call it being desensitised.'

She tried to get a sense of what he meant. What, anyway, was 'ordinary'? She had seen unborn lambs that had to be cut up alive in order to be delivered; she had seen a cow die of bloat and countless rats and rabbits killed by the farm dogs and cats. She had watched television news reports of carnage and unspeakable distress. She hadn't been especially sensitive herself. And yet—

119

'Then why do you look so queasy now?' she asked gently. 'Is it because you've never had to deal with a murder before?'

The word hung between them, threatening and alien. Each one of them leant back slightly, away from the very idea.

Den shook his head. 'The first week I was in the job, a chap stabbed his wife eighteen times. I knew her and identified the body. But this is different. Too much mystery, too few clues, and whatever anyone says, there is undeniably a killer out there somewhere, and I for one don't feel the least bit happy about that.'

'Then ask me some questions. Pursue your enquiries. After all, I must surely be a suspect, officially speaking.'

'Okay.' He was abruptly businesslike. 'How's this? Was your father's life insured?'

For a moment, she just stared at him. Then, 'Heavens, I don't know. Nobody's said anything. Probably not, knowing Dad.'

'Did he leave a will?'

'I think so, yes. The solicitor is supposed to be sending it to Mum any day now. He wanted her to go and see him, but she said it could all be done by post.'

'But you don't know what's in it?'

'No, Mum's in charge of all that. Except – Daddy did once say the farm would be mine when he died.' She looked at a shiny chromium urn behind the café counter and paused before adding wistfully, 'He probably didn't mean it.'

'But you believed him?'

'I think I did, yes. But I thought it wouldn't happen until I was at least forty.'

120

'But it could only be yours if he specifically willed it to you. Otherwise, it'll have to be divided between the widow and his children . . .'

'*All* his children?'

'That's right. Why, are there others we don't know about?' His laugh died when he saw her nod.

'Two. I've got two grown-up half-brothers. Mum thinks I've forgotten about them – she hasn't even mentioned them since he died – but I haven't. I've been thinking about them quite a lot lately. Do you think we'll have to share Redstone with them?'

'Probably not. He'll have covered all that in his will, presumably. We'll want to check, of course. They didn't come to the funeral, did they?'

Lilah shook her head. 'They seem to be completely out of touch. I suppose it's something you should explore.' She wanted to go, sensing deeper chasms ahead, too deep for her to confront right now. 'I think I'd better be moving,' she said.

'Right.' He looked relieved, and she felt offended. He slid his long body out from the cramped seat, paid for the coffees and left without waiting for her to accompany him.

Like someone in need of fresh air, she thought, as she gave him a little wave.

Father Edmund watched the little car disappear from sight, and stood without moving for another half-minute. He became aware of the muscle at the hinge of his jaw bulging rhythmically as he ground his teeth. It was a habit he had possessed for thirty years. It went with deep and uncomfortable thought.

That girl looked so – *blithe*. Her hair bouncing, a red T-shirt carelessly thrown on. It was all wrong. Where were the signs of suffering that there ought to be? Hadn't the wretched creature had *any* feelings for her father? Was life held so cheap these days that a bereaved daughter could swan half-naked round the countryside only days after burying her father?

He considered the wisdom of paying a visit to Miranda, knowing that she would be alone . . . The boy had gone back to school, he knew: more than one villager had reported seeing him on the bus that morning. A pastoral call, it would be – a humble enquiry as to the welfare of the widow, now that life was slowly pulling itself back to normal. Besides, it would perhaps help her to unburden her anxieties regarding the coming inquest. That, surely, must be weighing heavily upon the whole family; it was a matter that surely must require the support and encouragement of the parish clergyman.

The villagers were divided about the inquest. As far as they could determine, there would be no progress made on discovering the identity of Guy's killer. It was horribly exciting to have a double murder committed in their midst, and yet the lack of an obvious culprit was deeply disconcerting. Several of them were rendered very nervous by the events at Redstone and the Grimsdale place. Parents were keeping their children under firm surveillance. Nobody went for country walks in the Redstone direction. The taint of mystery and suspicion was deepening; Father Edmund had heard certain individuals clearly state that they wished there'd never been such a family as the Beardons.

Yes, he decided: he would drive himself up to Redstone and offer his services to Miranda Beardon. It was the very least he could do. It was the right and proper duty of any conscientious priest, redolent of former times, when his parishioners might have depended on him. The idea that it required a certain amount of courage on his part only enhanced the project in his own eyes.

He found her in the small patch of garden at the front of the house – if front it could be called. Like many farmhouses, the entrances were modest and could be termed neither 'front' nor 'side' nor 'back' with any certainty. People entered through any of them wearing dirty boots, carrying muddy lambs. He approached the straggly area, noting the nettles amongst the shrubs and the skeletal stalks of long-finished tulips, and stood waiting for Miranda to acknowledge him. He knew she had seen his car come into the yard, and must have realised who was visiting. The deliberate snub in the way she continued to wrench at the buttercup roots did not go unnoticed.

At last she stood up straight, thin and defensive in a baggy shirt and denim shorts. 'Hello,' she said, looking directly into his face. 'We don't see you here very often.'

He put his hands behind his back, trying to look priestly, half wishing he had worn his cassock instead of the thin grey suit.

'I came to see how you were getting along,' he lilted, honeying his words like any undertaker. 'I saw your daughter a little while ago, and she put me in mind of you.'

'Oh, well, you know . . .' she feebly answered his question. 'Life has to go on. The work keeps us going. No

123

time for brooding.' She laughed a little, mocking herself.

She isn't going to invite me in, he realised. *She doesn't need me. Blast the woman. Blast this idiotic anachronistic job of work. Wasting my time. Every day more futile than the last . . .*

'And how is young Roderick? I understand he's gone back to school.'

'That's right. He's got his GCSEs. We want him to take them, as planned, even if all this means he gets lower grades than he should. They're really important to him. He's got all sorts of ambitious ideas about a career.'

'I'm sure you did what was best. He'll have time for his grieving once term time is over. Boys are unpredictable in that respect.'

Miranda shrugged. 'Maybe.' Clearly, she was reluctant to discuss her son with him. Father Edmund wanted to scream at her. *Don't you care? Your husband is dead, woman! You seem to have forgotten all about that little fact.* But he said nothing, merely bounced slightly on his toes, and devoted some attention to the spiritual quality of his smile. He cast his gaze obliquely towards the murderous slurry pit, which was obviously much too close to the buildings. Sooner or later, there'd be a man round from the Council to tell them to fill it in and dig another one further off. In normal circumstances, Guy would have been fined for contravening the regulations so blatantly.

Frustrated by the growing silence, he knew he'd soon have to go. First, though, he had to penetrate the blandness of the woman he'd come to see. He wanted to get under her skin.

'Everyone has been wondering, of course, just how it was poor Guy came to such a terrible end.' He kept his tone silky and overwhelmingly sympathetic. 'They'll be very interested in the outcome of the inquest next week. It'll be an ordeal for you, I'm sure. Just tell me if I can offer you any assistance.'

Miranda did not react beyond a small frown of irritation. 'Oh, it'll soon be all over,' she said. 'I'm not particularly worried about it.'

'Well, that's very brave of you,' he purred. 'Most women would be worried sick. Especially after this terrible business with the poor Grimsdale brothers. I see that the good women of the village have taken it upon themselves to feed the cats and tend the place until Amos gets home. I understand that Phoebe Winnicombe is helping out. She was unwell, but it seems she's better now.'

'I hope you're not implying that *I* should be doing something? Good grief, as if there wasn't enough to do here.'

'No, no.' He raised his hands defensively, took a small step backwards. 'All I meant was . . . well, it has been a dreadful business and people are thinking there must be a maniac loose . . . and you really are very vulnerable here.'

'Vicar, it probably sounds strange, but honestly, I don't feel bothered. You seem to think I should be afraid of something, and I have to admit I'm really not. It's probably thanks to Guy. He was always so scathing about talk of murderers lurking in the woodshed, that he's convinced me – and Lilah – that there's not much to worry about. It was awful about the Grimms, I know. But I can't believe it had any connection with Guy's death, whatever people might be thinking.'

He was silent for a moment, before reverting doggedly to his original theme. 'An inquest is never a pleasant thing,' he stated, with a hint of defiance. 'So many questions . . .' He paused, waiting for a reaction.

'There isn't much I can tell them,' she said steadily. 'I was asleep until Lilah came bursting in with the news. I don't suppose they'll even want to ask me anything.'

'They will, my dear. You can be sure of that. You see, they'll want to know about his state of mind. How he was the day before. All that sort of thing. Surely, it must have entered your head that it wasn't an accident.'

'Rubbish!' she said, snapping her muddy hands together. 'Of course Guy didn't commit suicide. He was far too sane. Now, if you'll excuse me, I must get on with the weeding.'

Chapter Eleven

Miranda didn't want to go to Jonathan's barbecue. 'His friends always make me feel so dowdy,' she grumbled. 'And they'll be pussy-footing around, trying not to mention Guy. Can't you go without me?'

'I will if you insist, but it'll be the same for me. I don't know who makes you feel dowdy.'

'Cappy, for starters. She's dreadfully sophisticated. And Sarah's so slim and young. She'll be there, I imagine?'

Lilah nodded. 'He said he'd asked them. I don't know why, when she and Tim fight all the time. He must get some sort of buzz out of it. The Vicar's going to be there as well, which is a pain. He's been giving me evil looks, as if he thinks I'm some kind of demon.'

'That man isn't normal. And I think he's getting worse since Guy died. If that's what a pastoral visit's like, no wonder the church is in decline. He seemed intent on frightening me. And then he tried to claim that Guy committed suicide. Guy, of all people! He's obviously dotty. I'm glad Guy wouldn't let either of you go to his confirmation classes.'

'Maybe Roddy'll come with me to the barbecue.'

But Roddy pulled a face and shook his head. 'No way!' he spluttered. 'Not my thing at all. What do you want to go for, anyway? They'll all be decades older than you.'

Lilah shrugged. Anything for a change, she supposed. And she liked Jonathan. He frequently featured in her dreams, as a kind of romantic erotic figure, catching her unawares behind a hedge on sunny afternoons.

She set out at six fifteen, having swapped milkings with Roddy and done the rounds of calves and hens before she left. Sam had given her a reproachful look when she told him about the change. In recent days Sam had said almost nothing to her beyond the necessary minimum concerning the livestock. At the back of her mind, she knew something was wrong, something that would require her attention sooner or later. Until then, she pushed it away and concentrated on getting through the next in the endless string of farm tasks.

She took the cross-country route and walked across three fields in her open sandals, before emerging on to the lane that would take her to the Mabberleys' place. It was a rare summer evening, slow and soft, scented with young grass and new leaves. Dry without being dusty. She found herself calculating that there were at best twenty-five days in each year in which she could do this walk without wearing boots against the mud. Even if the field tracks were passable, there was usually a churned-up area in the gateways, or a boggy ditch too wide to leap without a foot sinking into noxious black liquid. The more orthodox route to the neighbouring farm was to go out of the Redstone yard, directly on to the narrow back lane which led to the Mabberleys. This lane was seldom used, and had a dark, inhospitable atmosphere to it. Lilah's automatic instinct had been to avoid it.

The Mabberleys farmed four hundred acres as if the new age of agribusiness had barely arrived. 'Lazy farming', Guy had called it. Beef cattle of all breeds ran free over much of the land, as if on the mid-west American prairies. Very few crops were grown, apart from some hay. Guy had devoted much attention to trying to work out how Jonathan managed to live as well as he did, given the poor beef prices. Resentment simmered between the two for more reasons than just the sloppy hedge-keeping between their farms. Jonathan's persistent good humour made it worse, for then Guy believed he was being mocked. It seemed that everything Mabberley touched turned to gold, where Guy regarded himself as perpetually only a few pounds away from bankruptcy.

Lilah could smell the charcoal before she could see the house. Fancy a Devon farmer giving something so vulgar as a barbecue, she thought with amusement. Especially one whose family had been here for generations – though Martha Cattermole had shown her how the social distinctions which once prevailed were hopelessly blurred now. Even the musical Devon accent was lessening, as comprehensive education worked its way down the generations.

In fact, Jonathan's worst crime, when it came down to it, was refusing to act the part properly. Mabberleys had lived in this house for centuries, farming much the same acreage in all that time. The property had remained more or less intact – no foreclosures made, no scandals or dramas. The grass was good, the extensive woodland against the north boundary a semi-public area for recreation. People came from town to picnic under the great Mabberley beeches and oaks, which might have gone back to Tudor or Elizabethan times. But it was as if Jonathan cared nothing for ownership, when other men across the world would have risked their lives to hold on to such an unspoilt and lovely piece of ground. His very casualness enraged people. His generosity was discounted, since anyone could be generous with something they didn't value. Holding a summer barbecue was *wrong*, somehow, for its very modernness. Better a big barn dance, or some long-lost folklore festival. But that was forgetting Cappy, of course, who could not be expected to understand the nuances, and who obviously couldn't have cared less about them in any case.

Lilah was the last to arrive. People were arranged around the patio on garden loungers, glasses in their hands, talking in relaxed fashion as if the initial formal overtures were long past. The main voice to be distinguished was that of Wing Commander Stradling, who spoke as if the words had to be forced violently from deep in his throat. He sounded more like a growling animal than a man, and everything he said seemed angry; an impression that was reinforced by his red cheeks and wiry grey hair. Lilah had always been shy of him, especially as Guy had consistently gone out of his way to provoke the man, but she did not dislike him. He could be funny, and kind, and she had sometimes felt almost sorry for him; a dinosaur left stranded by the removal of the respect which had once been his birthright. He was also a quietly heroic husband to an invalid wife kept invisibly at home. He was in the midst of addressing Sylvia, whom Lilah was very surprised to see. If Miranda had known that her one true friend in the village would be at the barbecue, thought Lilah,

130

she might have felt differently about putting in an appearance.

Tim and Sarah were positioned as far apart from each other as possible. Tim was chatting to Jonathan, his back to everyone else, his glass slopping as he waved it to illustrate a point. Jonathan was turning steaks on the barbecue, and only half attending. Sarah was the first to notice Lilah's arrival. She gave an over-bright smile and a silly little flip of her hand. 'Everyone!' she called, like a primary school teacher. 'Look, Lilah's here.'

Jonathan was the first to react. He dropped his fish slice and bounded across to greet her. His lovely dog followed, equally enthusiastic, and between them they lavished a warm welcome on her. She giggled with embarrassment as he gave her a big hug. The thin summer clothes ensured quite a bit of skin contact, which she found more provocative than she could have wished. The mixture of sexuality and security in his embrace left her with an ambivalence that rendered her speechless. All she could do was to stand back and concentrate on petting the dog for a few moments, to give herself time to regain her composure.

'You're late,' said Jonathan. 'You missed the aperitifs. You'll have to go straight on to the punch. Help yourself.' He waved at a great silver bowl on a garden table, and strolled back to his meat. She busied herself with pouring a glass of the cold punch. Some of it spilt, and she glanced round guiltily.

'Don't worry,' came a cool voice. 'That's the great thing about having all this outside.'

It was Cappy, Jonathan's wife, holding a big wooden bowl of salad. Her transatlantic accent made her sound detached and somehow superior. Dark-skinned and small, she came from some wildly exotic background which Lilah was never sure she fully understood. There was an Inuit parent, she was sure of that, but the other half seemed to vary from Creole to Chinese via Native American. Whatever her parentage, she seemed to have found her ideal man in her ideal place, and had been living in apparent contentment for five years now. Carelessly racist, Guy had called her 'Mabberley's half-caste', but he had always been charming to her face, and had been curious to hear stories of her early life, on the few occasions when he had talked with her.

'Here,' said Cappy now, 'let me wipe your glass.' She produced a damp cloth and deftly removed the stickiness. 'I'm sorry about your father, by the way. I thought the funeral went well, didn't you? We came straight home, of course, afterwards – we didn't think Guy would have wanted us to come to the bit back at the house. By the way, what *do* English people call that part of a funeral? Is it a wake?'

Lilah frowned. 'I don't know,' she said. 'Nobody called it that, as far as I know. It's just "refreshments", I suppose.'

Cappy laughed. 'Well, whatever, I'm still very sorry it happened. It must have been so strange, finding him like that.' She spoke easily, with no discernible embarrassment. She looked Lilah straight in the eye, as if searching for something, which had the effect of rendering the girl awkward and inarticulate.

'*Strange*,' she repeated. 'Yes, that's exactly what it was. Like something from a film. I still can't believe it.'

The woman laid a hand on the girl's arm. 'My father died violently, too, you know. It brought it back to me, when I heard about Guy. It makes life seem so – uncertain. Don't you think so? I saw Guy only the day before. Such a thing to happen, right next door. To a man so full of life! I would have expected him to live another thirty years.'

Lilah couldn't remember anything about the days before Guy's death. They seemed to have receded into a very remote past and to have lost any relevance. She didn't remember her last words to him, before that final 'Night, night,' which came every bedtime. But Cappy's remarks caused her to wonder for the first time just what Guy's last movements had been.

'Where did you see him?' she asked, with scant curiosity.

'In town. He was buying fruit, and said hello, for once. Usually he would just glower at us if he met us. Then I saw him again, from the car, when I was coming home. He was standing on the pavement with another man. They were having a bit of a quarrel, from the look of things. I felt a little embarrassed for him, to be honest. Though I do know – sorry, am I saying too much?'

'No, go on.' Lilah felt very odd, as if she were being shown something forbidden.

'Well, it's just that he was a man with a temper, and often shouted at people. At least, he shouted at Jonathan quite a lot. But it seemed strange for him to be doing it in the street. Out of character, perhaps? I'm sorry, I shouldn't judge. I didn't know him very well.'

'You're right, though. He was always sweet and charming in public. Who was the other man?'

'I've no idea. He had his back to me, so I couldn't see his face. It could have been anyone. Youngish, and quite thin, that's all I can recall.'

'But you could see that Daddy was angry?'

133

'Yes. He was quite red, and – *tight*, somehow. Like someone trying not to burst. I thought perhaps he would hit the other man. But I only saw them for a moment. Perhaps I got it all wrong.'

Lilah tried to dismiss the whole story. The man might have offended Guy in any number of ways: his temper was quickly sparked, and quickly assuaged again. Cappy had probably caught a brief glimpse of something that had meant nothing. She didn't seem to have connected it in any way to Guy's death, and Lilah tried to follow suit. Unfortunately, this new report felt more like a whole handful of important pieces for her growing jigsaw of suspicion than an irrelevant coincidence.

Sylvia seemed to be hanging back, as if unwilling to speak to Lilah. Firmly refusing to yield to paranoia, the girl went up to her and smiled. 'Hello, fancy meeting you here,' she said, exploiting the long-standing intimacy she assumed existed between them. 'It's been a while since I saw you.'

Sylvia's height gave her the same untouchable demeanour as Den's did. Tall people never seemed to be agitated or tense; like giraffes, their movements appeared calm and measured, even when in a hurry. Sylvia held a large glass tankard by its manly handle, and spoke in a rich contralto. The stance and voice contrasted, however, with something that looked very much like embarrassment.

'How's your Mum?'

Lilah merely shrugged, assuming that Sylvia knew the answer to that at least as well as she did.

'I really meant to call round today. I don't know why I didn't.' She stared vaguely over Lilah's shoulder at Jonathan's woods. 'You'd think I'd be there all the time, without Guy—' She blinked, and stopped herself.

For as long as Lilah could remember, Miranda and Sylvia had been close friends, meeting religiously every few days for a coffee and a chat. Sylvia had collected Lilah and Roddy from school when Miranda's car broke down, had swapped eggs for honey, tomatoes for clotted cream. Sylvia never stopped working, a fact witnessed by the obvious muscles in her arms and the absence of an ounce of surplus fat. In comparison with Sylvia, Miranda was a drone, lacking in skill or application.

'Is Sam behaving himself?' Sylvia asked, apparently changing the subject.

Lilah raised her eyebrows. 'He's wonderful. We'd be completely lost without him. He's not nearly as daft as people think, you know.'

'I never thought he was daft. Your mother doesn't think so, either.'

'No, of course *she* doesn't. But village people do. It's his own fault, I suppose – he plays up to it. I think he does it for an easy life. And Daddy often made him feel stupid.' She spoke dispassionately, about a state of affairs that had existed for as long as she could remember. Not until quite recently had she begun to feel a mild indignation on Sam's behalf, although she dismissed it as none of her business.

'That's true,' said Sylvia, carefully. 'And is your mother doing her share of the farmwork?' She smiled at the idea.

Lilah mirrored the smile. 'Not really. She never seems to get the hang of it. She feeds calves and does a bit of tidying up, but I wouldn't say she's a vital part of the workforce.'

Sylvia laughed aloud. 'Miranda's wicked, isn't she. Quite the wrong person to be involved in all this.'

'All this? Being widowed, you mean?' *Widow*. Now there was another strange word. Black cloth covering your head and a fairytale son off to sell the cow . . .

'And the rest. Coping with the paperwork, making decisions. I imagine you're taking on most of that, as well?'

'We're managing. Most of it's common sense, when it comes down to it.'

Sylvia looked at her, probing, as Cappy and Den had been, openly curious as to her state of mind.

'Don't stare at me,' Lilah said, itchy with irritation. 'People keep doing it, and it's awful.'

'Oh, Li, I'm sorry. I was just thinking about Miranda, and how you're getting to look like her. Your hair grows exactly the same as hers does – I never noticed before.'

'Don't tell me it's a widow's peak.' The joke seemed to come from somewhere else – Guy's spirit possessing her, never missing a chance to make a wordplay.

'Oh, my love. You'll be all right, you will. She's bloody lucky to have you, and I hope she knows it.'

Lilah couldn't think of an appropriate answer to that.

'Tell her I'll be round in a day or two, will you?'

Lilah nodded, still wordless, and the woman turned towards Sarah, who was making a commotion about a small cloud of midges dancing above her head.

The sun sank gloriously over Jonathan's nicely-framed horizon, and plates of steak and salad were passed around. Lilah tried to be sociable, but as Miranda had predicted, everyone but the Mabberleys seemed uneasy with her. She concentrated on the food, although an odd swollen sensation in her stomach meant that she could manage little of it. She

136

felt vaguely uneasy, as if tears could well up at any moment.

Father Edmund came over to her, somehow giving the impression that duty was forcing him against his will. 'I've been thinking about you,' he said unctuously. 'I do hope you're feeling a little better now, after your terrible shock.'

'Not much,' she said, with a little smile of apology.

He gave her a desultory pat on the shoulder before drifting over to the punch bowl. He seemed dispirited, even mildly depressed, and Lilah recalled with some amusement Jonathan's assertion that the vicar could be entertaining in his cups. Either that point was still to be reached, or tonight was an exception. Anyone less entertaining would be hard to imagine.

Next, the Wing Commander finally found some nerve, and huffed and growled an acknowledgement of her presence, but made no reference to Guy; his embarrassment was tangible, and Lilah released them both from the discomfort by suddenly deciding she should go to the loo. She spent ten minutes in the small downstairs lavatory, trying desperately to remember how it felt to be normal and relaxed among people she knew. Only the fear of attracting further unwelcome attention gave her the strength to go back to the patio.

When she resumed her place, Father Edmund seemed to be trying to act as self-elected marriage guidance counsellor to Tim and Sarah. He glided between them across the flagstones, carrying his plate awkwardly, offering to fetch a drink for Sarah, or suggesting to Tim that he might be working too hard. Lilah wondered whether he really cared about them, or whether it was all an act, part of the role he saw himself in as village priest. Tim seemed impatient with him, barely replying to the softly-voiced questions. He shot

137

furious glances at Sarah now and then, which she made a poor show of failing to notice. Lilah could think of only one occasion on which Tim and Sarah had not been angry with each other, and that had been before they were married. Since the big village wedding complete with marquee and orange blossom, they had generated a mutual fury which alternately amused and frightened anyone in contact with them.

Jonathan sent small friendly smiles across at Lilah whenever he was turned her way. The Wing Commander had him pinioned against a granite horse trough full of nasturtiums and begonias, haranguing him about the depredations of tourists. 'Grockles', he called them, apparently thinking he was being rather daringly original by so doing. 'Why they bother to come, I can't imagine,' he boomed. 'When all they do is clutter up the village shops and make a noise at night.'

Jonathan nodded and frowned, conveying perfect sympathy and commiseration. Silky-smooth, he let the older man believe that he was in perfect accord. Not by so much as a glint in his eye did he betray what he really felt. Lilah knew he liked the visitors – why else would he let them use his woods? She had seen him pretending to be the local Squire, chatting to Americans and city-dwellers as they got out of their cars in the village to photograph the pub or the War Memorial.

'They seem to gravitate here more all the time,' pursued the Wing Commander. 'We must be in some infernal guidebook or something. And the season starts earlier each year. Did you hear about that minibus, full of French housewives, on Easter Monday? Demanding teas at the Post Office, for some unknown reason.'

Jonathan laughed nastily, perfectly expressing his profound contempt for stupid French housewives.

'And that Irishman – I told you about him, did I? Tramping across my garden with binoculars. I'd have taken him for a spy not so long ago. Said he'd heard we'd got some lesser spotted something-or-other and had come for a look. Obviously tommy rot. I still wish I knew what he was up to.'

'A bit obvious, if he *was* a spy,' suggested Jonathan gently.

'Maybe so. I didn't say he *was* a spy. Just up to something. Or a damned fool, most likely. Thought he'd get a close view of Dartmoor from here, I shouldn't wonder. He had a backpack, sleeping bag, the whole shooting match. Hiked from Ballymajiggery by the look of him.'

Jonathan had done his bit to be sociable and stepped back. 'Please have another glass of the punch. It'll all be gone soon. I'll fetch you some.'

'No, no, my boy. I must be off. Doreen worries – well, no need to go into that.' He didn't move for a moment, while a lost look crossed his face. Then he made a big show of not breaking up the party, and thanking Cappy for her hospitality with elaborately old-fashioned formality.

Lilah took her chance. '*I'll* have that punch, then,' she said, bouncing up beside Jonathan. 'Gosh, doesn't he go on!'

'Sshh.' He glanced around to be sure the Wing Commander hadn't heard. 'Poor old chap – you have to pity him.'

'Maybe, but mostly he's just a pain in the neck. How could you be such a *creep* with him? You don't agree with all that stuff about grockles.'

'How do *you* know?' He pulled a childish face at her, a kid in the playground. 'Anyway, how's the detective work going? Last time I saw you, you were knee-deep in clues.'

This was dangerous territory. 'I was just being stupid. I decided to leave it all to the police.'

'Oh? What does that mean? Either that you've decided to get on with your life, or that I'm now one of the suspects. Trust nobody – that's what they say, isn't it?'

'I don't think I want to talk about it, if that's all right.'

'If that's what you want,' he said submissively, before striding across the patio to where Tim and Sarah were standing at arm's length, preparing to leave. 'Going so soon? And I hoped we were going to make a night of it!'

Cappy was beside Lilah again. 'Don't feel you have to go,' she said. 'It's early yet.' But it was almost dark and Lilah knew she must get home soon. Any later and Jonathan would insist on driving her the half-mile home, which she realised she didn't want. *Trust nobody* he had said, presumably in fun. Suddenly she felt cold. What would that be like – having nobody she could trust? Never accepting lifts or favours, never taking words at face value. Sam, Roddy, her mother, Sylvia, Jonathan himself . . . which of them could genuinely be trusted? Already Father Edmund caused her to question his motives, and everyone knew the Wing Commander had ample reason to abhor her father and his family. So who did that leave?

One person only, apart from friends who were all at college. One pillar of reliability seemed to stand out in a landscape of deception: Police Constable Den Cooper.

Chapter Twelve

The walk back was cool and the light faded fast. White daisies stood out luminously at the edge of the field, and a near-full moon appeared above the horizon. After a few minutes, away from the lights on Jonathan's patio, Lilah's eyes adjusted, and she could see her way quite easily. The choice to return by the way she had come had been greeted with mild concern by Cappy, but she had insisted, sturdily claiming to be able to get home blindfolded if necessary.

Nobody had said anything about the likelihood of a savage maniac hiding in the hedge, ready to jump out at her, and she hadn't given it a thought herself, despite Den's assertions the day before. She had wandered the fields since she was six or seven, a small pagan creature, finding birds' nests, digging for the elusive nut at the end of the sorrel root, scanning the ground for four-leaved clovers. The idea that there might be something to fear was unreal to her – it was the stuff of myths or nightmares, something that bore no relation to how things were in *her* fields, in *her* home village. This was a sparsely inhabited area, at best; if she were to meet anyone, it would be someone she knew. Later that night, she was forced to admit that she had been an idiot, that murder was something terrible and serious and not to be so easily brushed out of mind. But on this evening, after the reassuring session at the Mabberleys', she stepped lightly and fearlessly.

Her route did not lie through woodland, but through open fields. Even so, the hedges between the fields were high, and even Lilah's fearless heart beat a little faster as she crossed a small, neglected area which Guy had never bothered to cultivate. An old oak grew alone, close to the corner of the field; the twenty feet or so between it and the hedge was long grass, with docks and cow parsley in it.

A grunting sound was the first indication that the long grass concealed something alive. Lilah's stomach gave a little lurch of apprehension, mainly because she was unable to identify the source of the sound. Peering into the shadow thrown by the tree, she detected movement, and a sizeable shape, almost as big as a cow. But slowly the grunting became human, its rhythm connecting with her own bloodstream, until she knew with a flash of shock that it came from a man in the process of copulation. How she could be sure was beyond rational explanation. It was something a person just *knew*.

Torn between wanting to look away, pretend that nothing was happening, and a curiosity as to who these shameless individuals could be, she hovered, her heart thumping with the strangeness of the situation. The shape, as she glanced again, resolved into a woman on all fours, with the man behind her, gripping her hips, knees slightly bent, moving only a little. No violent thrusting, but a much gentler action, feeling his way, the grunts purely of pleasure. Lilah had no idea who they could be, after an initial wild assumption that the man must be Sam. Pondering this later, she wondered why she should think such a thing. This man had a frizz of curly hair, and narrow shoulders, and he was much taller than Sam. The woman was so hidden by the grass and the shadow, her head dropped forward, face hidden by a curtain of long black hair; it was impossible to recognise her. She was naked from the waist down. There was nothing to suggest coercion, no reason to storm in and create a fuss, or cry rape.

Still hesitant, Lilah concluded they must be a pair of grockles, enjoying the country air. It was the only explanation that made any sense. Gradually she edged away, anxious not to be seen, the potential embarrassment unbearable to contemplate. She was sweating, she realised, and the throb of her heart had spread through her body, in sympathy with the sensual pleasure going on so close by. Sex was no mystery to her; for the two years in the sixth form she'd had a boyfriend, to whom she had lost her virginity, and she had had a sporadic physical relationship with another boy since then. And nobody could possess a television set and not have a detailed knowledge of the process in a good many of its guises. But she couldn't avoid a stirring of excitement at this encounter; even her nipples were tingling, as she moved further away.

At last she dared to run, not caring whether she made a noise. It was close to ten o'clock and really dark as she reached the yard, and flung in through the back door. Roddy would be in bed, but avoiding Miranda might prove difficult. She was sure to want to know how the barbecue had gone, and who had been there.

Better face it, then, she thought, and went through into the sitting room. Her mother was knitting, all alone in front of the telly, cosy and domestic and middle-aged. 'You look like someone's Granny,' said Lilah, still breathless.

'And you look like you've run all the way back. What's the matter?' Miranda spoke lazily, as if half asleep, and only mildly interested. Lilah realised she need not have worried about explanations. Her mother was so detached these days, she hardly noticed anything.

'I was late. I thought you might be worried.'

Miranda shrugged. 'Was it fun?' she asked.

'Not bad. Sylvia was there. Says she'll be round in a day or two. Everyone was wary of me, as if I might have something catching. Cappy was nice, though.' As she spoke, the decision made itself not to mention the couple in the long grass. It wasn't something that was easy to talk about.

Miranda looked regretful. 'I might have gone if I'd known Sylvia was going.'

'Yes. That's what I thought. But you probably wouldn't have liked it much. It was quite dull, on the whole. Tim and Sarah didn't help.'

'They need their heads knocking together,' Miranda commented flatly. It had been Guy's line, and Lilah was irritated to hear her mother quoting him so unthinkingly.

'At least it was good to get out,' she said.

Miranda sighed dramatically, and tossed the knitting into a basket beside her. 'I can't stand much more of this,' she exploded, coming to life without any warning. 'It's no bloody way to live.'

'What on earth do you mean? What's happened?'

'Oh, nothing. That's the problem. It's as if everything's frozen. I'm supposed to believe that Guy's been murdered by someone who hated his guts, but for all I know the police have given up any hope of catching the person, or finding out why it happened. What a mess. I just keep thinking, if only Guy could see all this, how he'd laugh about it. Typical, he'd say. Typical British incompetence. I can *hear* him saying it.'

'I think they're doing quite a lot behind the scenes. They took all those papers and stuff from his office. And that's probably all they've got to go on, seeing as how they didn't find anything by the pit, apart from that shoe.'

'Well, how could they? Sam washed all the evidence away.'

'Did *you* think he'd been murdered, then? On the day it happened? Because I certainly didn't.'

Miranda said nothing for a long moment. 'I heard something,' she said. 'I didn't think anything of it at the time. And then I decided I should keep quiet.'

Lilah's heart skipped a beat. 'What was it? When?'

'Guy shouting at somebody. Nothing unusual in that, though it was very early. I've no idea what he was saying – probably just yelling at one of the cows.'

'No. The cows weren't in the yard when it happened. Why didn't you say anything?'

'Think about it, darling. Who does Guy shout at, more than anyone else?'

'Well – Sam, I suppose . . . Christ Almighty, Mum – you don't think Sam killed him. Do you?'

'I'm trying not to, but you must admit—'

Lilah hugged herself tightly, trying to think. Had she been a complete fool not to come to the same conclusion? Had she somehow put her mind on hold, refusing to allow it to see the obvious? She shuddered, and stared unseeing at the television.

'No. He couldn't have done that. Not just couldn't because of who he is, but *he* couldn't. I saw him, coming out of the privy. There was no muck on him. He was as shocked as I was. There wouldn't have been time.'

Miranda spread her hands. 'I expect you're right,' she said, meekly. 'Though if I'm forced to choose, I think I'd prefer it to have been Sam, someone we know, who wouldn't harm either of us, than some crazed outsider who might decide to pick us all off. And I suppose it would be possible to have done it without actually getting into the slurry. With a long pole or something.'

'What about that shoe? That wasn't Sam's.'

'Apparently not,' Miranda narrowed her eyes. 'Though I can't say I take much notice of his shoes.'

'But Mum. It's a *terrible* thing to think.'

'Well, maybe it is to you. I find it the lesser evil. I'm not scared exactly, but the thought has crossed my mind that we might be more vulnerable than we think.'

'Don't you think they'd have done it by now, if they were going to attack us? Everyone keeps saying we should be frightened, but if they really thought we were at risk, they'd protect us.'

'How? Billet a policeman on us, every night? No. If you ask me, I'd say they're fairly sure it's Sam or someone who

146

knows us well. They're just stuck for evidence.'

'So what about the Grimms? Where do they fit into your theory?'

'I've no idea,' sighed Miranda. 'I suppose it might just be a coincidence. It's not as if it was the same sort of killing. There wasn't a mark on Guy. If he was killed deliberately, the killer must simply have held him down until he drowned. Not a bit like smashing a person's head in with a blunt instrument. So maybe it was a tramp or a thief that attacked the Grimms, as people seem to be assuming.'

'Well, I'm going to bed. We're just going round in circles.' Lilah went to draw the curtains across the window, staring out warily onto the dark yard first. 'You know, Mum, it's a big relief to talk about it.'

'Is it? Just stirs everything up, if you ask me. Night, night, anyway. See you in the morning.'

Lilah still missed the goodnight kiss which Guy had always given her. Miranda had been dismissive of the sentimental ritual, never even noticing who was going to bed or when. Her recital now was unusual, and Lilah had a strange impression that her mother was, perhaps consciously, adopting some of Guy's persona, rather as she herself was doing. Perhaps it had to do with needing some of his strength, in order to cope.

'Night night, Mum. Make sure all the doors are locked, okay?'

'I just wish we still had a dog. Make a lot of difference, a dog would.'

Lilah didn't answer, but carried on to bed. The dark landing at the top of the stairs was suddenly full of man-shaped shadows, tucked in beside the big wardrobe that had overflowed from the bedrooms, or lurking in the space between Roddy's room and the old mullioned window that was the farmhouse's most interesting architectural feature. The bulb in the landing light had expired weeks ago, and nobody had replaced it. They seldom switched that one on anyway. Illumination filtered very faintly from downstairs, but until she could reach her own room, she was effectively in darkness. It annoyed her that she was frightened by this for the first time since she and Roddy had played Murder in the Dark as children, deliberately scaring themselves half to death.

Outside, amongst the farm buildings, not a single light was on. Guy had deplored the modern habit of keeping them on all night, and part of his nightly ritual was to ensure that everything was switched off. It struck Lilah for the first time that this meant that anything could be going on unobserved, since there was no dog to bark. With considerable force, a new fear flooded through her. As if waking from a coma, the emotion came like a dam bursting. They were all in real danger. Somebody had murdered Guy, and escaped free, his identity probably not even suspected. There were people in places where there should not be – the couple this evening had proved that.

She had argued with Den when he had tried to warn her. She still believed, in her rational mind, that she was not going to be murdered in her bed. But the encounter that evening had shaken her severely, and opened her up to a terror that made her weak.

Hurriedly she undressed, spent two minutes in the bathroom, and jumped into bed, pulling the blankets over

148

her head. Before falling asleep she concluded that the only hope of safety was to discover her father's killer quickly and produce evidence enough to convict him. Until then, surely it wouldn't be possible to feel easy. But – what if it *was* Sam? How would she feel if she discovered evidence that proved that Sam had killed Guy? Without Sam, the farm would collapse around them . . .

When she did finally fall asleep, she dreamt vividly of the copulating couple in the field. The man was the vicar and the woman was Sylvia, and they were grinning horribly as they made love, joined by a grossly elongated penis. His grey suit was covered in grass seeds, and his hair had slurry over it, like a cap. Sylvia had hitched up her skirt and her wide white thighs enveloped the man. Creeping up behind them was a kind of yeti, carrying a caveman's club, ready to bring it down on their heads. Lilah, as she watched, felt a thrill of anticipation, wanting them to be smashed to the ground, broken to pieces for their wickedness, destroyed for their sin.

Chapter Thirteen

Father Edmund had been the last to leave the Mabberley barbecue. He very much liked Jonathan, and knew how to please him. Jonathan valued outspokenness, and the vicar kept a small repertoire of stories for his delectation. He knew that Jonathan had hoped he would relate some of them as a kind of comic turn at the party. Instead, he had saved them for more private exposure.

'Interesting group of people,' he remarked, draining the last of the punch. 'I was surprised to see the little Beardon girl.'

'Not so little,' smiled Jonathan. 'She's probably running that farm now. Her mother's a bit scatty for the job.'

'Strange family, don't you find?' queried Father Edmund. His neck was mottled, and he was shifting his head and shoulders as if nervous. *Who's he to call someone 'strange'?* wondered Jonathan. He jerked an eyebrow to encourage further comment.

'I mean, they never quite seemed to fit in. Too much past history. I've noticed that with second families – they have a sort of insecurity. Not that Beardon ever said anything. I only found out through the church network.'

'Oh?' Here was a most juicy indiscretion, if Jonathan wasn't mistaken. What a pity everyone else had gone.

'You didn't know?' Jonathan shook his head. 'Well, I happen to be acquainted with the Rector at West Bridgford, which by coincidence is the home of the first Mrs Beardon. We found out the connection by accident – you know how you do. Mentioning names and so forth. I've known for a long time.'

'Does she know he's dead?'

'I imagine so. Even if she hasn't been informed by Miranda, she'll have heard it from my friend. Apparently she's quite a keen churchgoer and I did suggest he break the news, if necessary. Fascinating woman, by all accounts. Converted to Anglicanism from the Romans – unheard of. At least, I suppose she's still officially RC, but she's a pillar of his little church.'

'Maybe she's just in love with him?'

'Possibly,' conceded Father Edmund, rendered broadminded by Cappy's fruit punch. 'But you see what I mean about them being a strange family. Wherever they are, they seem to make themselves felt. Even young Roddy has presence. Those brooding eyes, like his father's. I often think that lad's a born priest. Inner depths. There were several like him at my theological college.'

'Nonsense!' laughed Jonathan. 'There's nothing spiritual about that lad. I've watched him mooching about the fields, swiping nettles and stamping on toadstools. He's a duck out of water, as Cappy would say. He should be in a town, with a gang, beating up old ladies and abusing substances.'

The vicar adopted a forbearing demeanour. 'Don't be

silly, Jonathan. You're just trying to be controversial. The boy lives an idyllic life, and you know it.'

'Idyllic perhaps. Lonely, certainly. There's trouble brewing for the wretched kid if I'm not mistaken. I'd bet he doesn't even know who owns Redstone now.'

The vicar waited for the relevation.

'Sam Carter is the joint owner with Miranda. My dad sold the place to them, all three jointly. He never got over the oddness of it. It was far too democratic for his taste. I've often wondered just who knows about it.'

'Fascinating,' said the vicar, with a gleam in his eye. 'But I'd better go now. You'll be getting tired of me. Shall I see you on Sunday?'

'Can't say, I'm afraid.' They both knew there was very little chance of the Mabberleys turning up for Sunday service. The congregation was static at nine or ten, all elderly, mostly from far-flung farms. Father Edmund had been given charge of two other parishes in recent years, which meant a circuit of three village churches. None of them boasted any real vitality or spirituality.

Jonathan and Cappy were restless when left alone. The glasses and plates were in the dishwasher, the remnants of the salads all thrown into one bowl. They made coffee and sat indoors, saying little. Jonathan was still thinking about the Beardons.

'Did you know Guy was married before? The vicar just told me.'

She shook her head. 'Any children?'

'I don't know. They'd be well into adulthood by now.'

'How did the vicar know? I can't imagine Guy confiding in him.'

'He's got a chum who seems to have a thing going with the first wife. Small world.'

'She wasn't at the funeral, was she?'

'I shouldn't think so. Someone would have said.'

'Is it important, do you think?'

'*Important?*' He wasn't sure what she was implying. 'How could it be important?'

'Oh – well, the whole thing's such a mystery, isn't it? This might be – you know – part of it.'

'I don't see how. How could it be?'

'I don't know. Don't get excited. I was just burbling. Didn't you think Sylvia was a bit . . . funny?' The change of subject was typical of her, and Jonathan had no difficulty in following the switch.

'When isn't she? I can't say I noticed her being any different from usual. But then she's not a woman I take much notice of.'

'You should. She's an example to you. All that hard work.'

'Ha ha. Why did you invite her, anyway? She didn't fit in particularly. I'm sure she despises Tim, for a start. And the vicar's terrified of her.'

'I wanted to see how she was. She's in love with Miranda, you know. I was curious to see whether Guy's death has changed anything.'

'Well, that's very odd—' His tone was mock-serious, his eyes wide open with pretended surprise. 'How extremely devious of you to keep the secret for so long!'

'Shut up. If we're to live in a village, it makes sense to

153

keep up with all the gossip. Isn't that what a village is *for*?'

'Perhaps it is, my darling – for an idle layabout like you, at least.' He leant across and kissed her, and thought once again that it was time they had some children. It was a thought he had almost every day, but Cappy perversely refused to consider it.

'Anyway,' he offered, 'I did overhear Sylvia and Lilah chatting, and it would seem that Sylvia has seen almost nothing of Miranda since this all happened. That holiday in Corfu seems to have made it all slightly unreal to her. Or maybe you think she's just biding her time until she can decently move in with Miranda?'

'She'd have Sam to reckon with.'

'Not to mention Lilah. Sounds as if there isn't going to be a lesbian love-nest next door for a while yet. How disappointing for you.'

'Very funny,' said Cappy cheerfully.

Next morning, the Mabberleys lay in even later than usual, rewarding themselves for their hospitality of the night before. 'Lazy farmers', Guy had styled them, and he had a point. 'Thank God we don't milk,' said Jonathan at regular intervals. 'Strictly for masochists, that.'

Cappy had her own little enterprise, a farm within a farm. It comprised peacocks, unusual poultry and cashmere rabbits. All her creatures reproduced themselves feverishly, in coddled conditions. The rabbits had to be frequently brushed and 'plucked', and the resulting hair sold to a spinner for the luxury knitting market. This work alone absorbed three or four hours each day. Her birds were moderately famous, and chicks were frequently despatched to far corners of the country. Some singular skill ensured that her eggs always hatched and her specimens were always perfect. The haunting alien cry of her peacocks fitted the atmosphere of decadence which was characteristic of the Mabberleys.

Jonathan too made money from breeding. His mixed breeds of beef cattle took care of themselves, calmly calving in the fields, and rearing the offspring to saleable size, fed largely on the lush grass for which the area was renowned. He had his animals killed and butchered by the last small slaughterhouse in the county, and sold the meat to specialist shops. The rewards were substantial. This had been another sore point with Guy, who although more or less officially organic, which should have given him an edge on Jonathan, felt himself to be always at a disadvantage. He lacked his neighbour's effortless luck and patrician relationships with everybody for miles around. Jonathan outdid him unfairly, in Guy's view. He openly accused him of being part of an upper-class network which absolved him from running his business according to the rules.

'Your trouble is that you resent him for being the real Squire around here,' his wife had accused him.

'He does everything he can to sabotage me,' Guy had grumbled.

'Don't be so paranoid,' Miranda had said, with a sigh.

At ten o'clock, Cappy and Jonathan got out of bed. Each went about their animal husbandry, Jonathan accompanied by the setter, Roxanne, as usual. First he strolled up to his top field, almost half a mile away, to count his bullocks and ensure that all was well. His route took in part of the path covered by Lilah the

155

evening before. As she had done, he noted how dry the ground was and how rare and few were days like this. His thoughts centred upon the passage of time and the rapid transience of each season. Approaching forty, he was discovering how easy it was to lose hold of time. A brief lapse of attention and a year had flown by. One reason why he had soon abandoned gardening as a pleasure activity was the tormenting brevity of each plant's glory. It seemed to be a matter of perpetual looking forward, which made him uneasy. Almost constant now was his nagging wish for children, their absence the single blot on an otherwise perfect life. Five short years ago, he had agreed with Cappy that they had no need to become parents, and no desire to do so. There were nephews or nieces to inherit the farm and carry on the Mabberley tradition. They would be sufficient to each other, they declared, and babies could only spoil things. Cappy continued to hold the same view, and both felt that Jonathan was a traitor to change his mind. He tried not to mention it more than once a month.

Roxanne ranged across each field, ever distracted by rabbits and birds, her extraordinarily keen nose leading her to cover awesome distances. Jonathan once tried to work out how many miles she ran each morning, and concluded that it could be as much as ten. One of his greatest joys in life was watching her in full stretch, red feathers flying, long ears streaming behind her like a girl's hair. The dog was five years old now – a wedding present from Cappy – and already he found himself dreading her old age and death. Now and then the anticipated pain of it would strike through him, bringing tears to his eyes.

The bullocks were fine. The grass was at its best, and their short, dense summer coats glowed with health. His favourite was a pure Hereford youngster, who had been special from a calf. They had reared him on a bucket, having bought him on a whim, and he was still very attached to his people. They called him Gregory, and now he came trotting up to greet Jonathan. Jonathan had planned to rear Gregory as a working bull, but he turned out to be a lean individual, with genes that even Jonathan would hesitate to reproduce. So Gregory had been castrated, and would eventually go along to the slaughter with all the others. Roxanne was fond of him too; the matching red of their coats made them a handsome pair.

Jonathan rubbed the soft folds under Gregory's neck, and slapped the broad, curly forehead, playing their customary game. Roxanne barked a little and ran round and round the steer, enticing him to run across the field with her. He bucked playfully, and Jonathan turned for home.

He took a different path, remembering that he ought to inspect a particularly neglected hedge bordering Redstone. That field was the next one to use for the bullocks, and he knew he would have to do some fencing before they could be turned in there.

An odd sound from the dog drew him to a particularly obvious gap in the deplorable hedge. She was pulling at something, which seemed to have been half-buried in the soft earth at the root of the few scrubby thorn bushes. It was very unusual behaviour for her: she would sniff and chase, but very rarely touch. A cold shiver ran through him as he strode over to investigate. Already he could see that she had some kind of cloth in her mouth, which was rapidly coming free from its concealing soil.

'Drop it!' he told her, trying to make himself look closely

at her find. He realised he was holding his breath, anticipating some horrible stench of rotting flesh. When none came, he let out a deep sigh, and nudged the object with his boot. Roxanne looked up at him, her liquid eyes concerned at his tension. She had been content to let the thing fall when told to. Already, she seemed to have lost interest in it.

With some reluctance, Jonathan extracted a bulky bundle from its hiding place. Loose soil fell away, along with large flakes of dry manure. With the tips of his fingers, he unfolded the material and held it out for inspection. As he lifted, he realised that garments had been bundled up and stuffed into an old rabbit hole, surrounding soil shovelled or kicked in to conceal them. Three items revealed themselves, as he peeled them apart. The first was a plain blue anorak in moderately good condition. No rips in it, both sleeves intact, nothing to justify throwing it away. The second was a pair of tracksuit bottoms, caked with manure. As the dry flakes peeled away, there was damper stuff underneath, especially lower down on the legs. When he tried to unfold them, he could smell the muck. Finally, a heavier object rolled free and fell to the ground. It was a shoe, so filthy with manure as to be impossible to describe.

It took very little time to link his find with the death at Redstone Farm. It seemed obvious that whoever had owned these clothes had gone into the slurry pit wearing them. And that person had removed them, still wet, bundled them up and hidden them here. Implications crowded in on him, filling him with foreboding. He almost decided to leave it well alone, to push his find deeper into the burrow and cover it properly, so no one would ever find it.

But he knew he did not dare. He would have to tell Lilah, and probably the police. He'd have to see the whole thing through, from the proximity of the next farm, and face whatever came of it. Murder was unreal, the stuff of stories. Mysterious murder, of a man whom few had liked, was fantastic and because of that, it carried its own excitement. Slowly his apprehension abated and a rather appealing sense of intrigue took its place. At worst it would mean answering too many dreary questions, and having ghoulish sightseers come to peer over his hedges. At best it would involve seeing more of Lilah, and an interesting intellectual challenge.

Carefully he wrapped up the bundle, mucky side in, as he'd first found it. 'Come on, you trouble-maker,' he said to Roxanne. 'The first thing you've found in your life, and it has to be Exhibit A in a murder mystery!'

Cappy's reaction to the find surprised Jonathan. 'Throw them away,' she said, her voice high and strained. 'Bury them somewhere. You'll do no good by going to the police. Leave it, Jon. Have some sense.'

'But why? What's the matter with you? Whose do you think they are?'

'Isn't it obvious? That poor man, bullied almost out of his wits, mocked and humiliated. You must have seen it. He doesn't deserve to go to prison. He's a countryman, used to open spaces. It'd kill him.'

'But *murder*, Cap. It's not as if he's been driving over the speed limit or poaching salmon. You can't just get away with killing someone.'

'Oh,' she moaned with an impatient despair. 'You soft

Europeans, all fine words and no spirit. Sometimes killing's the right thing to do. Death isn't the worst that can happen, despite what you people might think. Guy was sick, with his anger and guilt. He had violent death written all over him.'

'Lilah loved him. He can't have been so bad.'

'Lilah was his little princess. She had no cause to hate him, even though they had some rocky times ahead. Do you realise that girl has never had a serious boyfriend? Her precious Daddy wouldn't have allowed it.'

'Well, maybe – although I thought she was pretty thick with that boy when she was at school.' Jonathan was shocked at her insights; she had never said anything like this to him before. What was she quietly thinking about other people in the village? he wondered. But she hadn't changed his mind – not altogether, anyway.

'I'm going to show these to Lilah, for a start,' he decided. 'See if she can identify them. If she begs me to get rid of them, I'll consider it, I suppose.'

Cappy shook her head. 'You'll get hurt over this, my sweet, if you're not very careful. You're as daft as your dog, you know that?' She took him in a hug and pressed herself to him, in her favourite gesture. Her head came to his chin, and their two bodies fitted like jigsaw pieces. He stood there, feeling her warmth and rejoicing in her. When it came down to it, being married to Cappy was the only really important thing in his life. Everything else was just an amusing game.

'I won't get hurt,' he assured her. 'I'm bomb-proof, you know that.'

Chapter Fourteen

By morning Lilah's dream was still not entirely forgotten, leaving a jangled sense of something disturbed, something irrevocably wrong. She was irritable with everyone, even the postman when he drove into the yard just as she was walking back to the house and handed a bundle of letters to her.

'Save my legs, eh,' he said brightly. She just grunted at him, not even bothering to flick through the envelopes to see if there was anything for her. What would be the point?

They were all for Miranda, who opened them absently; letters from strangers had become a daily occurrence following her husband's demise. Guy had been a man of many parts, member of a number of societies, several of which seemed to have learnt by some kind of telepathy that he was dead. One was in a pale green envelope, addressed in plain handwriting, a second-class stamp in the corner. Having opened it, Miranda had to read it three times before the significance was fully clear to her.

It was handwritten on both sides of lined A4 paper in a spiky style using black ink and a thin nib.

Dear Mrs Beardon,

I presume you know that I exist. I have just heard from a mutual acquaintance that Guy is dead. Since I was his first wife, I think I ought to have been informed directly by you. As it is, I believe I am due something in his will. I am told that he lived well with you on a big farm and was well regarded in the village. He must have changed a lot in twenty-five years. When I knew him nobody had much respect for him. But that's all water under the bridge now I suppose. I don't want to upset you or anything like that, and I don't want to seem grasping. It's only that you might think of me if there's a shareout. I've been pretty hard up since he left me for no good reason, and now he's dead I think I should be remembered.

Perhaps you'll think better of me if I tell you something about my present situation. My eldest son Leo lives in France with his wife Yvonne and four children. He was always a bright boy – his father's pride and joy at one time. He's in his thirties now, and has a lot of trouble with asthma. It interferes with his work, and sad to say he hasn't much in the way of prosperity. He lives more like a gypsy than a respectable person.

Terry, the youngest, is over thirty, too, but you'd never think it. You might not know that I was ill after Guy left, and my aunt in County Monaghan took Terry on. He lived with her through most of his childhood, which is a great sadness to me now. But he came back to me when he was grown up, and we're good friends again by this time. He loves the land and animals, and is the living image of his father. He did well enough at school, considering, and has a sales job, covering the whole South of England.

So you see, both the boys, as well as myself, would much appreciate any small share of Guy's legacy. I never married again, and now I'm getting on everything seems to be falling apart. It's a bad world, these days, and I always think it was Guy who set me on the wrong path. Marrying too young, and him never happy with anything. He was never a very good teacher, in spite of all his cleverness and writing and everything. I have wondered so often how he was in later life. That's really why I'm writing to you, I think. Never mind money, I'd be thrilled if we could meet one day and talk about it all.

You can write to me at the address above.

With best regards,

Barbara Beardon (Mrs)

The address was in Nottinghamshire and meant nothing to Miranda. Her first reaction was curiosity about the 'mutual acquaintance' who had passed on the news of Guy's death. Curiosity – and a sharp pang of fear. There had been people spying on her. From one moment to the next her whole view of the village changed. This Barbara sounded seductively interesting. What had she done with her life? She had had twenty-five years as single woman, with very little childcare responsibili by the sound of it.

The references to money and legacies was worrying. Did this woman indeed have 'rights' of some kind? Had Miranda been wrong in not seeking her out and keeping everything open and legal?

'Lilah!' she called, glimpsing her daughter going into the barn, 'Lilah, come here and have a look at this.'

Lilah looked up, irritation plain on her face. 'What do you want?' she shouted. 'I'm busy.'

'This letter. You should read it.'

Lilah made a show of clumping crossly across the yard, where Miranda waited at the kitchen door. She snatched the letter, and glanced impatiently at it. Miranda watched her face register incomprehension, dismissal, then a sudden profound interest. The girl read it right through twice. 'Oh!' she said.

Excitement rippled through her. Despite knowing and wondering about her father's first family, she had never expected them to take the first step in making contact. It had always been as if they lived in Australia; or even that they were dead. They had never mattered, never seemed real. To receive a letter from them was very strange indeed, as if a famous personality had called round uninvited for a cup of tea. It was something unreal that you could never have predicted. She looked up at her mother warily.

'She sounds a bit peculiar,' she remarked.

'She didn't have much of an education, apparently. She married Guy when she was only nineteen. He always said that was why it went wrong.'

'How old is she now?'

'Oh, I don't know. Much older than me. Mid-fifties, I

164

think. Not much younger than Guy. What a terrible cheek she's got, writing like that.'

'"Mutual acquaintance". Who's that, then?'

'I've no idea. That's the bit I didn't like. Somebody's been spying on us and sending news of us to this . . . Barbara. It makes my skin crawl.'

'Scary,' agreed Lilah. 'She wants money, presumably. Has she got any claim, do you think?'

'I bloody well hope not. They were divorced ages ago. I saw the papers – I had that much sense. I made Guy prove it wasn't bigamy before I married him. He cut off all contact. We assumed she'd married again.'

'This is so weird, Mum. Ghosts from the past.'

'It's always the same when someone dies. All their secrets come crawling out. It was like this with my Grandad. He had another woman, that nobody knew about. She turned up at his funeral, bold as you like. I shall never forget my poor Gran's face. And my mum. I had to take her outside, before she could scratch the woman's eyes out.'

'How did anyone know who she was? She might have just been a friend?' Lilah had never heard this story before. She couldn't imagine her mother's frail parent wanting to savage anyone.

'It was obvious. She was crying. And she was wearing one of his old jumpers. Totally wrong for a funeral, but you could see she wanted it for comfort. Something of his to hold against her skin. I felt sorry for her. She was a nice woman, really. Surprisingly young. Grandad was nearly eighty when he died, and she was still in her forties.' Miranda was focusing on the memory, forgetting her daughter and the letter.

Lilah felt ensnared in the tangled family mysteries. All her life she had felt she belonged to a normal nuclear family. Both parents lived with the children, slept in the same bed, and more or less got on together. It was more than many of her peers could claim. Now one of those parents had died in bizarre and suspicious circumstances, and half-brothers were materialising as if by magic.

Miranda squared her shoulders. 'Give me the letter. I'll have to write back to her. What do you think I should say?'

'It's entirely up to you. I suppose it would be best to meet her. If you could stand it.'

'Why? What do you think might happen?'

'Nothing, Mum. What do I know about it?'

But Miranda was intent on the letter yet again. Lilah could see that there was some attraction in this voice from the past. Perhaps, she thought, there would be a kind of consolation in discussing your dead husband with a woman who had also been his wife. Lilah herself had wished since Guy's death that she'd had a sister, so that she could share with another daughter the precise nature of her loss. Watching her mother, she felt no resentment or criticism. But always, there was the pressure of the work, and she gave herself a brief shake.

'You might be able to go and see her when things quieten down a bit. When Roddy's exams are over, and the hay's all in. Though I'd say Sam deserves a break more than you do.'

'Since when did Sam ever want time off? He wouldn't know what to do with it.'

'You shouldn't assume that. It isn't fair.'

'Don't talk to me about *fair*,' Miranda suddenly shouted. 'That's the last word you should be using to me these days.'

166

'Okay.' Lilah turned an offended shoulder to her mother and strode back to the barn, full of resentment and confusion. Every time she got into some kind of routine or rhythm, another distraction happened. Some new turn to the nightmare sent her spinning all over again.

Take yesterday, she thought, as she threw straw bales about, trying to make space for a batch of new calves expected in the coming week. Cappy's story of Guy and a stranger arguing in the street; Jonathan hinting that he knew more than he would say; Sam so silent and watchful; disgusting goings-on in the Redstone fields. At least, it hadn't really been disgusting – that was her dream, making it in retrospect so violent and horrible. The dream had stayed with her ever since. What was there in her own mind that could transform a simple sex act into something so gruesome? The vicar and Sylvia, for heaven's sake! There could be no sane reason for that conjunction. The only thing connecting them was the fact that they lived next door to each other, Sylvia's smallholding running alongside the vicar's extensive garden. Neither had found Guy especially congenial . . . but that could be said of almost everyone who knew him.

Sam was greasing machinery, in a smaller shed next to the barn. She could hear him clanking about; for a mad moment she imagined it was her father. But Guy would have been muttering or singing to himself as he worked; Sam was completely silent. The grass was ready for cutting, for the hay; that meant the mower's blades had to be checked and probably sharpened, the hayturner dusted down, the baler set up with twine. Fortunately Sam knew the minutiae of these preparatory jobs; she certainly didn't.

Having finished her rearrangement of the barn, she strolled round to see exactly what Sam was doing. They hadn't talked seriously for days, except to share the farmwork and puzzle over which cows to dry off. Now, looking at him, she was shocked to see tears on his cheeks. He could only be crying for Guy, and she felt oddly reproached by this evidence of grief. Sam had known her father for longer than she had; he owed everything to the farmer, had been as close as a brother or son. Nobody had properly acknowledged this, and she felt painfully ashamed of herself, all the more so as she recalled her conversation with her mother the previous evening. Miranda seemed almost sure that Sam had killed Guy. Looking at him now, this seemed unthinkable to Lilah.

'Are you all right?' she asked him gently.

'You can't forget about it, can you?' he mumbled. 'I keep seeing it all, inside my head. Muck everywhere. I can smell it as well, and feel him, all weighted down with it. I can smell it on myself, now and then. Look – there's still a bit in my fingernails, and I've scrubbed them raw trying to get it off. I threw my moleskins away, you know, stuffed them in the dustbin. Couldn't abide having that smell on them.'

She looked, as invited, at his fingernail. 'That isn't muck, Sam. It's a little scar. You've got a Lady Macbeth complex.' Too late, she realised what she'd said. 'Not that I mean—' He didn't seem to have grasped any sinister implications, though he snatched his hand away, and turned back to greasing the blades of the mower.

Lilah pressed on, wanting to get some things straight, things she should have talked over with him days ago. 'Den said we ought to have left it all, for their investigation.'

'What – left him in there?'

'Perhaps not that – but not cleaned up, at any rate. They might have been able to work out exactly what happened, if you hadn't hosed down the edge of the pit.'

Sam shrugged. 'I thought it was best.' He fell silent for a moment, scratching his thick, greying hair. At forty, he looked much older. Although healthy enough, the outdoor life had not treated him well. Broken veins and rough hands, a slight limp from the time Guy had let an implement fall on his foot, and above all a permanently downcast glance: it all made him appear less than Lilah knew him to be. She noticed that he was wearing one of Guy's wax jackets and it seemed to her rather endearing that he should have taken on the boss's mantle like this. He was, in effect, the farmer now.

'There was muck everywhere, you see. I thought, well – I thought your Dad might feel a bit embarrassed, his yard in such a mess. With officials all over the place. Daft, I suppose. I didn't think.'

'I know what you mean.' She spoke the plain truth. Guy's first response to any kind of bureaucratic visit was to get Sam to hose down the yard, which did tend to accumulate manure and mud at a surprising rate from the brief twice-daily crossing made by the cows.

'It doesn't matter now, anyway.' They looked at each other, sharing the moment of despair and acceptance. Lilah had spoken for both of them, and he nodded slowly in agreement. Miranda had been right, Lilah realised: Guy was dead, killed by someone who had reason to commit murder. A dirty death, for a man who'd carelessly hurt a lo of people. It didn't matter, not in any serious way, whether or not that person was arrested, prosecuted, imprisoned. The facts would remain unchanged.

Sam squared his shoulders. 'I meant to tell you – I've taken Boss's gun, to keep with me. Thought it might be a good idea.'

She looked perplexed. 'What made you think of doing that?'

'The police said something about being careful. That gave me the idea.'

'Did you tell them about the gun?' He shook his head again. 'Show me where you keep it,' she said firmly.

With a sigh, he led the way back to his room. She followed him out of the barn, across a corner of the yard, past Miranda's modest front garden, still weedy and unimpressive, and up to Sam's door. As a young girl, she had gone in and out freely, visiting Sam as if he had been a brother or uncle. It had been Guy who noticed this one day, and ordered her to knock in future. 'Give the man some privacy, damn it,' he'd said angrily.

Sam had his own small cooker, a sink and tiny shower room. He had a bath in the big main bathroom every Sunday morning, a ritual for which Miranda heated the water specially. He kept everything clean and tidy, his bed under the far window, a table and upright chair close by the door, and a chest of drawers filling most of the remaining space.

'There,' he pointed. The gun stood discreetly in a narrow space between the bathroom door and the chest of drawers. 'So I can grab it quickly.'

'Is it loaded?'

He looked uneasy, and chewed his lips. Finally he nodded.

'Sam! Daddy would be furious. He never left it loaded.'

'I thought I might need it in a hurry,' he said. 'It's only for a bit, till all this is settled. Nobody's going to see it there. I'll clean it when I've got a minute, too. There's a pull-through thing in the barn.'

'I'm going to pretend I don't know about this,' she said. 'I'm sure you know what you're doing.'

Back in the farmhouse, Miranda slowly opened her remaining mail. A long white envelope proved to be from the solicitor, containing the contents of her husband's will. It took five lines to convey:

Mr Guy Beardon has bequeathed his entire estate to be shared in equal parts between his wife, Mrs Miranda Beardon; his daughter Miss Lilah Beardon; his son, Mr Roderick Beardon, and his partner Mr Samuel Carter. The executors are to be Mrs Beardon and Mr Carter.

Chapter Fifteen

Amos surprised himself at the effectiveness of his acting. Ignoring his pounding head, he began his campaign for release early next morning. Smiling cheerfully at the nurse who came to wake him twenty minutes before any possible reason could be found for doing so, he expressed a desire for a bath. Baths, he had observed, were held in high regard by these people.

He visited the lavatory, and untruthfully announced success in moving his bowels – another bizarre obsession amongst the nursing staff. When the interminable doctors' round finally reached his bed, he squared his shoulders, widened his eyes, and answered the brief questions clearly. It was amusing to see the surprise on the faces of the white-coated people. 'Well,' said the man in charge, 'you've certainly taken a turn for the better.' Amos managed a proud blush at this approval.

'At this rate you'll be able to go home in a day or two,' the doctor said. Then, abruptly remembering something of the story attached to this case, he switched on an expression of concern, and lowered his voice. 'Will you . . . er . . . be going back to the same house as before?'

Amos pouted a little, suggesting self-pity and indecision. 'Oh yes, sir, I think so,' he murmured. 'No choice, come to that.'

'Well, see Sister about it. She'll sort something out with the social services, if you need her to. Won't you, Sister?' He beamed down on a rotund woman of dark colouring who responded with the most imperceptible of nods.

It seemed to Amos that from then on he was on some kind of helter-skelter. Forms were brought for him to sign; the policeman visited yet again, trying to assure him that his house had been cleaned up and there was nothing for him to worry about; a woman with frizzy, grey hair bustled to his bedside at mid-morning teatime, smiling patronisingly and talking about post-traumatic stress, which he made her repeat three times, in revenge.

Next day, they took all the bandages off his head for the last time and replaced them with a neat sticking plaster. He was instructed to present himself at his local doctor's surgery in a few days for stitches to be removed and the whole wound examined. A young female doctor shone a torch in his eyes and said he was fit to be discharged. Just before lunch, they wheeled him into a lift, and out to the front entrance, where a car was waiting for him.

The house was scarcely recognisable. Nothing was as he'd left it. The toppling pile of official documents from Mum's bureau now sat squarely in the middle of the kitchen table, tied up with odd-looking tape; drawers which had been pushed in crookedly, overflowing with string and paper bags, were now closed properly, flush with each other; the kitchen, always cluttered with unwashed crockery and greasy pans, coats and boots kicking around on the floor, was impossibly clean and tidy. Amos sat down at the table, on a chair that had been brushed clear of cat hairs and mud, and laughed. It was the complete reversal of what he had expected. Every television show he could remember had depicted the aftermath of police investigations as a total mess. They hacked things down with axes, turned everything out onto the floor, tore pages out of books, tipped sugar, tea, rice in heaps onto the table. Was it possible that the reality could be so far removed from what he'd been led to believe? If so, surely those film people had a lot to answer for. He could hardly give credence to the idea that the new government, elected only a year ago, would have bothered to make such drastic changes as to insist on police time being spent on tidying up the scene of a murder. He laughed again at the procession of crazy ideas marching through his head.

The obvious explanation, of course, was that some friend from the village had come in and cleaned the place up for him. The presence of a vase of forsythia and long white daisies from the garden reinforced this idea. The only flaw was that Amos had no friends in the village. Amos and Isaac had made themselves into recluses, and apart from obligatory nods in passing, nobody visited them, or cared what became of them.

Fleetingly, he wondered whether Miranda Beardon would have taken the trouble to do all this. His heart lurched with excitement at the thought. Now that her husband was gone, she might be free to do that kind of thing. But regretfully he dismissed the notion. Miranda wasn't a cleaner, or a flower arranger. She would never even have given him a thought, so deeply immersed in her own troubles would she be.

Cautiously, he climbed the stairs. His own bedroom was much less changed than the downstairs rooms had been. The rug beside the bed had disappeared, and the sheets and blankets looked oddly smooth and flat, like those in hospital. The windows had been cleaned, and the cobwebs from the corners of the ceiling had disappeared. But his clothes were all in place, as were the ornaments on the shelf beside the bed.

It took considerable reserves of courage to enter Isaac's room. Amos's first inclination was to ensure that the door was tightly closed, and then never go in there again. His brother had lived in that room from a small boy, little changing apart from the size and nature of his clothes. Amos had passed on some of his own things to brighten up the room a bit – a model ship that he'd made, a dish to keep loose change in. Isaac had been fond of hoarding money, counting it carefully and planning small treats for himself.

But eventually Amos forced himself to look, prepared for almost anything. Splashes of blood on the ceiling, the smell of death, an uneasy ghost. What he found was quite an anticlimax. The bed was stripped down to the saggy old mattress. Isaac's clothes were neatly folded and piled on his big chair. The room smelt of some synthetic cleaning substance, perfumed with pungently artificial pine. It was nicely done, more as if Isaac had gone away on holiday than was dead and never coming back.

Downstairs again, he found cheese and eggs in the fridge, and a packet of cracker biscuits which had not been there before. A few tins – beans, tomatoes – had been added to their slender stores. He fingered them, moving them about to admire the breathtaking cleanliness of the cupboard. Other things had disappeared – ancient jars of chutney with the metal lids rusting through; leaking bags of sugar; jellies, which Isaac had been so keen on at one time, and then perversely refused, and which had softened and oozed and stuck themselves to the shelf. Well, he decided, from now on, he would keep it like this. No more mess or dirt. He was a reformed character. Looking round, he realised how free he felt, airy with relief and pride at the way his neglected house could look, with a bit of effort.

He ate crackers and cheese and made himself some black coffee. Then he remembered the cats. There had been five of them, at least, all Isaac's special darlings. They had run at will through the house, adding to the smell and untidiness, leaving muddy footmarks and hairs wherever they went.

So where were they? Who had fed them while he'd been away? Had that tortoiseshell hussy had yet another litter of kittens out in the barn? She'd looked imminent when last he saw her. Cramming the last biscuit into his mouth, he went out into the yard, glancing automatically down at Redstone as he did so. Most of the house was visible, just the lower half hidden by the swell of the field, down which he had hurtled on that dreadful morning. He could see the milking parlour, and the bright red splash of the smaller car sitting in the yard, close to the farm gate. He had thought f the Beardons as 'neighbours' ever since they'd come to

176

Redstone, even though it must be a good five hundred yards from one house to the other.

'Kitty, kitty,' he called, in a low voice. He could scarcely remember a time when he'd been here alone, and it made him nervous. 'Where are you? Cats! Come on.' There was nothing but silence. All the cats had gone. Perhaps they'd simply decided to seek hospitality at some other farm, or perhaps some officious RSPCA person had rounded them all up and impounded them.

They had other livestock: fifteen ewes, two Aberdeen Angus heifers and a donkey, all but the donkey kept for breeding and a small income realised from their offspring. In summertime, they would have come to no harm, grazing the few acres left to the Grimsdales after Guy Beardon's land purchases. Amos postponed the short walk necessary to check that all was well with them. His head was aching, the bruised flesh nagging for peace and calm and a cool flannel. Instead he turned back to the house, only to be arrested by the sound of a motor vehicle coming down the bumpy track which led nowhere but to his door.

He waited, forcing down an apprehension that it might be his attacker returning to complete the job. The policeman in the hospital had been reassuring, though vague. He had mentioned 'surveillance', with regular trips made to the area, and a close eye kept on any strangers. Surely no one would be daft enough to repeat the assault, at least not in broad daylight . . .

A battered yellow van came into view, then stopped beside his gate, so he could not quite see the driver. He dithered between retreating back into the house and waiting where he was, on the assumption that his visitor would eventually find him whatever he did. A few seconds' hesitation made the decision for him. The newcomer had already climbed out of the van and was striding towards him.

It was a woman, black hair flowing loose, a cotton dress tight across breast and thighs, a sturdy-looking forty-five or thereabouts. Amos stared. It had been five years or more since he last saw her as close to as this. Longer than that since they'd last spoken.

'Hello, Amos,' she said, a little breathlessly. 'You're home then.'

He spread wide his arms, leaving himself open, a gesture saying, 'As you see.' A gesture which also betrayed his bewilderment.

'They haven't buried Isaac yet, you know,' she said, hands on her hips. 'That's for you to see to. Time you shifted yourself, old man.'

He shook his head. 'Someone's supposed to be coming to see me. I ha'n't thought about it yet.' He stopped the head-shaking quickly as the pain intensified and gazed intently at his tormenter, still bemused at the sight of her. 'Why—?' he began.

She laughed. 'Someone had to see to the place, feed the cats, check those straggly ewes. Their bottoms are filthy, I might add.'

'But, *you*. What's it to you? I'm nothing to you.'

'Amos Grimsdale, don't act daft. You were never the daft one. Not that Isaac had so much wrong with him.' She laughed again, the sound jarring on Amos, making him want to cover his ears. Tears gathered, scalding, behind his eyes and nose.

'They were glad when I offered. The police. Awkward buggers, they were, leaving everything in a mess.'

Dread seized Amos. He felt weak like the newborn kittens which he knew now had been destroyed. She'd offered to feed the cats and then done away with them. She *would*. He searched his mind for what else she might have done to hurt him. What else did he have that he was afraid to lose? It was with a strange, wry relief that he realised there was nothing. And the realisation gave him strength.

'Did you kill the cats?' he challenged.

'Not all of them,' she retorted. 'You know yourself there was too many. The rest went to new homes.'

'Was it your business?' he said, as if he genuinely wished to know. 'They'd have got by.'

'Cats do no good,' she decreed. 'Messy, selfish, mean-minded things. My Elvira hates 'em.'

'And what's she got to do with it?'

She shrugged. 'You'll see. Now, I'm off. Will you come and visit me one day? There's a matter to talk over. But you're not fit for it now.'

'What matter?' he asked tiredly. 'Phoebe, I have nothing to speak to you about. You're not meaning me any good, that much I can see.'

'Ungrateful bugger!' she laughed. 'After I wore myself out cleaning this pigsty for you. Took me three whole days, and nothing from you but moaning about cats.'

'You didn't do it for me,' he said flatly. 'So what was it for?'

'I've told you. Come and see me when you feel better and we'll have a talk. And get that funeral seen to. It's not proper to leave it so long. After that, you should get those poor sheep shorn. They'll have maggots otherwise.'

Amos shrugged. Funeral rites were of scant importance to him. Phoebe glanced round, throwing a brief, passing look at Redstone, and stood still for a moment, a hand held oddly to her chest. 'I'll be off then. You needn't thank me for straightening the house, or getting in something you could eat. I don't expect thanks. But I'll be seeing you, Amos Grimsdale. Don't think I won't.'

She left him, almost running back the way she'd come. But at the van she stopped and looked back, throwing him a smile of triumph that stayed with him throughout that day and the long sleepless night that followed it.

Chapter Sixteen

The day of the inquest came after several days of comparative peace for the Beardons. The police had spent another morning questioning them about anybody they could think of who might have hated Guy enough to kill him, and they had made them repeat yet again every detail of what happened on the morning he died. Miranda then showed them Guy's will, its bleakness mirrored in her face. 'Does this surprise you?' the policeman asked her.

'A bit,' she admitted. 'I didn't think he would be so generous to Sam. It makes it more difficult to know what to do next. I was hoping I'd be free just to sell up and move. Now it's more complicated.'

The police warned all three Beardons, as well as Sam, that they would have to make detailed statements about how Guy was found, at the inquest. All four of them felt resigned about it by this time, regretting more the day lost from the farm work than the ordeal of speaking out in public. Even Sam, unaccustomed to making himself conspicuous, seemed relaxed as they piled into Guy's big car, to arrive in style.

'It feels very naughty of us to be driving this,' said Miranda, wriggling about on the wide seat. 'Guy would be furious.'

'He let me drive it once,' said Lilah. 'On the long, straight bit into town. It felt so *smooth*.'

The car was a Jaguar, almost twenty years old, kept polished and pristine, the perfect foil for Guy's character. He went to the races in it, and used it on the rare occasions when a long journey was called for. For short trips into town, he had used the smaller runabout, which Lilah regarded as mainly hers.

'I bags the Jag as mine when I'm driving,' said Roddy, from the back seat, next to Sam.

'Sounds fair to me,' laughed his mother. 'Except it'll cost about a thousand pounds to insure you for it.'

'That's okay. It'd cost that to get me another car, anyway.'

'True.' Miranda hummed a little as she manoeuvred the car out of the yard, pretending nonchalance. They all felt a shiver of concern at leaving the farm so unprotected. None of them could remember even an hour when there'd been nobody at all, not so much as a dog, to keep an eye out.

'It shouldn't take long,' Miranda said, trying to reassure herself as well as the others. 'We'll be back soon after lunch.'

'But everyone knows we'll be away.' Lilah gave a backward glance, wondering what could happen. The cows all massacred? The house burnt down? 'We should have asked the police to watch it for us.'

'Too late now.' Miranda spoke impatiently, her habitual refusal to worry asserting itself. Lilah, for the first time, began to see her mother as seriously irresponsible.

As they drove through the village, Lilah spotted Sylvia standing outside the Post Office, and she called 'Stop!' so suddenly that Miranda overreacted and sent everyone lurching forward.

'Bloody good brakes,' she remarked, ruefully.

'We can ask Sylvia to go and keep an eye on the farm,' Lilah said, inspired. 'She'd be glad to do that for us, wouldn't she?'

'We can ask.' Miranda wound down the window, and waited for Sylvia to trot the few yards after them. 'Hi,' she said. 'Lilah has a favour to beg of you.'

'Mum!' The girl was outraged. Sylvia's head appeared through the window, eyeing the car appreciatively.

'Didn't recognise you in the limousine,' she said. 'Very grand.'

'It's the inquest,' explained Roddy, in exasperation. 'And we'll be late at this rate.'

'Look, love,' Miranda smiled into her friend's eyes, 'would you be a real angel and go up to Redstone in about an hour's time. Make sure all's well. We've never left the place totally unguarded before. And, well, with all this . . .' She gazed round the innocent-seeming village helplessly. *All this* seemed hard to define.

'And get my head smashed in, you mean. Fine. Delighted to be of use to you. Lucky I'm so big and strong.'

Miranda raised her eyes skywards. 'You don't have to *do* anything. Just drive round the yard and out again. They call it showing a presence.'

'Course I'll do it. I'll go every half hour until you're back. Now scoot. And let's hope it isn't too gruelling for you.'

The Coroner was a small man with a curious pied moustache, giving him the look of some bristly hedgerow animal. He seemed not to enjoy his work. He listened with visible scorn to evidence from police, family and expert medical witnesses and frequently shook his head in exasperation. His summarising, when it came, was brief but passionate.

'This case,' he snapped, 'is a perfect example of the folly of assuming that a death is accidental, and failing to make adequate investigations at the scene at the earliest opportunity. Although no evidence has been found of any direct connection with the violent killing of Mr Isaac Grimsdale on the neighbouring farm, it has to be taken as strongly suggestive of a double killing. We do at least have irrefutable evidence for that death being a case for criminal investigation, and the police are actively pursuing a murder inquiry into that death.

'It is not, however, part of my brief to go into that. Mr Beardon's unfortunate decease is perhaps due in part to the accessibility of the lethal slurry pit, built in defiance of planning regulations which have been formulated solely for the purpose of avoiding just such a tragedy. If Mr Beardon had consulted the Planning Officer – as he was statutorily obliged to do, I might add – he would very possibly still be with us today. It would be pure supposition on my part, at this juncture, but the strong probability seems to me to be that this was an opportunist killing, probably by an intruder, who simply pushed the unfortunate man into the pit, and held him down until he drowned.

'But I must emphasise that there is no evidence so far discovered to indicate precisely what did happen. We have heard that there were no unusual sounds, the body showed no signs of a struggle, and aside from the single bruise on Mr Beardon's head which appears to predate the morning of his death, he was completely unharmed. We have heard the singularly distasteful details of what happens to a person having the misfortune to fall into a slurry pit such as this one. Despite the relatively shallow depth, and the common expectation that it would be a simple matter merely to stand up and wade out, the consistency of the material renders this almost impossible. It has a similar effect to quicksand, and we must allow for the possibility that this was in fact an accidental death – that Mr Beardon was unfortunate enough to slip over the edge of the pit, land face down, and despite considerable struggle, never to have succeeded in regaining his balance. We have had it amply demonstrated to us how this might happen, given the inevitable horror and panic that would accompany such a calamity. In the light of everything I have heard here today, I must record an open verdict and offer my most sincere condolences to the grieving family. Perhaps I need hardly add that there must be no further usage of the slurry pit as it now exists. Neither can I allow this opportunity to pass without giving the strongest possible warning to any other farmers . . .' here he raised his head and cast a sweeping glance around the crowded room '. . . of the *serious folly* of neglecting to respect the safety rules for such pits.' With a sigh and a businesslike stacking of the papers in front of him, he added, 'Thank you, everyone. This case is now concluded.'

Miranda and Lilah sat still for a moment, hardly aware that they had clasped each other's hands for the summing up. Hearing it stated so baldly that Guy had very probably been unlawfully killed was a greater shock than they had expected.

Clumsily the people in the room got to their feet to leave. They exchanged muttered remarks, almost afraid to shatter

185

the funereal silence – remarks born of a frustration that there were no clear answers to the mystery of how Guy had died, combined with resignation to the fact that finally the fun seemed to be over. A few people looked furtively at the Beardons; if anyone in the neighbourhood was destined to die violently, then Guy Beardon was the man. This was said with all the certainty of hindsight. Suspicious glances were thrown at Sam, who had been subtly but steadily chosen by the whole community as the most obvious candidate for Guy's murderer. Stories of his public humiliations, his relationship with Miranda, were whispered. If it had been Sam, then good luck to him, appeared to be the general feeling. A conspiracy of approval was almost tangible.

Lilah didn't know what to say to her mother. Miranda had not referred to the likely outcome of the inquest beforehand, and seemed disinclined to comment on it now. Her face betrayed no emotion, until Sam caught her up outside and said resentfully, 'Bit much, telling a man off after he's dead.' It took both women a moment to realise what he meant, then Lilah gave a short laugh.

Roddy joined in, 'Dad would have liked it, don't you think?'

'Can't see how you make that out,' grumbled Sam. 'It's like saying it's all his own fault. Makes me mad, that. Typical of those bloody stuffed shirts in offices.'

'You can see his point, Sam,' said Miranda, her voice oddly harsh. 'To them, Guy was a pig-headed fool who got what he deserved.'

'Mum!' protested Lilah. 'That's not very nice. How can anyone deserve to die like that? I still can't bear to think about it.'

186

'That's another thing,' put in Sam. 'Going into such detail with you two listening. It's not decent, if you ask me. After all, he was your dad – and husband.' The afterthought came with a glance at Miranda which Lilah found peculiar. Sam went on with his complaint, 'It made me feel sick, anyway.'

'I didn't really mind that,' said Lilah thoughtfully. 'I was impressed in a way that they did go into such detail and let us stay to hear it. It meant we were being taken seriously, somehow. Did you feel that, Mum?'

'I didn't *feel* anything. It's all *feelings* with people these days. I just kept thinking, over and over, how arrogant he'd always been about everything. Always overriding everybody, thinking he knew better. Always ordering people about, getting everything his own way. I was wondering what his last thoughts might have been. Do you think he might have acknowledged, at that very last moment, that he was partly to blame? Would that even have occurred to him, do you think?'

'Stop it, Mum. Don't be so callous. You can't say it's a person's own fault if they're *murdered*.' Even now, she could not persuade herself absolutely that this was the case. She continued to cling to the picture of an accidental fall, as definitely preferable. But too many facts pointed to the theory of a deliberate killing, and she spoke at least partly to try to convince herself.

Miranda was in pugnacious mode. 'You can. Of course you can.' She seemed about to say more, but after a glance at Sam, she fell silent. He seemed oblivious to what she was thinking, staring round at the dwindling crowd of people walking back to their cars or heading off to the shops. It was impossible to read his thoughts. But Sam wasn't stupid, that much was sure

Lilah jigged impatiently. 'Come on, we'd better get back. I'm hungry, and Sylvia might be worrying. And Chastity might be calving by now. She's due today. It's her first time; she might need help.'

'Chastity!' hooted Miranda, an increasingly angry look in her eyes. 'That's another thing – those stupid names he chose for the cows. What did he think everyone thought of him, calling a cow Chastity, of all things?'

Not to mention Hildegarde, Chionia, Undine, Theodora and Weatherproof, thought Lilah, a touch of sympathetic hysteria rising within her. Yet, where Miranda deplored the eccentric choices of names for the new calves, Lilah thought it was glorious.

'Let's get fish and chips,' said Roddy. 'I'm starving.'

'And eat them in Dad's car!' Lilah was horrified, but the others voted her down. They seemed to think something had been resolved, that there was cause for relief and forgetting. That even if Guy had been pushed head first into slurry and held there till he stopped breathing, it mattered less, now that the inquest was over.

They met Sylvia coming out of their lane, and awkwardly pulled up to speak to her. 'Open verdict,' said Miranda, before her friend could ask.

'As expected,' nodded Sylvia.

'Now we just get on with our lives, I suppose.' The bitterness in Miranda's tone was deepening. 'With the stigma of an unresolved death hanging over us for ever.'

'Bit different from how it goes in the films,' Sylvia agreed. 'Anyway, all's been quiet here. Though old Amos seems to be hanging about – must be lonely, poor old fella. Everyone seems to have forgotten about him. And there must be grockles in Mabberley's woods. I could hear voices from up there. Picnic season, I guess.'

'Sounds busier around here than usual,' Miranda remarked. 'Positively crowded.'

'You're not as isolated as you think. That should be comforting for you.'

'Depends who it is,' said Sam, something vigorous in his tone making them all turn to look at him. Miranda shrugged slightly.

'Well, thanks a million, Sylv. Come and see me tomorrow, and I'll give you a sandwich for your reward.'

'Right. Don't work too hard.' And she walked off.

'This car stinks of fish and chips,' remarked Roddy, with something like satisfaction, as they climbed out of it. 'Wouldn't Dad be furious!'

Lilah looked slowly at the faces of the three people she knew best in the world, and tears burst from her without warning. Sobs came explosively, choking her. The need for her father, his wit and his love, his strong arm and listening ear gripped her with a great violence. Nobody else would do. Nobody else understood her as he had done, and here they were laughing at him, angry with him. She felt herself drowning in loss and pain, flooded by her own tears, flooded with the whole terrible business.

Hating her family and their casual cruelty, she ran headlong into the barn and threw herself down on a pile of loose hay.

Chapter Seventeen

It took Lilah the rest of the day to recover. Miranda eventually forced her into the house, and sat her in Guy's armchair in the sitting room, bringing her cups of tea, and making forlorn efforts to comfort her.

'It's all been too much for you,' she said. 'I should have realised. But, darling, please try to stop crying. You'll make yourself ill.'

Tears ran like a leaking tap, until her eyes were almost closed and her lips swollen in sympathy. When she went to the bathroom for a pee and glanced in the mirror, she hardly knew herself. She tried, experimentally, to make herself stop crying, by gritting her teeth, forcing her jaw muscles to bulge with the effort. It worked for a few minutes, but then an image of Guy came back into her mind, and it all started again.

Roddy ignored her. When they sat down together for the evening meal, he gave one alarmed glance at her face, and kept his head down for the rest of the meal, eating quickly and then escaping to his room as soon as he could. Sam, who now ate all his meals with the family, where before he had sometimes fended for himself in his own room, tried to convey his understanding, making clumsy remarks about the farm and Chastity's imminent delivery.

Forcing herself, Lilah went out with Sam that evening, to help him decide whether the heifer was safe to leave for the night. They watched her quietly, as she took herself apart from the other animals, and stood patiently, head down, sides heaving from time to time.

'She's all right,' Sam pronounced, and Lilah agreed with him. By morning, there'd be a new little Jersey. With luck it would be female, and could take up residence in the area prepared for it in the barn. If luck went against them, the little bull would be despatched at a tender age, to become Pedigree Chum or Kit-e-Kat.

They walked back to the house, companionably silent. 'Longest day soon,' Sam commented, echoing Guy's acute awareness of the unfolding seasons. 'Best time of the year.'

'The long evenings are nice. I can't even imagine winter, with it getting dark at half past three.' She was speaking on auto-pilot, her head muffled with the aftermath of so much crying. Sam was an easy comrade, equally willing to talk or be silent. It was impossible to associate him with Guy's death, to cast him as the instigator of her misery and loneliness. She simply could not accept the general view that Sam had killed Guy. She *knew* Sam; she had seen his face when he first saw Guy in the slurry. Unless she was altogether useless at understanding people, then Sam had had nothing to do with it.

'Night night,' they said to each other, briefly, unemotionally, at the door to Sam's room. Early as it was, Lilah went up to bed as soon as she got indoors. Her bed had become a haven:

a refuge from the relentless events threatening her peace. It had become a habit now to pull the covers over her head, curling an arm in front of her face to make an air pocket, so she could breathe. Her nose was still sore and tender from all the weeping. She felt ill and sorry for herself.

But her last thought before falling asleep was of Chastity's calf, and the way nothing could stop the force of nature, that there was always birth to balance death. And in her dreams it was springtime.

Next day, the subdued, careful atmosphere persisted. 'Doubt there'll be any more police visits,' said Sam, in the middle of the morning.

As if waiting for a cue, they heard a car coming down the lane, the moment he'd spoken. 'It's Den!' cried Lilah, instantly recognising the car when it appeared. She was surprised at her own sudden enthusiasm.

'Speak of the devil,' muttered Sam, shaking his head. 'Should know better by this time.'

Once again the tall policeman unfolded himself from his car, standing over Lilah like a protective tree. She wanted to cling to him, weep on him, tell him everything in her unhappy heart.

'Oh,' she said. 'It's nice to see you.'

'I thought, after yesterday—' he began, examining her face. 'You look a bit . . .'

'Ravaged,' she supplied. 'Yes, I know.'

'That wasn't the word I would have used. Have you got time for a little chat?'

'Not really. There's a new calf. A little heifer. And we're starting the hay today. Terribly late, and the forecast isn't very good.' She spoke distractedly, desperate to leave it all and drive off with Den to a place where she had nothing at all to do.

He looked round, first at the buildings surrounding the yard, then up at the Grimms' house. From this distance, with a little imagination, it resembled a fairy castle on a hill, rather than a neglected, old stone farmhouse. 'I forgot you were so close to them,' he remarked. 'Practically next door.'

'We *are* next door. They're our closest neighbours. But we've never had much to do with them. We should be seeing to poor old Amos, I know. It's just – it's always so *busy*.' She looked at him helplessly, thinking of Miranda messing about in the house, with time enough to make all kinds of difference to the workload if only she'd put in the effort.

'Come and see the calf,' she invited, suddenly. 'She's in the barn. That's her mother you can hear, up in the top field.' The low, repetitive bawling was a distant throb of distress which Lilah had never grown used to, even though it happened every time a cow gave birth. Sometimes, at night, it was unbearable, the bereft mother calling and calling for her baby, the embodiment of despair. Sometimes it seemed to Lilah that in her short life she had been party to a fathomless ocean of pain and misery, that all this suffering was there inside her, barely suppressed by her flippant ways and habitual optimism. And sometimes she couldn't stop herself imagining every hurt and cruelty; every experimental laboratory; every horse used in war; every animal ill-used in the service of man; every creature sent terrified to the abattoir. All of it added up to an entire universe of horrifying anguish, and she had to breathe slow and deep to be able to carry on. At those times, she would seek out the company of Martha Cattermole, who believed passionately in animal rights. Martha shared the pain, while managing to make it bearable. 'It does more harm to the humans than it does to the animals,' she insisted. 'When we stop being cruel, then all kinds of wonders will be possible.' Lilah struggled mightily to understand and agree.

'Poor thing,' Den remarked now, and she could feel that he meant it.

He followed her, good-natured and patient, into the barn. The little fawn calf lay in a bed of straw, huge, liquid eyes turned towards the visitors, the bewilderment of its situation clear to see.

'I'm calling her Endurance, for obvious reasons,' said Lilah.

'She's sweet,' he said. 'I hope she'll be a good omen. Life going on, and that sort of thing.'

She gazed at the calf, thinking about the phrase he'd used. She'd heard it before and yet it was as if it actually *meant* something for the first time. Life *did* go on, like a ribbon unrolling from some immense cosmic spool, whatever else might happen.

'Yes,' she said. 'Life goes on.' She was astonished at how much better she felt.

The policeman moved away from the barn, after a few moments. 'You're too busy, then, for a talk?' he said.

'It depends. I don't like to leave everything to Sam. I could if it was important, but the work just mounts up. What's it about?'

'Just to keep you up to date, really. Amos described a chap who sounded like some sort of tramp or gypsy. He could be living rough round here somewhere. It would make sense to be careful.'

'I'm still not scared,' she told him.

'Okay. That's up to you. But I should also ask you again,

whether you've heard anybody mention a stranger about the place. Anything at all peculiar. It's easy to overlook things, so I'd like you to have a really good think. We're desperate for some leads on this.'

She frowned and tried to think. Her head felt thick and slow. 'Nothing comes to mind,' she said. 'I can't believe this man's still hanging round here, anyway. Surely he'd get as far away as possible?'

'He might. But that's assuming it was just a random bit of violence, for no reason. With your dad in the picture, that isn't very easy to credit. Wouldn't you agree with that?'

She nodded reluctantly, kicking at a stone, sending it clattering across the yard.

He smiled down at her. 'No more police talk. Let's hope you can get some peace from here on.' He paused, eyes on hers. 'Hey, guess who I saw just now, out in the road.' He was suddenly boyish, no longer the policeman.

'No idea.'

'Elvira Winnicombe! Remember her on the school bus? How we used to tease her. Awful, really, but she was always so gullible. I knew she lived around here, and I've been trying to catch up with her mother, but somehow I never expected to see her again.'

Lilah tried unsuccessfully to share his nostalgia. She managed a smile and a nod. 'Nothing's changed, really. Elvira goes to a day centre now, most of the time. She seems to be getting a bit more independent lately. Everyone keeps an eye out for her. Funny you've not seen her since school.'

'I'm not out this way very often. It took me right back, seeing her again. They should never have sent her on the same bus as us; we made her life a misery, poor girl.'

'I didn't. I just kept quiet. I was scared she'd tell her mother, and Phoebe's always been terribly fierce where Elvira is concerned. Besides, I wouldn't dare provoke Elvira – I was two years younger than her.'

'Still are, I should think,' he joked.

'No,' she said flatly. 'Now I'm about a thousand years older than she'll ever be.'

He took her between his big hands, holding her around the upper arms, and gave her a gentle shake. 'It's going to be all right,' he told her. 'I promise. Just take care. Don't go wandering over the fields by yourself without telling someone where you're going, how long you'll be. Take your brother with you, if you can. If it was just your dad's death, I wouldn't be so worried, but somebody treated the Grimsdales to a very savage attack. We can't just ignore that. We're going to be making an inch-by-inch search, starting from the far side of Mabberley's and working all the way down to your outbuildings. It'll take a while, but it has to be done. And if there's anything to find, we'll turn it up, sooner or later.'

He was sounding like a policeman again, and Lilah sighed. 'So there'll be lots of kind policemen to keep an eye on us, will there?' she said sarcastically.

'For a few days, yes.'

'But this is highly likely to scare the man away, surely, if he hasn't left the area already? He isn't going to sit under a tree and wait for you to find him.'

'That's probably true. Except we've got almost nothing to connect anybody with Isaac's killing. Unless we find the murder weapon with fingerprints on it – which would be a

196

miracle – our only hope is discovering some kind of motive. Even then, there'd not be much of a case.'

'It's hopeless, then, basically? Didn't you find anything useful in the Grimms' house? Footprints, or hairs, or something?'

Den shook his head, and laughed. 'Have you ever *seen* that house? It's knee deep in hairs, from the cats. And nobody's cleaned the floors for about six years. Plus you, Sam, Amos and all the ambulance men and our chaps tramping in and out. Yes, it's fairly hopeless. But we have to look as if we're doing something. And we don't want any more deaths. Above all, we don't want that. So watch it, okay?'

She nodded. Every time she managed to push away fear, someone reminded her of her vulnerability.

'And Lilah,' he added, dropping his hands, but looking intently into her eyes. She felt again the urge to lean on him, and shelter against him.

'What?' she whispered.

'Can we go out somewhere together, do you think? I mean, as old friends, nothing to do with police business. A film or something?'

A sweetness filled her. A surge of joy, spiced with excitement: the timeless response to a romantic proposition. Nothing anybody in the world could have said to her could have been more agreeable.

'Oh, yes,' she smiled. 'Oh yes, that would be lovely.'

Chapter Eighteen

Romance was given little chance to blossom, however. For a start, it was raining quite hard when Lilah got up next morning. Two cows needed the AI man, and she had to decide which breed of bull to use. It was a matter which Sam flatly refused to help with, which Lilah regarded as perversely obstructive.

Then her mother twisted her ankle on the wet step out of the milking parlour and announced that she couldn't possibly drive the tractor and trailer up to the top field, as she had originally offered to do. Roddy had insisted on going on the post-GCSE school trip to Alton Towers, which had entailed getting into school for 6 a.m. Lilah had driven him there, sleepily grumbling that he was needed on the farm, instead of gallivanting off on a pleasure trip at a time like this.

The weather continued grey and damp, which meant interrupting the hay harvest. Philip Jackson, from another neighbouring farm, had been contracted to come and assist, between his own crops, but Sam and Lilah agreed that it would be mad to proceed with rain in the air.

'This is *impossible*,' Lilah stormed at her mother. 'It's too much. We can't go on like this. I just want to walk out and leave the whole stupid place to rot. Why don't you phone Kippells and ask them to put it up for sale? We'll obviously have to do it eventually, so why wait?'

Miranda looked out of the window beside the armchair where she sat with her foot up. The view was of their closest fields with the Mabberley woods in the distance. 'Where would we go?' she said, weakly. 'What would we do for money? There's a mortgage on this place, remember.'

'When Daddy first died, you said you *wanted* to sell up and move.'

'I do. But I really can't face all the *effort* involved. I've never had to do anything like selling a farm. I wouldn't know where to start. Anyway – you told me you wouldn't move from here for anything.'

'Well I've changed my mind. I want to be like normal people, with nice, easy nine-to-five jobs, evenings and weekends off. Imagine staying in bed all day Sunday. Imagine never having to get up in the night for some animal in trouble. No more going out in a blizzard, or getting soaked to the skin three times in one day. Oh, Mum, I'm so *tired*.' And she slumped down opposite Miranda, like a small child.

'Oh, God,' tutted Miranda. 'Don't *you* go useless on me as well. Look, just have an hour's rest. It's too wet out there to do anything anyway. Sam'll do the feeding. Everything else can just wait for a day.'

'No, it *can't*,' shrilled the girl. 'That's what you never seem to understand. Farming isn't like housework. You can leave dust and washing up and cobwebs, but you can't leave animals. They get ill and die if you turn your back on them for a moment. And the hay will go mouldy if it gets wet. Then we'll have to buy some in, which we can't afford. We already buy far too much. Daddy called Jonathan lazy, but even Jonathan has to make sure his animals have something to eat.' She shook her head in frustration. Everything seemed to be slipping away from her into a chaos that threatened to engulf them all.

'You sounded just like Guy then,' said Miranda with pain in her voice. 'Working yourself up over a trifle, the way he always did. Overreacting. People like you two always seem to take life so hard – and make it hard for others in the process. You should learn the limits of your own power. That was something Guy never managed.'

Lilah thought about this, and smiled a little. 'You mean like he was with the weather? Enraged because it wouldn't do what he wanted.'

'I always expected him to die of a stroke – or a heart attack – in the middle of a tirade against the elements. It still seems all wrong to me, that he should have died the way he did. Wouldn't you think I'd have had some sort of premonition? My mother said he'd go off with a bang one day. She thought he was like King Lear. She was terrified of him.'

'Poor Granny.'

'She wasn't the only one . . .' Before Lilah could decide whether she had the courage to permit this piece of self-revelation, there was a noise at the door. Sam was kicking mud off his boots before removing them and coming in for his morning coffee. Miranda jumped. Normally, she would have it ready poured for him, knowing that he would appear punctually at half past ten for it. As it was, the water hadn't even boiled.

'Oh, Sam,' she called. 'We're falling apart in here. It seems to be one of those days when everything gets out of step. Lilah's coming to put the kettle on.'

The girl pulled a face. 'What happened to my rest?' she whispered, heaving herself out of the chair like an old woman. Her mother shrugged and smiled.

'Bring me a cup, there's a pet,' she said.

Sam was shining with the rain. His hair was flat to his head, and his face was wet. He had taken off his coat, but the shoulders of his shirt were dark where the rain had penetrated. 'It's getting a lot heavier,' he said. 'Can't think that Rod's having much fun on his big dippers, in this.'

'They'll hardly be there yet. The forecast was better for the east, anyway.'

'What's it say for us?'

'More showers all week. When can Philip come again?'

Sam shook his head. 'Hard to say. This has thrown everything out. He's worried about his own baling now. Your Dad would be in a state about it all.'

'I'm in a bit of a state myself,' she admitted.

'So I see,' was all he replied. It struck her then that they were all so locked up with their own grief and worry that no one had anything left over for the others. They were like the stone creatures in the Narnia book – all turned to cold, unresponsive statues by the death of Guy. What they needed was someone from outside to come and warm them up. Someone like Den, who had asked her to go out with him. Nursing the memory, she immediately felt better.

'Sam, do you think we're going to be able to keep on like this for much longer? So much depends on you, and you're supposed to have reasonable time off. There never seems to be a moment for any proper discussion. We're just staggering from one day to the next.'

Sam rubbed his face, taking his mouth and cheeks in his great hand and moulding them like a slab of clay. Lilah could remember him doing just this since she'd first known him. It always made her smile, the way he could be so rough with himself. It seemed to have a reviving effect; he straightened his shoulders and looked directly at her.

'That's all you need to get by on a farm,' he told her. 'Take the jobs as they come up, and don't worry about what hasn't happened. We can get through the summer easy enough. See how things look at the end of August, and have a think then. Things'll have settled down a bit by then. Your mum's the one with the say, don't forget. We can be patient and just let her take her time. Don't bother about me and my time off – I never knew what to do with it when I had it. My place is here, and it's pleasing to be useful.'

Poor Sam, she thought. *It's probably the first time he's ever felt like that.* One of Guy's favourite words for him had been 'useless', at times when he was slower than Guy required, or when he let an animal escape past him.

But the problems kept nagging at her for the rest of the day. There was no avoiding the fact that things wouldn't get any better. Never before had she worried about her future, or even given it any serious thought, but now when she glimpsed the years ahead, she quailed at the prospect. Despite her horror when Miranda had first mentioned selling up, it now seemed to her that she could only hope for a reasonable life if they sold the farm and moved away completely. If Sam couldn't have his due time away from work, then neither could she. There was virtually no possibility of any kind of respite for her in the foreseeable future. Grimly, she hoped that Roddy was making the most of his day at the theme park. At this rate, that would be the only break any of them would manage all summer.

Miranda had apparently been thinking along the same lines that day, but had reached a different conclusion. 'I've been thinking I might get over to Nottingham and see that woman,' she said when she and Lilah were drinking coffee after a hurried lunch.

Lilah had to think a moment. 'Who? Barbara, do you mean? What for? How would you get there? It's the other side of the country.' She half expected her mother to ask her to provide the transport.

'It's a small country. I'd drive.'

'I thought you had a bad ankle.'

'I'm not going *now*, you idiot. It's probably not much more than two hundred miles. I'll have to look it up. I went to Sheffield once. It's probably quite near there. Come to think of it, Roddy's gone to within a few miles of there now, and getting back all in one day. That proves it.'

'There were plenty of people outside school this morning grumbling that it's insane, actually. Chessington would have been nearer.'

'They enjoy the ride, though. Singing and fooling about.'

'He ought to be here, pulling his weight.'

'He's only young, Li. Be reasonable.'

But she didn't feel at all reasonable, or inclined to listen to her mother's blind optimism. And wasn't *she* young, too? She was quiet for some minutes, fiddling with a small hole in the knee of her jeans. Then she remembered her mother's initial remark.

'Why does she live in Nottingham, anyway?' she demanded, sullenly. 'Dad never lived there, did he?'

'Not to my knowledge. They were in Bristol when they were married, and before that Southampton, for a short time. Then she went to Liverpool after the divorce. I didn't know anything about the Nottingham bit. Your guess is as good as mine. But wouldn't you be curious, if you were me?'

'I might be, I suppose. I'm more interested in her children. They're my half-brothers. Didn't you ever see them?'

'No, never. You saw the letter. The younger one was born only a year or so before Guy left her, and he was only a toddler when she sent him to Ireland, poor little devil.'

'Ireland's meant to be a great place to bring up children. I'd be more likely to feel sorry for the older one. He knew more of what he was missing, presumably.'

Miranda hugged herself for a moment, as if cold. Lilah could see she didn't want to think too much about that side of the story. As Miranda grew less communicative, Lilah found herself feeling more so. She realised how much she wanted to ask her mother, how many details of Guy's life were a blank to her. And where exactly did Sam fit in? This evening, she promised herself, when everything was finished for the day, she'd broach some of these issues.

Meanwhile, there were things to do outside, as always.

* * *

Miranda was left wondering whether her ankle would allow her to finish reorganising the bedroom. There were still piles of shirts and underwear to be disposed of. The sensible thing would be to give them to Sam, but Sam was still in Coventry, so far as Miranda was concerned, and she could see no way of forgiving him enough to start handing him presents. She wasn't sure he'd take them, anyway. Apparently there was a vein of sensitivity within him that she had previously never suspected.

A 'Coo-ee' at the door saved her from this particular decision.

'Hello!' she responded. 'I forgot you were coming. What a relief.'

'Trouble?'

'Not really. I've hurt my ankle. Typical me. Lilah's exhausted, poor love. She spent all yesterday really *sobbing*, after we got home. It really hit her, all of a sudden, losing her Daddy. She hasn't got anyone to take his place.'

'She should have a boyfriend.'

'Well, she seems to like the tall policeman. It's Den Cooper. He was on the same school bus, umpteen years ago. Can't imagine what Guy would have thought about that.'

'He never seemed to encourage followers.'

'*Followers*! Sylvia, what a word. Positively Victorian.'

'Well, he was Victorian, when it came to Lilah and boys.'

They talked for their habitual three hours. Miranda related the story of Barbara's letter and the idea of a visit. Sylvia recounted the latest village gossip.

'Tim and Sarah are getting beyond a joke,' she said. 'I just hope neither of them has a gun. They sometimes seem intent on killing each other.'

'Does anyone know what their problem is?'

'I often think it's a kind of terrible game they can't stop playing.'

'Yet they're both quite pleasant, individually.'

'I know. Tim helps me now and then. He's good company on his own.'

'Even Guy rather liked him, which is saying something.' They lapsed into another Guy-centred silence, pouring more wine, sitting close together on the deep and well-worn sofa. Miranda never ceased to enjoy Sylvia's undemanding company, her obvious affection and the hint of a future where they could be together wherever they liked, free of the demands and disapprovals of husbands.

They were interrupted by Lilah rushing into the house. 'Mum! There are gunshots coming from Jonathan's woods, and somebody screamed. I think we should call the police!' The girl was white and trembling.

'Jesus!' said Sylvia on a long breath. 'Whatever next?'

'People are always shooting in the woods,' said Miranda calmly. 'And you're obviously safe.'

'And Roddy?' pressed Sylvia. 'Is he okay?'

'He's at Alton Towers,' said Lilah quickly. 'Somebody *screamed*. And Jonathan doesn't let people shoot in the woods, especially at this time of year. It upsets Cappy's birds and sends Roxanne psycho.'

'Call the police if you like,' said Miranda carelessly. 'But I still don't think it's much to worry about. Somebody's killing crows where they shouldn't. You could get Sam to go and take a look.'

'Oh, you're *useless*!' Lilah cried. 'Somebody could be lying dead out there and you wouldn't even care.'

She slammed out again, looking for Sam. He was in the big barn, making space for the coming hay bales. 'Did you hear those shots?' she demanded. 'Have you still got Dad's gun?'

'I heard 'em,' he said, slowly straightening his back. 'Some fool woman shooting rooks.'

'But she *screamed*,' Lilah said again.

'Laughing,' he told her. 'Listen.'

The woods were almost half a mile away and the air was thick with the last flurries of rain, but still the sounds carried clearly. As Lilah stepped out of the barn to stand in the yard, there came another shot and a startled cawing of rooks. A large cluster of nests filled the treetops in one corner of the woodland – nests that were full of baby birds at this season. It took a heartless person to persecute them at such a time. As Sam had predicted, another peal of excited female laughter burst out.

'You're right,' Lilah said in a small voice. 'I feel a fool, now. But you never answered my question – have you still got the gun?'

'Go and see, if you like,' he invited. 'You know where I left it. I haven't touched it since then.'

She did as he suggested, checking the corner of his room where she had seen him stand the gun.

It wasn't there.

Chapter Nineteen

Amos hadn't slept for three nights and was feeling light-headed. Every little noise terrified him, as he moved around inside his house, at a loss for something to do, feeling like a stranger in his own home. The tidiness, which had briefly felt like a kindness, a gift, was now a deliberate torment, reminding him that it had been done with malice by Phoebe who hated him.

He received a letter from the Coroner's Officer, informing him that his brother Isaac's body was now released for a funeral to take place, and would he please notify the Officer as to which funeral director he proposed to employ for the purpose. He knew he should go out to the public telephone in the village and answer the man's question, but it was too much for him. He couldn't remember the name of the undertaker who had buried his mother. He could hardly remember how to use a telephone, or which coins they took nowadays. He had got used to the image of Isaac's body lying in the metal drawer at the hospital, and was in no hurry to remove him. Sooner or later, something would surely happen to relieve him of the responsibility.

Although he daily expected her to, Phoebe did not come back again. Nobody came near him, except for a policeman who turned up one morning and introduced himself as Constable Den Cooper. Amos was still in his pyjamas, and paced the kitchen in embarrassment as Den asked him to describe again as precisely as he could the man who had attacked him and his brother. As the days had passed, the memory of the intruder grew fainter, until he was unsure of every detail. The light had been bad, his own sight filmed by shock and sleep.

'Youngish,' he said. 'Strong. A wild look in his eyes. Nose and mouth covered up.'

'And did he speak at all?'

Amos shook his head. 'Not a word,' he said.

'And can you think of anybody who might have had reason to attack you and your brother?'

Amos turned his face away, the image of Phoebe clear in his mind. He was tempted to confide in his questioner, to reveal his fear at the way she had spoken to him. But she was just a deranged woman. Nobody took her seriously. 'We never hurt anybody,' he said, in reply.

The policeman looked curiously around the clean kitchen, and peered into the equally clean living room. 'Someone done some tidying, I see,' he remarked. 'Who might that be, then?'

Amos saw his opening. 'It was like this when I got home from the hospital. Phoebe Winnicombe did it – I thought you'd have known? She must have had the say-so from you people.'

'Not my department,' shrugged the man. 'Friend of yours, is she?'

Amos laughed, the lines on his face deepening as he did so. 'Haven't seen her for years, till all this.'

'Then why—?'

'She's a madwoman.' Amos leant closer, his voice hoarse. 'Trouble, that's what she be. I'd have thought you'd know all about her.'

'Why do you think we should know about her?'

'She's deep. She . . . knows things.' He shifted from one foot to the other, wanting to say more, but having nothing specific to offer.

'Would you say there's reason to think she's involved in your brother's death?'

Amos slowly shook his head, which had begun to ache again. 'Don't know about that. I just wish she'd stay clear of me. Got rid of Isaac's cats, she did. 'Tis quiet here, without the cats.'

There being no obvious suspicious import in any of this, the policeman closed his notebook and prepared to leave. 'You look poorly, Mr Grimsdale,' he said kindly. 'Must be difficult here, after what happened. Isn't there someone you could go and stay with for a bit?'

'Not a soul. And I have to stay, for the sheep and that. Can't just up and leave, even if there was a place to go. Thinking of getting a dog or two, now Isaac's gone. Never liked dogs, did Isaac. Poor fellow.' He shook his head again, bowed with the strangeness of events and the burden of victimhood. Amos had never before regarded himself as a victim, and he found it heavy going.

He hardly noticed the policeman leaving, exhaustion hitting him so abruptly that he had to sit down in the old armchair and lean his head back. He fell into a deep sleep for an hour or more, before waking suddenly from a tormenting dream. If anything he felt worse for the brief oblivion.

He forced himself upstairs to get dressed, and then out to inspect his animals. The air was damp, a fine drizzle blowing across from one hill to another. Bad news for the hay, he thought, from long habit. Even though he and Isaac had not made hay for years, it still coloured his thinking. That and corn a month or so later, and ploughing, seeding, fertilising all in their due season. Giving all that up had been an unthinking process, brought about by the inexorable sale of their land, piece by piece, and the reduction in livestock accordingly. Amos had seen farmers ten years older than himself still working the land, wiry and indestructible, but he had not possessed their energy. He had been distracted and weakened by Isaac, who wasn't safe on a tractor, and who needed to be watched most of the time, like a little child.

A sudden storm swept through him. Grief for his brother, fear for himself, and a new sense of rage at his situation combined to galvanise him, as he stood there on the edge of his land, looking down at Redstone. He couldn't bear it, there with nobody to talk to, no cats to complain about, nothing where he'd left it, the house not feeling like his any more. Some instinct drove him over the big rotting gate which was never opened now, onto the land that had once been his and was now a part of Redstone Farm. This was where he had run, that morning, his head split open, blood wet on his face, mingled with tears at what had befallen his brother. He must have climbed the gate then, too, though he couldn't remember doing so.

They had been kind to him, the girl and Sam, that morning. He could go down and thank them. That was a normal thing to do. And he might get a sight of Miranda, of whom he had not thought for so many days. With a sense

211

of wonder, he checked back in his memory. It was true – he had forgotten Miranda until now. As if stored up out of sight somewhere, his obsession with her returned with new force. Beardon was dead and gone. She was free to talk to him, smile at him, even – was it possible? – come and drink tea with him in his pristine home. He smiled to himself, at that. What a snub to Phoebe that would be, if her mischief could be turned to something good and sweet after all.

He hurried down the field, slipping now and then on the wet grass. Before reaching the yard he paused to smooth back his hair with both hands, remembering that he had not brushed it for days. He hadn't washed his face, either. He shivered to think what he must look like. The dressing on his face must be grimy and coming unstuck, too. With sudden decision, he took hold of it and ripped it away. The stinging sensation abated within a few moments. Delicately he fingered the wound. It was dry and not unduly sensitive. *Thick skull*, he thought to himself.

The man Sam was moving about in the big shed that housed the implements. The mower was sitting out in the yard, attached to the tractor. He hadn't seen Amos, being intent on fixing something on the baler, a long screwdriver in his hand. Amos looked around for a dog to notice him and bark. Funny sort of a farm without a dog, he thought.

After a minute or so, he deliberately kicked at a stone, trying to make his presence felt. Sam looked up slowly, carelessly, a glance with no alarm in it. Odd, really, thought Amos. After the things that have happened. I could be standing here with a gun or a crowbar.

Sam's face showed clearly the succession of reactions to Amos's appearance. Blank failure to recognise him, followed by surprise, mild alarm and concern. 'Lord, man, you look poorly,' he said.

Amos smiled. 'I b'ain't so bad,' he said. 'Up and about, as you can see.'

'What can I do for you?' Sam stood up straight, subtly masterful. He spoke without a trace of Devon accent, something he had found both useful and embarrassing in his years at Redstone. The Midlands rhythms of his boyhood persisted only mildly, hidden by his almost eccentric habit of using good English. Guy had mimicked him, teased him, without effect. Miranda had once realised that it was Sam's use of language which redeemed him, and made him more than a simple farm labourer.

'Amos, what do you want?' he repeated.

'To say thank 'ee. For what you and the young girl did, for Isaac and me. You was neighbourly.'

'It was what anybody would have done. We're all sorry about Isaac. It must be very hard for you.'

'Ay.' Amos glanced towards the house. 'And things here can't be a lot better.'

'We're managing.'

'Strange, all the same. Police running over everything. Taking papers, nosing about. Seems like they think the same chap's done both killings. Is that right?'

Sam stood very still. 'Hard to say,' was all he would reply. It had struck him that this was the first time anyone had asked his direct opinion. Even the police, interviewing him three times, hadn't sought his personal view. They'd enquired about Amos and Isaac, their history and anyone they might know; they'd asked about his years with the Beardons, and what he might

213

gain from Guy's death. They'd looked at him strangely, and written a lot of notes. But they hadn't asked what he thought.

'Nobody's saying much, I reckon,' Amos commented. 'Not so easy to trust each other, time like this. For all they know, 'twas me, or Isaac, as chucked Beardon in the slurry. Or you.'

Sam made no reply. Something closed down in his face, and he became sullen and silent.

'See what I mean,' chuckled Amos, feeling rather better for this encounter. Again he looked towards the house. 'D'ye think I could go and say my thank yous to the little girl?'

'Nobody's going to stop you,' snapped Sam, discovering the screwdriver in his hand, and returning to his baler. 'But she's not a little girl. She's a grown woman, by any measure.'

Lilah's maturity was unimportant to Amos. Girls grew up, he supposed, but for him, she would forever be the cartwheeling child in the buttercups, that first day the Beardons moved in.

Boldly he strode to the farmhouse door, and knocked on it. After an interval that seemed unreasonably long, the door was opened by Miranda. For a moment Amos was speechless at the sight of her in front of him. Then he found the sense to utter, 'I came to say thank 'ee for being so good when we had our trouble.' He spoke haltingly, words whirling around in his head, everything difficult and different from his expectations. Miranda was closer than he had been to her for very many years. He had to hold his arms stiffly at his sides to prevent himself from embracing her.

'Mr Grimsdale!' she greeted him. 'What a surprise! Come in, you look terribly tired. Gosh, I'm so sorry we haven't come to see you, to tell you how dreadfully upset we were to hear about your brother. But – well, you can imagine it's been

214

a bit chaotic here. And how's your poor head? I didn't even know you were out of hospital. Isn't that awful! Except, yes, my friend did see you, a day or two ago, when the inquest was on. I should have paid more attention.'

He let the babble run over him, warm and sweet as it was. She sounded so genuine, as if she really did care about him. She sounded just as she had, all those years ago when she'd run up to visit him, and he'd fallen so ridiculously in love with her. She was a woman in a million.

'Oh, do come in,' she went on, stepping to one side to give him space to cross the threshold.

He stumbled past her, unable to believe what was happening. Never once had he been inside Redstone farmhouse. He hardly dared to raise his head and take in what her home was like. He was in a room with a Rayburn on one side, a big table at the end, under a window, and a dark dresser full of plates and a mess of other things, facing the Rayburn. Everything was untidy, cobwebs in corners, grimy windows. Without waiting for an invitation, he dropped into one of the upright chairs beside the table. Emotion was bubbling up inside him, and a weakness from love of Miranda and loss of Isaac.

'I just came to say thank'ee,' he mumbled. 'That's all.' And to everyone's horror, his own included, large hot tears began to slide down his cheeks, as he rested his injured head in both hands on the table.

Chapter Twenty

The day of Roddy's Alton Towers trip seemed to stretch for ever, comprising one bizarre event after the other. Sam's loss of the gun, which was less alarming than mysterious, to Lilah's mind; Sylvia's visit, which had lasted so long; and then poor old Amos turning up in such a state. There had been no time to slow down and try to grasp the import of each event until long after it happened.

Lilah didn't reproach her mother for neglecting to produce any supper, or to feed the calves, or close the yard gate, or to perform any of her usual tasks; she had clearly gained so much pleasure from Sylvia's company – and even, in a way, from Amos's as well. Miranda had taken an obvious satisfaction in soothing him, giving him tea, taking him home and promising to keep an eye on him in the future. But the girl could not postpone her plan to have a talk of her own with her mother that evening. As soon as she could, she settled them both in the sitting room and took a deep breath.

'About visiting Barbara,' she began. 'I can see that it would be intriguing to meet her, and it'll be fine when we've got straighter here – but don't you think you're being a bit premature? She sounds rather hostile towards us, in the letter.'

'She doesn't know us. And I didn't take Guy away from her; they were divorced before I met him. I suppose I just want to . . . well, compare notes.'

'That's ghoulish, Mum.'

'Is it?' Miranda spoke dreamily, not noticing or caring about her daughter's disapproval. 'I think it's nature. For me, it is, anyway. I was never jealous of her, like second wives are supposed to be. If he'd had a mistress, I'd probably have wanted to get to know her as well.'

'You're crazy.'

'Don't forget I grew up in the sixties. My whole generation is crazy. I never went a bundle on the idea of fidelity. It's too exclusive; too possessive. You wouldn't understand,' she finished with a sigh.

An awful thought struck the girl. 'Mum?'

'What? What's the matter?'

'You didn't . . . you weren't . . . were you?'

'Unfaithful?' Miranda avoided her daughter's glance and gently fingered her own neck. 'Not much chance of that, stuck away down here. I wouldn't tell you, anyway. You'd be on his side, you Daddy's girl.'

'You *were*, weren't you! I can see it from your face.'

'Not enough to be worth making a fuss about. Goodness me, why people get so upset about a perfectly harmless natural instinct, I shall never understand. People don't *own* each other, for heaven's sake.'

'He would have killed you if he'd found out. How did you have the *nerve*?'

'Well he didn't. Somebody killed *him* instead.' Miranda's face was suddenly hard and fierce, frightening Lilah.

The fear crawled with icy feet all over her. Anyone, *anyone*, could be Guy's killer. Even Miranda. Or Sylvia. The person hadn't needed to get right into the slurry with him – just pushed him down with some long-handled tool; something that would grip him by the back of his neck. It would take what – two or three minutes, or even less. Plenty of time to hide the tool, run back into the house and pretend to be asleep.

The growing panic generated by these suspicions was interrupted by a now-familiar sequence of sounds outside. A car engine; a slamming door; footsteps; then a knock. Frozen, Lilah and Miranda sat fighting their foolish trepidation, each trying to guess who it must be.

The sight of Jonathan was overwhelmingly reassuring. 'Oh, it's you!' Lilah breathed, on a great sigh of relief. 'How lovely to see you.'

'Steady on,' he laughed, a hint of warning in his voice. She checked her enthusiasm, instantly aware that he had come for something serious. A thump of foreboding went through her. Was there more trouble?

'Come in,' she invited. 'Mum's got a bad ankle. You can come and sympathise.'

'Can Roxanne come in too? She's got a story to tell you.'

'How are her feet?' The Beardons had rarely allowed dogs inside the house, because of their muddy feet, which could so easily turn an untidy and dusty house into a sordid hovel.

'Beautiful, except they need trimming. You can do it for her, if you like. She won't let me touch them.'

She didn't respond to the affable words. Jonathan had never come to see them in an evening before. Guy would not have welcomed him; it was even possible that he would have refused his neighbour entrance to the house. Lilah felt battered by so many changes, all carrying their own implications, all depriving her of peace. For the first time in her life, she felt an acute desire to jump into the car and just drive and drive until the land ran out.

Jonathan took several minutes to come to the point of his visit, but then he told his tale concisely. He hadn't brought the mucky clothes with him, despite his initial intention. Lilah asked him why.

'I wasn't sure you'd want me to. You might . . . recognise them.'

'Well, from what you say, we'd have at least found the brother to the shoe that was in the slurry. Not that that would have got us much further. I don't get what you mean. Wouldn't it be a good thing if we discovered who the stuff belonged to?'

Jonathan and Miranda maintained their silence – two wise adults waiting for the child to come to its senses. Lilah felt a rising anger. 'Well, *wouldn't* it? Christ almighty, Jonathan! You're as bad as Mum, wanting to deny the truth. We're talking about *murder*! That's the worst crime there is. You can't just stick your head in the sand. I'm phoning Den. This is evidence. The best evidence we've got so far.' She got up, and strode over to the phone. Her hand reached out for it, lifted the receiver, paused and then slammed it down again. Still the others said nothing.

'You're not being *fair*,' she howled, tears of rage burning her cheeks. 'You're not telling me everything. Den's the only straight person in this whole vile business. He's the only one I can trust.'

'Phone him, then,' said Miranda, coolly. 'We're not stopping you.'

'I can't. I don't know his home number. I'll have to wait till tomorrow. He's coming to take me out, anyway.'

'When?' Miranda demanded.

'One day soon. We didn't make a precise date.' Lilah kicked viciously at a pot of pampas grass, sending it rolling across the room. Miranda flinched at the violence. Jonathan and his dog drew closer together, ludicrously comic to Lilah in her hysteria.

'Steady on, kiddo,' he said, as she crumpled into a mix of sobs and laughter. He got up then, and went to her. 'Come on, now. It'll sort itself out. Maybe I should have waited to speak to your mum on her own. You're getting out of your depth with all this. At your age everything seems so black and white. The point is, I think, that there seems to be one main suspect in everyone's mind now. Cappy thinks the same and it's someone we're all fond of, someone we can see had plenty of provocation. We just can't really see how it would benefit anyone – not the cause of justice, or the greater good, or any worthy moral cause – if he was sent to prison for years. Some people survive prison more or less intact, but most don't. This chap wouldn't. It's a serious thing we're talking about here. We all know that. But your mother and I – and Cappy – know that it isn't black and white. Do you see?'

Lilah went on crying, clinging to his shoulder; Roxanne pushed at her with her nose, wanting to play this odd new game.

'Oh, God!' said Miranda suddenly. 'Look at the time!'

They both turned to stare blankly at her.

'Roddy,' she said. 'We were supposed to meet him at school twenty minutes ago.'

For Lilah, it was a fitting end to a day which had begun far too early. Awkwardly she disengaged from Jonathan and sat heavily on the floor. 'Well *I'm* not getting him,' she said. 'I should have been in bed by now. He'll phone in a minute. Tell him to get a taxi.'

'No, no,' said Jonathan, valiantly. 'I've got the car. Let me fetch him. I'll go right away. If he phones, tell him to stand where I can see him.'

Neither woman attempted to argue. All Miranda said was, 'Leave Roxanne here, then. We enjoy her company and I don't suppose she wants to go for a drive in the dark.'

As Jonathan's hand grasped the handle to the back door, Lilah said in a shrill voice, 'Jonathan! That man you were talking about, who wouldn't be able to bear it in prison – you *did* mean Sam, didn't you?'

Jonathan threw a quick glance at Miranda, shook his head at Lilah, as if to reproach her for voicing her thoughts, and left the house. They heard his engine start in the quiet yard and were left to face each other.

Lilah felt she was living a nightmare. At the same time, she was embarrassed by her own outburst. Without meeting her mother's eye, she stood up. 'I'm going to bed,' she said. 'I'll see you in the morning.'

Jonathan was glad of the night drive. He had been shaken by Lilah's behaviour, embarrassed and concerned. It struck

221

him that never before had he been called upon to cope with a sobbing woman; Cappy was volatile in her own way, but she would never have lost control to the extent that Lilah had just done. He drew several deep breaths, but nothing would shift the sensation of a hand stirring everything in his midriff and the warning voice in his head that predicted much more trouble yet to come.

As he passed through the village, he saw the dark outline of a man, leaning against the big beech tree which marked the top of the hill before plunging down into the valley that lay to the south of the village boundary. Something about the set of his head indentified the man as Tim Rickworth, whose house was a hundred yards distant. Jonathan stopped before he gave himself a chance to think. He pressed the button which lowered the window on the passenger side.

'Waiting for someone?' he called, already wondering whether he'd been an idiot to stop.

Tim was casual. 'No,' he shrugged. 'Just out for a little walk. It's a lovely evening. Have you noticed the sky? After such a foul day, it's quite a treat.'

Jonathan didn't even look; night skies didn't interest him. He remembered that he was supposed to be hurrying. 'Sorry to disturb you, then,' he said. 'I'm on an errand of mercy myself. Better get on.'

'Oh?' said Tim, slightly more animated. 'Problems?'

'Not really. Young Roddy Beardon is stranded at school. His Mum forgot to fetch him.'

'But—' Tim checked himself. Jonathan noticed the gaps in his own account.

'I'd dropped in earlier this evening. While I was there,

they remembered poor Roddy. I felt it was rather my fault, for distracting them. It made sense for me to go.'

'Better get on, then,' advised Tim. 'It's nearly eleven, I should think.'

'Surely not! Can't be.' Both men looked at watches, but found it too dark to decipher them. *Funny*, thought Jonathan, *you'd think he'd have one that lit itself up, yuppy like him.*

But he felt constrained to move on. The thought of the youngster waiting forlornly at the school gates spurred him on. What kind of a mother must Miranda Beardon be, anyway, to just forget the kid like that? For the rest of the drive, he considered the woman's character, and what he knew of her. Pretty and looking a lot younger than her real age, she'd never seemed to fit the role of farmer's wife. Odd, he discovered, that he hadn't given her more thought before this. His flirting had been automatic, her response as casual as his intentions. The farm had been dominated by Guy and his furies. The obvious assumption had been that Miranda was a pale character, overshadowed and cowed by her much older husband. Only now was he learning that there might be more to her; that some of the whispered rumours of her having a secret life might indeed be true. Almost he could believe that she might be conducting a love affair with Sylvia, as Cappy had suggested. He had always dismissed it automatically; Miranda was too feminine, for a start. And surely a woman married to Guy would not *dare*? He must remember to ask Cappy to elaborate.

Roddy was forced to swallow his indignation at being forgotten when he realised who had come for him. A couple of his friends, who lived in streets close to the school, had waited with him, in no hurry to get home. They'd promised themselves that in five more minutes, they'd phone Redstone to find out what was going on. All three had steadfastly refused to acknowledge that some further disaster might have happened. Instead, they'd reminded each other about the thrills of Nemesis and the Ripsaw and how dopey Paul Mathers had been sick after the Corkscrew.

At the sight of Jonathan, Roddy had felt a flutter of panic. 'Is Mum all right?' he'd asked, before getting into the car. 'Why've *you* come for me?'

'Everything's fine,' Jonathan soothed, giving a friendly wave to the other two boys. 'Nothing at all's happened. I'll explain as we go, okay?'

'I was waiting half an hour,' Roddy said, factually. 'We were due back here at ten, you know. We left Alton Towers at six, and it takes exactly four hours. Except we were late. There were roadworks on the motorway, or something.'

Jonathan accelerated into the night, feeling gratifyingly useful for once, and vital to the happiness of the Beardon family. 'It's all my fault,' he said cheerfully. 'I turned up unexpectedly, and made your Mum forget to collect you.'

'So nothing's wrong? Really?'

'Honestly. It's weird, isn't it, that feeling when you go away, even for a day, thinking something terrible's going to happen when you're not there. Cappy's like that.'

'Well, after what's happened . . .' Roddy stopped himself. It ought to be obvious to this fool that he'd worry. Why bother to explain? 'So why did you show up, in the first

224

place?' he demanded. 'You've never paid us a visit before.'

Jonathan laughed. 'That's true. A lot's changing without your dad around. I . . . had something to show your mum. She'll tell you about it in the morning, I expect. Ten more minutes, max, and we'll be there.'

Roddy was quick to notice Lilah's state of mind next day. He came in from milking to find her still in her pyjamas and her hair looking as if she'd been tearing at it like a Roman widow.

'What's the matter with you?' he demanded. 'Not ill, are you?'

'Shut up,' she told him.

He would not be deterred. 'That's nice. Aren't you going to ask me about yesterday? It was great, actually, even though it rained a bit. We went on everything. It's *huge* – the teachers kept getting lost. Thanks for forgetting to fetch me, by the way. I felt a right idiot with Nat and Ben staying to look after me, like a little kid.'

'One of the teachers should have waited with you.'

'That would have been even worse. I was safe enough – just pissed off.'

'What makes you think you were safe? There are murderers about, you of all people should know that.'

He pushed his lower lip out at her mulishly. 'I don't want to know anything about all that. It does my head in.' He half-turned away from her, hunching a shoulder defensively. 'I can still smell myself, sometimes, the way I stunk after getting him out with Sam. And I didn't even go right in, like Sam did. Even so, I got filthy. I'm going to throw those jeans away that I was wearing.'

'Where are they?'

'In a bucket outside. Mum chucked them in it on the day, and I don't think anyone's touched them since. They're probably rotten by now, anyway.'

How many pairs of mucky legwear *were* there in the neighbourhood, Lilah wondered. Guy's own twill trousers must have ended up in a bin at the hospital; nobody had offered to give them back. And Sam's moleskins had disappeared with the last dustbin collection.

'You have to listen to me, Roddy,' she insisted. 'You can't just run away from it.' She bent towards him, wanting to penetrate the shell he'd developed around himself. As if connected to her by a rigid rod, he leant away, keeping the distance between them unchanged. He put up a hand, to brush her away. From the lump on his jaw, she could see he was clenching his teeth, perhaps trying not to cry.

'Rod. Come on,' she coaxed, as if he were the toddler she could still clearly recall. 'There's something else, as well. Something important. I don't know whether Mum told you she'd had a letter from Daddy's first wife – Barbara. She wants to go and see her. We've got half-brothers.'

'We always knew that.'

'Well, yes, but it never seemed real to me until now. It seemed a sort of dream, something that happened a hundred years ago.'

'I wish I could go with her.'

'What?'

'I've always wanted to. I wanted to have brothers. If I can't have Dad back again, a big brother would be the next best thing.'

'She won't see the brothers – just the mother. They're grown up now, and living miles away from her. They've got wives and kids and houses.'

'But maybe she'll ask them to come and meet us. A family reunion! Hey, Li, that'd be cool, don't you think?' His mood was altogether changed, his eyes now bright and eager. Lilah was bemused.

'I don't think you *can* go. You're needed here. There's too much work to do.'

'Shit. Can't we go when the hay's finished? When's Mum thinking of making this visit anyway?'

'She didn't say.' She felt she was being unkind in not sharing Roddy's excitement. But to her, if anything, the other family seemed more of a threat than a source of interest. The mysterious half-brothers might have been fun to meet ten years ago, but now she had no wish to get to know them. Life already felt unbearably fragile to her, and such an unpredictable element crashing in on her would not improve anything.

'How did the milking go?' she asked him. 'Any problems?'

He shrugged. 'Nothing much. Sam isn't as tidy as Dad was. He leaves things in the wrong places. There's always something we can't find. It's annoying.'

'You haven't been rude to him, have you?'

He gave her a withering look. 'D'you think he'd notice if I was? After the way Dad was with him. He hardly takes any notice of me; you must know that.'

'He's got his own troubles.'

Roddy shrugged again, as if it was too much of a bother to think about, and returned to the matter uppermost in his

227

mind. 'I'm going to ask Mum about going with her. Where does this Barbara woman live?'

'Nottingham, or somewhere near it.'

'Alton Towers is quite near Nottingham. We could get there and back in a day quite easily.'

'You're not going, Rod. She won't take you.'

'Li, you're in a real stress today, aren't you?'

'Don't you think I have a *right* to be, with my father murdered by the farmhand and everyone acting as if that's perfectly okay?' Her voice rose and then cracked. She felt the previous evening's hysteria hovering somewhere, waiting to pounce.

Roddy's attention was finally held. All colour left his face. 'What do you mean? Sam? Are you telling me it was *Sam*? That's insane! The maddest thing I ever heard. He got Dad *out*, remember. You didn't see him as I did. How upset he was. *Of course* he didn't do it. I would bet anything – my life, even – that he had nothing to do with it.'

Lilah had realised, during the sleepless hours of the night, that Jonathan's discovery of the mucky clothes cast no real suspicion on Sam. The only pointer to him was that he lived at Redstone and the hedge where the things had been buried was bordering Redstone land. She thought carefully. If Sam had drowned Guy an hour or so before Lilah found him, getting into the pit with him, he could have found time to strip off those clothes and change into the moleskins, before going back to his normal routine. That's what Miranda and Jonathan assumed – but Lilah could think of several ill-fitting details: what about his hands, for instance? Not just his hands, but his *skin* would have been filthy and smelly.

'I know,' she said. 'I didn't mean to say that I thought it was him. When I found Dad, Sam was in the outside loo. He had his moleskins on. He didn't smell at all – and looked perfectly clean. But, Rod, someone *did* get right into the pit with him. Remember those trails of muck at the side of the pit? Before you pulled him out? They must have been made by someone climbing out, covered in the stuff. Someone held him down until he drowned.'

'It'd have to be somebody strong.'

Lilah nodded. 'Mum's pretty sure it was Sam.'

'*No!*' The cry echoed Lilah's own reaction, the day before. With deliberate melodrama, Roddy dropped his head to the table and banged it three times against the wood. Lilah reached out and held him still.

'Stop it, you fool. You'll hurt yourself.'

He looked up, with a dull stare that disconcerted her even more than his anger had done. 'Rod?' she queried.

'It's a bad dream, Li, all of it. A very yucky dream. That's the only possible explanation.' Tears filled his eyes. 'But Dad's not coming back, is he? Why is it so difficult to believe that?'

She left a silence, waiting for him to get the weeping over with. Then she said, 'So you definitely don't think Sam could have done it? He couldn't have forced Dad's face into the slurry?'

'Obviously he couldn't,' Roddy sniffed fiercely. 'Could *you*? Could Mum? Anyway, I don't want to talk about it any more.' He got up from the table. 'And you'd better get dressed. You'll be needed.'

Chapter Twenty-One

'I'm going for a walk,' Roddy announced, after supper. 'I need to get outside.'

'Can I come?' Lilah said, almost without thinking. 'We could go into the village and have a drink at the pub.'

Roddy and Miranda stared at her as if she had suggested an excursion to a strip club. The Beardons never frequented the local pub, which was unmodernised and unpretentious. Full of smoke and dark wood and elderly male villagers, it had never invited the attentions of tourists, women or children.

'Why on earth would we want to do that?' Roddy said.

Lilah blinked at her own madness. 'For a change,' she said, weakly. 'Because it's there, and a beer would be nice. It's what people do.'

'Guy would have had a fit if he'd heard you suggest it,' said Miranda.

'I don't think he would,' Lilah argued. 'What's to stop us? It's only fifteen minutes' walk away.'

Miranda widened her eyes and shrugged. 'It's fine by

me,' she said. 'Don't think I'm stopping you. It's up to you what you do.'

'Come on, Rod,' Lilah was suddenly resolved. 'Let's give it a go.'

'It's Saturday, remember,' he said, with growing reluctance. 'Everyone from the village will be there. They'll stare at us.'

'Let them,' said his sister.

Within minutes they were on the road into the village, side by side, the sun setting over the treetops to their right.

'You wanted to talk to me, I suppose,' said Roddy, after a while. 'You needn't have gone to such extremes. Mum thinks you're mad.'

'I don't care. We didn't say everything this morning.'

Roddy's pace slowed, as his mind began to work. 'Li, am I a suspect? Does Den think *I* killed Dad?'

'Of course not. Don't be stupid.'

'But I could be the one. If you're saying it might be Sam, it could just as well be Mum or me – or even you.'

'Or some passing tramp. That's my favourite theory. Has been from the start.'

'I can see why it would be.'

'I still want to work out how exactly it was done. Whether someone could hold him down till he drowned, and then just climb out and walk away afterwards.'

Despite obvious squeamishness, Roddy gave it his consideration. 'I suppose it wouldn't be so difficult, if you were really determined.'

'But surely he'd fight. There'd be wounds on him, and there weren't any, apart from that bruise on his head.'

'Not if he couldn't get his footing. It was horribly slippery in there. Sam could hardly stay upright when we were fishing Dad out. We used the long hook, and a fork, because we didn't want to get right into the middle. I pulled from the side, and Sam pushed him from the pit. We told all that to your policeman.' The boy was entering into the ghoulish discussion with more interest now; in spite of his qualms, it was a relief to talk about it at last.

'I'm glad I missed that. I was in the house with Mum. I think I must have missed quite a lot.'

'But *you* found him. You're the chief witness. We must have obliterated all the clues when we dragged him out.'

'So – we're going round in circles. Could it still have been Sam, or not? Never mind his character or motives – could he physically have managed it? And there's one other thing. Sam's got Daddy's gun. Except he seems to have lost it, or hidden it.' She told her brother how she'd discovered the gun was missing, and how apparently unconcerned Sam had been.

Roddy could make little of this information. 'This is a very nasty conversation. I wish we could talk about something else.'

'At least I can't smell muck any more. Can you?'

'No more than usual. I sometimes think I'll be able to smell it for the rest of my life.'

Lilah relented. 'All right, we won't talk about it any more – but it's not finished, you know. Not by a long way.'

'It's finished for me. Sam's our *friend*. More than a friend. If he married Mum, we could carry on pretty much the same as before. Did you think of *that*?'

232

Now it was Lilah's turn to be shocked. Her talk with Miranda came back to her – the hints of adultery and Miranda's reluctance to cast Sam as a villain, even if he was technically guilty. The idea of her mother and Sam having an attachment was not totally new to her, but she had avoided facing it for most of her grown-up life. Her mind ran a review of all the instances when the two had been together – firstly over the past few weeks, and then back for as many years as she could remember. She came up with very little that would confirm the suggestion. Except—

There had been an afternoon when Guy was ploughing, and hadn't been back for lunch. Lilah had come home early from school because snow was forecast, and the buses had been summoned to deliver the outlying pupils home before it could block the roads. She had gone straight to see the new lambs in the barn. Sam had been nowhere in sight, and a ewe was delivering unattended. She had shouted for him, and getting no response, had supervised the birth herself. Only later – perhaps fifteen minutes later – had he come sauntering into the barn, an odd look on his face.

'Where have you been?' she'd demanded. 'I called and called.'

'Oh, did you? I never heard you. I must have been too far away.' She hadn't noticed his evasiveness at the time, but something strange in his manner had made the incident memorable. It would have been the simplest thing in the world for him and Miranda to have spent an undisturbed hour in bed together, she now saw. Yet this thought was at least as hard to accept as was the one that Sam had killed her father. Now even she could see that here, as any detective would say, was a firm and obvious motive.

'Oh, God,' she groaned to Roddy. 'This is too much. You're right – let's just concentrate on keeping the farm going. That's all I can cope with.'

They sat self-consciously in the pub, surrounded by smoke and the disbelieving glances of the regulars. It was made worse by the presence of Hetty Taplow behind the bar; she nodded to them in a parody of politeness which did nothing to conceal her astonishment at seeing them there.

Roddy drank Coke, feeling young and completely out of place. Lilah ordered a pint of scrumpy, in an attempt to fit in. It came on draught, cloudy, the palest beige colour, like dilute urine, and tasted sharply acidic. She forced half the glass down, and then stopped, convinced that she'd be sick if she had another drop. Glumly, she watched the men ranged along the bar. She and Roddy were silent, unable to think of anything innocuous to say. Any words they uttered would be clearly heard by everyone present.

They knew the men by name, in most cases. Middle-aged workers for local businesses, and a solitary farmer, they were rough in every respect. Their language was full of expletives, their skin reddened with drink or weather. Most of them coughed and one or two spat. They talked loudly about the Lottery, their cars, the weather. They laughed exaggeratedly, which Lilah suspected was for her and Roddy's benefit.

'You two waiting for someone?' Hetty called, eventually.

'Oh, no,' Lilah returned, trying to sound blithe. 'We just thought it would be nice to get out for a bit.'

'Nothing better to do on a Saturday, then?' one of the drinkers chimed in, giving her a suggestive grin. 'No boyfriends?'

She forced a smile, and shook her head.

'That's a shame. First time I ever saw any of your family down here, and that's a fact.' As one, they all turned the full beam of their attention on the brother and sister, no longer feeling any need to be surreptitious about it.

'There's a first time for everything,' Roddy retorted, his tone defensive and loud.

'First time for getting your dad bumped off, and no mistake,' muttered Pat Brown, a slightly younger drinker. Everyone heard him.

Lilah took a deep breath. She knew now why she'd decided to come here: it was to test the mood of the village concerning the fate that had befallen Guy. Would they be treated as outcasts, or be given sympathy and support? Always balanced on the edge of the community, regarded as aloof and somehow peculiar, she understood that there had been scant grounds to hope that the latter response would prevail.

'That might be so,' she answered, her voice bell-like in its clarity. 'We miss him very much. He was our father, after all.' The final words quavered a little as emotion overcame her.

'Course he was, love,' placated Hetty. 'You're bound to miss him. Whatever others might have thought of him, you would have seen his best side. That's the thing with girls and their dads, isn't it.'

Lilah searched for hidden meaning, narrowing her eyes. But the words were simply true, and she decided to take them at face value. 'Well, yes, I think that's right,' she said, very solemnly. 'It's kind of you to say that.'

Hetty was clearly encouraged. 'And what about poor old Isaac Grimsdale? You reckon 'twas same person done both killings?'

'You tell us, Hetty,' suggested Pat Brown. 'Tell'un your notions on that subject, why don't 'ee?'

Hetty chewed her lip doubtfully and shot sideways glances at Lilah and Roddy. 'Go on,' said Lilah. 'It's all right. We'd be interested to hear what you think.'

'I'm not saying as this is gospel true. 'Tis gossip brings things together. It came to my mind what I was thinking, now who could have killed old Isaac?'

'They wanted to kill Amos as well,' Lilah pointed out. 'It wasn't just Isaac.'

'That's right!' Hetty was triumphant. 'And it came to my mind, that time, eight, ten years back, when Mrs Westerby's young'un had that accident.'

'You mean Sylvia's little girl? Ruth? That was when we'd only just moved here.'

Hetty nodded her agreement. 'Amos had got that new tractor from the money your Dad gived'e for the land. 'Tis the point, see. The ambulance couldn't get past that bugger of a tractor; got caught in a line of grockles, an' by the time it reached the house, the kiddie had bled to death. 'Tis my belief that woman never forgave they Grimsdales. That's all I be saying, mind. Your ma must remember it. She was a godsend to poor Mrs Westerby, cheering her up when the worst of it was done with.'

'Have you told the police about this?'

Hetty shook her head. 'Clean forgot about it till a day or so ago,' she said.

The exchange stopped as abruptly as it had begun. Roddy pushed his glass to the middle of the stained table and met her eye. 'Ready?' he asked. She glanced down at the abandoned cider and nodded. Together they stood up, smiled vaguely at the grouped men, and left. Outside, it was still not dark, though almost ten.

'That was *awful*,' said Roddy.

'It was interesting, though,' she assured him. 'We have some idea what they think of us now.'

'Do we?'

'Well, they obviously don't like us much. They resent all the trouble we've brought to their peaceful little village.'

'Well, we knew that anyway.'

'Mmm. But they're scared of us as well. That never occurred to me before.'

'You're barking, Li. Mad as – a mad thing.'

She slapped his arm, with a little laugh, and said no more. It was eerie, walking along the narrow lane in semi-darkness. Only a few days earlier she'd cheerfully crossed twilit fields after the Mabberley barbecue, but now it felt as if there were shadowy things waiting behind the hedges, evil people intent on harm. With Roddy beside her, she felt relatively safe, but nothing would have persuaded her to go out alone at night now. What precisely had changed her? she wondered. The encounter with the love-making couple? All the talk of murder? Den's warnings? Or did she truly believe that Sam had killed her father, and might therefore have some strange, twisted reason for killing her as well?

Miranda was waiting for them, curious as to what the pub had been like.

'It was dire, Mum,' Roddy burst out. 'They just stared at us for a long time, and nobody said anything. Then they were patronising, and sort of nasty. Not really rude or anything. But it was like being in a foreign country, being stared at by a lot of hostile locals. Hetty was the only one who tried to be nice.'

'Hetty! Good God, I forgot she works there on Saturdays. She must have been surprised to see you.'

'She was,' Lilah confirmed. 'You know she's got some theory about Sylvia hating the Grimms? She says their tractor got in the way of the ambulance when Sylvia's little Ruth died and she blames them. Sounds a bit far-fetched to me. Sylvia always seems so rational.'

Miranda went pale and put a hand to her cheek. 'What a thing to bring up after all this time. It was such a horrible injury – there was nothing the ambulance people could have done. The child's leg was sheered almost off. The artery was completely severed. Such a stupid thing to happen – no wonder Guy was always on at you two to be careful. Farms are lethal places.'

'What did happen, exactly? You never did tell me properly.'

'I thought it would give you nightmares. Ruth was climbing on an old grasscutter, and slipped onto one of the blades. Her brother tried to get her out, and just made it worse by turning the blade and twisting her leg somehow, so she was really jammed. He was dreadfully upset, poor kid. And then Humphrey left them, soon after. An avalanche of disaster. That's the way it seems to go – fate suddenly notices a normal, happy family and decides to torment them for a bit.'

238

'According to Hetty, you were a good Samaritan where Sylvia was concerned.'

'I did my best. Isn't that what friends are for? She's being just as good to me now.'

They went to bed within minutes of each other, each making sure the doors were locked firmly and the landing light left switched on. Miranda had replaced the bulb without any prompting, the morning after the Mabberley barbecue, and without discussion, all three had been careful to leave it burning every night since then.

Lilah slept well, despite a lingering acid in her stomach from the scrumpy. So when it came, the appalling shock of a gun being fired just outside her window sent her heart thudding with a violence that paralysed her.

Chapter Twenty-Two

The double gunshot rang out, deafeningly loud, as was the scream that followed it. Lilah couldn't remember afterwards exactly how long it must have been before she and Roddy crashed down the stairs together to investigate. It seemed at the time that she lay in bed, utterly paralysed, for an immense age, praying for a sign that it was all something perfectly normal after all. Guy had used a shotgun on foxes and pigeons from time to time; perhaps Sam was just warning off some predatory creature. But no – the gun had gone missing. When she remembered that, she knew something terrible had happened.

Then she and Roddy were outside in the yard, looking and listening with a mixture of fear and desperation for something to explain the shots. The complete silence made her aware that the dawn chorus had stopped. The shock must have sent all the birds winging across the fields to hide.

She was wearing only the T-shirt and pants that she slept in. Roddy had taken the time to wriggle into a pair of jeans, she noticed, as they both stared towards the empty slurry pit, where it seemed the noise had come from. For them both, the sense of history repeating itself was overwhelming.

At first there was nothing to see in the yard. Nothing moved or made a sound. Then one of the yard cats ran out of the office, scarcely touching the ground in its arrowlike flight. It seemed to Lilah like a living embodiment of acute fear. Yet she felt certain that there was nobody in the little room. Perhaps the animal had gone in there to hide when the shots rang out.

She and Roddy stood bewildered, in the middle of the yard. On three sides there were farm buildings, and behind them stood the house. Gates and openings led to fields, and to the approach lane, down from the main road.

'Where's Sam?' said Roddy. The door of Sam's room was standing open, as it did for much of the day. But at five in the morning, it should certainly have been closed.

Lilah understood then that she had known from the start who it was who had screamed. She knew that it was Sam she had come outside to find. A glance into his room arose more from a deferment of the inevitable than from any hope of seeing him.

'He's here somewhere,' she said determinedly, and began to make for the side of the milking parlour, a short weed-infested path to a little-used area between the parlour and the tractor shed. Roddy followed close behind her.

'Why are you going this way?' he demanded.

'The scream came from this direction. At least—' She slowed her pace and looked around. Old paper sacks and empty cans were often dumped there, as well as useless tyres and broken tools. Tall stands of nettles grew between the junk piles.

Her first thought when she found Sam face down in the nettles was that the stinging must be unbearable. But of course, the stings weren't worrying him, any more than the slurry all over his face had worried Guy. Her second thought was that she herself could endure no more, and she cried out, a low-pitched, groaning cry of pure anguish. Roddy put both arms clumsily around her, squeezing her, shaking her, wanting her to stop.

'Not again,' he said.

Lilah's moans turned to hoots of frantic and ghastly laughter. What was she supposed to do now? Make another telephone call to the police, rouse her oddly absent mother, persuade Roddy to get himself stung all over whilst examining Sam for signs of life?

They stood together, helpless children, staring at a thick patch of blood on Sam's back. It seemed to glisten and quiver like something alive that had landed on him from above and behind.

A car engine roused them, as a vehicle drove into the yard. A great terror filled Lilah. The man with the gun had come back, and was going to shoot her and Roddy as well. She screamed, a single high note this time, and Roddy jumped away from her. A door slammed, but they still had no idea who the visitor was, out of sight in the yard. Torn between running away and hiding amongst the tractor and trailers, or risking her life on it being some blessed rescuer, Lilah stood unmoving.

'Hello?' called a familiar voice, 'Sam?'

'Ohhhh,' she gave a long sigh, and turned to run to the friendly arms, when her mother's voice came from the house.

'Jonathan? What on earth are *you* doing here? What's going on?'

'I thought you'd be able to tell me. Cappy heard a noise, like a shot, and she thought she also heard a shout or scream, from this direction. She sent me to investigate.'

To Lilah, still concealed, his voice sounded different. Stilted, almost rehearsed. But then, if he was afraid he'd come on a fool's errand, he would have practised his explanation in advance, wouldn't he?

It was Roddy who acted. He ran around the corner into the yard, shouting, almost babbling, as he went. 'Jonathan, we're here. It's Sam. He's been shot. Amazing you hearing it all the way to your place! It *was* loud, though. I was almost deafened. He's in the nettles, and there's a horrible lump of blood . . .'

'Where's Lilah?' demanded Jonathan, striding up to Roddy, and putting a hand on his shoulder. The boy looked up at him with something close to adulation, so great was his relief that a grown man had appeared on the scene.

'Here,' she muttered, showing herself. 'It's this way.' Like a guide at a tourist attraction, she outstretched an arm in invitation. 'We haven't touched him.'

'Lilah? *Lilah!*' shouted Miranda, still in the kitchen doorway, 'What did you say has happened?'

'Come and see for yourself,' snapped the girl, suddenly shaken by rage. How did her mother always manage to avoid the worst of these moments, when everyone else was having their world turned inside out?

The woman hovered helplessly, in bare feet and a flimsy silk kimono clutched around what Lilah knew wa nakedness beneath. In unison, the three turned away fro her, and went around the side wall to view the unbearable.

If Roddy had expected Jonathan to take manful charge, creating reassuring order from chaos, he was disappointed. Their neighbour simply stood staring at Sam for what felt like several minutes.

Sam was wearing a khaki-coloured cotton shirt and a pair of old faded trousers which he favoured in warm weather. The belt was unfastened and the buckle end of it flopped loose, just visible through the leaves and stalks of the nettle patch. He had sunk further into the nettles since Roddy and Lilah had first found him; some of the plants had begun to spring back to their former position, partly hiding him from view.

'It is definitely Sam, is it?' said Jonathan at last.

'Of course it is,' Roddy was impatient. 'We have to *do* something.'

'We were told off last time for doing too much,' Lilah reminded him. *Last time* left a ghastly echo in her head – it was halfway to assuming that there might yet be a *next time* as well.

Belatedly Miranda joined them, her feet floundering in Guy's old wellingtons, making her look clownlike. 'I've phoned the police,' she said briefly, not looking at Sam, turning her head awkwardly away. 'God knows what they're going to think.'

'Who cares what they think!' Roddy burst out. 'This is *Sam* and he's dead.'

'Easy does it, Rod,' soothed Jonathan. 'It'll be all right.'

'It won't though,' said Lilah, her voice too loud in the agile morning. 'We'll really have to sell the farm now.'

'What?' Miranda queried, faintly. 'What do you mean?'

'Think about it,' said the girl, harshly. 'How can we possibly manage?'

'Don't worry about that now,' Jonathan told her. He seemed to have decided that his most useful role was as a calming influence in the midst of all the horror. All he succeeded in doing was irritating both Roddy and Lilah, who were beginning to realise that his presence was contributing nothing at all.

Three policemen came this time, which everyone immediately understood was unusual. Den was not amongst them, and Lilah crazily assumed that he had been forbidden to come because of the personal connection. She was sure he'd told her he was on duty today. Only later did she realise that his shift probably didn't start until eight or nine a.m. The three men had extremely serious faces. They walked all around Sam, and one of them pushed gingerly through the nettles to examine him, his hands raised to avoid stings. 'Has anybody called the doctor?' he demanded. One of his colleagues grunted an affirmative, and watched impassively as the more intrepid one felt Sam's neck for a pulse, and gently turned him to look at his face, befoe letting him roll back to his original position.

Jonathan's presence felt intrusive to Lilah now. An outsider, nosing his way into their trouble, breaking the boundary that would have kept this new death strictly in the family. *Thank God*, she thought, *that he didn't bring his dog.*

'Should we have called a doctor?' she asked.

The leading policeman shook his head. 'It doesn't matter,' he said. 'We've got someone on the way.'

The other two men muttered to each other, a rapid exchange of jargonised information. Lilah heard 'inquest' and 'a string of murders'. They looked even more serious now, if that was possible.

Then they all began to cast around for clues, or so it appeared to Lilah, looking at the ground; striding first to one corner, then another; peering into the tractor shed and the deserted and dusty winter cowshed. 'Any sign of a weapon?' one of them asked. Nobody spoke.

'It might've been Daddy's gun,' said Lilah, before she stopped to think. 'Someone stole it from Sam's room.'

Everyone stared around the yard again, as if expecting to see a gun propped neatly against one of the walls or gateposts. The man with Sam in the nettles stirred cautiously with his foot, trying to see whether it might be underneath the body.

The thought struck Lilah for the very first time that Sam might have committed suicide. He might have deliberately hidden the gun, planning to use it on himself one depressed morning, when the dawn brought nothing but dogged work and misery and hopelessness. She stared at each sombre face in turn, wondering if she'd been slower than everyone else and whether they'd all taken suicide for granted from the start. Only Miranda held her eye, and Lilah could see the same thought on her mother's face. 'Might he have shot himself?' she said, the question almost a whisper.

'Of course not!' scorned Roddy. 'Who'd shoot himself in the middle of a patch of nettles? Anyway, the gun isn't here.'

'Could you show me where the gun usually lives?' asked the man who'd raised the matter.

Lilah summoned meagre resources of energy to explain. 'After my father died, Sam said he would take care of it, and he put it in a little gap beside the chest of drawers in his room. It wouldn't really have shown to anyone who didn't know it was there. But it went missing. Sam and I noticed it was gone on Friday. We were worried, of course . . .' This wasn't true of Sam, she remembered. He had been strangely unconcerned. For some reason, she withheld this recollection, and seized on familiar excuses. 'Everyone here has been so busy, and we hadn't any idea who could have taken it, so we just sort of . . . forgot about it.' It sounded flimsy, even to her own ears. She didn't expect the police to understand that after everything that had happened, the loss of the gun had not seemed very important, even to her.

'Will you show us his room, please?'

Lilah waved a hand at Roddy. 'He can do it. I'm . . . just not up to it. Sorry.'

Roddy shrugged, and began to walk back to the house. The man followed him. They were gone for five minutes, and came back empty-handed.

'No sign of a gun,' confirmed the policeman.

'Lilah told you there wouldn't be,' said Miranda sourly. She looked at each policeman in turn, defying them to speak. Her kimono was coming open as she relaxed her hold on it. It seemed to Lilah that everyone noticed this at once.

'Mum, why don't you go and get dressed?' she said, briskly. 'You must be cold in that.'

Carelessly, Miranda looked down at herself. 'If I'm offending anyone, I suppose I should – but you're not so respectably dressed yourself, you know,' she said to Lila'

247

harshly, and turned to leave. She didn't react when another car squeezed into the yard and stopped directly behind Jonathan's, boxing him in. Instead she continued her clumping progress back to the house. Lilah immediately felt naked, exposed; she wondered whether she could get back to the house without making a fool of herself. Her whole body felt battered and sore from the tornado of emotions still raging through it.

'Now then,' said the junior policeman, emerging cautiously from the nettles, and pulling a pad and pencil from his pocket, 'time for some questions. Who was the first to find the – er, gentleman?'

'Sam. He's called Sam,' Roddy said. 'Sam Carter. Lilah and I found him together. We both heard the shots and the scream.'

'Is he a relative of yours?' The man had produced a notebook and pencil.

'No. He works here,' said Roddy, who was sounding confident and in control, getting into his stride. Lilah felt a surge of admiration for him.

'Is it all right if I go and get dressed?' she asked. The policeman with the notepad nodded. Jonathan was standing a little to one side, looking as if he felt superfluous. *Which he is*, thought Lilah, with a touch of bitterness.

The police doctor from the newly-arrived car somehow found his way to the spot and winced when he saw the nettles. Then with a deep breath he plunged in to begin his examination. Lilah didn't look. This was the part she had skipped last time, and her nerve was no stronger now. She hurried to the house, and made for her bedroom. Only after several minutes did she come out, and then it was to stay with her mother in the kitchen.

Miranda had made a pot of tea, and was smoking a rare cigarette. Lilah noticed that she was shaking. 'They'll be coming in for more questions in a minute,' Miranda said. 'Not that there's much to tell them. I can't work out the business of the gun, can you? Did Sam hear someone, and come out, and find someone with it, and then the person – whoever it was – shot him with it? With Guy's gun? Is that how it was?' Her words were staccato, sharp; shock and fear were plain on her face.

Lilah shook her head as best she could. She felt a tight pain beginning in her temples, as if she was going to have a terrible migraine. 'Poor Sam,' she said. 'Poor man. We had it all wrong, didn't we – Jonathan and you, especially? And you'd almost convinced me.'

'Oh, don't. I tried *not* to think it. I wanted to push it all away . . . Who knows what Jon really thought? What's he doing here, anyway?'

'He says he heard the shots – at least, Cappy did and sent him to see what it was.'

'Huh! He can pull the other one. There are shots all the time around here, with people rabbiting and pigeon-shooting. And crow-scaring things going off.'

'There was a scream,' Lilah pointed out, remembering for the first time the other element of déjà vu: there had been gunshots and screams only a day or two ago, in Jonathan's woods. Almost like a deliberate warning of what was going to happen. She felt like a bewildered mouse, caught between the paws of a malicious and murderous cat.

Miranda took a deep draw of the cigarette and then stubbed it out viciously. She looked out of the win hearing yet another vehicle arrive. 'How could anybody shoot Sam?' she wailed. 'How could they want to harm a man like that? A good man. Oh, God, it's not fair. It's not bloody fair.' And she sank her head onto her folded arms and wept long and loud.

Roddy was valiantly struggling to milk the cows, ineffectually assisted by Jonathan. Lilah watched as new rolls of official tape were fastened bizarrely around the nettle patch, as well as across the door to Sam's room. The men who had answered the 999 call remained, searching the yard and the buildings, as they had done before. New arrivals comprised a Detective Inspector and a middle-aged female sergeant who interviewed Lilah and Miranda formally in the kitchen. But before they could get properly started, a man came in, excitedly brandishing Guy's gun.

'Found it, ma'am!' he triumphed. 'Lying inside the gate of that first field, towards the woods, it was. Still warm, too.'

The sergeant responded with gratifying enthusiasm, jumping to her feet. 'Get it checked for prints,' she said. 'I assume this is your husband's gun, Mrs Beardon? The one that was mentioned earlier?'

Miranda shrugged. 'Looks like it,' she said. 'But all guns look the same to me.'

The woman gave her a severe frown. 'We're talking about a deliberate murder, madam,' she said. 'It seems to me that you're taking the matter rather lightly.'

Miranda laughed crazily. 'I can assure you that I'm not ‑ing that,' she said. 'Would you like me to tear out some of ‑hair, just to prove it to you?'

The sergeant shook her head, lost in disapproval. Lilah, watching from the end of the table, couldn't resist a stirring of admiration for her mother. She herself could barely speak or think, yet here was her mother shrugging at guns and dealing out sarcasm to officers of the law. It might be unwise in the circumstances, but it showed enviable spirit.

They had their own fingerprints taken, surprised at the inky mess as each fingertip was rolled laboriously onto the card, before the man departed with the gun. Jonathan also left at that point, with minimal ceremony. The interview struggled on. Times, unusual sounds, routines. When had they last seen Sam alive? How had he seemed? Did anybody have a motive for killing him? Had he kept the gun with him for a reason? Lilah worried about Roddy coping alone outside. He and Jonathan had been interviewed somewhat awkwardly by the Detective Inspector, who was also supervising the detailed examination of Sam's room and the nettle patch.

At about half past ten, there was a phone call for the Inspector. He listened with an avid expression, snapping 'Yes? Really! *Yes*!' at the person on the line. Then he called the family together. 'We have identified several sets of fingerprints on the gun,' he said. 'Yours, Mrs Beardon. And Mr Carter's. And a very recent set we can't identify, possibly Mr Beardon's, although they seem more like a woman's. Finally, there are those of Mr Amos Grimsdale. Two officers have already gone to his house, to ask him to accompany them to the station.'

Chapter Twenty-Three

Cappy made no attempt to hide her impatience when Jonathan finally got home at nine-thirty that morning, and gave her a detailed account of the new turn of events at Redstone. 'You could have phoned me,' she reproached him. 'You must have known I was dying to hear what had happened. And I was worried.'

Jonathan doubted the last part. 'Sorry, pet. I got carried away with all the goings-on. You could have phoned *them* if you were desperate for news. I told everyone it was you who'd sent me round there in the first place.'

'Did they think it was odd, at all?'

'Think what was odd?'

'Turning up the way you did, so quickly. So *early*.'

He shrugged. 'Didn't seem like it. It was light, after all. And I'm a farmer. Plenty of good reasons why I should have been awake.'

She examined his face, wondering whether he was as disingenuous as he sounded. Finding no sign of irony, she laughed at him. 'And did you have to answer a lot of police questions?'

'Some. It was all a bit disjointed, with me and Roddy trying to deal with the cows, as well as about a hundred police people. I'm supposed to be going in to make a formal statement later today. They'd just found the gun when I left. They did say I shouldn't go anywhere until they'd eliminated me from their enquiries.'

'And aren't you worried?' She shivered. 'I wouldn't like it, that's for sure.'

'This is England, sweetie. The cops are quite benign, really. And not terribly bright, in my experience. I can handle them easily, believe me.'

'Well, I've got some news of my own. As you might expect.'

'Wait. I've got to have coffee, toast and a pee, first. And your birds seem a bit fed up. Isn't it time they had some breakfast, too?'

With a little cry, part exasperation, part self-reproach, Cappy ran off to her poultry sheds and busied herself with sacks of corn and hungry fowls. Ten minutes later, she was back in her elegant kitchen, arms folded on the highly polished oak table, watching her husband eat two thick slices of toast and marmalade. Roxanne rested her long mahogany nose on his forearm, adoring eyes following every move from plate to mouth. He pretended to ignore both wife and dog until he was finished. Then he leant back, and gazed at Cappy. 'Okay, then. Fire away,' he said.

She hid her face in her arms for a moment, with a mock shyness at the full force of his attention. 'I don't know where to start,' she giggled. 'You've made me feel silly.'

'The . . . what should I call it? . . . *camp*'s still there, is it?'

'I would call it that, yes. It's just like something from my childhood, when we went out in the forest with my father and he showed us how to survive. I still can't believe it, how clever it is. Tucked right in the bracken, lovely and dry.'

'And there's nobody there this morning?'

She shook her head. 'That's why I went out so early, to see if I could catch them. After all, it *is* our land. I've every right to go where I like.'

'Nobody says you haven't. What do you mean?'

She shook herself slightly, irritated or confused. 'Well, yes. But it's somebody's *home*. There's a stone circle fireplace, blankets, very likely a food store somewhere, though I didn't see it. I felt like a trespasser.'

'Well, you've probably made them desert it, like a bird leaves its nest. If they're that clever, they'll know you've been snooping about. But I thought you said you'd got news. You haven't told me anything yet. Come on, angel. I've got work to do.'

'Well, it's news that there was nobody there. And the fire was cold. I was examining it when I heard the shots. I was really scared for a minute. I thought they were shooting at *me*. Amazing how the sound carries.'

'Well, I didn't hear it. Deep asleep, I was. I haven't got over my rude awakening, yet. You must have really flown down from the woods.'

'Four-minute mile, I think. How far would you say it is?'

'Less than half a mile. Still quite a run. Nice to know you're so fit. They'd only just discovered Sam when I got there, by the looks of it.'

'Poor Sam. What a thing. What have you told the police?' This aspect of the story plainly absorbed most of her thoughts.

254

'Nothing much more than I've said already. Least said the better, if you ask me. That's an end to any more mischief in the woods, anyway.'

'Oh?'

'Of course it is. Security, for a start. The place will be crawling with law-enforcers now. Redstone'll have to be sold, as well, or rented to someone who can run it. Roddy hasn't much idea – he and I made a real mess of the milking just now. It's all finished for the Beardons, believe me.'

She shook her head, her face serious. 'I don't think so, Jon. I think there's a way to go yet. It's all such a mess, with three people killed. If I were you, I'd be just a weeny bit worried about that interview at the police station. They'll want to know a whole lot of background. Gossip, hunches – the complete story. Now, go and count your beasts, and stop being so annoying.'

'Annoying! Me? That's impossible.' He laughed, but his feelings were ruffled by her words. As he and Roxanne made their regular trip around the bullock field, he wondered what she'd meant.

Before Jonathan got back, Cappy had a visitor. Tim Rickworth drove into the courtyard in his sporty car, and jumped out almost before the engine had died. Cappy saw him from the kitchen and went out to meet him. They stood several feet apart, assessing each other suspiciously, like cowboys preparing to draw.

'Something's happened at Redstone,' he said. 'Someth· else. This morning.'

She nodded. 'That's right. Sam's been shot.'

255

'*Sam*?' His voice was shrill with disbelief. 'Surely not! What on earth is happening to this place? It's like 1930s Chicago.'

'Not quite. But yes, it is terrible. He was such an – *innocent* person.'

'Was? He's dead, then?'

Cappy paused for two seconds before nodding. 'Instantly, by all accounts.'

'Perhaps he wasn't quite so innocent, then. I mean, somebody must have thought he deserved to die. This should mean the list of suspects is getting shorter, anyway.'

Cappy pouted her disagreement. 'I wouldn't quite say that,' she demurred.

'Come on. Think about it. This keeps it strictly local, surely? Something very nasty in Redstone's woodshed, if you ask me.'

Cappy made no reply. She turned away, moving slowly towards the big trough overflowing with nasturtiums and trailing begonia. Tim watched her flicking at fat stripey caterpillars which had infested the nasturtiums. When they landed on the ground, she crushed them under her sandal.

'They turn into butterflies, you know,' he said mildly, fighting not to let his disgust show on his lips.

'What? What do?'

'Those caterpillars,' he nodded.

She stared at what she'd done, and laughed briefly. 'But they eat my flowers first. I can't allow that, can I?'

Before he could respond to that, Tim was knocked violently from behind, and almost pushed off his feet. For a moment he t rigid, hands held out vertically as if ready for a karate . Then he span round in a blur of movement.

'Roxanne!' came Jonathan's voice, still some distance away. 'Put him down this minute.'

The dog ignored her master. Tim swung round and faced the dusty red creature raised up on hind legs, tongue lolling, unpleasant breath huffing into his face. Tim did not like dogs very much. He pushed it away, roughly, angry at the shock he'd received. Angry, too, at Jonathan's jokey attitude. The animal should be better controlled: it could hurt someone behaving like this.

'Come and have some coffee,' Jonathan invited, clapping Tim matily on the upper arm. 'Sorry about Roxanne. She can't believe you don't love her, you see. Neither can I, to be honest. You must be lacking in soul.'

And what about your wife, stamping on caterpillars? Tim silently retorted. *Where's the soul in that?*

'Heard about poor old Sam, then?' Jonathan continued. 'Chaos is come again, it would seem. Can't wait for this whole business to be over and done with. Ghastly for poor Lilah. I'm fond of that girl, you know. Hate to see her in such a mess.' He was breathing heavily, as if he'd been running, although he'd come walking at normal speed into the yard. He looked round for Cappy, but she hadn't followed them into the house.

'Well, well,' he went on thoughtfully. 'Maybe you can help with a dilemma, now you're here. Or at least tell me I'm doing the right thing.'

Tim sat at the table, waiting for more.

Quickly, as he made the coffee, Jonathan told his visi about the mucky clothes and shoe that he and Roxanne found. He explained that he had done nothing with on the assumption that he was protecting Sam. He related the agreement he'd come to with Miranda about it, and how there was little reason to help the police to prosecute Sam for murder, in the circumstances.

'But now everything's different. And of course we don't even know for sure that the things belonged to Sam. Thinking about it this morning, I realised they probably didn't. We just jumped to that conclusion.'

'Where's the stuff now?'

'In a bucket in the barn. I guess I'll have to produce it, and give the police all the help I can. They want me to go along for further questioning this afternoon.'

'Hmmm.' Tim stared into his coffee, trying to think. 'They'll want to know why you kept it back before.'

'I know. But I've got my story straight. More or less the truth, actually. How I'd felt a sense of natural justice, if Sam killed Guy, after years of intimidation and bullying.'

'Is that true?'

'Partly. I dare say it's all a lot more complicated than it looks.'

'They'll be furious with you. Withholding vital evidence. Obstructing the course of justice. I wouldn't be in your shoes.'

Jonathan shook his head. 'It won't be very nice, I'm sure. But I doubt if they'll actually bring me to book over it. They'll be too relieved to get the stuff now. It might make all the difference.'

Cappy drifted into the kitchen then. She'd obviously eard the last few words and looked intently at Jonathan. re you talking about those clothes?' she demanded.

He nodded. 'Why? What's the problem?'

appy leant back against the edge of the sink, the muscles

of her neck tight. 'I told you to *leave* it,' she hissed. 'Why can't you listen to me?'

'It's all different now,' he said mildly. 'And I don't think it can have been Sam's clothes after all. We should have another look. That shoe – it's a trainer. Can you see Sam wearing trainers?'

'Of course. Everybody wears trainers. I've seen old men in trainers.'

'Not when they're going out to milk the cows. Boots, pet. Farming people wear boots. Wellingtons. Big rubber things.' He laughed at her, the smooth English aristocrat tutoring the ignorant foreigner. She gripped the stainless steel with both hands, arching her back like a cat.

'You're a complete fool sometimes, you know,' she said, the words ice cold with rage. Then she pushed herself away from her support and swept out of the room.

Tim cleared his throat. 'Just like home,' he said.

Jonathan was pale. 'I've no idea why she's like that about it,' he said shakily.

'Probably just what I said. The police being upset with you. Getting involved in something like this – you never know which way it'll go. Maybe she thinks they'll take you in as a suspect.'

Jonathan shook his head. 'No chance. Whatever they find on that gun, it won't be *my* fingerprints.'

'They found the gun then?' Tim sounded surprised.

Jonathan nodded. 'Probably got a full list of prints on it by now. We all had to be done, look.' He held out both hands, smudges of black still evident on all ten digits. 'It was fun, in a daft sort of way.'

Tim drained the last of his coffee and got to his feet. 'Well, I can't stop,' he said. 'I'm supposed to be somewhere else.'

'Okay.' Jonathan didn't move. 'Didn't think you'd want to inspect the evidence. It is a bit niffy, even after all this time.'

'What is it now? Four weeks since Guy died? Doesn't seem as much as that. Weird business, the whole thing. And I thought Sarah and I were the biggest excitement the village would ever see.'

'You're deadly dull compared to a murder. And don't get ideas. It might be nice to have a truce for a while, come to that.'

'Some hopes. I married a harpy. A banshee. And yet . . .'

'I know. She's a darling deep down. Get help, man. It can't be healthy, going on as you two do.'

'Anyway. I'm off. See you. Have fun in your interrogation. And if there's any juicy news, let's hear it, okay?'

As Tim drove away, Cappy reappeared, and stood beside Jonathan, watching the car disappear. 'Sorry,' she said. 'He has that effect on me. No wonder Sarah's so screwed up.'

He turned to her, pulling her to his chest, rubbing his cheek against the top of her head, savouring the glossy black hair. 'It was me you were cross with, not Tim. Don't pretend.'

'Well, I'm all right again now. I just think—'

'I know. You're worried that I'm getting in too deeply. You're probably right, but I can't see much option at this stage.'

She rubbed his back, purring her affection. 'Never mind, J. It'll be all right. Now, let me go, will you. I want

260

to have another look at that camp. It's intriguing me terribly. I can't bear not knowing who's been there. Why haven't we heard anything?'

'There was some noise, a week or so ago. Remember? Shouting. Laughing. A woman. We were busy at the time.' He grinned wolfishly, to indicate exactly what they'd been busy doing.

Cappy giggled, and then shook her head. 'I don't even remember. Did you say anything at the time?'

'Possibly not. It was latish evening, and a weekend. I just assumed it was grockles. Anyway, if you're determined to go back, just be careful. I ought not to let you go at all, in the circumstances. I suppose we can at least be sure there isn't a gun lying around.'

The phone warbled from the hallway, stemming Cappy's mock outrage at Jonathan's words. He went to answer it.

It was Lilah. 'They got the fingerprint results,' she said, excitement plainly audible in her voice. 'All the obvious ones – plus Amos Grimsdale's and a mysterious stranger. They're going to arrest Amos, I think. I thought I'd better tell you.'

'Thanks.' He thought quickly. 'Do I still have to go in for questioning now?'

'I have no idea.'

'I suppose I do.' He thought again. 'But, *Amos*? Do they believe he killed your father as well? Why would he?'

'I suppose he's no less likely than anyone else. I hav taken it in yet. They'll need much more evidence, presum I must go now. Bye.'

'Bye.'

Cappy was watching him. '*Amos?*' she queried.

'So it seems.' They stared at each other, assessing this news. Finally Cappy spoke.

'Nonsense,' she said flatly. 'Absolute nonsense.'

Chapter Twenty-Four

Lilah was still light-headed with shock when Den's car came into the yard, close to midday. The frenetic activity had died down after the discovery of Amos's fingerprints on the gun. Sam's room had been thoroughly examined, and the door sealed, which had the effect of making the family feel the farm was somehow no longer theirs. They knew they couldn't keep it running on their own, anyway, beyond a few struggling weeks – a realisation that had dawned almost instantly upon the acceptance that they had lost Sam.

By the time of Den's arrival, Lilah felt as if she had been living with a police presence for months, and they would never go away and let life become even slightly normal again. Roddy and Jonathan had floundered through the morning milking with great difficulty, dropping units and making the cows nervous. The resulting milk missed the tanker, and had to be poured away. For Lilah that seemed to sum it all up. Everything was hopeless and futile, and out of control.

Den stood awkwardly, his face gravely concerned. 'Didn' think I'd see you today,' he said, quietly. 'I can't believe it

'No.' She understood, vaguely, that he couldn't allow himself to be unduly sympathetic or reassuring. After the morning's questioning and investigating, she knew that this time she herself could not be exempted from suspicion. Den had probably been told not to get soft with her – unless it was as a way of getting her to betray all she knew.

'Are you here officially?' she asked, boldly. 'You're obviously on duty.' She drew her gaze down his pristine uniform, thinking how distant it made him, how unsatisfactory as a potential comforter. He just nodded.

'So?' she persisted. 'What are you supposed to do?'

Still he was silent. Then he turned back to the car, as its radio spoke scratchily. 'Just lending a hand,' he threw back at her, almost over his shoulder. 'Seeing whether anything strikes me. Knowing the place already – Inspector Jennings thought I might come in useful.' He picked up his phone and muttered into it, his eyes on his colleagues, who were currently examining Miranda's patch of front garden. They were making no attempt to avoid damage, and the lupins and roses that struggled amongst the weeds were all looking bent and bedraggled. Lilah felt a flash of anger. What did they think they'd find – a footprint of someone who'd been stupid enough to scramble over a hedge when there was a perfectly good gate five feet away?

Den came back to her, slowly. 'I don't suppose you're allowed to tell me anything?' she challenged. 'Even though it's my life that's being turned inside out?'

He shook his head. 'Gunshot wounds. Very close range. One to the neck and one to the upper back. Died almost immediately—'

'Just had long enough to scream,' she spat. 'Not quite that immediate, was it?'

He waited, looking down into her eyes, examining her as he'd done in the coffee shop. *Not many people would face me like this*, she thought. *Not today.*

Then he spoke, as one human being to another, 'All I can tell you is stuff you know already.'

'I suppose all this is very interesting to you – the scene of a double murder. Triple, if you count Isaac.' Her tone was still obstinately sharp, almost spiteful.

'Very interesting,' he agreed mildly. 'I've never seen an operation like this before. They're bringing just about everyone in on it. The whole works.'

'Lucky us,' growled Lilah. 'And the neighbours haven't even heard about it yet.'

'Neighbours? I thought Mabberley—'

'Oh, yes, *he* was here almost as soon as it happened. I mean the people in the village. We were in the pub only last night. What on earth are they going to think? God, listen to me! That's exactly what Mum said, when we found Sam. What does it matter?'

Den rubbed his face with a broad long-fingered hand, in a gesture that reminded Lilah acutely of Sam. He seemed to be thinking hard, saying nothing for some time. Then he spoke slowly, carefully.

'Sam might not have died, if we'd been sharper.'

'Sharper about what?'

'Your dad. Remember? Nobody thought he'd been murdered at first.'

'It was Sam who swept away all the signs. Some peo think Sam killed Daddy.'

Den's eyebrows jerked. 'What about you? Do you think that?'

'Nothing makes any sense to me now. If Sam had shot himself, then yes, that would have been the obvious explanation. Now they're going after poor old Amos. Why should *he* kill Sam? That's as crazy as thinking Sam killed Daddy. There's just a horrible mass of possibilities. And . . . I don't dare to trust anybody. They all seem to have dirty secrets, twisted minds. In the pub, everyone was wary of us. It was horrible. I feel as though I've lifted up a stone and all kinds of foul things have come crawling out.'

'Who exactly are you talking about?'

She looked at him warily. 'Are you going to take notes? Make a list of suspects? Are you my friend, or Mr Detective Policeman?'

He spread his hands. 'Both, I hope. If you want to talk it through, I can listen intelligently. If you confess to the crimes, though, I'll have to take you in.' She waited for a laugh that didn't come, but an examination of his face assured her that he was at least partly joking. She paused and then started walking away from the yard, towards the nearest field. He followed her warily.

'There's a nice big rock over here, where I sometimes sit. It gets the midday sun. It'll probably be rather hot for you in that outfit, though.'

He smiled submissively, putting himself at her disposal. She led him to the spot and sat down at one end of the long granite seat, at a slightly higher level than the rest of the surrounding ground. Den patted it thoughtfully. 'Looks like n old gatepost,' he said. Lilah looked down at it in surprise. e'd always taken it for something natural, placed there by ire for her enjoyment.

'How's Endurance?' he asked.

'What?'

'The calf. Is she okay?'

'Oh! Yes, thanks, she's okay. A bit of a pest to feed, but Mum's supposed to be in charge of that. I have to make sure she remembers, though.'

'Sounds as if it's all go.'

'Tell me about it.' She sat in silence, grabbing at long grass blades growing against the granite, twisting them around her fingers. Then she frowned and began to speak.

'It's just so complicated. The obvious suspects are the ones I'm closest to. At the moment—' she glanced over her shoulder at the house, and reduced her voice to a whisper '—the one I'm most bothered about is my mother.'

Den smiled and stifled a dismissive laugh. He laid a hand lightly on her shoulder, and turned her half around. 'Let *us* worry about the suspects. You just tell me how all this is affecting you. I know a bit about debriefing.'

'I think I've been debriefed already. Isn't that what all the questions this morning were about?'

'Were there lots of questions?'

'Well, it seemed like a lot. Including yet more about Dad, and his first family. They wanted Barbara's address. That's his first wife. She's not going to be too pleased when the police turn up on her doorstep, is she? Is this going to go on much longer?'

'I shouldn't think so. By now they might have got confession from Amos, and the whole exercise will be over and done with.'

'I wish I could believe that. Though obviously I do

the idea of Amos facing a trial and prison and everything. If he did do all three murders, he must be mad, mustn't he? There's no other explanation.'

'I thought it was the brother who was potty, not Amos.'

Lilah nodded. 'So did I,' she sighed. 'I really don't think a set of fingerprints is enough to convince me it's him. Daddy might have lent him the gun at any time. Or just showed it to him, let him play with it—'

'*Play* with it? A gun isn't a toy.'

'I know it isn't. But we never took that gun particularly seriously; never saw it as something that could harm a *person*. It's something all farmers have, for shooting crows and things. Sam took it into his room because he was the head of the farm, after Daddy died. It seemed rather a joke at the time. It sounds ridiculous, but even when someone stole it, we weren't terribly bothered – least of all Sam.'

'Wait, wait. Nobody's told me anything about it being stolen. Explain.'

Briefly she ran over it again, finishing with, 'You don't think about guns killing people in this sort of community. I know there are accidents sometimes, but it's entirely the wrong sort of gun.'

'Do you think Sam just moved it to a better hiding place and didn't want you to know where it was? Would he have done that?'

She shrugged. 'I can't see why he'd want to, but it would ore or less fit with what's happened, so he might have done. might never know what really happened.' She sighed, sniffed back threatening tears.

ll me about him,' suggested Den. 'I saw hardly anything

of him when I came before. He struck me as a real countryman.'

'That's the image he liked to present. There wasn't much truth in it, really. He grew up in a town, and did pretty well at school, I think. My dad was his teacher originally. That's how they met. Daddy knew Sam before I was born. Before he met Mum. They go back at least twenty-five years.'

'That might be a key to the whole mystery. What is it that Adam Dalgliesh always says? The answer to a murder usually lies in the past. Something like that.'

'I don't read murder stories, and I don't expect I ever will now. But it's obvious, really. Unless it's some kind of fight about drugs, or a man killing his unfaithful wife on impulse. You have to hate someone to murder them. And hate needs a long time to build up and fester. People nurse it and feed it until it gets big and strong. Horrible.' She shuddered and looked round at the bright green of the summer grass, everything fresh and peaceful and reassuring. Somewhere, behind one of those hedges, over one of those hills, a murderer had walked away, a man who had held a gun a few inches from Sam's back and shot him. She tried for the twentieth time to fit Amos Grimsdale to this picture, and failed yet again.

'He must have known Sam would fall into the nettles. He must have done that on purpose.' She paused, staring at a big oak in the corner of the next field. 'Hate would make you do that. Just like hate would make someone enjoy the sight of Daddy drowning in slurry.'

'You're too young to be knowing about hate,' remarked, his voice full of sadness.

Lilah was annoyed. 'Don't patronise. I'm old enough

269

'Who do you hate, then?'

'Mr Rivers,' came the prompt reply. Den knew immediately who she meant, and the shared memory of school was a warm, comforting thing to Lilah. But Den spoilt it a little by laughing in disbelief.

'But he's just a harmless old buffoon.'

'That's why I hate him. Harmless old buffoons shouldn't be teaching history. It was his fault I got a D.'

'Me too. But I figured it was down to me, as much as him.'

'No, it was him. I spent every lesson loathing him so passionately – and working out ways of murdering him – that I never heard anything he tried to teach us.'

'He's retiring soon, surely?'

'This term. Yes. Not soon enough.'

'So Miss Lilah Beardon feels she might be capable of murder?'

'I think everyone is. But I didn't kill Daddy or Sam. And if I really decided to kill Mr Rivers, I'd use poison.'

Den plainly had more to say, but he swallowed it down, and maintained a light, bantering tone. 'I can promise you that nobody is going to regard you as a suspect. You come right at the very end of the list, if I'm any judge.'

She shifted closer to him, grateful for his efforts, her bare arm against his navy jumper. 'That's a comfort, I suppose. Though not much. I can't stop thinking about poor Sam. How could anybody be so cruel? I keep thinking how ightened he must be been. It's like one of those things ı hear on the news – people dragged out of bed in the v hours and taken out and shot.'

'An execution, you mean? So – was he being punished for killing Isaac? Or your father?'

'Who would do that? Nobody I know has much sense of justice. When Daddy died, they all just wanted to hush it up and try to carry on as usual.'

'Who are these people? Your mother, for one. And?'

'Jonathan, Roddy, Cappy, Sylvia. They all seemed to cope just fine with the idea that Sam pushed Daddy into the slurry, because of the way Daddy used to treat him – and perhaps for another reason as well, which I'm not going to tell you about. They said it would be wrong to say anything to the police about it. Sam had a lot to put up with, and not much of a life, and was no danger to anyone else. And Daddy simply got what he deserved,' she choked. 'Isn't that terrible.'

'But you went along with it?'

'I never managed to *believe* it. Even when it did seem logical, I couldn't convince myself that Sam had committed murder. Remember, I saw him when Daddy was first found. I saw the horror on his face. I feel in my gut that he didn't do it.'

'So someone has killed three times now? The same person?'

'I think so, yes. Someone with a very sick mind. Ruthless. Evil. Someone I am starting to feel very, very scared of.'

'So if it was Amos, you'll feel much safer.'

'Of course.'

'The minute he confesses, I'll let you know,' he promised. 'It's what everyone's hoping for now.'

Lilah shuddered, and leant more heavily against him, seeking protection. For the first time, the coming night became a potential time of terror for her. The disgust and shock she had been feeling had modified into fear.

recent days. Now she saw herself as impossibly vulnerable, trying to sleep in a house where two murders had happened. Guy as a victim had made some kind of sense. A strong, difficult man felled by a nemesis partly of his own making. But Sam – a harmless individual whose acts had never appeared to attract malice or resentment – was an altogether more appalling quarry. It was entirely unfair that he should be murdered. And worse than unfair: it contravened some cosmic regulation, which once breached could only lead to catastrophe. If Sam could be brutally murdered, then anybody could.

'I think you'd better consider moving out – all of you – if we can't pin anything on Amos. Get someone to do the milking for the time being, and go and stay in town. Nobody would expect you to go on sleeping here after all this.'

'It's not just the milking. There are calves, and heifers in the fields. And there's hay to cut. It won't all just *stop*, however much we might want it to.'

'Send the calves and heifers to market, and forget about the hay,' he suggested in a sensible, rational tone. He was totally unprepared for her response. Her face tightened, and then suddenly she exploded into loud sobs. She didn't even try to explain to him the anguish that he had triggered with his words. She had faced the idea of moving away from the farm permanently, and selling off the stock, earlier that morning, but it had been an idea for the future and a mildly appealing one. It had spelt freedom from work and worry then. But to think of her own calves, reared largely her, known intimately by name and character, being n round a noisy market ring with red-faced farmers bidding casually for their lives, was intolerable. It was as if Den had suggested she take them out one by one and shoot them.

Silently, he handed her a large paper tissue, and waited for her to subside. 'Sorry,' she sniffed.

'It's too soon,' he said. 'I should have known.'

'No, it isn't. I'm okay, really. It's just . . . sending young animals off to slaughter is always dreadful.'

'They wouldn't be slaughtered, though. Someone would buy the heifers to join another milking herd, and the calves would be reared, just the same as they would here.'

She gave him a wordless look of respect at his easy knowledge of dairy farming. Even at school, she had had to explain to most of her friends how it all worked.

Den went on, 'And whatever happens, at least you'd be safe. The whole force is taking this seriously now. You'll be given five-star protection now, if you want it.'

'That sounds awful. Armed guards at the door.' She shuddered.

'Not quite. Anyway, we're getting ahead of ourselves. I'm going back to the station now, to see how they're getting on there. I'll phone you as soon as there's any news. And I haven't forgotten about taking you out. I'd make a date now, but I have a feeling life is going to get pretty busy over the next few days.'

'I'll look forward to it,' she said, with a weak little smile.

He turned his car in the yard and set off up the driv in second gear, thinking about the Beardons and the avalanche of trouble, trying to imagine what it must be living in the middle of something so cataclysmic. He noticed the figure of Sylvia Westerby on a bike at the last minute, where she was leaning into a bush to give him space to pass. She looked innocuous enough, waving cheerily at him, and pushing off again as soon as he was past her. It was interesting, he mused, how often she seemed to turn up and how close she seemed to be to the Beardon family.

Chapter Twenty-Five

Sylvia came cycling into the yard like a racer, glancing curiously at the few remaining police officers and the vivid tapes they'd stretched around the nettle patch. She went into the house without knocking.

'My God, what's all this?' she demanded of her friend. Miranda was sitting at the table, a cold mug of coffee beside her. 'The village is buzzing.'

'It's just like living in a nightmare, Sylv. Thanks for coming. I didn't hear the car.'

'I came on the bike. I thought the yard might not take another vehicle.'

She spoke quickly, slightly breathless. Miranda barely responded.

'I gather it's Sam. What happened exactly?'

'Somebody shot him. They think it was Amos Grimr̄ Why, Sylv? Why would Amos – or *anybody* – do that just makes no sense to me. I thought he might kill hir̄ when I realised he'd taken Guy's gun. But I couldn̄ anything – how could I? I didn't even dare to be him, because he'd think I was trying to seduce him again.'

'So you were horrible to him, were you?'

'Not at all. Just – neutral. He seemed all right. With so much to do, and being in charge. I thought he was coming into his own. It was all looking fairly manageable, these past few days.'

'So why think he'd kill himself?'

'Oh, well – it seems so stupid now. This was definitely murder. You can't shoot yourself in the back, even by accident.'

'Tell me.' Sylvia moved a chair close to Miranda's and sat sideways on it, only a few inches away. Miranda kept her gaze on the table.

'I was an idiot. I came to the conclusion, you see, that Sam killed Guy. It seemed obvious – there wasn't anybody else. At least . . .'

'At least nobody else you could bear to consider,' finished Sylvia softly. She put a hand lightly on her friend's arm. Miranda moaned.

'It'll be all right,' Sylvia reassured, leaning forward and taking Miranda's hand. 'They're being terribly thorough out there.' She glanced through the window towards the yard, almost nervously. 'I've never seen anything like it.'

'Lilah's got very friendly with one of the policemen. He's a nice boy, I think. He seems to be helping her. I hope it makes her feel safer, anyway.'

'Come on, Em. You're not in any danger.'

'How can you say that? Let me tell you, it feels very much as if we're being picked off one by one. I don't know we'll get through the next few nights, if it turns out wrong about Amos. And I can't help feeling they are. I mean – *Amos*. He wouldn't hurt anybody, surely?'

Sylvia pursed her lips and gazed out of the window. After a while, she said, 'Do you want me to come and stay with you? I could manage it for a bit.'

'No, don't be silly. You can't leave all your livestock. That's the trouble with both of us – all these damned *animals* hanging round our necks. You know what Lilah said, when we found Sam? *We'll really have to sell the farm now.* It's always the first thing she thinks about – the farm.'

'She might be right, though,' Sylvia commented. 'You certainly can't go on like this, even if some of us organise a rota to come and help you for a bit.'

'Who would be prepared to do that?'

Sylvia made a sweeping gesture. 'Oh, several people, I should think. They'll all be curious to see what's going on up here, for one thing. You're celebrities now, you know.'

'Oh.' Miranda was flat again. 'You mean Hetty, I suppose. She'll be around again for Sam's funeral, no doubt.'

'Not Hetty, no. Me, for one. And Jonathan.'

'And Wing Commander Stradling for good measure? And the vicar? God, I'd rather we just sent all the cows to market tomorrow than that.' She noticed Sylvia's recoil. 'Oh, sorry, love. I didn't mean it like that. I'd be thrilled if *you* came to help – of course I would. But I can't think about it yet. Not with all those policemen under our feet, and the children having to cope with everything. Poor Roddy – what'll this do to him? I've been sitting here all morning, totally useless, with all these thoughts coming at me. Every few minutes there's a whole new lot. Things I've got to decide and d● And there's nobody I can turn to about any of it.'

'There's *me*, Miranda. I keep telling you. I can milk cows as well as anybody.'

'Yes,' sighed Miranda, as if defeated. 'Yes, I'm sure you can.'

Amos had given up any attempt to understand what was happening. Nothing made any sense. The policemen, who wanted him to say he had killed Sam Carter and Guy Beardon, and would probably be ecstatic if he'd confess to the murder of his brother while he was at it, were kind to him, so he could find no cause for complaint there. They brought him tea and biscuits and scrambled eggs. They gave him a little bed with warm blankets, and took him to the lavatory when he asked them to. They let him sleep until well after sunrise next morning. In many ways, it was preferable to hospital, apart from the talking, which hurt his head in a worse way than the bashing it had received. This time, it hurt deep inside, where he tried to understand why anyone should think he was a killer. He got the impression that the police thought he was daft, when surely everybody knew that had been Isaac, not him.

They showed him the gun, and asked if he'd ever seen it before. He shrugged. A gun was a gun. It wasn't his. He'd had one, years ago, but had thrown it away when the barrel got wobbly, and any shot would be liable to hit him in the face if he tried to use it. This one was Beardon's, they said. And it had his, Amos's, fingerprints on it. How did he explain that?

He couldn't remember ever touching the thing. He never went to Redstone, until that morning, a few days back. He adn't seen the gun then. He stared at the floor, clutching his ad between his hands, trying to remember. It didn't help that these men kept talking, nagging at him, never shouting, never bullying, but just going on and on, encouraging him to own up to something he surely hadn't done.

Just when he felt he might recall something, they switched to Beardon. Amos had pushed him in the slurry, hadn't he? Drowned him in the stuff. *Why? Why did you do that, Mr Grimsdale?*

He spread his hands, as if inviting them to find slurry on them. 'It wasn't me,' he said, eyes wide. 'It's daft to say it was me.'

He lost any sense of time. They talked at him on the first day, and then put him to bed. Next day a man turned up who said he was a solicitor, and would advise him what to say. And then *he* started asking questions and talking, just as bad as the policemen. And then, soon after, they brought him a bag of clothes, covered in dried-up flaking muck.

'Have you seen these before?' they asked. He looked. There were trousers of some sort, very mucky, and an anorak, not so bad. And a shoe. He could see it was nothing like any shoes he'd ever possessed.

'No I haven't,' he said. 'I truly haven't.' And it seemed to him that the policemen believed him. They sighed and shook their heads, and didn't ask him anything more for a while.

Den Cooper had always been interested in forensics. It had been his initial ambition to concentrate on that side of police work, and he spent as much time as he could watching the activities. The clothes that Jonathan Mabberley had brou in were a godsend, in all sorts of ways. Den had been to get them to the lab people right away, and wait for wh information they could give him on an early examination while he waited and watched.

'Women's stuff,' they said, after barely a minute. 'Tracksuit bottoms. Size sixteen. The anorak could be either sex, but look – there's a long hair on it. And another. Could be a chap, but unlikely. The collar isn't greasy. The shape's female – see how it's a bit baggy at the front? A woman with big bazongas, by the looks of it. The trainer's size seven. Small for a man. Big for a woman. But see how it's worn down at the heel. Women walk like that more than men do.'

Den went back to his superiors at top speed. 'A woman!' he said. 'Guy Beardon was killed by a woman.'

'Steady on, lad,' was the reply, or words to that effect. 'All this shows is that a woman was in that slurry at some point. No certainty that she did the farmer in.' They were fairly committed to the idea of Amos Grimsdale being the answer to everything at that point.

'What? Even Isaac?' said Den, when he realised. They sucked their teeth a little at that. After all, Amos had been hospitalised himself. And he had run bleeding down the fields to get help from Redstone.

'Could be,' they nodded. 'Stranger things have happened.'

'Rubbish,' said Den, rudely.

The file on the Beardons became unwieldy. Secretaries rattled away at keyboards, producing transcripts of interviews with Lilah, Roddy, Miranda, Jonathan, which were added to those already produced after Guy Beardon's death. Isaac Grimshaw had his own much thinner grey file but on almost every page there was a cross-reference to someone at Redstone. 'Might as well amalgamate them,' said one of the detectives, leafing through the sheaves of paper yet again. 'They're obviously the same case.'

'And yet, they're very different,' demurred his mate. 'Totally different *modus operandi*, as they say. Completely different *feel*.'

'Connected, Dave. Definitely connected. Nobody's going to tell me that two neighbouring houses can be the scene of violent death within a few weeks of each other, and *not* be connected.'

'Course I'm not saying that. After all, we've got the chap from the one place about to be booked for knocking off two victims from the other place. Except these clothes don't help. If it *was* a woman – well, a woman's not going to bash two old chaps over the head with a crowbar, is she?'

'It's not beyond the bounds of possibility, Dave. Not these days. You get some very violent women these days. And see what Cooper's put in these notes. Sylvia Westerby, for example: she's tough and strong – tall, too. Half the women in the area work outdoors, lugging hay bales up and down ladders, lifting trailers on and off towbars. Got good muscles, most of them.'

'We're not getting far, here, are we? I mean, it's close. I can feel it getting close. But we're not *there* yet. It isn't hanging together.' He banged the flat of his hand down on the bulging file. 'In fact, when you really think about it, we're making quite a pig's ear of the whole messy business. No motive, not much evidence. The long-shots have g cast-iron alibis. That son of Beardon's, the grown-up – Terry; ten thousand witnesses could say he was a

Cup Final the day his dad was killed. His brother lives in France – we've checked he hasn't been over here for the past three months. We've been thorough there. And look at the women we'd have to bring in – that Mabberley lady, for a start – not to mention the Westerby lady. Can't see either of them making a quick confession.'

The detective shook his head. 'If it has to be a woman, I'd go for Beardon's wife. Striking to look at, a fair bit younger than him, up to something with the workman . . .'

'Where did you get that from? That's not in the file.'

'The vicar let something drop, early on. Wasn't a formal interview. Just chatting to him.'

'It ought to be in the file. It's pertinent.'

'You're right, Dave. Good word, that. Very possibly, it's pertinent.'

They went back to Amos. The legal chap was making noises about letting him go if they weren't going to charge him; muted noises, however, since somebody had killed three people, and it wasn't good policing to let a prime suspect loose on the community. If necessary, they could hang on to him for a while yet.

'Women,' said Dave, before they went back into the interview room. 'Let's get him talking about women.'

So they asked Amos what he felt about the Beardon ladies, mother and daughter. He squinted at them warily and made no reply.

'Nice looking, both of them,' said Dave, casually. Amos alled his long hours of television viewing with their cop/bad cop routine, and was unmoved. His feelings for Miranda had nothing to do with these youngsters and their clumsy obtuseness. Torture wouldn't persuade him to speak about her. There was only one woman he would be prepared to talk about, and that was with a view to saving himself from further intimidation. But it wasn't easy to introduce her name into the conversation. Especially as they seemed so intent on Miranda Beardon.

'You must have seen quite a lot of her, over the years,' one of them said. 'Got friendly with her too, I dare say?'

Amos shrugged. 'Not specially,' he muttered. 'Hardly spoke to her.'

'But you went to visit her last week. What was that all about? She said you were in quite a state about something.'

The small betrayal stung Amos. Could Miranda have been cruel enough to tell these men about his tears? Had she had any idea what had caused them? Surely not, since he scarcely understood it himself. He merely shook his head at the question.

'Are you acquainted with Mrs Mabberley at all? Or Mrs Westerby, next door to the vicarage?'

Amos stared at them, impatience rising from chest to throat, so he could barely speak. 'I see the Mabberley woman now and then. She gives me a lift to the shop once in a while. Mrs Westerby blames me and Isaac for her little kid dying, years ago. Haven't hardly spoken to her from that day to this. Her's best friend with Miranda.' He shook his head again slowly.

The men exchanged glances; one jotted down a note 'Miranda? You know Mrs Beardon as Miranda, do you?'

Impossible to explain, without admitting too much.

kept his eyes on the table in front of him, and said nothing. He *thought* of her as Miranda, of course he did. But he would never say it to her face.

The man prompted. 'Mr Grimsdale? Could you answer, please?'

'It's a pretty name,' he mumbled. 'I tell you, I hardly ever spoke to her. Just a bit of a wave over the hedge, if she came to the top field. Which she didn't often do. Blackberrying, maybe. Mushrooming. She didn't do much farmwork, that I could see.'

'And you *could* see, couldn't you?' put in the other. 'From your yard, you can see right down into Redstone's.'

This was touchy territory for Amos, and he tensed. 'S'pose so,' he muttered. 'No time for staring into other folks' yards, all the same.' Mercifully, the men let it go, and moved to another topic.

'With Sam Carter dead, everything'll be different there now, won't it?' This didn't sound like much of a question to Amos, so he merely nodded. He didn't care about Sam Carter, beyond a persistent thump of surprise at his killing which never seemed to go away. Sam's death didn't seem to Amos to be part of any conceivable pattern.

'My brother's dead, too,' he said quietly. A hint of reproach reached his questioners. It was true they had given Isaac Grimsdale much less attention than he warranted. They looked at each other and grimaced briefly. 'Do you think I killed *him*?' Amos sat up straighter and looked from one to the other. 'I've told you, it was a man with his face covered up. Tall and thin. Dark eyes.'

'That's all right, sir,' said Dave, soothingly, meaninglessly. 'Now, if we could go through the Redstone murders one

284

more time. Is there anything else you think we should know about that?'

Amos sighed. It was at least a better question than the others had been. Treating him for a change as if he had some sense. But he knew nothing about the Redstone murders. He had no opinions about what had happened.

'It's got nothing to do with me,' he said finally. 'I've got troubles of my own.' Again he looked at them, willing them to listen properly. But they didn't. They thought he was simply talking about Isaac again, and they put on kind, patient expressions, sitting back in their chairs and staring at the ceiling.

'Am I going to be charged?' he asked.

'Well, we'll see about that,' Dave answered quickly. 'There's still a lot of work to do.'

Amos sighed again. He didn't mind. He wasn't in any great rush to go home; and things weren't so bad here. If he went home he'd have to do something about Isaac's long-overdue funeral. He'd have to make a whole lot of decisions about what to do next. And he'd probably have to face Phoebe again. Facing Phoebe was by far the worst thing he'd have to do. Compared to her, being interrogated by policemen was nothing.

Chapter Twenty-Six

By mid-afternoon, everyone was exhausted after their early awakening. Roddy and Lilah drifted about outside, trying to decide which jobs were the most vital. Taking food and water to calves, keeping the cows milked and the milking equipment clean were the only things that couldn't be postponed, they concluded. Put like that, it didn't seem so bad. 'Well, we can probably survive another twenty-four hours,' said Lilah. 'That seems like quite a long time, from here.'

'It does when you think back a day,' Roddy agreed, with a doleful shake of his head. Then he grinned at her. 'But we're coping okay for now. I think we're pretty brilliant so far.' The friendliness of him was like a warm blanket, and she slapped at his arm. He butted his head into her shoulder, in an intimacy they hadn't known for a long time.

At three o'clock Miranda announced that she was going to the supermarket outside town to get some much needed supplies of groceries. Roddy and Lilah drifted into Guy's office, to try to make sense of a number of letters that had ed up since Guy had died, and somehow seeing it as the best place to avoid thinking about Sam. The police had taken nothing further, and a small mound of papers now lay on the table in front of the computer. Miranda had merely opened letters addressed to Guy and thrown them into a chaotic heap.

'Funny how much easier it is to think about Daddy now,' remarked Lilah, as they sorted his correspondence. 'He hasn't faded in my mind, or anything, but it doesn't hurt so much. I dreamt he was still alive last night. I'd forgotten it, with all this drama. He was all big and warm and clean. It was lovely. Although when I woke up, I was in a panic that I hadn't done any of the things he'd expect me to. I knew he'd be cross and sarcastic, even more so with me than with you and Sam. So then I felt a sort of relief that he wasn't really alive. Quite a lot of relief, to be honest.'

'Yeah,' growled Roddy. 'I've had that dream as well. I've got used to him not yelling at me all the time. There's a kind of space where he used to be and it's getting bigger every day. I can just do what I like with my life now, without him being in control of everything. Mum won't even care what my exam results are.'

'Are you sure that's better? At least Dad paid us some attention.'

Roddy looked at her, more serious than she had ever seen him. 'Believe me, Li, it is.'

She put her hand on his arm and squeezed hard. 'He was nicer to me,' she admitted. 'It's different for me. I've got that great big space as well, but I don't think I like it much, in spite of what I just said. I don't know if I can manage without Dad giving me orders.'

'Course you can,' he said roughly. 'You're not a kid any mor whatever he might have thought. Now you can act your age.'

She removed her hand and for a moment felt like slapping him. But he stood his ground and his words echoed in her ears; she knew they were true. She even permitted the idea that without Guy's disappearance, she might never have been able to act her age. She might have been stunted all her life, trapped in the little-girl act that she'd never been aware of until these past few days.

Roddy changed the subject. 'I still feel numb about Sam. It's as if I was already full up, and there isn't any room to properly cope with what happened to him. Except those nettles . . .' He shuddered. 'And the way he screamed.'

Lilah pulled a face. 'He probably would have married Mum, like you said. They were already joint owners of Redstone. It would have kept things neat.'

'I wonder. Can't see Sylvia being too pleased about that. She wants them to be all girls together.'

'Don't start getting paranoid about Sylvia,' she advised.

'According to Hetty, she's Prime Suspect for the killing of Isaac.'

'I can understand the theory, but it feels completely wrong.' She shook her head, and went back to sifting through the letters. 'They're almost all bills,' she concluded. 'Mum will have to pay them – I can't write farm cheques.' She found a letter at the bottom of the heap that caught her attention. She turned it over, and took the sheet out of the already opened envelope. 'Hey, look at this.'

'What is it?'

'It's the bill from the undertaker for Dad's funeral.'

Roddy took it from her with a macabre snort of laughter.

'Father Edmund charged a hundred and eighty pounds for his services,' she went on. 'That seems a lot for what he did.'

'It does include the organist,' Roddy pointed out, wryly. It was then that the two heard a throat being cleared outside.

Lilah's first reaction was sheer terror. Her heart turned over and she stared wildly at her brother.

Roddy put out a reassuring hand and went to the door. He was confronted by the black-garbed vicar, his attire seeming ludicrous in the hot summer farmyard. When Lilah saw him, she gasped; she knew he must have heard them talking about him. Surely he would exact some sort of revenge?

Father Edmund looked hot and uncomfortable. 'Have you walked here?' Roddy demanded, his voice loud and accusing. 'We didn't hear a car.'

'My aggravating motor is out of action again. I got a lift to the top of your lane with Mrs Mabberley. She is a kind lady, haven't you found?'

Roddy shrugged. Cappy Mabberley was not a significant character in his life. 'I suppose you heard us just now?' he challenged.

'Roddy!' Lilah was horrified. It seemed to her that they'd successfully put the moment behind them; why in the world had he returned to it?

Father Edmund fluttered his hands in an attempt to pacify them both. He smiled, a twisted, unfriendly grimace. 'Listeners never hear well of themselves,' he told Roddy, as if this were a new-minted observation. 'But it isn't quite fair to criticise me in this instance. The church sets the fees – and takes most of them. I see almost nothing for myself, believe me. You don't begrudge poor Mrs Simpson her little bit as organis

I hope? I always think she gives us an especially magnificent performance for funerals. Now, my dears—' the two flinched at his pseudo-affection '—it's your mother I ought to speak to. Is she about somewhere? Busy, I suppose, after this morning's terrible business. Such a dreadful thing to happen. Police all over everything, I imagine, too?' He cast his eyes around the yard, taking in the official tape and the barrier across Sam's door. 'Such a very unexpected turn of events.'

'That's a strange thing to say,' frowned Lilah. 'What *did* you expect, then?'

He avoided her questioning stare, turning his large face up towards the Grimsdale house, appearing to be deep in thought. Lilah wanted to shout at him angrily, to make him go away and leave them alone. He brought with him an aura of some secret satisfaction, as if he privately relished the whole catastrophic business. A twitching smile pulled at his mouth, and his elaborate speech about the church fees could be interpreted as mocking, even cruel.

Slowly the man turned back to them. 'Your mother?' he repeated.

'She's gone into town,' said Roddy. 'What did you want her for?'

'Well, young fellow, your man Sam Carter will be needing a funeral, will he not? I just dropped by to offer my humble services once again.'

Lilah finally found her voice and seized at random on words which would make him leave. Words which would protect them all from this intruder – and that included Sam, even if he was dead. 'He has family, you know, besides us. They'll have to decide what's to happen. If it's the same as Daddy, we'll have to wait for the Coroner's Officer to give us permission to go ahead, anyway. We'll phone you when there's any news.'

'And where might this *family* be living? I understood that he'd been with your father since he was little more than a boy.'

'The police are still trying to find them, I think,' said Lilah vaguely. 'Now, if you don't mind, we're desperately busy here.'

'I suppose you'll have to walk back?' said Roddy, with obvious malice. 'Lucky it's not muddy in the lane. Hot, though.'

The vicar gave another grimace, and turned to go. They watched him pick his way through the scattered cowpats on the yard, as if it were a minefield, and slowly move out of sight up their lane.

'You could have driven him back,' Roddy said, quietly.

'There's only Daddy's car here, and I'm not insured to drive it.'

'*And* we never asked him to come. Why didn't he phone us, instead of trogging all this way? And why did you fib about Sam's family?'

'I didn't think it was any of his business. He already seemed to know too much. This is a serious business now, you know. A real murder. No shadow of a doubt, like with Daddy. You have to be careful what you say to people.'

'I don't see why. Not unless you're the murderer. *You* didn't do it, did you, Li?'

'Shut up.'

'Sor-*ree*,' he snarled, obviously hurt.

'Oh, Christ, I didn't mean it, Rod. Come on, let's sort these damned bills out and get outside to something more interesting. I wish Mum was back. I keep thinking something else awful is going to happen with just us here.'

'You are scared, aren't you? Scared of the vicar, of all people. I just hate him – always have done. Smarmy bugger. How anyone can smile like that, I don't understand. As if he wanted to hit you.'

'I remember you said that about him, when you were little. "Why does that man smile when he hates you?" you said, every time you saw him. We all thought you'd put your finger right on what he was like. No wonder I find him scary.'

Fed up with the stuffy office, he went outside and stood in the yard, looking lost. After a moment, his sister followed him.

'Doesn't it seem quiet,' she said. 'I wish Mum would hurry up.'

'I don't think I've ever been here with just you before. There was always Dad or Mum or Sam around. We're like babies, aren't we. Wanting our mother.'

'You know what I hate most about all this?' she said, thoughtfully. 'Not being able to stop thinking about it. After all that stuff with me trying to convince you that Sam killed Dad – when I never really believed it myself? Well, that's all wrong now. But the things that made us think it are all still true. They might give us some idea of who killed Sam.'

'I'd have thought you'd have had enough of detective work,' he said. 'And you don't know for sure that Dad and Sam and Isaac were all killed by the same person. It might be much more complicated than that.'

'I think it's a reasonable assumption,' she said. 'Don't you? You said there was no way in the world that Sam could commit murder. I'd have thought that what happened yesterday proved you were right. And I prefer to think it's some sort of psychopathic vagrant than one of our friends or neighbours.'

'Well, I'm going to bed really early tonight, and I'm locking my door,' he said.

'There isn't a lock on your door, idiot.'

'Then I'll barricade it with a chair. Remember what happened to Isaac.'

'No, I'd rather not. I'm much too tired for that. Let's get the milking done, quick as we can, and then off to bed.'

'We can't do it yet. The cows will think we've gone bonkers. Why don't we go in and have a little rest, and wait for Mum? We could make some tea.'

'That's a very civilised idea, Rod. Except I know I'm going to fall asleep the minute I sit down.'

When she got back with the shopping, Miranda was initially alarmed at the lack of movement in the yard or barn. Hurriedly she ran into the house, not daring to call out. It was two or three minutes before she found her children, side by side on the sofa, like exhausted toddlers. Roddy's head was on Lilah's shoulder, and both had kicked their shoes off. They were soundly asleep.

Affection for them brought tears to her eyes, as she tiptoed back to the car, pausing to take the telephone off its cradle. She carried the bags of groceries into the kitchen, stowing tins and loaves and butter and cheese in the appropriate places.

Everything was quiet, no animal sounds, no motors running. Every time she glanced out of the window, she felt she had just missed glimpsing Sam crossing the yard, intent on some task. In contrast to Lilah and Roddy, Miranda had plenty of emotion to spare for the most recent loss. Guy's death had faded, conferring a kind of status on her as his widow, and was turning out to be much less difficult to accept than she had expected. Sam was entirely different. She had unfinished business with Sam, and to have him suddenly dead was both a shock and an outrage. She cursed herself for being so slow to talk to him. Sam had been joint owner of Redstone, a fact she had never allowed herself to forget, even though it was never mentioned between them. She and Sam would surely have formed a partnership in every sense of the word, given time. To lose both her menfolk was a serious blow, and not one from which she would quickly recover.

But Miranda was not a person to succumb to ostentatious displays of grief; nor was she inclined to weep and wail. The farm would go, she had already realised that. And then she would have money and freedom – as long as she could placate Lilah.

How strange death is, she mused. Like a great brick thrown into a pond, sending ripples out, far and wide. And by some linkage in her thoughts, she was moved to put the phone back for a moment, before picking it up again and pushing the 01 memory button. Her call was answered quickly.

'Mum?' she said, trying to sound normal. 'It's me. There's some more unpleasant news from here, I'm afraid.'

It wasn't a particularly distressing conversation. Her mother had never felt anything for Sam, had barely spoken to him over all the years he'd been with them. Miranda saw no reason to betray her own complicated relationship with him. She talked for a few minutes before she understood why she had made this particular call.

'We'll have to sell Redstone, Mum,' she said. 'And that's going to mean a lot of work. A sale of livestock and machinery, showing people round, packing up, moving. I think I'll need your help.'

The reply was prolonged. Her mother reminded her that she was over seventy, and that she had all the work she could manage dealing with her father, who was getting more forgetful every day. She wondered, with some sharpness, what Miranda thought she could possibly do to help with a farm sale.

Eventually, Miranda interrupted her. 'Well, I think I get the message. Would you be interested in having our new address when we have one, or shall I just get out of your life completely?' And she slammed the phone down with a crash, wiping her hand across her eyes.

'Mum?' came a small voice from the doorway. 'Who was that? What did you mean about our new address?'

Lilah looked like a tousled child, and Miranda held out a hand to her. 'Nothing,' she said, with a quivery smile. 'I just proved to myself yet again what a lousy judge of character I am, that's all.'

Chapter Twenty-Seven

Later, after the milking had somehow been accomplished, Lilah began to speak to Miranda of her fears. 'I don't think I'll sleep very well tonight,' she began, with a strained little laugh. 'Even if Amos *was* the one who shot Sam, there's probably still someone out there who bashed Isaac to death. Where do you think he is now?'

'Far away from here, I hope,' said Miranda, with a yawn. 'Not scared of him, are you?'

'Den said I had a right to be. He said we ought to get a relief milker to take over, and someone else to keep things going, and move into town until everything's settled.'

'All right for him to talk. What about all our things? And the hens. If we're going to do something like that, then it'll be properly, after we've sold the whole place.'

'That's what I thought, too. Except I don't want to sell up. I can't imagine living anywhere else.'

'Well, I think we'll be forced to sell in September.'

'Why September?'

'Isn't that when farms are always sold? Something

to do with Lady Day or Michaelmas. We bought this in September, and moved on October the tenth. My birthday, God help me.'

'Whatever happens in September, we can't manage properly *now*. Not just the three of us. I keep thinking *Sam'll know how to do that*, and then remembering. We're completely lost without him.'

'So we can have a relief milker, but stay here and do the rest. That'll take the worst of the pressure off.'

Lilah said nothing. Her mother wasn't listening properly, refusing to understand just what trouble they were in. But all Lilah could think of was how tired she was, and how it didn't really matter if someone came and shot her in the night, if she was fast asleep and knew nothing about it. Then her mother surprised her.

'Sleep in with me tonight, why don't you? It's been a horrible day, and you've coped fantastically with it all. You can have Daddy's side of the bed, if you promise not to snore. Sylvia offered to come and stay with us, but I think I'd rather we faced it on our own, for now.'

Lilah wasn't sure how to respond to that. There were elements of her mother's friendship with Sylvia that she had always found unsettling. She smiled faintly at her mother's uncharacteristic solicitude. 'That'll be nice. Thanks.'

'Good. Now, go and have a bath and get to bed.'

'But it's barely eight o'clock.'

'So? You've been awake since five – that's long enough for anybody. Get along with you. I'll be up myself in a bit, when I've got Roddy in.'

'Where is he?'

'Outside, shutting up the hens, I think. If he hasn't fallen asleep somewhere.'

'Aren't you worried about him?'

Miranda sighed. 'Of course I am. But I can't say anything, can I? He's an adolescent boy. If he's not scared, that's something to be thankful for.'

'But—'

'Hush now. Leave Roddy to me. I won't let anything happen to him.'

'Is he sleeping in with us as well?'

Miranda laughed. 'No, but I might suggest he puts a chair across his door.'

'Don't bother. He's already thought of that for himself.'

Lilah dropped off to sleep in the bath, and dreamt vividly of a catlike figure lurking in the shadows of the yard, waiting to pounce and kill. She woke with a jerk of panic, splashing the cooling water and taking a moment to realise where she was. Heavily, she got out and dried herself, then pulled on a long T-shirt and padded into her parents' bedroom. Guy's side was no longer as it had been when he was alive. The bedside table had gone, replaced by a bookcase. A clean, plump pillow awaited her, and she let her head sink into it, feeling young and frightened. Her insides were hollow, as if she'd been filled with some kind of cold gas. Her last thought was for the morning milking, inescapably looming up. And then tomorrow evening's milking. And the morning after that. It seemed impossible. She knew she wouldn't do it properly. *Maybe*, she thought muzzily, *maybe Sam'll come back*.

* * *

Miranda's mother phoned back the next day, and got Lilah. 'Your mother sounded very upset,' were the cautious opening words. 'I hope she's over it today?'

'It'll take a bit longer than that,' the girl replied, only half her attention on the conversation. She was watching Roddy outside, trying to get the tractor into reverse gear. It had taken him ten minutes to start it. Roddy had never been very good with the machinery, and had only driven the tractor in times of crisis.

'Well, dear, I didn't mean to make her so cross. It was just . . .'

'Oh, I don't think it's you, Granny. It's everything here. She told you about Sam, I suppose.'

'She said you'd have to sell the farm. I don't really understand why. It all sounds like some kind of nightmare.'

'That's exactly what it's like. Everything's falling apart. Except—' She had woken with a faint stirring of optimism, after a long and peaceful night's sleep in her mother's bed.

'Well, I don't know what to say,' twittered her grandmother. 'It's all too much for me, at my age.'

'Too much at any age, I should think.'

'So what are the police doing about it? Haven't they arrested anybody yet?'

'Well, sort of. Though we haven't heard anything definite. I don't suppose it'll be long now.' Outside, Roddy had found reverse gear, and the tractor had taken a sudden leap backwards, narrowly missing the corner of the barn. Lilah gave a small yelp of alarm.

'What, dear? What's the matter?'

'Oh, nothing, Granny. Look, I can't really talk to you now

'Well.' The voice was decidedly offended. 'I just thought . . .'

'I know. I'll tell Mum you rang. Bye.'

She blew out her cheeks with exasperation as she put the receiver down. What a waste of breath *that* had been. Poor Roddy was still wrestling with the tractor controls, his face pale, as she went outside to help him, giving the back of the tractor a very wide berth.

'What are you grinning about?' her brother demanded. 'This bloody thing's impossible.'

'Leave it,' she called, over the engine noise. 'You're going to cause an accident. What were you trying to do, anyway?'

He switched it off, but didn't move to get down from the cab. 'I've got to be able to use it. I was practising, that's all.'

'Well, it's pretty stupid to do it on your own. I could have shown you how to work it.'

'I *know* how to work it. I got it started, didn't I? I twiddled all the right levers.' Lilah walked to the open-sided engine and peered in.

'So you did,' she said. And she turned them all off again. 'Now let's get down to something useful.'

'Who was on the phone?'

'Oh, Granny. She's such a pain. Silly old biddy, waffling on. Mum yelled at her yesterday, and I suppose she's fishing for an apology.'

'Everybody's silly and stupid to you today.'

Lilah paused a moment. 'Yes, they are,' she agreed, and marched off to the barn. 'And these stupid calves need feeding!' she called over her shoulder.

* * *

300

Lilah found her mother mildly stupid that day, as well. After the restful night, where exhaustion had swamped every emotion, she'd woken feeling infinitely better, and at first assumed that everyone else would be the same. Even before the call from her grandmother, Lilah had found that this was not the case.

'God, I wish I could get away from here,' were the first words she heard Miranda say when she woke up. 'I'm going to have to find a way of escaping, even if only for a few hours.'

'You went shopping yesterday,' Lilah pointed out.

'That doesn't count.'

'So where might you go, leaving me and Roddy to the wolves?'

'Don't worry, I'd come back and defend you at bedtime. But I'm useless here anyway. I could go and see the land agents, for a start. And think about where we might move to. With Roddy going on to A levels next term, the timing's really not too bad.'

'Oh, Mum. Don't start that again.' And Lilah had run downstairs, refusing to listen to any more.

After the phonecall, and Roddy's awful attempts at tractor driving, the final remnants of Lilah's good mood evaporated. She thought about Sam, dead in the nettles, and now lying on some cold metal tray, being probed by pathologists. It was not much more than twenty-four hours ago, and already it felt like weeks. Unlike Guy, Sam had left few physical traces of himself behind. The police had asked them not to go into his room until they'd finished examining it, and Sam had been meticulous about keeping all his things in there. Everything around the farm had been used equally by the two men, but somehow Guy's mark was still the one left on everything. His quirky names for things, his rage if anything was left out of place, his make-do-and-mend with lengths of wire and string – everything still shouted the fact of his existence. It was almost as if Sam himself had never been much more than a ghost.

After lunch, when there was a brief lull in the farmwork, Lilah remembered her father's will. 'Did Sam make a will?' she asked her mother.

'I shouldn't think so. Not to my knowledge.'

'So who inherits his share of Redstone?'

'I was rather imagining it must be me.'

'Is that how it works? Surely he did have relations somewhere, even if he never talked about them?'

Miranda rubbed her brow, between the eyes. 'He did. He had a brother, quite a lot older. I met him once, before we moved here. Let's hope he's dead by now.'

'He wouldn't be *that* old. The solicitor will have to look for him.'

'I wish you hadn't raised this subject,' Miranda sighed. 'Now I'm going to worry that we'll *never* afford to buy a new house. Not if we have to give a chunk of what we get for Redstone to some strange Carter man. The law of inheritance is very unfair – I've always thought so.'

'If Dad hadn't made a will, would Sam have inherited anything?'

'I assume not. But can we stop this please? I had to go over it all with the police yesterday, including Sam's brother. They seemed to think he might have to be investigated, which is stretching it a bit, if you ask me. I can't believe he'd have heard about Guy, guessed Sam had inherited something and come out here to kill him. It's preposterous.'

Lilah shook her head at this diversion. 'I'm not talking about motives for murder. I'm talking about what's going to happen to *us*.'

Miranda shrugged. 'We'll figure something out; we'll have to, won't we?'

Lilah put both hands to her head. Somewhere there was a thread leading out of this mess, but all she could see so far was a fog of hopelessness, with destitution at the end of it.

The phone continued to intrude into the day. Midway through the afternoon, Den called, and asked for Lilah when Roddy answered.

'Lover boy,' he said, with a rude face, handing Lilah the receiver.

'There's been a development,' Den said. 'Yesterday, Jonathan Mabberley brought in some mucky clothes he'd found. We think they must have been worn by someone who'd got into the slurry pit.'

Lilah drew breath to tell him oh yes, she knew all about the clothes, but she found the sense to keep quiet. 'Oh?' was all she said.

'And we're certain they were worn by a woman.'

'Ah.' It jolted her, fear and surprise filling her throat, swelling her heart.

'So that's the way the investigation's going now. They want me to tell you and your mother that there'll be someone along to ask you a few more questions. Not sure when.'

'Any chance that it'll be you?'

'Not an earthly. I'm not even in the running. It'll probably be Dave Spooner. He's okay.'

'So when will I see you?' She sounded pathetic to her own ears, but was well beyond caring.

'Not sure.'

She paused, giving him time to say something personal, something friendly, but he didn't. Disappointment added to the leaden sensation inside her. How stupid of her to expect anything else.

'Bye then,' she said, and put the phone down before he could say anything else. Only then did she realise that he must have been in a roomful of people, not daring to say anything more.

She went to find Roddy and told him what Den had said. His reaction came so quickly, Lilah could hardly register what he'd said.

'A *woman*? Somebody Dad was having an affair with, you mean?'

She gazed at him, trying to follow his thought processes. 'Maybe,' she finally agreed, trying to ignore the sharp pang of denial that pierced her at the very idea. If her mother could have adulterous relationships, then why not her father, too? 'But who? I can't think of any likely candidates, can you?'

Roddy snorted. 'Only about a dozen. Let's see – there's Hetty, Phoebe Winnicombe, Mrs Axford from the shop, your friend Martha Cattermole. We all know how much she liked him.'

'Stop it,' Lilah exploded, half amused, half horrified. 'A woman could never have held him down in the slurry – could she?'

Roddy shrugged. 'Women are sometimes pretty strong. Look at Sylvia.'

Lilah was about to dismiss this remark when it echoed oddly inside her head. People had been saying similar things to her over the past few days. 'Okay,' she said slowly, looking her brother in the eye, 'let's do just that. We'll look at Sylvia. Come with me to wash down the parlour and we'll talk it through.'

The conversation was broken by the clashing of metal equipment and the slooshing of water as they hosed down the walkways between the milking stalls. It was very different from talking to Den, with his careful attempts to avoid hurting her, and his even more careful loyalty to the secrets of the police investigation. Roddy knew no such caution.

'Sylvia's quite poor, isn't she,' he began. 'Perhaps she thought Mum would ask her to move in here, if Dad was out of the way. And Sam. It would all work out for her, if she sold her place and used the cash to keep Redstone going. She could become an equal partner in the farm.'

'So why attack the Grimms?'

'Hetty told you the answer to that in the pub.'

'But it isn't working out, is it? Mum says she's selling up.'

'That's because Sylvia hasn't made her proposition yet. She's biding her time. She doesn't want Mum to make any uncomfortable connections. That would really wreck it.'

'But how did she get the gun?'

'Either she tricked Sam into giving it to her, or she nicked it the last time she was here. Easy, either way. Sam wouldn't expect her to shoot him, would he?'

'Rod, I don't like this. It all fits too neatly.' Lilah threw a bucketful of water over the floor and then brushed at a patch of resistant muck. 'And there isn't the slightest bit of proof.'

'I bet you she hasn't got alibis for any of the three mornings,' he continued. 'And I bet your Den hasn't given her a thought. If the same person killed Dad, Sam and Isaac, then she's the only one with a motive for all of them.'

'Okay, I can just about go along with the idea of her drowning Dad, assuming she could somehow get to catch her flight to Corfu that same morning, but whacking people's heads with a crowbar? And Amos said it was definitely a man.'

'Did he? I haven't heard that.'

'Den told me. Somebody wearing a balaclava, and rough clothes.'

'Sounds as if it could be anybody,' Roddy commented. 'Including Sylvia.'

Chapter Twenty-Eight

Lilah went to see Jonathan and Cappy that evening, curious about his interview with the police, and how they'd treated him.

Roxanne came to meet her at the curve of the lane, scenting her approach with the infallible nose of the gundog. But her greeting was subdued: a wag of the tail and a sniff of Lilah's jeans. Together they went across the tidy back garden, where the barbecue had been held, and on to the patio. The house stood sideways to its driveway, making the rear as accessible as the front. In summer, the French doors stood permanently open and Lilah had long ago been invited to use them without formality. Now she stood for a moment, preparing to call out. Before she could draw breath, Cappy's voice came from inside the room.

'Honestly, darling, you are making a fuss.'

'You haven't any idea what it was like,' came the reply, much harsher than Jonathan's usual relaxed drawl. 'Those men, like pigs, rummaging about in things they can't begin to understand. You should have heard them. Asking all about the Beardons, how often we see them, whether we knew how Sam fitted in.'

'And what did you tell them?'

'That's what's so foul about it all. I turned into a complete jelly – told them everything. All that stuff about Guy's first wife – finding the mucky clothes – everything. I feel sick at myself now. I thought I had more guts. I was scared. I just wanted them to think what a co-operative chap I was. Above suspicion. They seemed to be hung up on my driving round there so quickly the other morning, which I hadn't expected. As if shots and screams were normal country sounds, not worth bothering with . . .'

Lilah knew she mustn't eavesdrop any more. Deliberately she scuffed her sandal on the stone patio, and then clapped her hands foolishly at the dog. 'Hello, Roxanne!' she chirped. 'Jonathan? Cappy? Anybody in?'

'In here,' Cappy called. 'Is that you, Lil?' As she entered the room, both the Mabberleys stood up to greet her, which felt oddly rebuffing. Ranged side by side, they presented a united front, which made her falter and pause only a few inches inside the threshold. But she spoke up boldly.

'I came to see if Jonathan's all right. Den phoned this afternoon and he told me you'd taken the clothes in.' As in her conversation with Den, she bit off the urge to tell them more, to share everything that the policeman had told her.

She was looking brightly from one to the other, covering up the peculiar hot shudders that were surging through her at having heard them talking about her family. It struck her that every household in the village might be discussing, gossiping, surmising about every detail of their lives. She wished then that she had tiptoed away again, to think over what she'd heard before having to speak to them.

'Den?' said Cappy. 'Who's Den?'

'One of the policemen. I knew him at school, sort of. I see him sometimes, since Daddy died.' She shrugged awkwardly, wondering how she was sounding. The couple seemed to be looking at her with something like anger. Cappy had lines around her mouth which were new, and Jonathan was far from his normal self. It was as if the sheen had been wiped off them, revealing the pale flesh beneath. Something unhealthy hung in the air. Even the dog was subdued and glum.

'So?' pursued Lilah, with a sense of having little left to lose. 'Tell me about it.'

'Oh, well—' Jonathan flipped a hand, in one of his old gestures. 'You know. You've seen it all on the telly. You sit one side of a table, and they sit the other, and they ask about a hundred daft questions, and make you sign something and then you can go. All a great waste of time and taxpayers' money.'

'I feel sort of responsible for you being hassled. If you didn't live next door to a family that keeps getting itself murdered, none of this would have happened.'

'True,' said Jonathan, rapidly recovering his normal urbane composure. 'We'd never have let you buy the place if we'd known what it would be like.'

'*You* didn't own it before us, did you? Nobody ever told me that.'

'Well, it was no secret. You were just too young to be interested. It was all done through agents, and we'd never lived there. It was more of a technicality than anything. My dad bought it from an old chap in 1940, and never farmed it himself. There were tenants before you.'

'But Daddy never once mentioned it. That's really strange.'

'Well, it isn't important,' Cappy interrupted. 'Have they still got poor old Amos locked up?'

Lilah and Jonathan looked at each other, each expecting the other to answer. Then both shrugged. 'Don't know,' said Lilah. She'd forgotten Amos since Den's phonecall. The implication had been that he was no longer a prime suspect, but Den hadn't actually said as much. She wanted to tell the Mabberleys that the clothes had belonged to a woman, that the police were now giving this most of their attention. But Cappy was a woman, and Cappy was deeply unknowable. Lilah hesitated, and tried to think.

It was more than possible that her neighbours already knew that they were female clothes. But if they'd been Cappy's it made no sense whatsoever that she'd have allowed Jonathan to take them to the police. And it made even less sense to imagine the restrained and immaculate Cappy Mabberley wallowing in a slurry pit. Even so, Lilah kept the information to herself. She had come to glean, not to divulge.

The silence grew awkward, all three standing stiffly, tense with unspoken ideas and suspicions. Then Cappy swung her arms, as if limbering up for a race. 'Tell you what,' she said. 'I've got something to show you.'

Jonathan darted a quick glance of warning at her. 'Err,' he said.

'Oh, it's all right,' Cappy laughed, purpose shining from her. 'There's no reason to keep it secret from Lilah.'

'What?' The girl was intrigued, even excited.

'Come with me,' Cappy beckoned, heading past Lilah

to the French windows. 'It's still light enough, but we can't waste any time.'

'Can I come?' asked Jonathan.

Cappy looked back at him, considering. 'No. You stay here.'

'Well, be careful. If you see anyone, you're to come right back. Especially if Lilah's with you.'

'Phooey,' was all Cappy replied. 'Come on, Lil.'

Nobody else called her 'Lil'. It was strangely affectionate. She followed the woman past the bird sheds, down a deep, ancient lane, between high Devon hedges; the official entrance drive to the Mabberley farm. After a quarter of a mile, covered at a brisk walk, they turned through an open gateway into a field of lush grass, apparently destined for hay. 'Are you making hay this year?' Lilah queried. 'That's unusual.'

'Jonathan's getting someone in to do it, I think. There's another couple of fields like this, over there.' She waved a vague arm. 'We'll soon be there.'

The whole walk took fifteen minutes, and ended in the Mabberley woods, criss-crossed by paths and open to anyone in search of sylvan encounters. Off the paths it was dense with bracken, brambles, hawthorn and holly, as well as the larger, older trees, and thus almost impossible to traverse. 'Nothing like the woods of my childhood,' Cappy remarked, in a low voice. 'It's all bare between the trees where I grew up, and none of this endless stinging and scratching stuff.' Nonetheless, she plunged off the path they'd taken, striding confidently over snaking brambles, and sidestepping horribly reminiscent clumps of nettles. 'Tread where I do,' she instructed Lilah.

'Why are we whispering?' asked Lilah.

'We're going to a secret place. In a minute we mustn't talk at all, not even in whispers.' They plunged on, making some noise in the evening quiet. Lilah wondered who there might be to hear them. She had never taken much interest in these woods, preferring open fields and hedgerows. The presence of holidaymakers had always been off-putting to her, with their loud laughter and silly picnics.

Without warning, Cappy stopped and pointed. 'There,' she sighed. 'By the witch's tree.'

Lilah could see nothing remarkable. A mountain ash grew straggly beside a broad, green sweep of bracken. It was a relatively light spot, with no large trees to blot out the sun, and it seemed to be clear of brambles. In fact, the ground underfoot was mossy and springy. She peered in the direction of Cappy's pointing finger, but soon gave up. 'Where?' she said. 'What witch's tree?'

The woman indicated the rowan. 'I'll explain later,' she mouthed, close to Lilah's ear. 'Now follow me carefully.'

She led Lilah straight towards the bracken, and then began to skirt round it to an area that had been out of sight to them. Lilah began to notice signs of human interference. A circular ring of stones contained a scattering of wood ash and singed ground. There was a visible path leading directly into the bracken. Following it, she realised that it ended in a shelter, formed from bracken and young ash and elder limbs. So cleverly was it made that it took her some time to recognise it for what it was. There was a smell about it, too, of sweat and smoke and something sweet. *Dope*, she thought suddenly.

Cappy watched her, and then spoke in a normal voice. 'Clever, isn't it. There are some things hidden away, too. Drinking cups, and a blanket.'

'How on earth did you find it?'

'Oh, well, I thought I saw someone coming down here one day, and being a nosy cow, I kept a lookout. And – well, I know Jonathan doesn't care who uses the woods, but they are *ours*, after all. I do feel we should know what's going on in here.'

'Smoking dope, by the smell of it,' said Lilah. 'It's lovely, though. Like a fairytale.'

'Don't you feel it's a bit sinister?'

Lilah considered. 'Not really. But perhaps I'm not very sensitive to atmospheres. They probably don't use it much. Have you ever seen them properly? Who are they?'

Cappy shook her head. 'I just saw a man, and then only from the back. Youngish.'

'And you haven't said anything to the police? After all—'

'You think it's got something to do with the murders? Well, yes, that's why I showed it to you. But it isn't much, really, is it? Probably just some local lad coming to get away from it all. I mean, that's what these woods are for.' She seemed defensive and somehow frustrated. Lilah wondered whether she had been expected to react differently.

'But don't you think they'd want to know about it?' she persisted. The failure to tell the police struck her as quite seriously neglectful.

'I have a good reason,' Cappy replied evasively. 'It's growing about three hundred yards away, but I'm not telling you where.'

Lilah blinked, and then understood. 'Oh, Cappy!' she laughed. 'How brave of you!'

'Purely for personal use,' the woman said primly. 'But it wouldn't be funny at all if I got caught, now would it. It's well hidden, but even so, no sense in asking for trouble. Besides, I've never actually told Jonathan.'

'Well, thanks for showing me the hideout, and trusting me with your secret. I'd never be able to find it again on my own. Hadn't we better go before it gets really dark?'

Cappy nodded and turned to lead the way back. Lilah couldn't even work out where they'd come from, or where the paths were: without her guide, she'd be completely lost. 'How many acres are these woods?' she asked.

'Fifty or so, altogether. That's quite a size, by English standards.'

'You can say that again. I had no idea they were so big. Stupid, when I've lived next door for most of my life. It never occurred to me to wonder before.'

'Hush!' The sound came sharp, aggressive. Lilah stopped still, and caught the sounds of swishing that meant someone was ploughing through undergrowth, much as they were. *Too late,* she thought. *Our voices must have carried far enough to be heard.*

Cappy surprised her by suddenly crouching down behind a small, dense holly tree, flapping at Lilah to do the same. Feeling rather foolish, she squatted where she was, assuming she wouldn't be noticed in the fading light.

The sounds came closer, obviously made by a single person, treading confidently along a known route. *Why are we hiding?* Lilah wondered. *What on earth is this all about?*

A woman came into view. Her face was a pale disc, framed with long, untidy black hair. Two distinct facts were immediately obvious to Lilah. Firstly, this was Elvira, the simple girl from the village, Phoebe Winnicombe's daughter. Elvira, who had travelled the daily school bus with Lilah and Den and all the others of their generation.

Secondly, this was the female half of the copulating couple she had seen in the field after the Mabberleys' barbecue. How this became such a certainty to Lilah was unclear. The swinging black hair, the broad, round hips, were the only physical pointers. But Lilah was sure. And it seemed suddenly very important to find the identity of the man who'd been with her.

Chapter Twenty-Nine

She let Jonathan drive her home, without any argument. He dropped her at the farmyard gate, turning round and leaving her without saying more than a muted goodnight. Cappy's revelation of the lair in the woods had only made Lilah more obsessed with her own preoccupations. 'I must get home,' was all Lilah had said, once they'd got safely back to the Mabberleys' house.

As she let herself into the Redstone kitchen, she was greeted by a fevered Roddy. 'Where have you *been*?' he demanded, as soon as he saw her.

'Why? What's the matter?'

'We left Particular out of the milking. She's hurt her leg, and didn't come in with the others. Now she's bawling her head off because she needs to be milked. Her udder's bursting. Mum was up in the orchard and heard her. We went to try and get her in, but she's too lame to walk.'

'We'll have to milk her by hand.'

'Can you do that?'

'If I have to. Remember that little course I did when I

was seventeen?' Roddy looked blank. 'Never mind,' she said impatiently. 'The point is, I was quite good at it, compared to some. She won't like it, though. And it's *dark*, Rod. What a bugger.'

'Well, it's your fault. If you hadn't stayed out so long, we could have got it sorted by now. Where *were* you?'

'At Jonathan's. I told you.'

'You didn't.'

'Roddy, I *did*. You can't have been listening.'

'Oh, it doesn't matter. I just want to go to bed, but I suppose I'll have to come with you, hold a torch or something.'

'Why isn't Mum doing something?'

'She was going to phone somebody to come and help, when someone phoned her first. I don't know who, but she must still be talking.'

'If Particular's leg's that bad, we ought to get the vet out.'

'I don't think she's too bothered about the leg – except when she tries to walk. Just the udder.'

'Did she come in this morning?'

'I don't remember. The order did seem to go wrong near the end. No wonder she's bawling if she's missed *two* milkings.'

With a deep sigh, Lilah took charge. The cow was approached, soothed, milked by hand just enough to ease the worst of the pressure, and her leg deemed sufficiently non-urgent to wait until morning. Before this was accomplished, Miranda joined them, hovering and making suggestions until Lilah sent her back to the house. The rhythm of the hand milking would have been quite pleasant if it hadn't been such a strain on the unaccustomed muscles.

Soon both hands were aching unbearably, and one teat still hadn't been touched. Milk spread across the ground in a widening pool, somehow horrible in the torchlight. As the torch battery faded, the silvery light of a half-moon made the milk shine weirdly against the dark grass.

At last, it was done. The two stumbled back across the fields, exhausted and resentful. Lilah felt giddy with the relentless succession of crises overwhelming her. But she was grateful to Roddy for staying with her and told him so.

'That's okay,' he mumbled. 'She's stopped bawling, anyway, so we must have done something right.'

'It's funny I didn't hear her from the Mabberleys'. I was outside most of the time – you'd think it would have carried.'

'What were you doing there, anyway?'

'I didn't go for anything special, but Cappy showed me a secret camp, out in their woods. I'm not sure what to make of it.'

'Why would she show it to you? Whose is it?'

'Well – I probably shouldn't tell you that part just yet. I need to have a think first. Okay?'

He slashed the stick he carried across the tops of some young nettles, and both were reminded of Sam.

Miranda was in her pyjamas when they got back, a pan of hot milk keeping warm on the Aga for them. 'Pyjamas, Mum?' smirked Roddy. 'Aren't they Dad's?'

She hugged herself and wriggled into the brushed cotton. 'They feel wonderful,' she said. 'I want to wear them all the time.'

Lilah was beyond speech. She took her mug and started

up the stairs. 'Oh—' Miranda stopped her. 'You'll never guess who phoned.' Neither of her children responded. 'Barbara!' she announced, with a dramatic flourish. 'You know – Guy's first wife. Barbara Beardon, that wrote the letter. She phoned. I told her I wanted to go and see her, and she said fine. So I am. She sounds nice.'

'Great, Mum,' said Lilah, wearily. 'Can we talk about it tomorrow? I think I'll die if I don't go to bed this minute.'

When she woke, her hands still ached. They felt big and hot. When she rolled out of bed and started to pull on her jeans, her fingers worked stiffly. It was worrying to be so disabled and she envisaged a day of pain and incompetence. Particular's troubles were not yet over, either: if she wasn't properly milked out, the supply would dry up and they'd lose the yield of one of their best milkers, only a month into her lactation. Not until she was in the kitchen did she remember Miranda's announcement about the first Mrs Beardon.

Initially her reaction was one of exasperation that her mother could seriously consider leaving the farm when they were so obviously under huge pressure. It was unthinkable that she and Roddy could be left to do everything on their own. Even if they abandoned everything except the cows and young stock, it would be too much for them. At the prospect ahead, she almost gave up and crawled back into bed to nurse her throbbing hands. Instead she poured two mugs of tea and went to the bottom of the stairs to call Roddy. A muffled response assured her that he had woken up.

Getting through the morning milking gave them no chance to talk to each other. Miranda came out when they'd started and intercepted some milk for the younger calves who were already calling for their breakfast across the yard. What semblance of routine there was had to be patched together as they were forced to put the tasks in order of priority. All three realised that the only way to manage was to begin early in the day, working all morning, and give themselves at least part of the afternoon to pause for rest and reflection. Lilah knew they were achieving the impossible, out of a sort of lucky ignorance, which couldn't last. None of them knew how to maintain the milking machine, how to operate some of the implements or even keep the tractor in proper order. Lilah was fairly familiar with the basics, but there were serious limitations to her knowledge, in spite of her experience. Thinking about it now, she realised what poor use she had made of her opportunities, and how Guy had conspired to prevent her from genuinely sharing in any decision-making.

As she shut off the milking machine and went to put the equipment in to soak, her mind sought tirelessly for some escape, a way out of their intolerable position. It kept coming back to the cows. Everything else could be shelved or sold. Even the calves could go to market at a few days' notice, distressing though it might be. But the cows were too important for that. Many of them were very dear to her. She had known them all their lives, knew how they were related, and which had been difficult to feed as new calves, or which had been slow to take to the rigours of twice-daily milking after nearly two years' freedom out in the fields. She had seen markets – the callous men with their sticks and loud voices, and the great bulging eyes of the animals showing their panic. She knew how established herds behaved towards a newcomer – worse than children in a primary school playground. *Not the cows*, repeated a small voice inside her. *Please don't let us have to sell the cows.* This fear, perhaps, was the single factor which kept her going through the hot June morning with its dust and flies and grass seeds. Miranda might make remarks like, 'When this lot's sold . . .' or 'Roll on market day', but she wouldn't do anything about it. There didn't seem to be time to pick up the phone to summon the cattle truck or consult the auctioneer. There were too many aspects to selling which she didn't understand. Somewhere, they all hoped there would be an expert on hand to help them. Perhaps if they waited long enough, this rescuer would turn up in the yard in a glossy white Land Rover.

Lilah continued to feel Guy's presence at every turn. In the hot June sunshine, with heavy black shadows in the corners and the background buzz of insects, she regularly thought she saw him, heard his voice. He would be just out of sight, behind the barn door, or calling her from one of the fields. The cuckoo didn't help. More than once she was convinced it was her father's distant voice, calling 'Li-lah!' needing her for some urgent task.

Had the person who killed Guy and Sam understood what he was doing? That he was destroying Redstone, forcing the surviving family out into the unknown? Had that been the purpose, all along? If so, where was that person now, and how did he hope to gain from what he had done?

321

He or she, Lilah corrected herself. It might have been a woman. A woman who had a score to settle with Guy. That much was just credible. But Sam? Who could possibly have any grudge against poor Sam? The theory about Sylvia hardly extended that far, surely? What difference would Sam's existence have made to her plan? She wouldn't inherit his share of the farm. Rather than being any sort of impediment, wasn't he a vital element of the farm, his contribution ensuring that it remained viable?

The morning passed, with feeding and cleaning and automatic release of the cows back into the same field they'd occupied for weeks. Miranda phoned the vet for Particular's bad leg, which looked worse in daylight, and then lent a brief hand, before disappearing into the house and eventually calling Lilah in to lunch at twelve. The girl fell on it voraciously.

'Thank goodness it's summer,' said Miranda, as she watched her. 'Otherwise you'd still have the mucking out to do.'

'If it wasn't summer, we'd have given up by now,' said Lilah. 'Or the RSPCA would have forcibly closed us down.'

'We'll have to get someone to help us. We should have done it before. There must be at least one person out of work in the village. Preferably a man who understands machinery. It's stupid to struggle on like this. Something will blow up because we haven't oiled it, or the milk will be rejected because it's got something nasty in it. And if I go to Nottingham, there'll obviously have to be someone.'

'Yes, but who? Have sense, Mum. You can't possibly be serious about going off now.'

'I won't just abandon you. I'll ask Sylvia to come and do the things that I've been doing. Let's face it, she's far more competent than I am.'

Lilah sighed. Too many disjointed thoughts were whirling around in her head, and she felt exhausted with the strain of it all. 'I forgot to tell you what Cappy showed me last night,' she said. 'It was all very peculiar.' Having engaged her mother's attention, she told her briefly about the hideaway in the woods. She also described seeing Elvira making her way back to it, although there was a strong feeling of anxiety attached to that part of her revelations. Her words sounded inconsequential in her own ears as she related the scene, and yet she knew it was important.

'Elvira was always rather fey,' said Miranda. 'It's the sort of thing she would do.'

'I know. Cappy said there was a witch's tree.'

'A rowan? Fancy her knowing about that.'

'Fancy *you* knowing,' said Lilah. 'I've never heard them called that.'

'I thought everybody knew about rowan trees,' said Miranda in surprise.

Lilah pressed on doggedly. 'I do get the feeling that there's something wrong about her being there, especially if she's with a boy. Phoebe can't be very happy about it.'

'If she knows. It's a wise mother that knows everything her daughter gets up to.' She pulled a silly face. 'Anyway, don't get yourself in a state about it. You're living on your nerves as it is, if I'm any judge. You're all keyed up. Your imagination's working overtime. It's all beginning to look much clearer to me. Some stranger – it might even be Elvira's boyfriend, I suppose – pushed Guy into the slurry, maybe because he shouted at him or abused him – you know what he was like with that sort of person. So, then he went off to try and burgle the Grimms, and laid about with a crowbar in the process. Then he came back here – don't criminals always return to the scene, to check they didn't leave any clues? Well, Sam must have seen him, and got himself shot. Awful. Horrific. But not a conspiracy, or anybody we know. Isn't that the most likely explanation?'

Lilah folded her arms tightly around herself. 'I'd really like to think so,' she said, with a faint smile. 'But somehow I can't believe it's as simple as that.'

'Well, leave it for now. Maybe this will cheer you up. Look, I've found an advert in one of Guy's magazines for a relief milking agency. I'll get onto them. You two can't go on like this. I'll try to get someone to do the mornings, at least.'

'Mum! Have you any idea how much these agencies *cost*? You can't do that.'

'I don't care. We can always apply to the Council for a house, and the state for some money. Or live in a caravan. Or I could get work as a live-in housekeeper somewhere.'

Lilah guffawed unkindly. 'You, Mother, are the last person in the world to find work as a housekeeper. Who's going to provide you with references?'

Miranda gave her daughter a half-hearted slap. 'I'll fake them,' she said.

'We don't know for sure we're selling up. Wait before phoning the agency. Why don't I try the college? There

324

might be an agriculture student looking for work. I should have thought of that ages ago. We just need another pair of hands.'

'That's not a bad idea. But I'll phone, not you.'

Lilah was suspicious of her mother's helpfulness. 'Is this all because you're so keen to get to meet that woman?'

'Lilah! What a nasty thing to say. It's not true at all – just that last night's phone call was the spur I needed. It sort of brought me to my senses, I suppose.'

'I still don't see what the attraction is.'

Miranda pouted and said nothing. Lilah knew she'd have to let it go at that.

Sylvia came back that afternoon, when Miranda and Lilah were sitting outside with cups of tea, barely awake in the warm sunshine.

'Only me!' she called, the moment she cycled into the yard. Miranda waved a brief welcome. Lilah sighed.

The visitor came and stood in front of them, hands on her hips. 'This isn't what I expected to see,' she commented. 'You're supposed to be rushed off your feet.'

'We are,' said Lilah. 'You see us collapsed from exhaustion.'

'It's all go at my place, too. The goat's kidded already, and one of the cats looks as if it'll die any minute. It ought to be knocked on the head, really. And everyone else seems to be rushing about, too – crazy on a day like this. I passed young Tim just now, driving much too fast for these lanes. The Wing Commander's taken Mrs out for a spin, as well. They are funny. More of a menace than Tim, if anything. She can't sit up properly any more, and he rams her into the front seat like a doll. Then he drives with one hand supporting her. This whole village is a madhouse these days. Redstone seems quite a haven, by comparison.'

Miranda gave a grunt of derision. 'Yes, we must be. We've just got muck and murder and—'

'Misery,' finished Lilah. 'Which reminds me – I haven't phoned the vet about poor Particular yet.' She went to get up.

'I did that,' said Miranda. 'He ought to have been here by now. Sorry, I forgot to tell you.'

'What's wrong with her?' asked Sylvia, and the whole story was recounted to her. 'Poor thing,' was her brief response. 'Now, surely there are things I could be doing?'

'Just talk to us,' said Miranda. 'Just at this moment finding work for you is almost as exhausting as doing it ourselves – eh, Li?'

Her daughter looked at her in surprise. 'Yes,' she agreed. Miranda was exactly right. Finding work for Sylvia felt wrong, in a number of ways. Her mother's friend's role was as confidante and consoler, not farm worker. Until the vet arrived, everything could wait. She sipped again at her tea and thought about the things she and Roddy had said about Sylvia. Now the woman herself was here, it all seemed sillier than any game; the product of fevered imaginations and too much horror.

'Oh, and I forgot the biggest news of all,' Sylvia continued. 'They've released poor old Amos. I saw him being driven home in a police car. Looked rather green, I thought. Somebody should go and see that he's all right.'

'Well, it isn't going to be me,' said Miranda. 'I've a feeling he's been nursing some sort of crush on me, ever since we moved here. Though don't tell anybody I said so.'

'And it isn't going to be me, either,' said Lilah. 'I nominate the vicar.' Their laughter brought Roddy from the house to stare at them in disgust.

Chapter Thirty

Amos had very mixed feelings about being returned home, especially as he had been forced to promise not to leave the immediate area of the village without police permission. 'You still think I did it then?' he said bitterly. 'Just can't find enough proof, I suppose.' He had grown bolder during his days in custody. It seemed to him that there was less and less to lose, as time went on.

His house was different again. There had been a renewed police examination, since he had become implicated in the Redstone murders. Silvery powder marks showed where they had taken fingerprints, and his bed was not at all as he had left it. 'Don't suppose you found anything,' he said. The policeman wouldn't meet his gaze.

'Will you be all right, sir?' he asked, for form's sake. Amos felt like telling him no, of course he wouldn't be all right. There was no food in the house; he had the ghost of Isaac on one hand and the threat of Phoebe on the other; and that murdering thug somewhere out there, planning God knows what. He just nodded, with a surly scowl, and shut the door firmly behind the constable.

He had no idea of the date, and wasn't even sure what day it was. His old van, which he and Isaac had used for their infrequent journeys further afield than the village, was very unlikely to start, which meant he'd have to walk to the local shop for groceries. With something like yearning, he gazed down at Redstone from his bedroom window. They'd have milk to spare. He had a passion for hot chocolate made with full-cream milk, and more than anything, that was what he craved now. Something sweet and warm, to assuage all the pain and confusion of the past weeks. They'd given it to him in hospital, though watery and tepid, but at the police station all he'd been offered was tea.

What would it be like down at Redstone now? he wondered. With Sam Carter dead, they'd be struggling. He could go and offer them some help. But he remembered that he was suspected of killing Sam, and possibly Guy Beardon too. Miranda would look at him with suspicion, perhaps even revulsion. He wouldn't be able to abide that.

But neither could he abide hanging about here, scared of every sound, shaking with the fear of unknown attackers. And known ones. Someone had come into his house and clubbed his brother to death. That was real, although he still couldn't fully believe it. His own head had been broken, too. Slowly, standing there at his upstairs window, watching the sweep of fields down to Redstone, and then up again beyond, to woodlands and moors in the far distance, his fear turned to rage. What had Isaac ever done to deserve that? What had either of them ever done? His conscience was clear as a bell. Neither of them had ever hurt a fly without good reason.

There was no movement in the picture he contemplated, beyond the swirl of a group of birds on the edge of the far woods. Amos had excellent eyesight and the light was good. A pigeon on the roof of Redstone was clearly visible to him. Pity he hadn't been standing here that morning when Guy Beardon was pushed into the slurry.

With a sigh, he turned away and restlessly paced the room, trying to think what to do next. Something had to be done to settle this murder business once and for all. None of it made sense to him, except that there was a natural urge for revenge taking root in his mind. There didn't seem to be much prospect of the police catching anybody. Their daft questions had shown how lost they were. Well, then, he'd have to get out there and see what he could find out for himself. Rather than continuing to be scared of Phoebe and her mad ways, he decided to tackle her head on. She had to be at the back of it all somehow. Why else would she turn up after all these years and take over his house? He thought again of those eyes, glaring at him through the grey woollen slit of the balaclava. Was it possible that it had been Phoebe herself and not a man at all? How could he be sure of his description, when he'd been woozy with sleep and terror and bewilderment? If Isaac hadn't been dead, Amos could easily have convinced himself now that the whole thing had been nothing more than a dream.

And yet he could not imagine why Phoebe should want him and Isaac dead. Nor could he credit the idea that she had somehow induced a young vagrant to do the deed for her. Even Phoebe Winnicombe would need a powerful reason for such an act and Amos knew of nothing in the world to account for such a theory.

Just the same, she had said and done enough crazy things in the past days to warrant his going to see her. If he didn't do so, he thought the questions pounding at his head would drive him mad.

He went to the top drawer of his tallboy where he'd always kept a stack of cash, and pulled it open, half expecting it to have gone. But it was all there, in the pink plastic bags that the bank had given him. Five-pound notes were rolled up tightly together and secured with an elastic band. Deftly Amos took three from the roll, and replaced the rest. Then he took down his canvas shopping bag from its hook on the back of the kitchen door. Amos had a deep aversion to plastic carrier bags and would never accept one with his shopping.

There were a few lettuces in the garden, just starting to bolt. He pulled one up and shook it clean. Discarding a few outer leaves, he began to eat it, there in the garden, until it was all gone. It had a refreshing effect, but did little for his nagging hunger. Without bothering to lock the door, he set off towards the village, the shop and Phoebe's cottage.

She had lived here all her life, just as Amos and Isaac had always done. Thinking back, as he walked, Amos could remember the first time he'd noticed her. He had been twenty-five and she was ten or twelve. A smiling child, with skin like honey and long black hair. She had always been loud, shouting orders at the village boys, arguing, complaining. Her parents had been half-gypsy, though seemingly not inclined to travel. She had not been trained in any of the usual conventions; the cottage had no hot water, no bathroom, no heating. It stood high on a bank, halfway up a stony track beside the churchyard which led nowhere. The cob walls were always stained with damp, the window frames ragged with rot. Phoebe had had a young sister, who died one winter, as everyone watched helplessly. That had all been forty years ago, but only the superficial things had really changed.

Phoebe had done poorly at school, like Amos. Nobody cared, at that secondary modern, whether they stayed at home to help with digging potatoes or carting hay. They had grasped the basics of reading, and could write neatly when required to do so. But even now, in a world gone mad with writing and reading, there was precious little necessity for it in their daily lives.

The cottage was in a better state now. In the long, slow years of her life, Phoebe had enjoyed some success and made herself some money by being an expert in more than one field. Nothing so obvious as basket making or herbal concoctions, with the inevitable twee stalls at craft fairs calling for gingham decorations and fancy labels. Phoebe was, or had been, the best thatcher in the area. She could also lay a hedge as fast and straight as anyone in the county. Such skills were rare, and the payments for them high. Her cottage now had a new damp course, weatherproofing and central heating.

Amos had been taken with the young Phoebe, and watched her grow, year by year. He heard her pour scorn on men and their ways, and announce to the world that she would never marry. That suited him nicely; his mother had decreed that he should never marry, either. He had Isaac to care for. That was his child, his family. He had submitted with little sense of outrage or deprivation.

So it was that he and Phoebe had a history, and as he came close to her cottage, knowing somehow for sure that she was in, waiting for him, it seemed that he must finally confront her with it, and take hold at last of the consequences.

He had no need to knock. The door stood open, the weak sun, obscured by a layer of cloud, casting a soft shadow across the threshold. He stepped into the living room, which lay immediately beyond the door, paused, and cleared his throat. 'Hello?' he said, in a normal tone. 'You there?'

He braced himself for the worst – a sudden leap from behind the door, a knife poised to stab him; a torrent of cruel abuse and contempt; tears; insanity. There was movement in the room beyond the one he now stood in. He heard a voice whispering. 'Phoebe,' he said. 'It's me.'

Some scuffling and another spate of whispering preceding a flurry of female bodies, and then there were two of them standing side by side, across the room, looking at him without expression. One of them nudged the other, who grinned foolishly. Then she said, 'Hello, Daddy.'

He had, of course, come across Elvira from time to time, over the years. She had never seemed to be any of his business. Like her mother in appearance, although much heavier, with a wide, pale face, she trudged around the lanes, her gaze mostly downcast. She appeared always to be in a world of her own, often intent on some incomprehensible matter of her own, sometimes muttering to herself. She carried a basket, and gathered berries and mushrooms. As far as anyone knew, Phoebe was a satisfactory mother, keeping the girl clean and fed in somewhat better fashion than her own experience had been. Nobody had the slightest idea who Elvira's father might be.

Amos stared stupidly at the two women. Something crumbled inside him, some walled-up knowledge that he had not so much struggled to deny, as simply forgotten about. Elvira must be somewhere over twenty by this time, he supposed, though an exact calculation was beyond him. The years were all so alike, there was nothing he could find to pin down dates with any accuracy. The girl's simple mind was forever fixed in childhood, so that it made little sense to count the years. He had known, in a vague way, that he could technically be her father. And the knowledge meant scarcely anything to him. A pang of shame, a tweak of pity would perhaps grip him on a wakeful night when the thought of a wife and child came warm and inviting to his lonely bed. To be followed all too swiftly by the awareness that only one person in the world could ever be that wife, and she had vowed never to marry. But though she remained steadfastly single, Phoebe would never have permitted Amos to marry another woman. This he knew for certain, without ever needing to be told.

'Wh-what?' he stuttered. 'What did you say?'

'She's your girl, Amos,' Phoebe clarified, her voice like broken glass. 'And 'tis time you confessed it.'

He stood up taller, the anger slowly returning. 'When have I had a chance of that?' he demanded. 'Confess, is it! Seems I'm to spend my days confessing, just now.'

The words were muddled, but the feeling was clear. All his life, this woman had played with him, spoilt everything for him. She had taunted Isaac in their younger days, whilst having her own daft girl, even worse in the head, some might say.

'I am not in your debt,' he said. 'Too late now, Phoebe, to try to make out that I am.'

'Time has no meaning in this,' she said, taking her daughter's arm. 'This is your rightful child. And you've always known it to be so.'

'She could have been once,' he said, suddenly sad and soft, thinking of the might-have-beens. 'But you kept her for your own. You, Phoebe Winnicombe, always so strong and proud. People said you'd found her in the churchyard or stolen her from a pram. Or that you got her from some passing stranger who never knew what he'd done. If you say it was me, then that's just words now. The time has long gone when I could have cared about her.'

'No! All you ever cared for was that useless brother. Now he's gone, and Elvira's to take his place. I'm decided.'

Amos felt a derisive laugh struggling to burst out. But he dared not laugh at Phoebe. Something was becoming clear in his mind, a terrible thing, which he did not want to face. He struggled against it, insisting to himself that he must be wrong. Whatever she might say, however harshly she might say it, he still would not believe that she had had Isaac killed.

He remembered again the murdering figure with the mask across his face, swinging the crowbar. There had been nothing familiar about him, in his youth and the blaze of his dark eyes. It had been a look of purpose, an intentness to finish an unpleasant job.

And yet. Whereas before there had been no motive as to why Isaac should die, now something was forming in his mind as he observed his one-time lover and her daughter standing there before him, and it changed everything.

Chapter Thirty-One

The vicar had private business which was causing him profound anxiety. Since Guy Beardon died, things were getting worse. The first wife had somehow got hold of his address and had been contacting him by letter and phone more and more in the last week or so. Yet he still wasn't sure what she wanted. What had begun as a bit of minor mischief, a sense of putting one over on the arrogant Guy, by knowing unsuspected details of his early life, had turned into something much darker and more dangerous.

Guy had died a dirty, disgusting death, and Father Edmund was still unable to feel any personal sorrow for this fact. He had been much more affected by the killing of Sam Carter, in spite of his profound disapproval of the man's ungodliness. It had been with motives of genuine concern that he had visited Redstone that afternoon; hearing those children talking about him so disaparagingly in the office had come as a very unpleasant shock. Any sympathy he might have been fostering had evaporated in seconds. How in God's name was he supposed to care about heathens and pagans like them? Running half-wild all their lives, not understanding the normal constraints of modern existence, they were barely the same species as others of their generation. There was nothing at all he could do for them, and it was futile even to try.

And yet he had tried, in a feeble way, to divert the tidal wave of trouble they were facing. And, heaven help him, he was still trying – though since Sam's death, he had realised that he was groping more blindly than he'd believed at first. There was some substantial piece of the jigsaw that he was missing, and it was an attempt to grasp this which preoccupied him now.

Sylvia Westerby seemed to him to be a good place to start. Living next door, she and he had struck up a workable relationship, which Father Edmund found oddly satisfying. He enjoyed her directness, her easy strength. Although she never came to church, she would sometimes lend a hand at garden parties and bring and buys. A good-natured woman was a precious thing, in his opinion, and he made a special effort not to alienate her.

The boundary between the two properties comprised a substantial hedge, reinforced with a wire netting fence, to prevent Sylvia's livestock from straying. But at the upper end, adjacent to the road running into the village centre, there was only a fence, leaving a clear view of each other's front doors. If Sylvia's door stood open, it meant she was at home. He went to look. Not only was the door open, but her bicycle was propped against the wall of the house. 'Hello!' he called, standing just outside the threshold. 'Are you there?'

She came through from one of the main rooms, appearing slowly, her expression neutral. 'I'm here,' she said and waited. He felt her silence as hostile, almost aggressive. *Serves her right for leaving the door open,* he thought.

'Ah, yes,' he began, clasping his hands together in front of his stomach. 'I just thought I should come and ask you how things are at Redstone. I did call in, but Mrs Beardon was out, and the children – well, I didn't get much sense out of them.'

'They're not *children,* vicar,' she corrected him sternly. Then her tone mellowed. 'They're all very shocked. Obviously.' She leant a shoulder against the doorway, and seemed in no hurry to be rid of him – but neither was she inviting him in. Obstinacy kept him there; he was intent on seeing this through.

'They can't manage the farm now, surely? I thought perhaps we could find someone to help them. Rally the community.'

Sylvia laughed a little, a chuckle of muted scorn. But her words were friendly. 'Yes, I had the same idea myself. I have been going over nearly every day, but they seem too disorganised to be able to help, if you see what I mean. It's difficult to know how to be of any assistance. And who is there in the village who's not already as busy as can be?'

'There must be people. Youngsters. Retired . . .'

'Don't suggest Wing Commander Stradling, whatever you do. We've already considered him.' She laughed again, and Father Edmund allowed himself to join in fleetingly.

'There's Phoebe and Elvira. They'd be ideal.' He felt a rare sense of inspiration. Where had that idea come from?

He cocked his head pensively, looking at the thought again. Surely it was brilliant.

Sylvia pursed her lips and widened her eyes. 'My goodness,' she said. 'I would never have thought of them. They don't know much about farming, surely?'

'We could ask them,' he said. And that matter seemed to be closed. After all, the farm work had not been his main worry.

'The police—' he went on. 'Are they still examining the place for clues?'

'Oh, no, I don't think so. I gather it's all being done from their offices, now. Laboratories – whatever. I have no idea what it is they're doing.'

'I saw the car here—' he paused delicately.

'That's right. They asked me some questions, as well. Didn't you get a visit?'

He shook his head. 'Not since Sam died, no. I was interviewed after the Grimsdale death, as was everyone else, so far as I know. They didn't seem to think I had anything useful to contribute.'

She looked at him sharply. 'And were they right?' she asked.

Father Edmund put his head back, and breathed deeply. 'They were indeed,' he said stiffly. Something had gone wrong with the conversation. He hadn't expected to be put on the defensive like this. He had come to elicit information, and only now did he realise how incompetently he was going about it.

He breathed again, steadying himself. 'Well, as I say, I am very concerned about that poor family. Perhaps you would convey my sentiments to them. I would willingly help in any way I can. It's hard to imagine how it is for them, with so much tragedy falling upon them. Murder is a terrible thing.' Words were coming more easily now. 'Just think what hatred there must have been. Something must have been desperately wrong up there, for this to happen.'

Sylvia said nothing. When he looked into her face again, there were tears in her eyes, gathering heavily on her lower lids, trembling on the brink before spilling over. Father Edmund was appalled.

'Well,' he flustered. 'I won't keep you any longer. I'm sorry to have intruded. Sorry to . . . er . . .' She blinked, and scraped a forefinger from each hand harshly across each cheek. She seemed angry, but still she said nothing.

He left, knocking glancingly against the bike as he went. *Typical*, he thought furiously, as he regained his own property. *Wretched women, retreating into tears just when you thought you might get something out of them.*

He made himself tea and laid two homemade ginger biscuits on a small plate. One of the few perks of this job was the never-ending stream of good food provided by the church ladies. A bachelor vicar was a magnet for such things, and it was a lean day when some little tin or jar or packet of cake, jam, or biscuits did not appear in his porch as if by magic.

He reviewed his plan as he crunched, torn between wishing himself completely removed from the whole business, and excitement at the special nature of his involvement. The first Mrs Beardon had asked him for help, and he could not easily refuse it. She was keen to meet Miranda, and to ascertain the precise legal position regarding Guy's estate, without alerting either Miranda's children or the police. This had seemed innocent enough to Father Edmund. He had his doubts as to whether she could be entitled to any property, and had told her as much, already. But he supposed that she had a much more emotional motive, namely sheer curiosity as to how Guy's life had turned out after he'd left her. This he could understand. This, he told himself, was why he was willing to assist her. After all, she had only requested that he keep her informed as to whether it appeared possible for Miranda to leave Redstone for a visit to Nottingham. Barbara did not seem much interested in the murders, presumably under the impression that some inscrutable local feud lay behind them. People, as Father Edmund well knew, had strange ideas about life in the deep countryside.

Fortified, he washed his teacup, and stepped outside once again. This time he would need the car. There was an element to this mystery that he had so far overlooked, despite its nagging presence at the back of his mind. That all three deaths were connected seemed both obvious and impossible. The paradox had apparently struck most people in the same way, and had the same effect. The murder of Isaac Grimsdale had been so incomprehensible that scarcely anyone even had a theory about it. And without a theory, they had been rendered wordless on the subject. 'Poor old Isaac,' they said, shrugging helplessly.

This would not do. At the very least, Amos must be in need of succour. Another non-churchgoer, he was barely known to the vicar. But this was not a good reason for neglecting him. There were pastoral duties to perform, as well as a rich vein for amateur sleuthing. Besides, Isaac had not yet been buried. The Council would take charge at this rate, bundling him off to the crematorium early one morning with none of the due ritual. Perhaps Amos simply needed a helping hand, to guide him through the process. Father Edmund was more than satisfied with this excuse for a visit.

The track to the Grimsdale farmhouse was overgrown and bumpy. It ran between high hedges, beyond which was land which had long belonged to Redstone on one side, and a different farm entirely on the other. Father Edmund was only dimly aware of the history of land ownership in the area, although the church ladies had been more than happy to explain it to him, many a time. Rounding a sudden sharp bend, he found himself in a large rutted yard outside the house, which was set on high ground. Automatically he stared at the view falling away to his right, sweeping down to the hollow where Redstone and all its outbuildings clustered, and then up the far side to the Mabberley woods. It was splendid, he acknowledged; more than splendid. How odd that nobody had ever mentioned it to him! The Grimsdales' house must have the finest vista in the whole area. It did him good just to stand for a moment and appreciate it.

When he turned back, remembering the reason for his visit, Amos was standing in the doorway, at the front of the house, staring at him. 'Good God!' he said, thickly.

'My dear fellow, how are you?' Father Edmund gushed nervously. 'I'm afraid this visit is badly overdue. I've come to offer my condolences over your brother.'

Amos went on staring. Father Edmund could see the wound on his head; it looked as if it ought to be covered with a dressing. Had the man's brains been addled? he wondered. Wasn't there mental trouble in the family, anyway?

'I'm glad to see you,' said Amos, then. 'It's like magic.'

'Pardon?'

'I was – in a way – praying for someone like you to come. I need help, you see.'

To the best of his recollection, Father Edmund had never been the answer to anyone's prayer before. It was a highly disturbing feeling. Warily, he smiled. 'Then you must tell me all about it,' he said. 'Shall we go in?'

The inside of the house was astonishingly tidy. He realised that he had expected a hovel, full of animal hair, mud, unwashed crockery. He gazed about him, and then looked questioningly at Amos. 'Do I detect the hand of a woman?' he said, with a knowing smirk.

Amos shuddered at that, and almost ran into the living room. Father Edmund followed, noting that this room was equally pristine. Amos threw himself down on a large armchair and gestured his visitor to find a seat. Then a long silence ensued, with the vicar unable to find a safe opening to a conversation he could not begin to predict.

At last, Amos spoke. 'A woman,' he said. 'That's it, all right.' And he began to tell a strange, disjointed story, full of ancient grievances and present day terrors. The vicar listened, uncomprehending at first, but afraid to interrupt with questions, in case some tenuous thread be lost.

At the end, he sat back, and stared hard at the unnervingly clean ceiling. *The woman even washed his ceiling*, he thought, irrelevantly. 'I think we'll have to go to the police,' he said at last. 'If I've understood you correctly, they'll be most anxious to hear everything that you've just told me.'

Amos nodded resignedly, almost mournfully. Father Edmund felt something flutter inside him, and his head hummed strangely. What could this sensation be? he wondered. Suddenly he understood. It was sadness. Pure overwhelming sadness, for the things that could happen in the world.

Chapter Thirty-Two

While Amos was unburdening himself to the vicar, Miranda was doing something similar to Dave, the young police sergeant. He had been detailed to interview her one more time, with a view to confirming the facts about her relationship with Sam, as well as eliciting any other information which might be 'pertinent'. 'We'd like to know a little more about Mr Carter's background,' he began. 'It strikes us as rather . . . well, *thin*. A few discrepancies seem to be showing up, too.'

Miranda fought down a surge of irritation. Talking about Sam's 'background' seemed pure irrelevance to her. She waited restlessly for the questions to start.

'Basically,' said the man, with a small smile, 'we can't seem to get hold of any motive for his killing. None of the people we've spoken to can suggest any reason at all why Mr Carter should be murdered. Here we have someone turning up on your farm in the early hours of the morning, having presumably taken your husband's gun from Mr Carter's room on a previous occasion, and then shooting him in the back with it. No sign of a disturbance, nobody reporting a fight or even an argument. That does seem to suggest that the killer was quietly waiting for his chance – that this was all carefully planned. Would you agree?'

Miranda felt panic. How was she supposed to reply?

'Er, well . . .' she stuttered. 'I haven't really thought about it. At least, not in that sort of detail. You'd be better off asking Lilah. She's the amateur detective, not me.'

'Well, let's go through it slowly, shall we?' His patient persistence seemed sinister, like a cat silently watching the mousehole. It was worse somehow that he was so young. He ought not to be this confident at his tender age. At times he behaved almost paternalistically, though never enough for her to feel she could trust him.

'Firstly, the gun. Your daughter saw it in Mr Carter's room a few days ago.'

'Yes, she mentioned it,' confirmed Miranda.

'So, how do you think the killer could have got hold of it?'

'Sam never locked his door. Anyone could have slipped in and taken it. There's been a lot of coming and going since Guy died.'

'Could you give me a few names?'

'Oh, heavens.' She felt daunted. 'Let's see. Jonathan, Sylvia, Amos, the AI man, the milk recorder, about four reps, the vicar . . . any number of police people. And there are times when nobody's in the yard, when it would be easy to sneak in on foot. There are plenty of hiding places and we haven't got a dog to warn us.' She looked up as a shadow crossed the sunlit floor. Lilah was standing in the doorway, as the policeman had done earlier.

'Can I come in?' she asked. 'It's just that I've found something in the office.'

Miranda sighed. 'Oh, Lilah, not again,' she protested.

Ignoring her, Lilah held something out to the policeman. 'I've never seen it before. I don't understand why it was there,' she said simply.

'Have *you* seen it before?' he asked Miranda.

It was a photograph of Guy, standing on a beach, a coat jacket slung over his shoulders. He looked young and handsome and arrogant. Miranda looked at it for a long moment and shook her head.

'Could it have been Mr Beardon's?' the Inspector asked.

'It could have been,' said Miranda, with a nod. 'In fact, surely it *must* have been. He's got an old album somewhere. If I was a suspicious wife, I'd say he'd been showing this to some lady friend, showing off what a handsome chap he'd been in his prime.' She spoke lightly, dismissively. Lilah was horrified.

'Mum!' she protested. 'Don't make jokes like that.'

'I wasn't joking, love. You know how vain your father was. And it's a very nice photo.'

The policeman looked from one to the other, assessing their reactions. 'Right, then,' he said at last, slipping the photo into an envelope. 'Could you fetch the album, please?'

With some difficulty, Miranda found it. It took very few minutes to establish that the photo had not come from its pages. There were no empty spaces, no recent removals. Dave licked his lips and chewed a corner of his mouth with suppressed excitement. 'Thank you very much,' he nodded to Lilah. 'Now, perhaps I can carry on with your mum for

348

a bit?' She looked hard at Miranda for a moment, and then went outside, closing the door behind her.

'Tell me more about Mr Carter,' he invited. 'Anything that comes to mind.'

Miranda, soothed by the relaxed approach, found herself pouring out a jumble of information about herself, Guy and Sam. She briefly went over their early history, when Sam had been a favourite pupil of Guy's, and when he left school Guy had kept a fatherly eye on him. 'I suppose he was a sort of substitute for Terry and Leo,' she said thoughtfully. 'Even though he was much older than them.'

'Who are?' the policeman prompted.

'His sons, by his first wife. We told you about them.'

'Oh yes,' he said. 'We checked them out. They've both got the strongest possible abilis.'

'I'm impressed,' she said with a faint smile.

He encouraged her to finish the story, asking about personalities and relationships. Guy had been a difficult man, she admitted. Everyone had had cause to resent him, including herself. And yet she hadn't at all minded being married to him. Having him die like that made her genuinely sad, if not entirely surprised. 'It was an awful way to go,' she added. Yet every time she thought about it, the horror was mixed with a very tiny glow of amusement. That the mighty Guy in all his arrogant confidence should come to that end was a little bit of a joke; a joke she planned to revisit with Sylvia and other friends, over the years to come.

She confessed with a wry smile, that she really had supposed that Sam had done it, out of a mixture of all-too-understandable reasons.

'Which were?' he prompted.

Firstly, she explained, there was the way Guy treated him. Even a worm will turn, and Sam was several stages up from a worm. People always assumed that because he wore shapeless and tattered clothes and had rough hands that he must be an ignorant semi-human yokel. Guy himself, although he knew better than anyone that this was wrong, behaved as if it were so. The unvarying humiliations could easily have become too much to bear.

'And secondly?' He asked the question almost idly, as if he had all the time in the world. He leant back in his chair, folding his arms. He had even stopped taking notes.

Well, Miranda plunged on, *secondly*, there was the curious matter of the ownership of the farm. Guy had behaved badly over that, she supposed, although on paper it must seem perfectly fair. When they had found Redstone and decided to buy it from the Mabberleys, it had been clear that every penny of the milk cheque would have to go to pay the mortgage every month. There simply was nothing to spare for Sam's wages. At that time, Sam and Guy had been as close as father and son, and neither could bear to be parted. Sam wanted to get away from his domineering widowed mother, and Guy was aware that he had actual biological sons growing up forever out of his sight or knowledge. Each filled a gaping need in the other. Miranda formed the third side of the triangle, and was not always comfortable with her position. Casually, Guy offered Sam part ownership of the new farm in return for the most minimal of wages. He would have free accommodation and food, and occasional use of the car. It was more than many a farm labourer might have

350

expected in generations past. Sam had shrugged and nodded agreement. From the start, he had seemed content, and never once had Miranda heard him complain about money in all the subsequent years.

'So, strictly speaking, he was a man of some considerable means?' the sergeant summarised. 'And he might possibly have taken exception to the way your husband treated him as only a humble employee?'

'We all forgot about the original arrangement,' Miranda assured him. 'I suppose Guy felt – I don't know – *embarrassed*, almost. I don't really think he deliberately slighted Sam, or anything like that. Although – well, he was never very nice to him, I suppose. I always assumed that Sam accepted it, as Guy's manner. I mean, they were obviously fond of each other, in a funny sort of way.'

'So, to your knowledge, nobody in the village knew that Sam Carter was part owner of the farm?'

'That's right.' She nodded. 'None of us would ever have talked about it. I don't think we can treat it as a motive. Not even Lilah or Roddy knew. And I had honestly forgotten until the will arrived the other day.'

'Right,' he said slowly. 'And is there a thirdly?'

'Pardon?'

'We've had firstly and secondly. Reasons for thinking that Sam might have killed your husband. Is there anything else?'

Miranda felt her face growing red. Hoping to avoid his gaze, she stood up. 'Let me get us some coffee,' she said.

He nodded acceptance. 'There is, isn't there?' he persisted.

'I don't think so,' she muttered, with her back to him.

'I should tell you that I've talked at some length to your

351

neighbours, as well as the vicar and Mrs Axford in the shop. And a person called Hetty Taplow. Routine questions, but there did seem to be hints. I'll put this as delicately as I can, Mrs Beardon, but it must be mentioned. One or two people seem to think that there were . . . relations . . . between you and Sam Carter. Is there any truth in that suggestion?'

She sighed, and turned back to him. 'It isn't like you think,' she began.

'I expect it is,' he said, with a direct look. 'Don't worry, it won't go any further. At least . . .'

'It might, if we get to a court case. I don't mind, really. I've never cared much about what people think of me. Yes, Sam and I had sex sometimes. Do I have to say any more than that?'

'Did your husband know?'

'God! Of course not! He'd probably have taken us both out and shot us if he'd ever found out. The only person who knew was Sylvia, and she wished she didn't, I think. It wasn't anything important. Just sex. Sam didn't have anyone else, and . . . oh, what's the use of trying to explain?'

'But it's definitely a thirdly, all the same. A reason why Sam might have wanted your husband out of the way?'

Miranda said nothing. The memories were irresistibly coming back to her. The 'affair' – if that's what it was – was something she almost never thought about between encounters, but which she found quite extraordinarily pleasurable when it was actually happening. The inevitable Lady Chatterley overtones – utterly inappropriate though they were – only added humour to it.

For Sam had not been in any sense a 'good' lover. Urgent,

apologetic, hasty, clumsy – like no character in any book she'd read, she had still found it thrilling. She loved the way he'd *needed* her so inescapably; she more than loved his moments of climax, the long, relinquishing gasp and brief collapse onto her welcoming breast. Always then she cradled him, calling him baby names and shushing his groans of guilt and shame. They parted every time with her on a warm, self-satisfied high and him stumbling awkwardly away, mumbling that he wasn't going to do it ever again – he'd find his own woman, be damned if he didn't.

But he never did, and he grew all the more dependent on her, until he started taking risks –dropping back to the house when Guy assumed he was hedging or ditching – and telling her he loved her. Although he never voiced it, Miranda assumed that he suffered agonies of jealousy towards Guy, the rightful husband.

Perhaps he had calculated that with Guy dead, he could marry Miranda and assert his rights on a number of levels. In the weeks following Guy's death, she had allowed herself to believe that he would get over his guilt and allow himself to move into her bed permanently. The idea even had some natural justice to it, although she suspected there could definitely be too much of a good thing where Sam was concerned.

The policeman had finished. He drained his coffee mug and got to his feet. 'Thank you very much indeed for being so frank,' he said, and smiled the warmest smile so far. 'You've been extremely helpful. So has your daughter. I'm sure we'll have something to show for the investigation before much longer. Meanwhile, please do contact us if there's any more you feel we should know.'

Miranda nodded, then remembered something. 'I meant to ask you – would it be all right if I went away for a day or two? There's somebody I want to go and see. And it would be wonderful to get out of this place for a bit.'

He smiled paternally. 'That would be no problem, providing you came back again. Just let us know when and where.'

When he was gone, Miranda felt drained. What had possessed her, telling him everything like that? He must be a hypnotist, to have got it all out of her so easily. And poor Lilah, banned from the house, what must she be thinking? A quick look around the yard suggested that she had found some work further off. The hens were clustered around the gate, crooning earnestly, and Miranda realised they hadn't been fed. As she scattered corn for them, she watched with scorn their desperate dashes from grain to grain. *Stupid creatures,* she thought. So dependent. Like everything else here, a millstone around her neck. The desire to escape was like a physical sensation. Like running away from a great fire. She had to get away, to a place where nobody and nothing needed her.

This was the chief motive in wanting to visit the woman in Nottingham. She hadn't been completely honest with Lilah when conveying the subject matter of last night's phone call. Barbara had sounded as if she had something important to discuss, and Miranda was happy to clutch at any straw.

She knew that she was probably taking a foolish risk. She was, after all, a woman of property, and if Barbara was living in relative poverty, the discrepancy might call for action that would be unwise or worse. Though she had had the sense to speak to her solicitor, in order to give herself at least a modicum of ammunition prior to making the visit. If she could honestly state that everything was mortgaged, or tied up in some sort of trust, or rightfully due to Lilah and Roddy, she would feel more confident.

But escape was not going to be entirely simple. First she had to ensure that Lilah and Roddy would survive without her. The very least she could do was to ensure that they had some help with the milking. She took up the phone and dialled the number of the agricultural college. It rang and rang in vain. 'Damn it!' she exclaimed, dashing the thing down in a gesture worthy of the irascible Guy. But still she couldn't quite take the step of phoning for a proper relief milker. Somehow, it was just too much of a commitment. Somehow, there had to be a simpler answer.

Then, as if to confirm her hesitation, a car drove into the yard. She didn't immediately recognise the sporty red model, and even took a moment to identify the young man who jumped out with remarkable energy. Then she realised who he was: young Tim Rickworth, the husband of Sarah, the overworked computer whizz kid who did little but dash hither and yon in his fast red car.

Bewildered, she went to meet him at the door. 'Hi!' he greeted, as if he regularly paid her a visit. 'How's it going?'

She expelled an expressive sigh.

'Just as I thought,' he trumpeted. 'Well, sigh no more, fair lady. Sir Galahad is here at last.'

'Er—' She'd heard that Tim and Sarah were both on the unpredictable end of the spectrum. She wondered now whether he might be seriously unstable.

'Sorry,' he grinned, dropping the medieval act. 'It's simple really. I finished a contract yesterday, and have promised myself a whole month off. I did book us a farmhouse in the Dordogne, actually, but Sarah's refused to go, so that's off. It's an ill wind – because I honestly would love to come over and lend a hand, if you think I'd be any use. No strings, no need to pay me or anything. I guess it's just a romantic gesture on my part – reading too much Laurie Lee, if you like. I like cows, especially your sweet little fawn ones with the long eyelashes. If someone can just give me a couple of lessons in milking, then I'm your man. No hour too early, no task too mucky. Well, within reason.'

'Gosh!' said Miranda. 'Don't pinch me. I don't want to wake up from this one.'

Tim's laugh was a little forced. 'So?' he said, after a moment. 'What do you say?'

'I'm tempted to say I don't believe you, but that might be rude. I think we'll have to find Lilah, and see what she says. She's really the boss around here, these days.'

'She's over there, look, doing something manful with those bales. Hey, Lilah, put that down. Let Sir Galahad shoulder thy ponderous burden!' And he ran across to where she was struggling with some hay and took it from her. Astonished, she could only stare at him, mouth wide open.

Chapter Thirty-Three

Cappy had left the house just as it got light, to the sound of hectic birdsong and Jonathan's gentle snores. Summer mornings were magical to her, coming as she did from northern latitudes where the light was something precious, to be celebrated extravagantly. It was also a time for secret activity, unobserved by others. A time to defy the senseless laws of her adopted country, and pursue her own ends undisturbed.

In a remote corner of the great Mabberley woods, Cappy had cleared a piece of ground, tilling it and letting in the sunlight. Then she had planted a forbidden herb and kept her seedlings safe from potentially marauding deer or squirrels with cleverly camouflaged netting and sheets of polythene. It was a minor indulgence, a small-scale business, which occupied little of her time. But it accounted for her presence in the woods, and how she came to notice the hidden camp in the bracken. It had not taken long for her interest to be diverted to the goings-on there.

This morning, she crept silently along the invisible path, until she could see the hideaway. There was a canvas bag on the ground beside the fire circle, and a pair of Doc Marten boots. Someone was at home – and unlikely to stir for some hours yet, she assumed. Squatting out of sight, she considered her alternatives, slowly and methodically. It was beginning to worry her that this camp existed; it seemed now that it had to be connected to the Redstone murders, and was therefore sure to implicate her and Jonathan in some way. It would suit her very well for it to be gone and the people driven well away. And now that she knew the identity of one of them, she could take steps to orchestrate their removal.

Elvira had always fascinated Cappy. A great lumpen girl, with striking black hair and a meaningless grin, she had seemed to hang about the village doing nothing for as long as Cappy could remember. Phoebe, her mother, was an alarming woman, snappy and independent, seldom responding to Cappy's friendly waves and smiles. Together the pair resembled something from an old English novel: a Thomas Hardy or Charles Dickens. But they were only too real, and when Jonathan had mentioned seeing Elvira with a strange young man, showing every sign of being her boyfriend or lover, Cappy had worried. And Cappy did not like to worry. She actively sought serenity, smoothing out wrinkles in her life almost before they happened. Jonathan's regular pleadings for a child was one of these wrinkles, the biggest of them all. Knowing how disorganising and unpredictable children were, she shuddered at the idea. Knowing her own paradoxical nature, harsh in many ways, but unduly sensitive in others, she shuddered even more. And the presence of this camp in the bracken was another source of the anxiety she tried so hard to avoid.

She wanted them gone for her own selfish reasons. Yet now that she knew that one of the campers was Elvira, she was also anxious for the girl's welfare. She had to do something *now*, this morning, before the turmoil inside her became unbearable, although doing it would in the short run only create more turmoil. With a deep sigh, she stood up, and carefully trod the zigzag route back to the main path through the woods.

It was a mile and a half to the village, where she now had to go. Taking the car would wake Jonathan, so she would walk. She was still too early, anyway. The path came out onto a stretch of road leading to the village, past the northern boundary of Redstone's land. The Redstone buildings could not be seen from there, but the Grimsdales' house could, on the crest of the opposite hill. There was no high hedge on either side of this road, it having been widened in recent years, and the great banks bulldozed away, to be replaced by an ugly fence of posts and wire. Nobody, it seemed, had been willing to pay for a new hedge to be laid. Not Guy and not the Council. Pity, thought Cappy, not for the first time. It would have been several useful months' work for Phoebe.

It was still twenty minutes or so short of seven o'clock when she reached her destination. The door of the cottage, high on its bank, was firmly closed, and there was no sign of life. No whistling kettle or mumbling radio. She tried the door, confident that it would not be locked.

Inside the living room, she walked to a door in the corner, and unlatched it. It opened onto a flight of stairs, steep and uncarpeted. She went up, not caring that she made a noise.

Phoebe was asleep under a great heavy eiderdown,

surely far too hot for a June night. Her badger-striped hair was all that Cappy could see. There was a sour smell, tinged with something offensive: rotting meat, thought Cappy, glancing round the room for some clue as to its origin. She went to the bed, and laid a hand on the woman's shoulder, under the bedcover.

'Phoebe. I want you to come with me,' she said.

The woman turned over, her eyes immediately locking onto Cappy's. She showed no surprise. 'What did you say?' she grumbled.

'I want you to come and get Elvira. She's not safe where she is.'

Phoebe sighed, and sat up, in a great heaving motion like a walrus bursting out of the sea. She was naked, and Cappy suddenly found the source of the smell. Phoebe's right breast was at least twice the size of its partner, ulcerated and discoloured. 'Oh God,' said Cappy.

Phoebe glanced down at herself, and gave a little shrug. 'Yes. It's going to get me pretty soon now, the bloody thing. That's why—' She stopped abruptly, staring suspiciously at her visitor. 'And don't say it. Just don't.'

'You underestimate me,' replied Cappy quietly. 'I'd do exactly the same in your position.'

'Ah. I might have known.' She swung herself out of bed, stomach flat, legs muscular and lean. Cappy felt a pang of admiration. And sorrow. She couldn't remember when she last felt such sorrow, and it made her angry.

'Come on,' she urged, brusquely. 'You still have to think about Elvira.'

'Don't I always think of Elvira,' said Phoebe, suddenly

savage. 'It's all I ever fucking think about. What's her trouble now?'

'I'll have to show you. Have you got something we can drive?'

'I've got the van. Can't promise it'll start, though.' She pulled on a pair of jeans, and then turned away to bind her swollen breast in a kind of modified bra, which kept it close against her body. She sprayed herself with something perfumed, which struck Cappy as grotesquely incongruous, then a T-shirt followed, and a baggy sweatshirt, and Cappy could see why nobody would guess at Phoebe's cancer.

The old van started first try, and Phoebe drove it jerkily down her rutted track, and out into the road leading through the village square. Nobody was about. Cappy directed her to the edge of the woods, next to the opening used by picnicking tourists, and ordered her to turn off the engine. 'We have to walk from here,' she said.

Phoebe sighed. 'Trouble, is it?' she said, sounding achingly tired. 'Can't pretend I didn't know it'd come in the end. Though nobody can say I didn't do my best. Lead on, then.'

Amos hadn't slept well that night, running again and again over the kaleidoscope of events of the previous day. The vicar had taken charge, driving him to the police station, standing over him while he explained about Phoebe and his suspicions concerning her and Elvira. They had written some of it down, nodding and shaking their heads, sucking their pens, exchanging glances.

'I hope you're taking this seriously,' the vicar had said

to them, sternly. 'This is extremely important information – you do realise that.'

'It could be, sir,' they said. 'But we'll have to take care how we approach it. It isn't as if you've produced any hard evidence here, is it?'

'*Motive*, man!' Father Edmund had shouted. 'Don't tell me you haven't realised there is now a motive.'

'I'm not quite sure I follow you, sir,' said one of the detectives. Amos had been amused by the vicar's exasperation. It hardly mattered to him now, whether the police believed him or not. He knew in his own mind what this whole miserable business had been about, and that was all that really mattered.

The vicar had spelt it out. 'Phoebe and Amos are Elvira's natural parents. She always rebuffed any approaches from Amos in the early years, until he assumed that she wanted nothing from him – if he was indeed the girl's father, which he often doubted. Now, when Elvira is too much trouble, and she thinks an easier life might be nice, Phoebe suddenly remembers that Amos has money in the bank, and wants it for her girl. She told him as much – didn't she, Amos?'

He nodded slowly. 'Sort of,' he agreed.

'So,' went on Father Edmund, 'she had to arrange that Isaac was put out of the way, so Elvira could take his place, and live with Amos, as housekeeper and acknowledged daughter.' He faltered, realising that his imagination was running away with him. He caught the look of amused contempt on the policeman's face.

'Are you telling me, sir, that Phoebe Winnicombe killed Isaac Grimsdale?'

'No, 'twasn't her,' said Amos more firmly than he felt. 'But could be she put someone up to it.' He stared at the wall, trying to convince himself that this was the case. 'But he tried to kill me, as well,' he pointed out. 'That's a facer, now isn't it?'

The conversation had become increasingly disjointed after that, the police repeatedly trying to glean some hard facts and the vicar shouting one minute, and stammering over some silly notion the next. In the end, he'd been taken home again. They told him that the new information had been 'very useful', but they'd have to process it first before taking any action.

Now, on this early morning, with the pigeons having long, burbling conversations right outside his window, and from somewhere the annoying sound of a returning cat mewling for food, Amos abandoned any further attempt to sleep and got out of bed.

As always, he went to his window, and looked out to check the weather. There wasn't a single cloud to be seen, just a thin haze above the Mabberley woods opposite. A fine day, then. A good day for getting back to something like normal, checking on the neglected beasts and deciding on how to proceed from here. If one of Isaac's cats had escaped from its new home and come back, perhaps that was not such a terrible thing, after all. It could at least catch a few mice.

Then a movement in the distance caught his eye. Someone was walking along the road, below the woods, alongside the new fence. A tiny figure, moving at a comfortable walking pace. It seemed to him it must be a woman. And whoever it was, he knew for certain that it meant trouble, and another day of chaos, vexation and fear.

He could think of no suitable action, other than a continued vigil at the window. Scanning Redstone, he could see no movement at all. The pale-yellow cows were slowly beginning to cluster at the gate of their field, away to the right, but it would be half an hour or more before anybody got up to milk them. His mind reran, yet again, the whole course of events since Isaac had died. Then he went back to the killing of Sam Carter and his own subsequent arrest. And something new occurred to him; something which gave him a momentary sense of gladness.

Sam had been in the barn tinkering with some machinery when Amos had gone down to Redstone. He hadn't been very friendly, Amos remembered; so that when Amos had accidentally kicked over a shotgun left carelessly propped against the barn wall with a pull-through rag next to it, he'd quickly stood it up again without saying anything. It had all been over in a second, and Sam hadn't even seen what happened.

He wiped a hand across his brow, lingering over the lump on his temple, which was still tender. The blow had affected his memory; he was sure of that now. The days before Isaac's death were a blur to him. And, so it would seem, some of the things that happened since then were also slipping about in his head, loose from their moorings. Hadn't something strange happened to him in hospital one night, for example? Or had that just been a dream? An old woman crawling about on the floor did not seem very probable.

364

He sat there, forgetting where he was; forgetting the time of day, watching a succession of images from his memory and imagination; a waking nightmare in which he lost all sense of his immediate surroundings.

But his eye was alert for activity outside. A van went speeding along that same woodside road, and Amos thought he knew whose it was. The colour was distinctive: a light mustard hue which had been in his own yard not many days before. It brought him out of his reverie. If he was right, and Phoebe was driving around the countryside at this hour, then perhaps things really were finally coming to a head.

The van slowed, just at the point where his view was obscured by a high old hedge, and passed out of sight. Perhaps, after he'd had some breakfast, and attended to that persistent cat, he'd walk over there, towards the Mabberley place, and see if he could discover what might be going on.

Jonathan was not at first alarmed when he woke to find Cappy's side of the bed deserted. She did this often, and would usually appear at about seven with a cup of tea for him. It was only seven fifteen now. No reason to be concerned.

But as he lay there, he realised that there was no sound of movement from downstairs, which *was* unusual. He got out of bed and went to the top of the stairs to listen more carefully. Nothing.

It hit him then that she had gone back to that camp in the woods. And something must have happened there, because she would not have stayed out so long, knowing he'd worry.

Okay, he admitted to himself. *I'm worried. Now what do I do?* He realised that although she had told him about the camp, he had no idea where it actually was. If he went looking for her, he could spend all day searching and still not cover more than half the whole area of woodland. Unless there were some helpful noises, like gunshots or screams.

'Damn it!' he said aloud. 'This is getting beyond a joke.'

With a strong sense of doing the wrong thing, he lifted the telephone receiver and pushed the 9 button twice. Then he quickly put it down again. No, that very definitely wasn't right. He should find the number of the local station and call them direct. That would be better. Why hadn't those stupid men given him a card with the number on it? He flipped through the directory, peripherally aware that his sight was now bad enough to need glasses for something like this. He had to hold the book at arm's length to read the 'Police' entry.

A tired-sounding woman answered. 'Could I speak to someone dealing with the Redstone murders,' he said urgently.

'What?'

'Surely you've heard about it? Two men killed on their own farm.'

'Oh. Right.' She woke up a bit. 'Hold on, sir.'

A long silence ensued. Finally a man spoke, warily. 'Can I help you, sir?' he said.

Jonathan tried to be brief, yet urgent, although it took a while to establish his identity to the man's satisfaction. 'I think my wife could be in danger. There are people hiding in our woods. She found a sort of camp there, a few days ago.'

'But never reported it, is that right sir?'

'Yes, yes. Now I think she's gone there, and might be – well – in danger.'

'Can you show us this secret camp, sir?'

Jonathan cleared his throat. 'Well, not precisely. But if you'd send someone, we might start a search.'

Another silence. 'All right, sir. Someone will be with you shortly. Where should we meet you?'

'At the entrance to the woods, on the village road. The one they widened. There's a parking area that the tourists use.'

'Right, sir. We'll see you there.'

As she led the cows down into the milking yard, Lilah heard a car speeding along the road below the woods. It was going unusually fast and she tutted to herself. A few minutes later, another one followed, just as quickly. *Something's happening*, she thought.

Chapter Thirty-Four

Cappy and Phoebe arrived just as the occupant of the bracken hideaway was stirring. Perhaps they had been less than silent during their approach. In any case, Phoebe gave no time for assessment or gentle awakenings.

'You bloody girl!' she cried. 'Come out of there!'

A rounded backside emerged slowly, as Elvira reversed into the open on all fours. Something pathetically childlike in the clumsy crawling struck Cappy painfully, and renewed her sense of sadness at what was happening. She opened her mouth to caution Phoebe to be gentle with her daughter, but closed it again. What did she know about it? Standing there, watching these two bizarre countrywomen, she felt more alien than at any time since arriving in England, ten years ago.

Before Elvira could stand up, Phoebe had seized hold of her and pulled her upwards. 'Mum!' squawked the girl. 'Leave me alone.' Then she turned to face her mother and Cappy saw a look of pure malice fix itself on her features. 'Why don't you leave me *alone*?' she repeated. 'Why'd you come chasing after me?'

Phoebe released her hold and looked at Cappy. 'This lady said you weren't safe here.'

Elvira laughed harshly, maniacally. The sound rang through the woods, silencing the birds. Cappy wanted to cover her ears; she had never heard such an inhuman sound. The girl was obviously not merely backward; she was seriously deranged.

'Well?' Elvira demanded. 'What're you going to do now?' She spoke thickly, as if her tongue were too big for her mouth. Phoebe looked to Cappy for assistance, an anxious, doubtful look coming into her eyes.

'You ought not to be here,' she told her daughter. 'It's trespassing.'

'I'm not hurting anyone.' Elvira was defiant.

'Come on, girl,' said Phoebe. 'Remember what we talked about. Remember yesterday, when he came to see us? There's no need to live out here, like some animal, when you can have a lovely new home. Remember?' She spoke soothingly, almost hypnotically, but Cappy knew that she was being careful not to give anything away. She seemed unsure as to whether Elvira would understand her. Her face was tense and desperate.

The girl narrowed her eyes, so they almost disappeared in her plump cheeks. 'Don't need a new home,' she replied. 'Getting married, I am.' She laughed again. 'Yeah, I am. Really and truly getting married.'

'What do you mean?' Phoebe's voice was high with shock. 'Who's been getting at you? Who's been out here with you? I heard stories of you being with some man. What's been going on?'

Before she could reply, Elvira's attention was drawn by the sound of heavy footsteps crashing through the undergrowth. All three of them turned towards the noise.

'Here they are!' came a man's voice. 'Over here!'

In no time there were three policemen – one of them alarmingly tall – confronting them, standing with their arms held out from their sides as if ready to head off escaping animals. Cappy took a deep breath to steady her pounding heart, then walked towards them.

'It's all right,' she said. 'Nobody's been hurt. I'm Mrs Mabberley. My husband owns these woods.'

'And your husband is very worried about you,' said one of the men. 'He asked us to come and make a search for you. Is there anybody else here?' He looked round, eyes darting here and there, but Cappy shook her head.

'And who are these ladies?' the man pursued.

Like a hostess, Cappy introduced them. 'Phoebe Winnicombe and her daughter, Elvira.'

Phoebe threw an accusing look at Cappy before reaching out a hand to Elvira. 'We were just going home. Weren't we, love?'

Elvira nodded very slightly, and bent to pick up the canvas bag which was lying beside the mouth of the bracken cave.

'Has someone been sleeping here?' pursued the man. 'Would you mind showing us?'

Elvira shrugged and flapped an arm briefly towards her hideout. She said nothing.

Slowly, the policemen seemed to come to the conclusion that they had been directed to something important. They became mutedly excited, glancing at each other, muttering briefly, as they examined the area. The women stood passively watching, although Cappy was anxious to move away. At last she said, almost pleading, 'Am I free to go home now?'

'Well,' said the man doubtfully, 'I think, in the circumstances, I'll have to ask all of you to come with us for questioning.'

'What on earth do you mean?' Cappy spoke stridently. 'We haven't done anything to justify that. You don't mean to say you're arresting us, surely? I've made no complaint against Elvira.'

'No, madam, we're not arresting you, but you must be aware that there is a murder inquiry going on. Three people have been killed within half a mile of this spot, in recent weeks. The existence of this camp, so close by, is something we must take seriously. We need to know exactly who has been here; when; for how long. If you would be kind enough to help us with our enquiries, I'm sure it will be in everybody's best interests.'

Cappy sighed. 'Well, could we get on with it, then? And could we first tell my husband that I'm all right? Where is he now, anyway?'

'He went in the other direction, with our sergeant. I can contact them, if you'll just give me a moment.' He unhooked a small mobile phone from his belt and tapped its buttons. Before he spoke, he walked some paces away, but Cappy could still hear that the signal was poor, and the voice at the other end very crackly.

She looked at Phoebe and Elvira. They were standing apart, Phoebe looking ill and bewildered, Elvira pale and

371

frightened. *What have I done?* Cappy wondered. *Why on earth did I get myself involved in this?* She moved towards them. 'Come on,' she said. 'Better get moving.'

With a sudden shriek, Elvira backed away from her, before turning tail and running into the deepest part of the woodland. In an astonishingly short time, she was lost from sight. Heart in her mouth, Cappy realised that she was heading right for the cannabis patch. *'Catch her!'* she screamed at the stolid policemen. 'Go after her!' She danced up and down in her anxiety, stopping only when Phoebe went up to her and clapped a hand on her shoulder, shaking her roughly.

'Why?' she demanded. 'Why are you so keen for her to be caught?'

Cappy ignored her, still frantic, watching two of the men begin to give chase. The third one finished speaking into his phone, and began to tap in new numbers. 'How far can she go?' he asked Cappy.

'A long way,' she said. 'It comes out over by Roadworthy Cross, in that direction. Assuming she goes in a straight line, that is. She seems to know her way around. You could get someone to head her off . . .' She faltered. It was too difficult to explain to someone who didn't know the area. There were tiny lanes and tracks, nameless in most cases, criss-crossing the woodlands and surrounding fields. Elvira would be at a huge advantage.

'We're not doing any good here,' decided the man. 'Would you both come with me, please?' He led the way purposefully and almost accurately, back to the main path through the woods. Cappy saw Jonathan fifty yards away, coming towards

372

them, and ran to meet him, flinging herself in his arms.

'I've been a fool,' she said breathlessly, before anyone could come close enough to hear. 'But let me do all the talking, will you? It'll all be a ghastly mess otherwise.'

The policeman came up behind her. 'Mr Mabberley, would you please take your wife home? We'd like you both to stay there until we can sort things out here. I've called for reinforcements and another vehicle, so we can take you all in for questioning. But my priority must be to examine that hideaway. Can I rely on you, sir?'

'Of course,' said Jonathan, easily. 'Come on, darling. We'll go and get some breakfast.'

Cappy smiled up at him, acting the innocent, then looked at the policeman. 'We'll be waiting for you at the house,' she said. 'But I don't think you'll find anything important there. That poor girl isn't right in the head, you know. She wouldn't do anybody any harm.' She looked back at Phoebe. 'She's ill,' she added, in a low voice. 'Don't be hard on her. She hasn't done anything, either.'

The man did not smile. 'We'll be along for you in a little while,' he said, and nodded at Jonathan to take her away.

Amos met the Mabberleys in their yard. He could see that something strange was going on, and it came to him with total certainty that it had been Cappy he had seen walking along the road at six-thirty that morning.

'Where's Phoebe?' he said, surprising himself at the question. Cappy's answer was even more of a surprise.

'She's gone with the police,' she said. 'They want to question her.'

'High time,' he growled. 'They should lock that woman up.'

Cappy wouldn't be drawn. Her flurry of concern had burnt itself out, and she no longer cared what happened to the Winnicombes. 'Well,' she said vaguely. 'I don't know how we can help you.'

Amos gave Jonathan a pleading look. He could see himself through their eyes: old worn-out clothes, and the body inside them not much better. 'Will ye listen to me,' he said. 'I've things to tell.'

Jonathan shifted uneasily, holding Cappy close around the shoulders. 'My wife's had a shock,' he said feebly. 'I ought to get her into the house.'

'Shock?' echoed Amos harshly, and put a hand to the wound on his head. 'Shock, is it?'

'Honestly, my friend, I don't think we're the people you should speak to. It's the Beardons, or the police, don't you think? I can see you're troubled about Phoebe. And Elvira seems to be in some trouble . . .' He glanced at Cappy for confirmation, but she did not respond. 'Anyway, it's all in the hands of the police now.'

Amos turned to leave. 'This the quick way to Redstone?' he queried, indicating the track down to a gate and across the fields; the one Lilah had used on the night of the barbecue.

'That's right,' said Jonathan.

The chase through the woods did not last long. Den's long legs soon gained on Elvira, despite her superior knowledge of the terrain. She was wearing only socks, which did not effectively shield her feet from the many sharp and prickly plants in her path. He caught at her arm as she hesitated on the edge of a dense patch of brambles, and pulled her to a standstill. She screamed and punched at his chest, but he held on. His colleague was soon holding her other arm, and together they started walking her back the way they'd come.

'You *can't*, you *mustn't*,' she wept, hanging heavy between them like a baulky toddler. 'I bain't going with you.'

'Come on, Elvira,' said Den. 'Don't you remember me? We used to go on the same bus to school.'

She squinted up at him. 'I never went to your school,' she said.

'No,' he agreed. 'But you went on our bus.'

'Hmmm,' she grunted. He could see her trying to remember, and in the process forgetting to obstruct their progress. He kept up his amiable chatter.

'Nice camp you've got there. Must have been fun, 'specially in the nice weather.' She grinned, but said nothing. 'Got yourself a boyfriend then? Is that right?' he pressed on.

'Getting married, I am,' she agreed.

She was walking with them now, yelping occasionally when something stabbed at her feet. 'Forgot your DMs,' remarked the other policeman. 'Look like new ones, too.'

'He gave 'un to me. For a present,' she simpered. 'Ma said I couldn't have any, so he bought 'un. Shows he loves me. He do love me,' she repeated earnestly. 'Really and truly.'

'I should hope he does,' said Den, and found himself meaning it.

They stopped at the camp, giving Elvira time to put her Doc Martens on and gather up her bag. Then they drove her to the police station. She became agitated in the car, turning to look out of the back window, watching the road behind them intently.

'Is she fit to be interviewed?' the desk officer asked when they arrived.

'We've got no choice,' said Den. 'I think she'll be okay if we're gentle.'

'Gentle!' repeated the man, but a more careful look at Elvira gave him pause. 'I see what you mean,' he said. 'Poor little bitch. Should we get a woman to do it?'

Den considered briefly, then shook his head. 'She seems all right with men,' he said.

Den was asked to sit with Elvira while a senior detective interviewed her. She seemed at first not to need him, striding into the room in the clumping boots for a minute or two, before plonking herself down on one of the chairs. Den realised that she must have been sent for assessments of various sorts for much of her life, and had grown accustomed to strange rooms full of strange people. She waited quietly for something to happen.

'Please tell us your full name,' began the interviewer.

'Elvira Mary Winnicombe,' came the prompt reply.

'And your address?'

The reply to this was equally forthcoming. Encouraged, the man moved swiftly on to the main business. 'Would you tell us, please, Elvira, if you know anything about the way Mr Guy Beardon died?'

She narrowed her eyes at him and shook her head. 'Never heard nothing,' she said, and then frowned doubtfully.

'You do know who I mean? The man who fell into the slurry pit.'

Elvira giggled, and folded her arms tightly across her chest. 'He never fell in,' she said.

The room went still and silent and the interviewer read Elvira the convoluted wording of the newly-revised police caution.

After that it was easy. For Den, it felt too easy. They didn't even have to trick her into telling the whole story. He wanted to stop her, to say, 'Hasn't anyone warned you not to tell us all this?' She seemed to feel no caution, no hesitation about revealing what had happened. It was disconcerting and more – like a very young child confessing to evil deeds, with no sense at all of having done something wrong. As she went on, Den found it almost unbearable.

At last, the important question came. 'Who told you to do this, Elvira? Who said you should push Mr Beardon into the muck?'

'Somebody,' she said, abruptly switching into a cunning demeanour. 'Don't you ask me that.'

'All right,' agreed the man. 'I won't. Now, what about the other man? Sam Carter. Somebody shot him, didn't they? Do you know how to shoot a gun, Elvira?'

Her laughter was genuine. 'I do,' she said. ''Tis easy. He fell in the nettles.' She laughed again and Den's skin crawled.

'How did you get the gun?'

'I went into his room when he was milking. They was all busy, even the missus. Then I kept 'un till 'twas needed.'

'And then you went back to Redstone?'

'He was bad, that Sam. Taking things not his'n. I knew I should shoot'n, so I did. He was talking to me, then he got running, so I shot'n. By the nettles.'

'But—' The man bit back his puzzlement. His question would have been beyond her understanding.

She ignored the interruption. 'Then I threw it away and ran back to the hideout.' Den tried to visualise the scene of Sam's killing, but failed. Surely the man could have snatched back the gun, or talked her out of her intention.

'Were you all by yourself?' he asked, before he could stop himself.

The cunning look came back and she clamped her mouth shut. Then she nodded. 'I pulled both the triggers,' she said. 'One first, then the other. Triggers, they're called,' she repeated cheerfully.

'That's right,' confirmed her questioner. 'They certainly are.'

There was little enthusiasm for further questions after that and Elvira herself seemed to have exhausted her supply of information. They took her fingerprints, and escorted her to a cell, giving her a generous breakfast. Nobody rejoiced when the prints were found to match those on the gun which had killed Sam. Neither did they when the muck-covered trainers were found to be Elvira's size, with marks inside matching the impressions of her toes found in the Doc Marten boots.

'Means, opportunity, confession, evidence,' listed the man who had interviewed her. 'All that's missing is motive.'

'And for that, we need to locate this chap who says he's going to marry her,' said Den. 'And that shouldn't be too difficult. If anybody wants me, I'll be at Redstone.'

Lilah was waiting for news. She had seen a third police car speeding towards the Mabberley woods only a few minutes

378

before the milking was finished, as she went out to send a heifer in. Tim Rickworth was there for the later stages of the milking; he was now sloshing water about, brushing out the parlour, whistling foolishly as he worked. She had to admit, though, that he had been a big help. The cows were sent back to their field, Roddy appearing to follow them up and shut them in.

'Breakfast time,' Lilah announced, and she and Tim kicked off their boots at the back door and went into the house.

'What a time for a visit!' remarked Miranda, glancing out of the window as she stood over the toaster. 'What on earth does *he* want? You'll have to talk to him, Li. I'm too busy.'

Lilah shook her head, unable to see anyone through the window. 'What are you talking about? Who's here?'

'He's crossing the yard now. And before he knocks – I hope you haven't forgotten I'm going to Nottingham.'

'Not much chance of that,' said Lilah, pulling a face. 'I still think you're mad.'

'Well, think what you like. Now you've got Tim, you can manage without me, and with the offer of a lift, it all works out perfectly.'

'What time's he coming?'

'Not sure exactly. Ten or eleven. It was very nice of him to offer, and if you're here, you can come and meet him. He is your half-brother, after all. Aren't you curious to see him?'

'I am,' offered Roddy.

'I don't mind seeing him. Later on, I'll be happy to get to know him. It's just . . .' Lilah stopped. How could she explain the sense of overload, of struggling from hour to hour, deliberately closing her mind off to anything new? Any distraction now might make her release her hold on the work, the sense of danger, her own sanity.

They waited for the knock on the door, and then Miranda went to open it.

Chapter Thirty-Five

Amos looked wearily round the crowded kitchen, and seemed overcome. For several minutes he said nothing, his head hanging, the picture of misery. 'Everybody out,' Miranda suddenly ordered. 'Leave this to me. There are too many of us in here anyway. Roddy, take Tim and get the calves done. Lilah, you must have things to do.'

'I'll just finish my toast first,' she said calmly. 'Then I'll go and see if Jezebel's calved yet. She didn't come in with the others this morning.'

Left alone, several minutes later, Miranda sat down with Amos, pushing yet another mug of coffee towards him. 'Have you come to tell us something?' she said.

Amos shook his head helplessly.

'You didn't come from home just now, did you?' she pressed him. 'You came from the wrong direction. Where have you been?'

'Up there.' He nodded towards the Mabberley land. 'They've had trouble there. I saw her – early – walking. The police came.'

'Yes, Lilah said she'd heard them. Do you know what's been going on? Have they found somebody?'

'Phoebe! They've arrested Phoebe. I know about that. The Mabberleys told me.' He was suddenly eager, animated. 'I came to explain to you, why she did it. Why she had Isaac killed, so that that girl of hers would have to come and live with me.' He paused, and rubbed his head, all around the swollen bruise. 'At least . . .' He subsided as suddenly as he'd revived. 'Yes, that must be it,' he frowned. 'She wants the girl to live with me, and have my money when I go. It's my daughter, you see.'

Miranda sat down opposite him, and put one hand on his arm. 'Amos? Say that again, would you?'

'Elvira. Phoebe's girl. The simple one. She's mine.'

'Oh my God.' Miranda wanted to take him in her arms and rock him, but had the sense to resist the urge. But pity rushed through her, in a confused torrent. Pity for Amos, for Elvira and for herself.

Lilah walked briskly through two fields in search of the missing Jezebel, who was another first-time mother. When one of the heifers was due to calve, it would be brought down to join the herd a few days ahead of her time, to become accustomed to the new regime and her new sisters. Then the calving would take place in the company of older animals, which seemed to have a calming influence. It was usual for the new arrival to be found by whoever went to fetch them in for milking, morning or evening. Lilah had heard Guy labelled old-fashioned for this *laissez faire* system, many a time, but he insisted that it worked, and calving difficulties were rare. The heifer, unlike cows on their second or third calf, would sometimes scarcely seem to notice when her baby was removed from her, and she was added in at the end of the milking session, and given quantities of feed to boost her milk yield. It was a source of some self-satisfaction to Lilah that she had accomplished all this herself, in the midst of all the turmoil, when little Endurance had been born.

Lilah wondered whether Miranda's lift had turned up yet. The road snaked around the perimeter of this field, and two or three cars had passed within the last few minutes; perhaps one of them was Terry, she thought. Perhaps after she'd found the heifer, she could climb out onto the road and wait there to wave. Having said goodbye to her mother, she was in no hurry to return to the house and go through it all over again, even if that did mean she could have met her half-brother.

The animal she was seeking came into view amongst the trees. It was standing, head down, sniffing at a blur of pale brown. 'Ah,' Lilah said to herself. 'Too late!'

The calf was dry, probably born the previous evening, and it stood up quite competently when she came into sight. The huge black eyes turned apprehensively towards her, and its mother turned to face the intruder. Lilah could see already that the calf was a bull. From long habit, she sighed. Another trip to market, selling him at a few days old for cat meat. There was no animal so redundant as a male Jersey calf. Though perhaps he was lucky not to be wanted for veal. At least his end would be quick.

He looked a good size, and Lilah doubted whether she

could carry him the whole distance back to the yard. The simple way to get him and his mother back would be to pop him into the link box on the back of the tractor and drive slowly home with the heifer following anxiously behind. But that entailed walking back, starting up the tractor, driving up to the field again . . . quicker, probably, to see whether she could manage him now.

Guy had always slung calves across his shoulders and marched along as if they were featherweights. Lilah could never balance them, and her instability caused panic in the passenger, whose kicking and struggling made it impossible. Instead, she preferred to hold them to her chest, the four legs bunched together, and the head hanging free. It wasn't easy, but at least they kept still that way.

'Come on, my lad,' she grunted, getting hold of him. The heifer protested softly, only a few feet away. 'Oof, you're a heavy one!'

At least it was downhill. Most of the fields sloped down towards the yard, in its natural hollow. Taking it steadily, Lilah managed to get across the first field. The heifer followed her, nosing at the calf once or twice, and mumbling at Lilah in a low voice, trying to make her put the baby down.

She had to drop him, to rest her shoulders and get her breath back. She thought she might try driving them for a bit, although it was famously impossible to persuade a bull calf to do anything you wanted. Neither pushing nor pulling would work. But every few yards they covered would be a gain, and she didn't think she could carry him again for a while.

When Den came into view from the next gateway, she

could hardly believe it. She had never, ever, been so pleased to see anyone, and the grin that spread across her face must have been visible a mile away.

'Can I help?' he said, once in earshot.

'You certainly can. Do you think you can carry this little chap? He's a bit heavy for me.'

'I might manage him. I'm beginning to get used to your calves. This one looks rather cuddly.'

'He's clean and dry, anyway. And he doesn't struggle, like some. We don't get fond of the bulls, though. They're not with us long enough.'

'Sad.' He hoisted the calf onto his shoulders, as Guy had used to do.

'Is this a social call?' she asked, as they began to cross the field. The heifer continued to trot behind her calf, but kept more distance now the man was carrying him. Lilah also had to trot to keep up with Den's long strides.

'We have someone in custody,' he said, without any preliminaries. Lilah could hear the excitement in his voice, and looked at him searchingly.

'It's early days, but we've taken fingerprints, and they match the set on the gun that we couldn't identify. And there's been a confession, for what it's worth. And the clothes – it seems they were hers.'

'*Hers!*' said Lilah, feeling the thrum of a host of strong emotions. *Sylvia!* 'Who?' she demanded. 'Who are you talking about?'

Den huffed a little, and shifted the calf into a better position. 'This isn't how I'd imagined telling you,' he said wryly, his face pink and boyish.

'Never mind that,' Lilah exploded. 'Tell me, will you!'

'Elvira Winnicombe,' he said flatly. 'When I left, she'd already made a full confession. I didn't stop to hear all of it, but we're sure. There isn't any doubt about it. Elvira killed your father and Sam Carter.'

'But—' Lilah's head was whirling. Now that the moment had come, it was dreadful, being told like this that a particular person, someone she knew, had deliberately murdered her father. There was no satisfaction to it. She stopped in her tracks, gazing around at the woods and hills, and down at the farmhouse, the slurry pit, the barn. Nothing made sense. Her head rang with the madness of it. 'But *why*?' she said fiercely. 'Why on earth would she *do* that?'

'That's where we're stuck, for the moment,' he said mildly.

The effect of his tone was twofold. One part of her wanted to lie down and drum her heels and scream and scream. But his forbearance also reminded her that he was sharing information with her that she was not yet entitled to. She owed it to him to behave rationally. She should be grateful.

'Were you there?' she asked him, after a minute or two. 'When they arrested her?'

'Yes. I chased her through the woods. She was very fast for her size. But we caught her soon enough. She didn't have any shoes on. She began jabbering away, when we interviewed her at the station, although it didn't make much sense at first. In the end, she told us quite easily. She couldn't have known what she was doing, poor thing. Seemed quite pleased with herself, as if she'd been really clever.'

'It sounds horrible. I mean – Elvira! She was on the school bus.'

386

'I know.'

'But Sam. How could she have shot Sam? How could he *let* her?'

Den shook his head minimally, hampered by the calf.

'Can you really believe her?' Lilah said, after a while. 'Is she fit to make a proper confession? Somebody might have put her up to it.'

'There's evidence. We don't have to rely on the confession.'

'She has a boyfriend,' Lilah suddenly remembered. 'A lover. I saw them together. So did Jonathan, I think.'

'Yes. And I have a feeling he was there when she shot Sam. Otherwise, as you say, it doesn't seem credible. Who is he? That's what everyone wants to know now. She thinks he's going to marry her.'

'I have no idea. I saw them when it was dark. I didn't see his face.'

Carefully, he took her hand, holding the calf unsteadily with the other one. Behind them the heifer made anxious noises. 'When this is over . . .' he began. 'Do you think—?'

'What?' She felt a mixture of impatience and submission. 'What will we do?'

'Forget all this. Be ordinary.' He smiled down at her. 'Does that sound good?'

She nodded. 'I think it will, one of these days. When I can dare to feel hopeful again.' She wriggled against his protective arm. 'But, God! *Elvira*!'

A sound drew their attention back to the farmyard. A bright red car drove through the gates. 'Heavens! That must be Terry,' she said.

'Terry?' He spoke sharply, suddenly all attention. 'Who's he?'

'My half-brother. He's taking Mum to see his mother in Nottingham. The two Mrs Beardons want to meet each other.'

'Have you told anybody about this?'

'What do you mean? Who would we tell?'

'Us, you fool. The police. She can't just go off like that.'

'Oh, I think she did say something to that Dave chap. Nobody's going to stop her, surely. It's only for a day or two.' Suddenly, for no reason, she felt scared. 'Come on. I want to meet him. He is my brother, after all.'

'So do I,' said Den urgently. 'But we've got a few minutes. If it is him, they'll take a minute to load up, won't they?'

'Probably. Even so, I think we should get a move on.'

From halfway down the field, they gained a clearer view of the yard, perhaps three hundred yards away. Lilah could see the car already turned round, ready to leave; beside it was her mother and Amos and a man whose face she couldn't see. Miranda paused halfway between the house and the car, and went back to Amos. Lilah could see her speaking earnestly to him, patting his arm. He began to walk away from her, his head bowed. His direction was roughly that of his own house, across one of the other fields. As Lilah watched, now jogging ahead of the burdened Den, she saw the man open the car door and help Miranda in. There seemed to be something forceful in the way he did it, an unnatural haste. He slammed the door shut and began to walk round the back of the car to the driver's side. Everything was getting closer. She could call out now, and her mother would hear. She would soon be able to see the man's face clearly . . .

'Den!' She stopped. 'There's something wrong.' She felt her world slowly collapsing around her, like a castle built of toy bricks. In that instant she knew who and why and how, vividly, as if the truth had been punched into her.

Den started to run, the calf still around his neck, and the startled heifer also running to keep up. 'Stop!' he yelled, in a deafening voice. And then again, even louder, 'Stop, I tell you!' The man in the yard looked up. Lilah wondered later what he made of the immensely tall man charging along with a calf on his back and a cow cantering alongside.

However extraordinary it may have looked to him, he didn't hesitate. He leant over Miranda in the passenger seat; she seemed content to sit there at his bidding. Den paused, to set the calf on the ground. Lilah was moved, even in that moment, by how carefully, how tenderly, he did it.

Then he resumed his charging run, reaching the car in seconds. Terry met him, something long and apparently heavy held in both hands. Like a baseball player, he swung his club, making contact with Den's head before the policeman could do anything. Lilah, frozen, clenched inside with horror, half expected to see the head go soaring across the yard. Instead, Den simply dropped on the spot, folding up like a collapsing deckchair. Terry ran round the car to the driver's seat, jumped in and set the car quickly in motion, taking Miranda away. Lilah saw her begin to turn back, her mouth open, her eyes wide. The car engine seemed violently loud. She half noticed Amos coming back again, at a shambling run, almost exactly as he had run down to Redstone on the morning of Isaac's death. Somehow she knew that Amos too had understood in those moments exactly who, and why and how.

The next sound was the strangest of all. A terrible broken screaming came from somewhere, as Den lay there on his back, the side of his face already disfigured and purple. It took Lilah nearly a minute to understand that she was making the noise herself.

Chapter Thirty-Six

Lilah's next thought was for Roddy. A searing terror flashed through her that the killer had found her brother and killed him. Where was he, otherwise? And Tim? Why hadn't they been there, to save Den and Miranda? She gazed at Amos, who stood looking after the car, as if unsure whether it had really existed. His helplessness only fuelled her sense of panic. Den's gurgling moan brought her back to reality and she cautiously approached him; one eye was open and focused on her, but the other side of his face was a mess she could hardly bear to look at. The crowbar had caught him at an angle, smashing his cheekbone and jaw.

'Don't scream,' he mumbled, the words thick, but audible. 'It gives me a headache.'

'Just don't move,' she ordered him. 'You'll damage your brain if you do.' A snort from Amos triggered a rising hysteria.

'Same crowbar he used on me,' he said. 'Didn't damage my brain so much.'

She wanted to say something about Isaac and the permanent, terminal damage done to him, but restrained herself. Then she realised that she should go and call for help. The prospect of dialling 999 yet again from the Redstone phone was too much for her. It was like living in a time warp. Kneeling next to Den, she stroked ineffectively at his hair.

'Ought to fetch someone,' Amos observed.

'Go and see to it, then,' Lilah snapped. 'I'm not leaving him.'

Then everything happened at once. Jonathan's Land Rover came charging down the Redstone lane like cavalry in a western. Before it could properly slither to a stop, Tim came tumbling out of the passenger seat, looking oddly different. Immediately taking charge, he knelt beside Den and began to examine the wound. Lilah looked to Jonathan, bewildered, and saw Roddy, white-faced on the back seat, making no attempt to leave the vehicle.

'Where's your mother?' asked Tim.

'She's gone. With that man – Terry, I suppose. It was him who attacked Den.'

'Are you sure? Did you see him?'

'*Yes*, I saw everything. I saw them driving away. He was *kidnapping* her. Go after her, Jonathan. Please. He'll murder her next.' Her voice had risen to another scream, all control lost in the face of total nightmare. Den started to gurgle again, but Tim waved a hand to hush him. Then he addressed himself to Lilah.

'It's all right,' he soothed. 'There's a whole lot of police officers waiting at the top of your drive, with two squad cars. They'll catch him.'

'How on earth did they miss him just now, then?' she demanded. 'He's only been gone a couple of minutes.'

'Longer'n that,' said Amos reproachfully.

'Pity they didn't stop him on his way in,' Lilah snarled. 'What makes you think they'll manage it now?'

Tim frowned. 'They're bound to realise . . .' Interrupting himself, he extracted a phone from his pocket and made a hurried call. 'He's in the car that left just now,' he said. 'Don't lose him.'

Lilah stared at him for a long moment, and then gave up. 'Where have *you* been, anyway?' she demanded of her brother.

Roddy leant his head out of the Land Rover. 'The police phoned, trying to get hold of Den. We told them he'd gone up to see you, and left his phone in the car.' For the first time, Lilah noticed the police car parked unobtrusively beside the barn. Roddy went on: 'They said they wanted him to phone back. Tim and I were going to go up the field and get him, but then Jonathan phoned and told us what had happened with Phoebe and Elvira. He said we should keep Amos here, and he'd come round and drive him into town, because he had things to tell the police.'

'God, Roddy, get *on* with it,' Lilah shouted in frustration. 'I don't care about all this stuff.'

'Well, basically, we haven't been anywhere,' he retorted loudly. 'We were running after that red car with Mum in it, when Jonathan came down the lane, and we came back here with him.' Roddy glared at her, still pale, his lips shaking. 'Satisfied?'

The explanation fitted almost nothing that Lilah thought she had witnessed. The time frame seemed entirely wrong. 'Well, what do we do now?' she cried, looking round at the three standing men, and back to the prostrate Den. 'We've got to help Mum.'

'There'll be an ambulance here in a minute,' said Tim, holding his mobile telephone in one hand.

Lilah turned her attention back to Den, in an agony of indecision. 'I can't leave him. But I have to be sure that Mum's okay. She might be dead as well by this time. We have to follow the red car.'

Jonathan looked to Tim for an answer. 'Come *on*,' she screamed. There was a moment of hush, as the men seemed to commune silently.

'I don't think so,' said Tim, at last. 'It might be dangerous.'

'*Might?*' she demanded, increasingly hysterical. 'After all this?' She swept an expressive arm to embrace the entire farm, and finished by looking down at Den, lying on the ground, wounded and in pain.

In the car, Miranda faced the man who was abducting her. 'You killed Isaac,' she accused, her glance darting to the crowbar, wedged between the front seats. She could hardly speak for terror. 'Why? You didn't even know him.'

'Shut up,' he snapped, his voice unexpectedly Irish. 'Why should I tell you anything?'

'And Guy. You were involved in killing Guy, weren't you? Even if you didn't do it yourself.'

'I said *shut up*,' he repeated.

The bulging eyes and chewed lips warned Miranda that he was on the edge. Anything could happen. Her mind was blank, apart from a desperate need to understand. The car was going much too fast, swinging her painfully against the door, and then forcing her to brace herself to avoid falling onto him. She had undone her seatbelt, in a futile attempt to be ready to jump out of the car if it stopped or even slowed sufficiently.

Something forced her to keep up the questions. If he was going to kill her anyway, surely he owed her an explanation first? Wasn't that always what happened – the murderer revealed everything, on the assumption that his hearer would never live to share the secrets?

'Did you want Guy dead? Your own father?'

It didn't work. He merely turned to her for a second, and sneered. 'I won't tell you again. If you say one more word, I'll bash *your* head in as well.'

The high hedges, flashing pink and white with the summer flowers, skimmed past as he kept the accelerator hard down. There was a junction less than half a mile ahead, with a sharp bend just before it. They would be lucky to avoid disaster if he didn't slow down.

She wished she could see him better, and confirm the impression she'd had that he was uncannily like Guy to look at. But the reckless pace kept her gaze fixed mainly on the road ahead, willing it to remain clear. At least he was in no position to carry out his threat to bash her, so she risked further speech.

'Where are we going?' she asked.

He made no reply. She asked again, and he shook his head rapidly, side to side, as if shaking water from his hair; it was the craziest gesture he had made so far.

'You don't know,' she interpreted, dully. 'You haven't got any idea. Not to see your mother, I assume?'

'She's got nothing to do with this.'

'They'll catch you. You've killed someone.'

'Let them try.' He took the next bend faster than she could have imagined, and she reproached herself desperately, while clinging tightly to the door handle, shouting at him to slow down.

Jonathan and Tim were saved from more of Lilah's wrath by the strangely exciting throb of a helicopter engine coming rapidly closer. Everyone looked up. The panic died in Lilah and she sqautted beside Den, passive and wooden, waiting for the next impossibility to happen.

Somehow, the injured policeman was taken up into the deafening machine. When it lifted slowly, magically, up into the sky, she held her flying hair away from her face and watched.

She looked around yet again at her home, then up into neighbouring fields where the heifers galloped frantically to escape the terrifying noise in the sky. *They'll slip their calves*, she thought, and the idea seemed unbearably sad. In a rush, great hot tears began to run from her eyes at this final piece of destruction. For a few minutes, she couldn't see anything, but when she looked again, Tim and Jonathan were joining Roddy in the vehicle, and she followed automatically. They paused to speak to Amos.

'Go home, old chap,' said Tim, kindly. 'When this is over, someone'll come to see you're all right.'

Amos nodded submissively. Lilah wondered whether he had any idea what was going on. She couldn't remember where he fitted into the story, had no idea why he'd come to speak to Miranda. She felt no curiosity as to what might happen next. Her powers of reasoning seemed to have died. Huddled on the back seat of the inexplicably fast-moving Land Rover with Roddy, she let the tears flow. Everything was over now, the whole matter was at an end. If the helicopter fell out of the sky onto the Land Rover, it would be no more than fitting.

But gradually she became aware of how very rapidly they were travelling.

'Where are we going?' she asked, in the little-girl voice she'd sometimes used with her father.

'It's not over yet,' Tim threw over his shoulder. 'This guy is really something. Do you know him? Terry, you said his name was?'

'He's my half-brother. Mine and Roddy's.'

'Good God.' Jonathan whistled, then went quiet. After some thought he said, 'This is all very strange. There's something going on that I can't fathom out. Did this bloke kill Guy and Sam? Or what? And where does Elvira fit in?'

'He killed Isaac, I suppose,' said Lilah. 'But Elvira's been arrested for killing Daddy and Sam. Den just told me that.' In spite of herself, Lilah was reviving. 'Roddy looks as if he's going to be sick.'

As they left the village, heading towards town, she saw two police cars on the steep road some distance ahead of them, driving much too fast, one behind the other. She heard Jonathan say, 'They must have lost him.'

The view was patchy, but the road snaked for some distance between the hedges, destined to meet a much larger and busier road just over the brow of the hill. Everywhere felt oddly deserted to Lilah. Just two incongruous police cars, chasing madly after an invisible quarry, and themselves in the jolting Land Rover gaining on them all the time.

'Where the hell is he?' snapped Tim.

The inexorable climax built as she waited with a cold, numb horror. On the main road, they could see the police cars ahead, lights flashing. There was no traffic, making her feel again as if they were in a time warp, or some different reality altogether. 'They've stopped the traffic,' Tim said. 'I'm impressed.'

They came upon the final scene with devastating abruptness. The road dipped gracefully down into a shallow valley and up the other side, visible for a good distance, giving the occupants of the Land Rover a panoramic view of events. Halfway up the opposite side, a tractor was toiling along, evidently oblivious to the drama unfolding behind it. A red car was closing rapidly on it, and began to pull out to overtake it, just as the tractor itself began to make a right turn.

It was obvious that the car was travelling too fast to stop. For two or three seconds, Lilah was transported into her mother's body, seeing the whole encounter through Miranda's eyes, feeling the breathless, tingling fear that went with speed and that terrible sense of knowing that an impact was inevitable.

Afterwards, they concluded there must have been a moment of telepathy, which caused Miranda to duck her head and protect it with her arms, pressing herself against the firm side of the car and closing her eyes tightly. When the car swerved and then pitched and rolled, grinding through a thick hedge and plunging into a bramble-filled ditch, she gave herself up to it and simply waited for the sickening motions to stop.

The next part was lost to Lilah, the car obscured by a large beech tree, which it had mercifully avoided hitting. She saw the tractor driver climb down and walk unsteadily to the hole in the hedge, staring uncomprehendingly as first two police cars and then a Land Rover pulled up in the road. Overwhelmed, he stood passively, an insignificant bystander.

Lilah wanted to curl up tight and close her eyes, avoiding any further misery or responsibility. Would she have to watch her mother being lifted unconscious or dead from the car?

'Everybody out,' ordered Tim, urgently. 'You might be able to help.' Lilah and Roddy fumbled in unison with door handles, clumsy and slow, neither in any hurry to witness their mother's fate.

Tim held out a hand to each of them. Lilah took one, blinking at the strangeness of it. Surely Tim had desk-bound, white hands, with slim fingers and narrow wrists? This was the arm of a very different individual. She looked hesitantly into his face, almost afraid that he would peel off a latex mask to reveal someone wholly other underneath.

In a way, that's what he did. His eyes, formerly so casually friendly and eager to please, were now full of a mature intelligence, combined with a kind of apologetic understanding. His whole bearing had changed in one smooth transition from an unfit yuppie to a lean military professional. Lilah felt simultaneously betrayed and relieved. Meekly, she waited for him to assist her to her mother.

The door of the crashed car on the passenger side was now open, the angle it made transforming the car into some monstrous alien machine, a metal contraption with no purpose other than to crush its occupants. The door was being propped open by one of the policemen, and Miranda's legs in tight blue jeans began to emerge, apparently of their own volition.

Concerned male hands and arms caught her as she unfolded from the capsized seat and pushed herself up and out, like a strange birth from an experimental new species. With a curiously awkward wriggle, she stood upright, breathing deep and squaring her shoulders. Lilah watched, tense with apprehension, as her mother lifted first one foot, then the other, walking on the spot as if to test her legs. Three men hovered round her, hands fluttering, ready to catch her if she fell.

Lilah knew then that she had been doubly blessed. 'She's all right!' she screamed, alarming herself and Roddy at the force and volume of her words.

Miranda gave a little shrug. She was paler than Lilah had ever seen her, with strange mauve smudges under her eyes. She was gripping herself by the upper arms, as if cold, and kept glancing at the car quickly, then away again.

Lilah turned to the numerous policemen. 'She's cold,' she said accusingly, nodding towards her mother. One of them caught her eye.

'Right,' he said, as if receiving an order. 'John, there'll be a blanket in the back of your car.' Another man headed vaguely for the gap in the hedge and the parked cars.

Lilah realised that the apparent inactivity was because everyone's attention was drawn to the proceedings in and beside the car. They seemed tensely coiled, waiting for some climax yet to come. The siren of an ambulance preceded the vehicle along the lane, but nobody turned away from the man inside the car. With Miranda out of the way, two of them were able to crawl in and assess his condition. *He's sure to be dead*, thought Lilah, dispassionately.

But slowly, a second miraculous birth was being enacted. Inch by inch, feet first, he was being extracted from his metal womb. As a pair of clean blue trainers appeared, a new sound filled the void: an eerie, despairing shriek from the emerging man. Not so much pain, Lilah felt, as misery and failure and fear.

All in a moment there was a man lying on the ground, moaning and cursing, blood on his face and head, and something seriously wrong with his right shoulder. Two men knelt beside him, two more approached. One of them dangled a pair of handcuffs. 'How is he?' he demanded, his tone impatient and gruff.

'He'll live,' somebody said.

'That's all I wanted to know,' growled the man. Then he took a breath, and intoned the police caution, familiar from countless television dramas. And Lilah tentatively stepped closer for a proper look at Terry's face.

He was younger than she'd imagined, looking no more than twenty-six or seven, and his face was shockingly, agonisingly, familiar.

Chapter Thirty-Seven

Miranda had received a letter from Barbara, which she showed to anybody who might be interested. 'That'll explain it, I expect,' she said to Sylvia, who had remained by her side throughout Sam's funeral. She pulled the blue envelope from her bag and handed it to her friend. She knew the contents off by heart, and recalled it as she watched Sylvia read.

My dear Miranda,
I hardly know what to say. It feels just now as if the whole world has collapsed about our ears and I know you must be thinking the worst of me and my son. The truth is that Terry always had a bee in his bonnet about his dad. Guy became a sort of bogeyman to him, to blame for every bad thing that ever happened. He's been spying on you for a year or two now, thinking he could have the farm for his own. He hung around your village, using the vicar as a pretext. Maybe you didn't know that Edmund is a good friend of our man here, who is

a special companion of mine. Small world, as they say.

I tried to talk sense into him, truly I did. I said we'd do better to get things into the open, make friends with you. When Guy died, I did believe it was an accident. Terry swore to me he had nothing to do with it. Then the man Sam was shot, and I suppose I knew what must have happened. So I tried to turn a terrible situation into something good, which was why I wanted to meet you. But it all got beyond my control, and the rest you know better than I do.

Spare a thought for me, dear, if you can. Terry's in for a life sentence, and that's a heavy thing for a mother to bear. You have your son and your daughter alive and well. We all have to get through it the best we can.

Believe me, after all, your friend.

Barbara.

Tim Rickworth also had a letter, which he showed to Jonathan. He had found it on the kitchen table when he finally got home after the great chase.

That's it, chum. I put up with lies and deceit for too long, never knowing where you were or what you were really doing. Well, your cover's blown now, and serves you right. What happens now? That's your problem. I'd love to be able to say I was running off with . . . well, there isn't anybody. I'm just leaving. Please address all communication to my solicitor, as per card attached.

Lilah made her apologies to her mother as they left the churchyard and Sam's grave. 'I promised I'd go and see Den this afternoon,' she said.

'Of course,' Miranda acknowledged. 'I thought you went every afternoon, anyway.'

'I do,' smiled the girl. 'Shall I give him your love?'

Sylvia glanced from mother to daughter, surprised at the banter. 'You two seem remarkably happy,' she commented. 'In the circumstances.'

It was early afternoon before Lilah located Den in his new room, lying in a high metal bed. She leant over him; the side of his face was covered now, from temple to jaw. He was awake, staring at the ceiling. Then his eyes turned to her, and she watched a smile dawn. She reached out a hand and found his. 'Does it hurt?' she mouthed, not sure whether any voice came through the choking emotion in her throat. He shook his head, making the slightest movement, and winced. The contradiction seemed amusing to her, and she grinned.

Then he winked at her, the self-consciousness of it making him appear boyish, vulnerable. To her, he wasn't any longer a policeman, but a valued ally in the insanity that had exploded all around them. And more than that, he was someone who had nearly died, because of something rotten in her family, and for whom she now felt responsible.

'How was the funeral?' he asked.

She grimaced. 'It was horrible. But I'd say the case is now closed, apart from a few lingering questions.'

'Don't ask me for answers,' he whispered. 'I'm meant to be resting.'

404

'Just one thing, if you're up to it.' He waited. 'What's happened to Tim Rickworth? He's turned into a completely different person.'

'That's an easy one,' he said. 'He used to be in the SAS – still on the payroll, as far as I know. It makes him good in a crisis.'

'Are you saying that the police asked him to come and help out on the farm? As a security thing?'

Den nodded and grinned crookedly. 'Good idea, eh?'

Lilah pursed her lips thoughtfully. 'I'd rather you'd told us,' she said. 'But yes, it was quite a good idea.'

On the day after his capture, Lilah had obtained permission to visit Terry, escorted by a policeman. He was in the same hospital as Den, kept under twenty-four-hour guard. He had a smaller facial dressing than Den's, and his arm in a rigid splint.

'I'm Lilah,' she told him. 'Your half-sister. I wanted to meet you and try to understand what you've done.'

He stared at her through furious brown eyes, set in their sockets exactly as Guy's had been. His mouth went thin, pulled straight at the sides, so that he looked just as Guy would look when enraged by a disobediant farm animal.

'I didn't touch your old man,' he snarled. 'I wasn't even in the county that night, and I can prove it.'

She stared at him. She had thought she was ready for anything, but it was a bad shock to find that he was stupid. Guy would have tolerated almost anything but stupidity in his children.

'We know you didn't kill him,' she said coldly. 'It was Elvira. Hasn't anybody told you she confessed?'

Terry's face went blank, and then he began to try to sit up, wrestling with the bedcovers. 'Where is she?' he demanded. 'What have they done to her? I told her to stay safely in the woods.'

His concern was another surprise. 'They found the hideout,' she said, a spark of pleasure igniting at his panic. 'That all happened yesterday. She's been charged with killing Daddy and Sam. She *confessed*. The police are assuming that you were with her when she shot Sam.'

The policeman sitting near the door cleared his throat. When she looked at him, he shook his head. 'Er—' he said, worry puckering his face, 'I don't think . . .'

'Oops. Sorry.' Lilah said unapologetically. She turned back to her half-brother. 'I'm not supposed to tell you. They probably didn't know that I knew, come to think of it.'

Terry continued to struggle. The policeman opened the door and called a nurse. 'Calm down, lad,' he admonished. 'There's not a thing you can do about it.'

Terry threw himself back against the pillows, knocking his head on the metal bedhead. 'Elvira!' he moaned in anguish.

'I saw you together,' Lilah told him. 'You make a funny couple, I must say.'

'She's a darling,' he said, the Irishness of his voice making the word rich and warm.

Oh my God, he really loves her, Lilah realised. The desire to hurt him dribbled away. He'd made enough mess of his life already, without any help from her. But she had more to say yet, and despite a nagging sense of wrongness, she blurted it out.

'He was a good father to us,' she said. 'Though he had

406

his faults. I can understand that it wasn't like that for you. I know you got Elvira to kill him for you, which makes it your crime at least as much as hers. He didn't deserve that. I hope they put you in prison for a long time, for what you've done to me and Roddy. However bad things were, you've only made it much worse.'

He stared at her, his mouth twitching, and said nothing. She could see no remorse on his face.

'I'm going in a minute,' she said quietly. 'But first I must ask you – why Sam? That still doesn't make any sense to me.'

He closed his eyes and she thought for a moment he might refuse to answer her. But then his eyelids snapped up, and the look of hatred was there again. 'That should have been *me*,' he spat. '*Me* living on the farm, being his son. Leo never wanted any of it, but I did. I remember that Sam when I was little, when Dad lived with us. It was always *Sam Carter's ten times brighter than you'll ever be*. I hated him for as long as I can remember. Then, when I knew he was going to run the farm, that finished it. He remembered me, too. Said I looked just the same.'

'So we were right – you *were* with Elvira when she shot him.'

He shook his head slightly. 'Got more sense than that,' he said. 'Made sure of an alibi, like the last time. I visited your precious Sam a week or two after the old man's funeral. Told him not to say anything. Showed him a picture of his boss the way I remembered him. Told him I'd get you and your little brother too, if he said a word about me visiting. Scared stiff, he was.'

All Lilah could do was turn away in sorrow.

* * *

Father Edmund wondered whether he was the first person to fit the whole puzzle together. Motive, opportunity, means. His inadequacy had lain in failing to convince the police when he had taken Amos to speak to them two days earlier, although at that point the truth was still partially obscured. He had needed to speak to Phoebe before the veil was ripped away completely.

She had been sitting on a garden chair on the scrubby patch of grass outside her cottage when he arrived. She barely even looked at him.

'They have Elvira,' he said, to show her that he knew. 'I'm sure they'll treat her gently, a girl like her.'

'They'll be saying she's evil, to do what she did. They don't understand that she can't tell right from wrong. That's your department, isn't it, Father? Can you explain it to them? That she was just a pawn in that man's hands?'

'Of course,' he assured her, more robustly than he really felt.

'He told her he'd marry her. That they'd be rich with her inheritance from Amos. You know the man I mean?' She was clutching herself, with both hands, and her face was grey.

'I do,' he said. 'I know him and I know his mother. And I see it all now.'

He went to call at Redstone that same evening. When Miranda answered the door to his knock, limping from a bruised leg, he walked in before she could refuse him entry. 'You might be interested in what I have to tell you,' he said.

Together they went into the living room, where Lilah and Roddy already sat, watching something mindless on

408

television. 'Switch it off,' said Miranda, and invited the vicar to sit down in Guy's armchair.

'Hello, Mr Larkin,' said Lilah with unconcealed hostility. 'What brings you here?'

'He says he's got something to tell us,' her mother explained.

'Can't think what,' said Roddy. 'It's all obvious now.'

'What do you mean, boy – obvious?' The vicar was already losing his fragile composure.

Lilah interposed. 'There's a pattern to the whole thing,' she said slowly, tiredly. 'It's all about fathers. Fathers and people letting each other down.' She sighed. 'Funny, you call yourself "Father" as well, don't you? And you've been just as useless as the others.'

'I beg your pardon,' he blustered. 'I didn't come here—'

'It's true, though,' said Roddy.

The vicar sat back, fighting an urge to get up and run away. He was horrified by what was happening. The last thing he'd expected was that it would all rebound on him. Any tracks he might have left had been carefully covered – or so he believed.

Roddy resumed the attack. 'You haven't been *fatherly* at all, have you? Jonathan says you knew Terry was hanging around here. You knew he'd come to confront Dad about being abandoned as a kid. You just sat back and let all this happen.'

The boy was on his feet now, fists clenched, pouring out a lifetime of dislike for the man in front of him.

Lilah took over, more gently. 'You see,' she said, 'all this happened because people failed as fathers. Amos was

409

Elvira's father, but he never faced up to it. He just carried on, hoarding money for no reason, cutting himself off. Now Phoebe's dying—'

'What?' The vicar didn't try to conceal his amazement. 'I've just seen her, this afternoon.'

'She's got cancer. So she needed someone to look after Elvira, and she told the girl who her father was, and said they'd find a way to make him take care of her. Phoebe didn't know about Terry. She just thought she could bully or shame Amos into doing what she wanted. When Isaac was killed, that must have seemed pure good luck to her – or witchcraft. Elvira repeated her mother's intentions to Terry, who decided it made more sense to kill both Isaac and Amos, so Elvira could have all the money directly. After all, Terry really does love Elvira. He wanted to look after her. He decided to kill both the Grimms, but he made a hash of it, which is probably typical.'

The vicar felt the ground disappearing from beneath his feet. He hadn't dreamt that the Beardons would be so well informed. But he fought to regain some credibility.

'Terry told Elvira he'd marry her,' he offered, in a humble tone. 'Isn't that something just a bit . . . redemptive?'

'They fell in love,' Lilah confirmed. 'So perhaps that's right. Redemptive,' she repeated slowly. 'That sounds rather nice.'

'They had a camp in the Mabberley woods,' she went on. 'From about Easter onwards. He was backpacking, pretending to be an ordinary tourist. That's when the Wing Commander saw him. He must have met Elvira somehow. And he saw Dad in town and confronted him. Cappy was there, but couldn't see Terry's face.'

'And Guy told him to bugger off, which was a great

mistake,' Miranda contributed. 'A fatal mistake, in fact.'

'We're only guessing on that, but Cappy did think there was a major argument going on,' Lilah went on. 'He had an old photo of Dad, which might have helped him recognise him. Or Elvira could have pointed him out.'

'Anyway, they plotted to kill both their fathers,' Roddy summed up. 'Only they swapped, to confuse everybody.'

'Which was quite clever,' said Lilah. 'I just wish Daddy could have known about it. In a weird way, I think he'd have been rather impressed. And I suppose it would be easier to kill someone else's father, rather than your own,' she added.

'What I don't completely understand is Sam,' said Miranda, with a forlorn sniff. 'I'm still confused about that. I understand Terry's jealousy. I always thought Guy was unfair about that, the way he would talk about his own boys in comparison with Sam. But how did Terry know that Sam was part owner of Redstone? Lilah thinks that was the final straw for him.'

The vicar's neck grew mottled. 'Well, of course, these things can be ascertained—'

'*You* knew, didn't you?' Roddy suddenly accused. 'You came snooping round here, and overheard us in the office that day, when we found that letter. Bloody hell – did *you* tell him?'

The vicar cringed back, his face a dark red, the picture of guilt and fear.

'Roddy, wait,' Lilah stopped him. 'That was *after* Sam died, remember? That wouldn't explain it.' She paused, and her eyes widened. 'But Jonathan knew. He's always known. Redstone belonged to his father before we bought it. He *must* have known. It would have been on all the sales paperwork.'

'And he told Mr Larkin, and Mr Larkin told Barbara and *she* told Terry.' Roddy stared at the vicar. 'Which means it was *your* fault that Sam was killed,' he added viciously.

'Roddy, don't,' said Miranda. 'Facts are facts. It wasn't the vicar's fault.' She looked at the miserable clergyman with a kindly scorn. 'Perhaps you'd better go now,' she said. Like a rabbit released from a snare, he leapt up and bolted for the door. Without a word he was gone, though there was clear expression of his feelings in the slamming sound which echoed through the house behind him.

'He'll get over it,' said Miranda. 'His sort always do, especially when God's on their side.'

'But what about us?' demanded Lilah. 'When are *we* going to get over it?'

Miranda moved to the sofa, and sat down in the middle of it. 'Come here,' she told them. When they joined her, one on either side, she put an arm around each pair of shoulders.

'We've got each other,' she said. 'And I've decided to try and keep the farm. It's what Guy would have wanted. And Sam. We're going to keep the cows, and make a go of it. We've got friends who'll rally round. We can't give up now, can we?'

'Not even now that everything's over and done with?' queried Roddy, uncertainly.

'It isn't over and done with, Rod,' said Lilah, hugging her mother. 'It's only just beginning!'

It was true. Lilah felt as if she were emerging from an overlong childhood, to begin her adult life. Day by day she watched Den recover, sitting quietly with him, playing gently with his long fingers, thinking of nothing. Before going home, she would lean over and kiss him. His mouth was dry, tasting of hospital and the bland food they gave him.

Jonathan took Tim to the village pub that evening. 'Come on, man,' he encouraged, as Tim stared morosely into his beer. 'She'll come back. You're the sort of couple that thrives on breaking up and getting back together. You've done nothing but fight since you got married.'

'I don't blame her, really. It's a bugger living with someone like me. She'll never forgive me for not quitting the service altogether. I thought a compromise would work, but I was only fooling myself.'

Jonathan shook his head, and drank some more beer, grimacing as it went down. 'This stuff's vile. This must be the worst pub in England.'

'It's not meant for enjoyment. Just a place to be quiet after a day's work. I like it. It's real. Sarah loathes it.'

'Well, I'm on her side in that.'

Jonathan forced down the rest of his beer, musing on the events in which he'd become an unwilling player. All they could do now was pick up the pieces and carry on as best they might.

Cappy had taken it upon herself to befriend Lilah, offering her a listening ear and a shoulder to cry on. After a few days, the girl had given into her insistent offers and gone over for a talk. But when it came to it, she could think of little to say. Only one unresolved emotion remained.

'It's Sam,' she blurted. 'That's what makes me saddest. We were his whole life and we killed him, between us. I don't

413

think I'll ever get round that.' She wept then, fast-flowing tears, with scarcely a sound to accompany them.

Cappy got up and put an arm round her shoulders.

'I know, Lil,' she said. 'I know.'